Emma Redux

Happily Ever After

Helen Heineman

DEDICATION

This book is dedicated to the spirit of Jane Austen
and her memorable characters

Emma and George Knightley

ACKNOWLEDGMENTS

I owe thanks to many for help along the way with this novel. Like Jane Austen before me, I have shared the manuscript of my book with members of my family whose comments, suggestions, and edits have been enormously useful to me, especially my son George and his wife Jennifer, Daughters-in-Law Andrea and Liesa, and Grandson Nicholas. Grandson Alexander also listened patiently to the many family readings of the emerging chapters of Emma Redux. Grandson Christopher drew and designed the cover illustration, a stylish woman in Regency dress reviewing the marriage portrait of Emma and Mr. Knightley, her pages of writing visible on Jane Austen's own table.

Other members of my family have also helped keep my spirits up, especially since the passing of my husband John in 2017. From him, I learned what good marriages are all about.

AUTHOR'S NOTE

As is typical in Jane Austen's novels, there is no specific year in which *Emma* is set. The book was first published in December 1815. I have chosen to fix 1836 as the date of Emma and Knightley's marriage, the year before Queen Victoria came to the throne.

Look for more Knightley family adventures in soon-to-appear sequels as the story of Emma and Mr. Knightley and their families and friends continues.

Emma Redux

Happily Ever After

Part I

CHAPTER 1

"Mr. Knightley will never marry!" said Emma.

"She always declares she will never marry, which,
of course, means just nothing at all," said Mr. Knightley.

On August 6, at St. John's parish in Highbury, Emma Woodhouse, handsome, clever, and rich, took George Knightley, a man of good looks, great moral probity, social prestige, and stature, as her lawful wedded husband. A few weeks earlier, in the same parish, and under the auspices of the same clergyman, Harriet Smith, pretty, amiable, and the natural daughter of a tradesman, took Robert Martin, a tall, rugged man, intelligent, and an enterprising farmer, as her lawful wedded husband. Some months later, after a suitable period of mourning for his aunt, Frank Churchill, personable, witty, and a man of recent good fortune, planned to take Jane Fairfax, elegant, bright, and a woman of high character and no fortune, as his lawful wife.

After some time, Emma's father partially recovered from the shock of his daughter's announcement, and their friends and relatives began to adjust to the idea of a union between the two who had always been considered as brother and sister. Then after the wedding bells rang out, and Mr. Elton had duly married them, Mr. and Mrs. Knightley stepped into their carriage and departed from Highbury for a mystery honeymoon in unknown parts.

"It's miraculous, really! Everything went so easily," said Emma, herself astonished at the smoothness with which all had been managed so quickly. "I do believe that all these years of your visits to us have somewhat accustomed Father to you, Mr. Knightley."

"Yes, indeed. But I've never taken his beloved Emma away from Hartfield. And for two weeks!"

"'An eternity,' my father said, but I assured him I'd be back," said Emma.

"As will I," said Mr. Knightley with a smile.

"It was good of John and Isabella to come and stay with him," said Emma.

"And that someone had broken into the poultry roost," added Mr. Knightley. "My brother and your sister, of all people, understand both the animal and human geography of Hartfield. It was Isabella's turn to care for your father."

"It was the best gift they could have given us," replied Emma.

"You have kept the faith for so many years now, enabling John and Isabella to have their large family and my brother to build up his thriving law practice in London. It was not so much a gift, as a debt that needed repayment."

"Well, they were more than willing to do it," said Emma. She was so happy she was not going to quibble over a word.

As she said, everything still seemed miraculous. She had finally found her knight—Knightley—in shining armor. How distant now, her many protestations that she would never marry, and here she was, driving away with George Knightley in his carriage to who knows where. A mystery honeymoon. Well, he too had made his protestations about marriage. When Mrs. Elton offered to do the invitations to his strawberry party at Donwell—What was it he said? "No, I thank you. There is but one married woman I would permit to select guests for Donwell."

"Oh, Mrs. Weston, of course," Mrs. Elton guessed. Then, Emma felt an odd kind of start at his naming 'Mrs. Knightley.'

"And until she is in being, I will handle the invitations myself." He had referred to that fictional Mrs. Knightley more than once— even on one occasion lightly suggesting she might fill the role—and each time that feeling of shock had come. All that was a mystery, solved as of late, after the engagement of Frank Churchill and Jane Fairfax helped them both to better understand their feelings.

"What are you thinking about?" he asked, still holding tightly to the hand with which he had helped her climb into the carriage, miles back now.

It couldn't be explained at present, she thought. "I'm wondering if Isabella is getting Father's supper ready—soup and gruel and his glass of wine. I hope she will remember to prop his back with a pillow when he eats and keep the fire warm during his early dinner."

"I'm sure she'll do a creditable job. You must think now of *our* comforts, at least for the next two weeks," he said, smiling.

Emma's thoughts raced to what lay ahead.

"Do you know, it will be the first time I've ever slept away from Hartfield." She rested her head on his shoulder. "Indeed, it will be the first time I've shared a bed with anyone. Even as children, Isabella and I had our own rooms and tucked ourselves in without assistance."

She lifted her head and looked at him.

"I'll be taking care of that task now," he said, still cradling her hand and stroking it gently.

She was ready for him to take her to himself. He had always been a part of her life, during her many years of growing up and becoming a woman. She felt sure he would lead her now into the happy fulfillment of marriage.

Despite her great imaginative abilities, she'd never really imagined what marriage would be like. For her, being 'handsome, clever, and rich,' had been enough to make a life. Her own mother died so early; she had not witnessed conjugal love at home. And her father expressed such negative views: 'People should not marry, Emma! Mothers die!' Recently, she'd observed more when 'poor Miss Taylor' became Mrs. Weston. And though she hadn't been present for Isabella's five deliveries—How could she have left her father?—she'd been present for Mrs. Weston's. She hoped she was ready for her own.

But she was the first to glimpse the attraction between John and Isabella during their courtship at Hartfield, indeed, even predicted their marriage, but their removal to London made them available only as visitors. Now she wanted these two weeks with Mr. Knightley.

"Emma." He interrupted her reverie. "I think you should call me George now."

"How can I? After sixteen years of calling you, Mr. Knightley! That's just who you are," she smiled.

"We'll see how it all evolves. You never were Miss Woodhouse to me, only my beloved Emma."

And so, the carriage ride continued, long and quite bumpy, but she didn't mind. Whatever she would call him, he belonged to her now, not to Harriet Smith, as she had briefly feared. She was at least grateful to Harriet for revealing to her how much she loved him. She owed Harriet this much: she must never tell that last secret, Harriet's attachment to Mr. Knightley and her conviction that he returned her feelings. That private matter she would not disclose, though she came close to revealing it in the confusion of the moment when he confessed his love for her.

She never resented his scoldings and lectures. Oddly enough, she sometimes even looked forward to those encounters. Only lately she realized that it was at those moments she felt most passionately connected to him, even though she misunderstood the nature of the passion, both his and her own. But passion it had surely been. She always hated it if he left abruptly after one of their disagreements. Often, they made up right on the spot. "Can we be friends again?" one of them would say. Now all was clear. She was his, and he was hers. Nothing else mattered. She didn't care where they were going, as long as they were going there together.

"I've planned our two weeks carefully, dear Emma. If you take a look to your right, you'll see something quite new."

She turned. As the carriage pulled up over the last hill, there it was.

"The seaside!" she cried.

It had been his first consideration when seeking a place to stay. "Of course. And we'll be within daily sight of the sea. Box Hill may be the most beautiful view in Surrey, but we're in Kent now, near the sea!"

The source of his choice came from an odd direction. In recent weeks, he'd been enjoying installments of *The Pickwick Papers*, by the new and upcoming young author Charles Dickens, when he learned that Dickens favored the seaside resort of Broadstairs and was staying there this very year. Broadstairs was not far from Highbury and was reachable by coach. Once the idea came, he wrote ahead, finding out everything he could about accommodations and activities. Donwell's library contained *A Guide to All the Watering and Seabathing Places*, including a section on Broadstairs. What he learned about the place appealed to him, and so he booked rooms at the Albion Hotel.

On the way he directed the coach to drive along the white cliffs of Dover, giving Emma that first dramatic sight of the sea. And it was quite wonderful when they got out and stood together at the edge of the rise of cliffs, hearing the thunder of the waves and seeing the majesty of the ocean.

"You've given me the greatest wedding gift, this view of the sea," she said, as they stood a long time, breathing in the kind of air that even healthful Highbury had never given her. "Better even than the one Frank Churchill gave to Jane. I didn't tell you this, but when he briefly apologized for using me as cover for his engagement to Jane, he told me he had convinced his uncle to give Jane all his aunt's jewels as his wedding present, newly set, of course."

"Would you have wanted some of the jewels left to me and John by my mother? I confess, I had not even thought of it. Nor had John, for that matter. Maybe it's time we took a look," he said. He did not want Emma to think he did not properly honor her. Not only could he not make speeches, he thought, but he wasn't very good about giving gifts, either. He turned to her.

"My dear Mr. Knightley," she answered. "There will be plenty of time for those observances. In the meantime, this view of the sea, and our two weeks together, alone, are the very best gift you could have given me. Remember, I have my own mother's jewels to wear, whenever I want them."

"These two weeks mean much to me as well," he told her. "It's been a long time since we were alone and at peace with one another. When we return, I'm quite prepared for my residence at Hartfield, and even ready to share you with your father. As I told you, my heart will always be with you, and wherever you are, that will be my home."

For a man who said he couldn't make speeches, she thought, he already made several she would remember all her life.

"You always said you took your walks over to Hartfield 'for your constitution,'" she said. "Or to oversee Father's accounts."

"I hadn't known myself, in those days, that it was glimpses of you that brought me over. Hartfield was like a magnet, only I never completely understood the true attraction at first."

"Your purpose was often to scold me—often quite justly, I'll admit."

"In retrospect, I might have secretly enjoyed that," he said. It was amazing, really, thinking of himself as a rational person, how often he had failed to understand his own motives. "Now," he said, "I want these two weeks to be as perfect as possible. I'm hoping Broadstairs will be the perfect place. I've chosen a room overlooking the harbor and the Bay. People say it's the pride of the Kent coastline. The town is quiet and old-fashioned, steeply built on a half-circle of cliffs, in layers, with gardens in front and charming streets behind. We'll enjoy walking along the clifftop, with the sea on one side, and the interesting houses on the other. If it's good enough for this new phenomenon, Mr. Charles Dickens, it should be good enough for us!"

With that as an introduction, the coach pulled up in front of the Albion Hotel, looking exactly as the guide book described it, 'a newly built house, conveniently fitted up.' And so here, away from both Hartfield and Donwell, their life together was about to begin.

CHAPTER 2

Mr. Knightley was reading Keats.

Many the wonders I this day have seen...
The ocean with its vastness, its blue green,
Its ships, its rocks, its caves, its hopes, its fears,
Its voice mysterious, which whoso hears
Must think on what will be and what has been.

Yes, he thought. It was on this coast that John Keats first glimpsed the sea. And Broadstairs, near where Keats stayed, was a good location, with all the charm and virtues of a quiet seaside town. They took a pleasant walk along the clifftop almost every day. Mr. Knightley collected some fossils for his collection, sea urchins which, he read in a geology book, were trapped in the chalk cliffs ages ago. And there was a lively birdlife here, especially now, when migrating birds were making their landfall on these shores, before flying off to their far-away homes elsewhere.

"Just like the birds, we've migrated here for two weeks," he told Emma. "Still, while it isn't our final destination, I don't think we'll ever forget our days here."

"Never," she readily agreed, pressing his arm. "It has been a hidden place for us to rest, before returning to our home at Hartfield," which they both knew, would be different. But today, they were not thinking about future arrangements. Here, they walked along the clifftop and through the gardens, with stunning views of Viking Bay, guarded by the pier on one side, and the headland on the other. Here, they heard the gulls scream and watched the fishing boats coming in to the pier.

"I've enjoyed everything here, the concerts, and especially the one ball we attended," she said. "Dancing with you has been a new discovery!"

"Indeed, it has. I also found the Colonnade library an interesting place. I must admit I was surprised to find it so good, with some selections I don't have at Donwell."

"And the curious little shops," she added. "We must pick out some gifts for Isabella and John's children. Maybe even Father would enjoy one of those miniature objects made of shells that pretend not to be shells."

"I like walking around the pier best—there are always boatmen, talking, or drinking their mugs of beer. Makes me think of the days when they salvaged the valuable cargoes of wrecked ships and helped to save people, as well. When we return to our room in the evening, and you're doing your toilet, I like going back down there for a few minutes. If the tides and waves are strong, you can feel the force of the winds and waters."

"You would enjoy that kind of thing. I prefer our lovely room. I can feel the cold air there when I open the French window to our balcony." She smiled at him, taking his hand. "You'll have plenty of wind and waters to contend with when we get back, I fancy."

"Nothing too much for me to handle, with you at my side," he said. "I rather like rough weather. It never interfered with my daily constitutionals, especially if you were there as the day's reward." He held her hand tightly. There was a part of him that still could hardly believe how all this had come about. He was a man accustomed to planning, acting rationally, knowing in advance what he was about to do. He felt swept into his new happiness, Emma herself providing the force of the winds, even when they strolled in the cultured garden settings of Hartfield. On that last, fateful day, he hurried back from London and went to see Emma, thinking to console her for her regrets on the announcement of Frank Churchill's engagement to Jane Fairfax. Within the hour, he returned to Donwell securely possessed of Emma's heart, his whole future arranged in a way he hardly dared to hope.

"I watch the children on the sands, making castles with such labor which the next tide overthrows," she said, wondering to herself when their children would come, and what kind of mother she would be. That too lay in the future. For now, she loved holding little Emma, her niece. Isabella said Mr. Knightley always enjoyed rough-housing with her boys and often sat for hours with little Emma on his knees.

Given his talk about migrating birds, he had begun to wonder what their life together at Hartfield would be like. Mrs. Weston once told him Emma needed female companionship, and longed for more of it when she left to marry Mr. Weston. That had prompted Emma's adoption of Harriet Smith as her bosom friend. The culture around them seemed to have distinctly male and female spheres. Isabella was occupied with her five children, his brother John with his London law practice. Emma arranged her life around her father's needs, and he occupied himself with running Donwell and its surrounding properties. What spheres would he and Emma now inhabit?

Whenever he came to Hartfield, she always seemed glad to see him, even when they were sparring in disagreement. Mrs. Weston said that since he lived so much alone, he could not understand Emma's need for female companionship and advocated for Harriet Smith as Emma's friend because they could read together.

He wondered if they could be all in all to each other now. He never pined for a male friend, though he was close to his brother during their younger years. But after John married Isabella, he indeed lived mostly alone. He was sure Emma's companionship was enough for him now. He would have to wait and see how she fared.

As for her old attempts at rivaling Jane Fairfax with her reading program of 100 titles, Emma made only brief starts at Mr. Milton's *Paradise Lost*. But he took up the book himself, and now especially remembered Adam's loneliness, assuaged by God only when Eve was created. Now he appreciated the full force of Adam's words to Eve, after the Fall: "Flesh of flesh, Bone of my bone thou art, and from thy state, Mine never shall be parted." Indeed, Eve was created out of Adam's rib. He never believed that literally, but now, quite unlike his former self, he thought he could feel the very spot on his chest from which the rib creating Emma had been taken.

Strangely enough, during that unexpected acceptance of his declaration of love in the gardens at Hartfield, she spoke of their proposed union in words close to Milton's: "I was talking to Harriet of a secret matter of her heart, and I examined my own heart, and there you were, never I fear, to be parted."

For the rest of their stay, they walked, talked, shopped, ate together, and, of course, most fulfilling of all, bedded together. It happened with an ease that still surprised him. In Broadstairs, they became truly all in all to each other. The arrangements in Hartfield would wait for their return. At any rate, he resolved to make up for his negative words about Harriet Smith. On their return, he would take the initiative, suggest a dinner at Hartfield to which they would invite the Robert Martins. He had done all he could to advance the marriage between Harriet and Mr. Martin. He became something of a matchmaker himself, sending Robert to London with a commission for his brother, while Harriet stayed at the John Knightleys, by Emma's request. The rest had worked out just as he hoped, as his brother's letter stated.

He'd tell Emma about it tomorrow. He hoped she would be pleased!

On their last day, they enjoyed their usual English breakfast: poached eggs, grilled tomato and toast, on the pink and green bordered dishes and placemats that said 'Albion Hotel.' As if they could ever forget where they were!

They took a final carriage ride to Ramsgate to visit St. Augustine's Abbey, with its famous Madonna and rood screen. At lunch in a little cafe run by a couple married fifty years, they ate ham sandwiches. One more stop at the Albion Book Store—*Sketches by Boz* was available, and purchased by Mr. Knightley—and one more glimpse of the beach, people walking dogs, even a woman in a bathing cap and rather red cheeks coming back from one of the bathing machines. The seaside would provide many memories: children playing, hunting for treasure, kicking balls, mothers wheeling baby carriages, young people laughing and running into the water as far as their ankles, splashing water, fishing, digging in the sand, waving to friends and feeding the gulls. They took it all in.

"It will be hard trying to describe the trip to Father and the others," said Emma. "They'll listen, but how can they understand? Yesterday I took a few stones from the ocean to bring back and when I looked at them this morning, they were dried and had lost their luster and beauty. It will be like that, I suppose," she said, clinging to him tightly as the carriage left Broadstairs.

"We won't need any stones to remind us. This time together will always be part of us," he said, waving his hand toward the sea. "There's no need to explain to others." He was ready to start another subject. "Now, it's time to talk about any plans we might have on our return to Hartfield."

She nodded. Her mind went to her father and how he had fared in her absence, and what their new routine would look like. They talked about domestic arrangements and agreed they would not have separate bedrooms, as many couples did. There would be little privacy in the household, so evenings together would be much desired by them both. For his part, in addition to deciding on which books to bring over from Donwell to Hartfield, and which room he would outfit as his study, he resolved to work on reinforcing Emma's old friendship with Harriet Smith, now Mrs. Robert Martin. On that score, he was determined to make amends.

CHAPTER 3

The blissful two weeks were over. Mr. Woodhouse had been waiting for them all day, getting more anxious as time went on, even though Isabella reminded him that carriage travel could be slow. And the horses would have to be rested.

"Seven miles an hour, with stops, is all we made from London at Christmas," she said. "You can't stand outside waiting for them all day. And since we don't know where they're coming from, we really can't calculate how many hours it will take for them to get back home."

"The later it gets, the more possible it is that Emma may be chilled. I told her before she left, that it's never a good idea to travel after dark," said Mr. Woodhouse. "And Isabella, would you please bring me an extra scarf? Emma always did that when I was out toward evening. If we had only known where they went, we'd know more about the conditions of the roads." There was no end to the dangers in store for his daughter. "I've read in the papers about recent accidents, some even fatal! Just yesterday, a woman was killed when her carriage overturned."

Isabella saw no hope in continuing that conversation.

"And what about highwaymen?" he continued, "I've read about that too."

"Father, Mr. Knightley is with her, and he will never let anything happen to Emma." She wished her husband back from his quick day's trip to London. Maybe he could think of consoling things to say, though he was never good at such things.

"Travelling in a coach is a bone-rattling experience," Mr.

Woodhouse went on. "That's why my advice is always to stay at home."

"Yes, Father, that's right. I know you're not a good traveler. But Mr. Knightley is. Emma is in good hands."

"Has cook made up some broth for when she returns?"

"Yes, Father. We'll have supper as soon as they walk into the house."

"I hope they didn't stop somewhere on the way. These wayside inns are dangerous. If Emma were to lie down in a damp bed, she would surely catch a cold."

"They are not stopping anywhere, I'm quite sure. Come inside and let me fetch you another scarf if you insist on waiting outside."

Fortunately, neither robbers, tempests, nor overturning had occurred, and just before dark set in, the sound of Mr. Knightley's coach was heard outside. Nothing alarming had beset them and now, here they were. Emma emerged first, and her father, raising his arms in a dance of happiness to greet her, ran to meet the coach.

Mr. Woodhouse kissed his daughter and bowed to his new son-in-law. John Knightley arrived from London shortly after, and in a few moments, the small group assembled and entered the room where supper was waiting.

At first, no one spoke. It was as if they were strangers, meeting for the first time, trying to find some subject that would release conversation and get them started in their new relationships.

John and Isabella were leaving on the morrow, eager to return to London. Little Emma had come with Isabella, while the older children had stayed behind in London with their nursemaids and tutors. Tonight, Isabella and John were part of this new family circle, ready to help smooth this difficult transition for Mr. Woodhouse.

"You mustn't leave until we've unpacked the gifts we've brought for the children," said Emma, making a start. "And there's something special for you, too, Father."

He nodded, with one of his half-smiles which, she knew, often meant he had not fully grasped what had been said.

"Lovely, Emma," said her sister, "thinking of us during your honeymoon time. Wasn't it, Father?"

"Honeymoon?" Mr. Woodhouse seemed startled, as if he were learning of their marriage for the first time. "Oh yes, your honeymoon," he repeated.

"How did you like Broadstairs, George?" asked his brother, attempting to cover Mr. Woodhouse's odd remark. "Did you find any trace of the great Charles Dickens? Was he there himself? I've heard he often goes down there for a day or two, just to take the air and sit in his room watching the waves. No doubt the place will get into his next book."

"I don't think we've ever heard of someone by the name of Dickens," said Mr. Woodhouse. "It sounds like a common name. Do we know anything of his family, Emma?"

"We had no sightings of him," said Mr. Knightley, hoping to forestall any research into the Dickens family tree. "But Emma and I read a bit in his *Sketches by Boz*. We've begun making a list of one hundred books we plan to read together, and Boz is on the list. There are many scenes of London life in it, John, and I think you might like it."

"Too busy for fiction, George. You and Emma will have to tell us all about it." John relapsed into eating his dinner.

"Broadstairs was an interesting place," said Mr. Knightley. "Mr. Turner, the artist, was residing in Margate, the next town over. We went over there one day. How the seaside draws us all. Well, why not. No one in England is more than 70 miles from the sea," Mr. Knightley continued. "I'm going to buy one of Mr. Turner's watercolors or a print of them. That way, even here at Hartfield, Emma can always have a look at the seaside, whenever she wants."

"As long as she covers up properly. Sea air is cold," added Mr. Woodhouse.

An awkward silence followed. No one seemed interested in Turner's seascapes, or pursuing the habits and works of Mr. Charles Dickens, least of all Mr. Woodhouse. Mr. Knightley hoped John would not bring up the *Pickwick Papers*, which he was still eagerly following in the monthly parts. Not the type of book his father-in-law would like, he thought, though he was grateful to John for keeping the conversation going.

Mr. Woodhouse had still said very little of a positive nature. He was seated at the head of the table, in his usual position, but Emma had taken his right side, and Mr. Knightley his left, leaving John seated at the other end, the place usually occupied by Emma. Somehow the configuration felt odd, not only because they were an uneven number, but rather because Emma was not in her usual place at the table's opposite end. How such a simple thing as table seating signaled the many hurdles which lay ahead.

"Mr. Woodhouse," began Mr. Knightley, "We must go over your accounts tomorrow. Time to catch up with bills and correspondence."

"Yes, indeed. What time do you plan on coming over? You are always so good about taking the walk over from Donwell most days. Even in cold weather, when the cold northeast wind blows."

Here was a challenge to the conversational efforts. Mr. Knightley hoped Emma might help. If not, he was carefully considering the best way to answer. Maybe Mr. Woodhouse thought they planned to wait a bit before consolidating their residences.

"Father," said Emma. "I know you can't have forgotten something so important." She smiled her brightest smile and gently laid her hand on her father's arm. "You must remember that Mr. Knightley is to live here now, with us. You won't ever have to wonder about when he's coming—he'll always be here. How wonderful! Now that John and Isabella are leaving, we'll always have protection, and won't have to worry about any thefts in the barnyard!"

Mr. Knightley also smiled, nodded, and said how convenient it all was, and no trouble to him at all. Mr. Woodhouse nodded too and smiled, and for the moment, everyone sighed with relief at the first obstacle overcome—the mention of Mr. Knightley's permanent residence at Hartfield. The rest of the meal continued in amiable silence to its conclusion.

"After our long journey back home," said Emma, "we probably should retire early tonight. John and Isabella must be off early in the morning."

"Surely you must have things to see to at Donwell," said Mr. Woodhouse, turning to Mr. Knightley. "William Larkins must be eager to go over your accounts with you." He smiled. "We don't want to be keeping you here too late."

Emma could not make it out. Was her father just ignoring the fact of her marriage? What should she do? Then her new husband showed the first signs of his determination to make his residence at Hartfield a success. Imagine—calling Mr. Knightley her husband, if only in her thoughts!

"Not at all, sir," said Mr. Knightley. "Emma and I are planning on retiring early ourselves. I think we should all be heading upstairs." He rose, bowed politely to all, and, as in the old days when transporting Mr. Woodhouse by carriage, offered his arm to his father-in-law. There was a moment's pause, and then, as if recalling something he had forgotten, Emma's father stood and, leaning heavily on Mr. Knightley's arm, they climbed the stairs to the upper rooms together.

John Knightley turned to his wife and remarked, "I always did enjoy watching George handle difficult people. He's a master at it. Too bad you never were witness to the way he managed our father, rest his soul. It was a beautiful thing to see and saved me from many a scrape. I was different. My mother used to say I came out of her womb arguing. It was good training for my life as a lawyer. But George always won the day just by being his own charming, truthful, and determined self. I've never seen Emma's father leave without a parting word of some warning or other. Time for bed for us too, my dear. I can see George will manage here just perfectly. He always does."

CHAPTER 4

The next morning, Mr. Knightley and Mr. Woodhouse were seated downstairs at the desk with letters, books, and documents, doing their usual financial work. All had gone quiet after John and Isabella left bearing the gifts for the children, and Mr. Woodhouse put the shell creation on his dresser, and breakfast was served and eaten. With Mr. Knightley's chair in the drawing-room now unoccupied, Emma found herself alone. She went in to them.

"I think while you are both busy, I'll take a walk over to Randalls to see how Mrs. Weston is coming along. I'll stay only a short while."

Both seemed engrossed in a pile of documents. Her husband nodded, and she was on her way. While the fall weather was approaching, the garden still had some blooms. As she walked through the shrubbery, Emma viewed the spot where she had almost stopped her husband from declaring his love. With more self-knowledge than ever before, she had recovered, run after him, and told him to tell her whatever he wanted. She would hear it all. Yes, for once, she had put him first, as his true friend, forgetting her fears that he was about to reveal his secret love for Harriet Smith and ask for her approval. Had that happened, she must have told him of Harriet's feelings for him. He should never know the unselfish sacrifice she had been ready to make. It had been a near miss, saved only because of her persistence in calling him back. She was rewarded now, beyond her hopes and fears, and it was time to forget all that. Harriet's secret—her declaration of love for the third man in the same year—would be Emma's secret forever, the only one she would ever keep from her husband. She still was at a loss as to how she could face Harriet the first time she would see her after her marriage.

Her musings complete, she turned down the path toward Randalls, the lovely country home of the Westons. Though she was repentant about everything concerning her blunders with Harriet Smith, she still prided herself on bringing the Westons together. It had cost her greatly at the time, for it meant the loss of 'poor Miss Taylor's' company (as her father still sometimes continued to call her), even though she was happy that her former governess had found a good husband and home, aided, she still believed, with her help. Her father still thought Mrs. Weston might better not have married, living with them until, still at Hartfield, she died of contented old age!

She was welcomed with Mrs. Weston's usual warmth and friendliness. In her later years with Emma, she had been more friend than a governess.

"Hello, my dear Emma. I'm so glad to see you. I hope you've come to tell me all about your honeymoon!" said she. "We have been wondering about your destination. Though I'm sure Mr. Knightley will have chosen the best possible place!"

"Indeed, he did. Can you believe it? The seaside! And Broadstairs! Oh, how wonderful it all was. The two weeks flew by, and now it seems like a dream. Even better, we seem to have survived our reunion with Father. In fact, he's closeted with Mr. Knightley this morning, going over his accounts. That's why I've come over to see you." And after telling her friend all about the sea, their walks, dinners, dances, and tour of the coast, she finished with, "Now what news do you have for me?"

"Actually, dear Emma, I do have news. Frank has taken Jane to Enscombe to be introduced to his uncle. I received a letter from him yesterday, telling me that he and Jane have arranged, when the months of mourning his aunt are over, to be married here, in Highbury, at St. John's. Is not that wonderful! And his Uncle Churchill plans to attend the ceremony. With the death of Mrs. Churchill, all the old differences have disappeared. Frank hopes they will have a honeymoon in Switzerland before they settle in for good at Enscombe."

"I remember he spoke once of his desire to see Switzerland. I'm so happy that he will have his dream come true, along with his marriage to Jane. How exciting! He was always talking about traveling. Have they set a date?"

"Indeed, they have. Just three months from now. So, Mr. Weston and I can start the planning now. Of course, Mr. Elton will marry them, but Frank wants a big party afterwards. He writes that he thinks Randalls may be too small and wants us to look into a reception at the Crown. What do you think, Emma?"

She had a suspicion that Mr. Knightley would find it an inappropriate and extravagant way to celebrate their union. Their own nuptials had been very simple and celebrated at Hartfield. Of course, part of that decision had been to make it all easier for her father. But Frank had no such restrictions anymore. Given his easy temperament, Mr. Weston would agree to anything Frank wanted, though she wondered if Jane would like it. After all, the Crown could hardly be a source of happy memories for her. Frank had made such a show of ignoring her that night at the Crown ball and making much of his regard for Emma. The more she thought of it, the more she was sure Mr. Knightley wouldn't approve.

"Whatever will make them happy," said Emma, "will be fine with me. I am glad that they will be married here. It will make it so much easier for the Bates to attend. I may even coax Father to come, now that he so readily takes the arm of Mr. Knightley to steady himself. I was amazed last evening, that he did so. It had always been my task, but last night, Mr. Knightley took it over. I was so happy to see it. I still may be the choice to adjust his many scarves and serve his early dinner, but his taking of Mr. Knightley's arm signals a healthy division of labor and a visible sign that all is well with Father." Emma smiled. "Would you like to walk outside a little? The way we used to? Or will your advanced condition prevent you?"

"Thank you, dear Emma, but just today I am a little tired, and must decline your invitation. As soon as the baby arrives, we can continue our walks. And today it looks a little like rain may be coming."

"Very well," said Emma. "It's just as well. I think I had better head back to Hartfield. You certainly shouldn't be caught in the rain."

"Would you like one of our umbrellas, dear Emma?" she asked, smiling.

"Like that day I borrowed one from Mr. Weston and left the two of you to share the other. I knew you were destined to be together!"

said Emma. "I even told Mr. Knightley when I got back, though he scolded me for taking any credit for prompting the two of you to fall in love!"

"Falling in love is such a mystery, Emma. It's always hard to say when it starts, or why it continues. Often, we don't recognize it at first. I don't think I did," she said.

"You are right," said Emma. "But I always loved Mr. Knightley, from the time I was about ten!"

Mrs. Weston smiled again. "Your love for Mr. Knightley couldn't have begun when you were only a child—though you always liked to see him, I'll admit. But ten was a bit early for love to start, don't you think?"

"No. Just because I didn't always call my feelings for him by the proper name, I know it was love. And for him, too. We talked it all over one day at the seaside in Broadstairs and agreed that we had always loved each other, while not recognizing it as such for many years. Though he was first in knowing, I wasn't far behind. He told me he knew for certain at the Box Hill outing when I so recklessly flirted with Frank."

"I think you were a little in love with Frank when he first came, don't you agree?" said Mrs. Weston.

"Not really. I was flattered by his attention and did enjoy his company and his playfulness. But I don't think I'd call it love, that strong connection I've always felt for Mr. Knightley, even when we were calling it friendship. But I recognized my true feelings when I was talking to Harriet Smith." She stopped abruptly. She almost slipped into telling her old governess how Harriet's declaration of love for Mr. Knightley was the final means of her enlightenment. She told herself then, "Mr. Knightley must marry nobody but me!" But that was a secret she would never tell.

"Well, I'm off for now. I'll send for you by carriage tomorrow. Do come over and see all the changes we've made to accommodate Mr. Knightley's residence. So many books! Fortunately, we have room for a library just for him! And—you may not believe it—but we've started on a list of 100 books we plan to read together."

Mrs. Weston laughed. "Neither I nor Harriet Smith ever succeeded in making you realize that goal. I wonder if Mr. Knightley will!"

They laughed together, and Emma set off on her way back home.

While she enjoyed her visit, there was something about Mrs. Weston's manner that bothered her. As always, she continued to pride herself on being able to detect people's feelings. Mrs. Weston didn't look like herself. Emma would ask about her tomorrow.

When she reached Hartfield, she found her father reading beside the fire. "Where is Mr. Knightley," she asked.

"He is performing his daily constitutional, dear Emma," her father replied. "He has walked over to Donwell and says he will be back within the hour."

Emma marveled at the way her father seemed to have accustomed himself to their new living conditions. She wondered, though, if her husband missed Donwell. It had been in his family for so many years, indeed since it became a private home after Henry VIII dissolved the monasteries of England, selling them off, or granting them outright to noble families. The Knightley family purchased the house in 1561.

She had always liked Donwell. It was a large, handsome structure, with some sections still dating to medieval times, most of the improvements, however, dating to the 17th century. The house even had an old chapel, complete with the original stained glass. She remembered being impressed, when she was a child, with the large parlor, hung round with its portraits of ancient ancestors. In those days, Mr. Knightley used to tell her their stories. Once, in one of his attempts to amuse her, he had dared her to count the windows on the front, a task which had kept her occupied for at least an hour.

She decided to walk over to Donwell, and of course, found Mr. Knightley in his large, well-stocked library.

"How did you find Mrs. Weston? Well, I hope," he said, adding with a smile, "Have you come over to find another book for our list? Though we are not even close to being finished with Milton." She kissed him and sat down across from him at the large library table. "No, my dear. I've come over to get you back for lunch. Can you come?"

He put aside his work and took his wife's arm. They walked together across the green meadows, shaded by trees more ancient and less trimmed and cultivated than those at Hartfield. "I was going to visit the Martin farm, but that can wait for another day." They continued hand in hand through the beautiful landscape, amid the towering and spreading woods, past rock and meadow, to their mutual home at Hartfield.

"Are you regretting your departure from Donwell?" she asked.

"I thought I told you—I wish to live where my heart is, and that is with you," he said, holding her hand tightly. No more was said until they reached Hartfield and found Mr. Woodhouse anxiously awaiting their return. In that respect, nothing had changed.

CHAPTER 5

Back at Enscombe, Frank Churchill and Jane Fairfax sat in the ornate drawing-room of the Churchill home planning their future together. For them, a time of waiting lay ahead, the three months' mourning due to Mrs. Churchill, following her sudden death.

"Well," Frank began, "Emma and Knightley seem to have begun their future together," he continued, as Jane finished reading to him his stepmother's most recent letter. "Imagine! The great Knightley has moved into Hartfield. And very quickly, indeed. That's a bit of a come-down for him, don't you think?"

"I think it's quite a lovely solution," replied Jane, detecting criticism both in his tone of voice and in his words. "It shows his great love, giving up all his comforts for her."

"I certainly could never have done that," he replied. "Imagine, a man like George Knightley not being master in his own house!" He thought ahead to eventually becoming master at Enscombe. "Well, I suppose Knightley has ruled over his own establishment at Donwell for so many years, he can put it all away from him for a while." He added, in thought, but not in words, that if bringing Emma to bed was the immediate reward of the move, it might have been worthwhile. "I think he's as besotted with Emma as I am with you," he concluded, laughing and pulling her to him.

"I don't think you would have moved into the Bates home for me," she said with a smile. "My dearest Frank, you have not the possession of Mr. Knightley's patient kind of endurance," she said, "though you have great powers of persuasion," she added, recalling how he had pressed their secret engagement upon her. Enjoying his caress and kiss, but pulling back a bit, she added, "We will have our time soon now."

"Yes, but we must suffer these dreaded three months of waiting, my dear. And with you staying here for a few days in the house, only a handful of steps away from me, it's a hardship to await the consummation of our love." The warmth of his passion for her rose and seemed to taunt him.

Frank felt as if most of his life had been spent waiting for what he wanted. He supposed he loved his aunt in the way he might have loved the mother he never knew. But in recent years, as her health worsened, and as she demanded more and more from him, he began to feel trapped by her possessive love. He wondered how Emma had, for so long, borne that kind of possessive love from Mr. Woodhouse, even after her marriage. It was madness, he thought. She claimed she loved Highbury and never wanted to leave it. He supposed she was being truthful, as far as she knew herself.

"You'll have much to distract you, my dear, during our waiting period. And, while we are at Enscombe, like the constant presence of Mr. Woodhouse at Hartfield, your uncle's presence will be a reminder of the need to forestall our happiness until the proper period of mourning is over," said Jane.

Frank made no reply but was unconvinced. As he had approached his manhood, he had grown more and more restless, and sometimes tired of Enscombe. Mrs. Churchill, finally recognizing her need to let go a bit, had permitted his various trips, never too far away, of course, which somewhat relieved the tension and the feeling of confinement, that had been growing on him. Weymouth had been the permissible place, and then, on the latest of those trips there, he met Jane and fell in love with her. Now, with his aunt's timely death, he should be able to do almost anything he wanted. Mr. Churchill never interfered with him, and his quick acceptance of Frank's engagement to Jane, boded well for the future.

Frank was no novice at love-making and had managed to enjoy the comforts of female companionship whenever he wished, especially on those brief trips to Weymouth. Even here at Enscombe, he had enjoyed a long relationship with a local woman, employed at the house. But as soon as he saw Jane, she became his one desire. He succeeded in making her agree to a secret engagement, though for the foreseeable future, she would be out of reach. When she went to

Highbury to stay with Miss and Mrs. Bates for the summer, he contrived several visits there. But visiting his father and ostensibly paying visits to the Bates had been frustrating. He could hardly touch Jane, except for some brief stolen moments when Miss Bates was out. Fixing Mrs. Bates' spectacles had given him his longest afternoon with Jane.

His enjoyable flirtation with Emma Woodhouse somewhat relieved the tedium. Sometimes he thought of trying to go a bit further with her. He thought he saw some stirrings in Emma that might perhaps mean more serious feelings for him. At that last interview at the Westons, he had taken her hand, but then she so quickly pulled it away, that he realized he must have been mistaken. He supposed that would be going too far, even for him, especially with a lady like Miss Woodhouse. As he was saying his goodbyes, he toyed with the idea of telling her the truth about his engagement with Jane. But he still had some problems to resolve at Enscombe with a certain Miss Sharpe, employed at the great house as attendant to his aunt. When his aunt relaxed and granted him trips to Weymouth, Miss Sharpe followed him there, procuring a position as a governess to several visiting families. He had not yet completely disengaged himself from her, though his love for Jane quickly replaced his former affection for Miss Sharpe. That was an issue he had to resolve, and soon.

Now, back in Enscombe, he longed to consummate his love for Jane. What difference could it make to anyone? Speaking for himself, none at all. But he wasn't sure how Jane would react.

She had broken her moral code so far as to be secretly engaged to him. But the lies and subterfuges tortured her even to the point of injuring her health. For himself, he enjoyed the game, especially when Emma became involved in their mutually developed fantasy of a love affair between Jane and Mr. Dixon, the Campbells' new son-in-law. To him, there was something about secrets that was delicious and made relationships much more exciting. To Jane, the secrets gnawed away at her and spoiled relationships. She hated it when he joked about how the secret had almost come out when he mentioned Dr. Perry's intention of setting up a carriage, something he could not have known without a letter from Jane. He covered it up with talk of an extraordinary dream, telling Jane he could never think of it without laughing but was silenced by her retort: "How you can bear

such recollections, is astonishing to me…how can you *court* them?"
He was sure she would eventually see things his way.

Amid these recollections and resolutions, he felt his old
restlessness returning. He turned to the matter of planning their
honeymoon journey. Switzerland awaited them! He started to tell
Jane about his plans for a trip abroad.

"But that is so far away, my dear," said Jane. "Don't you think
somewhere closer would be better for our first weeks as a married
couple? The letter from your stepmother describes the Knightleys'
trip to Broadstairs. How beautiful it sounds. I have always loved the
sea. Have you ever considered returning to Weymouth for our
honeymoon? It would be something to revisit those scenes where we
first discovered our love for one another. Weymouth is quite as
beautiful, in its way, as the Alps, I think. I understand that the artist
Mr. Constable has painted some wonderful seascapes of the place.
Might not we rather think of Weymouth?"

Frank was determined that their honeymoon travel plans take
them further away, something he had been dreaming of, even before
he had fallen in love with Jane. He was unconvinced about
Weymouth. The fact that some artist had stayed there meant very
little to him. He also had other, more compelling reasons to stay
away.

But a day or two later, Jane had taken the subject up again. On a
visit to the library at Enscombe, she discovered that Mr. Constable
and his wife had honeymooned at Weymouth, staying at the vicarage
at Osmington in Dorset, on the Downs, overlooking Weymouth Bay.
Constable had painted Weymouth Bay with swirling movements, the
mountains merging with sea and sky. The book contained an
engraving of the painting, and made her fall in love, all over again,
with Frank and their time at Weymouth. She so loved the place, with
its tempestuous sky and wild and attractive coastline. In her further
reading, she discovered that Constable suffered greatly from his long
engagement with his wife, whose father had forbidden their marriage.
It made her think of Mrs. Churchill, and how she would have resisted
Frank's marriage with her. Constable's father finally conceded, and
the two married happily, honeymooning at Weymouth.

The book went on to say that the *View of Weymouth Bay* was one
of Constable's finest paintings, either 'because the occasion of his
viewing it was a particularly happy one or simply because the natural

grandeur of the scene appealed to him.' The writer concluded that the painting was 'a most dramatic composition and passionately expressed the wonder and glory of the elements.' Yes, she thought, 'wonder and glory,' indeed. That was how she felt then, and still did now. When she and Frank spoke of such things again, she would repeat her thoughts about a honeymoon in Weymouth. It was where she wanted to spend her first weeks as the wife of Frank Churchill. She was happy they would be married in Highbury, among her old friends and family. She must be content with that, for the present.

CHAPTER 6

'People should not marry, Emma! Mothers die.' She remembered her father's words when he heard of Miss Taylor's acceptance of the offer of marriage from Mr. Weston. Now, it seemed, there was some truth to her father's caution. Mrs. Weston had given birth to a lovely little girl, named Adelaide. But after the first days had gone well, Mrs. Weston began to feel unwell and took to her bed. Emma visited every day and found Mr. Weston more than naturally gloomy. Dr. Perry had performed the delivery which, unfortunately, had to be by Caesarian section, an additional concern as such surgeries were relatively new.

Emma was glad Mr. Knightley lived at Hartfield and was able to entertain her father while she made her daily visits to Mrs. Weston. He ordered William Larkins to bring some of his collections over for Mr. Woodhouse to amuse himself with and cheerfully kept him company. Miss Bates was recruited for games of backgammon, and even Isabella was contacted in London, with an invitation to Hartfield. Each day, when Emma returned, she kept up her daily cheerful smiles and demeanor, saving her dark thoughts for the evening, when she and her husband were alone.

"She does not look well," said Emma to her husband, when Mr. Woodhouse was duly escorted to his room by his son-in-law and the door to their bedroom was finally closed. "I wonder if John and Isabella know a London doctor who might come and have a look."

"These so-called geriatric pregnancies are never easy, I'm told," said Mr. Knightley. "Mrs. Weston is nearing forty, not an easy age for child-bearing. But she has been a healthy woman all her life. There's no reason why she cannot recover, given time and rest." He knew much about his estate and its administration but had never made any inquiry into the current practices of the delivery of children.

"Isabella has never had any trouble bearing children," Emma said.

"Yes, my dear, but she began at a younger age," replied Mr. Knightley. "If you wish, I'll ride to London tomorrow, and see what kind of medical connections John might have. Perhaps he knows a doctor who could come to Highbury and examine Mrs. Weston."

"I wish you would," said Emma. "I'm uneasy about her."

News of Mrs. Weston's delivery and subsequent ill health had reached Enscombe as well. Mr. Weston had written, hoping Frank might leave Enscombe and come to Randalls to see his stepmother.

The letter quickly produced the desired results. "It would give me something to do," said Frank, "a distraction during this ordeal of waiting for our marriage," he said to Jane after the letter arrived.

"I will go with you," she said. "Perhaps I can be of some use in taking care of the baby."

"As you wish," he replied. "I'll call for the carriage tomorrow."

So it was that Frank Churchill and Jane Fairfax returned to Highbury. Jane wrote to Miss Bates, and to her father-in-law to be, and he relayed the news to Emma.

"While Jane is with her aunt, he will probably stay at Randalls, but, if you agree, we can also offer Donwell during their time here," said Emma, pleased at Frank's concern for Mrs. Weston, who had been so supportive of him during the late revelations of his secret engagement to Jane. "You see," she continued, "he's quite a different person now that he has been able to display his love for Jane openly."

"We'll see. It is good that they are coming. During this time, Mr. Weston needs all the support he can get. He's already lost one wife. I'm sure he doesn't want to lose Mrs. Weston as well."

"Don't even think of it," said Emma. "It couldn't be borne. And that lovely little baby. She needs her mother, as Frank needed his. Is there anything else we can do for them?"

"I don't know. With Jane coming, there will be someone to stay there all day and care for the child. About nursing, I don't know. I'll ask Robert Martin if he knows a wet nurse in the neighborhood. His elder sister is married, with a young baby herself. She may be able to help if Mrs. Weston worsens."

After Frank Churchill and Jane arrived, Emma stayed back for a few days, not wanting to be in the way. Jane stayed once again with her relatives and Frank at Randalls. Soon, she heard from Miss Bates that Frank was worried about his father's mental state, and suggested a change of scene for Mr. Weston, who declined.

Mr. Knightley disapproved. "How could Frank even contemplate leaving everything to Jane? It's not good. Emma, you should resume your daily visits. If more help is needed, you will let me know."

And so, Emma rode or walked to Randalls every day, while Mr. Knightley continued managing daily life at Hartfield. His brother wrote that Isabella and baby Emma would be coming to give more help if needed. John could not come at once, as he was in the middle of a legal case. But he had procured the help of a London doctor, who would be arriving with Isabella, a Dr. Proctor, about whom John had good reports. In the meantime, Frank had to be content with more limited excursions, taking his father out for walks or a carriage ride every day.

They had done all they could. Jane spent every day at Randalls, and Emma was a daily visitor. Mr. Martin's oldest sister was engaged as a wet nurse, and everyone hoped that each day would bring improvement in Mrs. Weston's condition.

On his trip to London, Mr. Knightley spoke to several medical experts about Mrs. Weston's condition. What was dreaded above all things, was the so-called 'childbed fever,' or puerperal sepsis. He was told it could be spread by midwives, or by so-called 'gentleman' doctors, who did not wash their hands. He was determined to question Dr. Proctor on his arrival. There wasn't much more he could do. He too remembered his father-in-law's dire predictions, upon learning of 'poor Miss Taylor's' projected marriage. 'She could have stayed with us until she died.' Indeed, that is almost what she had done. He longed to bring Emma good news, but truth-teller that he was, he could not. With his tasks in London completed, he headed back on the 16-mile ride to Hartfield with a heavy heart.

CHAPTER 7

Once arrived at Hartfield, Mr. Knightley and Emma now faced the task of informing Mr. Woodhouse about Mrs. Weston's condition. Predictably, he reminded them of his oft-expressed opinion that people should never marry. But once past that, he became more like his less apprehensive self and told Mr. Knightley to offer whatever help was within their power to give, whether the assistance of carriages or offers of food, healthy preparations, of course.

Isabella would arrive the next day, so they all decided to retire early, Mr. Knightley leading his father-in-law up the stairs, with Emma following. She knew that her father had always enjoyed seeing Mr. Knightley as an almost daily visitor. Now past her husband's transition from visitor to resident, he became increasingly comfortable with the new arrangements. Especially in this time of impending trouble, it was a relief to see Mr. Woodhouse settled comfortably at Hartfield. Emma quite expected him one day, in a moment of forgetfulness, to counsel Mr. Knightley never to marry!

That night, however, Emma and Mr. Knightley could not get themselves to sleep from worry. Trying to find some means of distraction, he reminded Emma of their projected reading list of one hundred books.

"Why not work on our list tonight," said Mr. Knightley. "I always liked reading before going to bed."

"Well," said Emma, "Now that you are no longer living alone, that might not work as well."

"True," he said. "I certainly am not suggesting it as a habitual bedtime practice. But tonight, it might help us forget our worry about

Mrs. Weston. Would you have a suggestion from your old list? The one you made when you were fourteen? I confess that I saved it and could probably find it again. But I seem to remember you once showing me your newer list. If I'm correct, it started with Milton. Why not begin there? You know, I studied *Paradise Lost* with my college tutor, and could take the work up at any point with ease."

She thought for a moment. "That's a story that turns out tragically. Would that be best tonight?" She wasn't sure about this suggestion.

"Oh, in the end, they come through their ordeal, even somewhat improved. And some spots speak of happy things, most especially, of the joys of conjugal love."

"That sounds good," said Emma with a smile. "Why don't you read me some of that part. I remember getting stuck right at the start, on justifying the ways of God to man."

"Indeed, that would be a tough order, especially at the moment. There are other parts that might better suit us tonight." Mr. Knightley was a good reader with a fine voice, and in the old days at college, loved to intone Milton's sonorous lines. Turning the pages of the leather-bound copy he had brought over from the Donwell library, he soon found the lines he wanted, and Emma settled back to listen. He had been so good about everything since his arrival at Hartfield, the least she could do was listen to Milton, if that's what pleased him.

"I always liked this section," he began, "though at the time I first read it, I hardly had thoughts of marriage. Here we are." He read aloud. "Hail wedded Love, mysterious law…Paradise of all things." In a short while, he saw that Emma had fallen asleep. Milton had worked his spell. Before putting the book away, he repeated some words to himself: Marriage—'Paradise of all things.' Indeed. He had finally found it.

In the morning, he went back to the passage, reading aloud more of Adam's words to Eve, without thinking that his wife still slept beside him. "Awake, My fairest, my espoused, my latest found, Heaven's last best gift, my ever new delight."

Shaken suddenly into wakefulness, Emma pulled herself up. Almost embarrassed by the poet's words, he said, "I wasn't trying to wake you up. But in those distant days, when you were but a child, I never thought I would find myself reading such things to you as we awoke together as man and wife. Quite incredible, it still is to me. And 'Heaven's last best gift, my ever new delight' fits my current situation quite nicely."

She asked him to read that part to her again. She was almost getting to like Milton.

Yet, happy as they both were, the troubles at Randalls soon replaced these thoughts, and dressing quickly, they went downstairs to breakfast. Since Isabella had not yet arrived, Emma decided to walk over and find how Mrs. Weston fared since yesterday. Jane and Frank were settled in by now, he at Randalls, she in her old place at the Bates home. Upon her arrival, Emma learned at once from Jane that the news was not good. Mrs. Weston's fever continued unabated, and she was now in additional pain.

"It's fortunate that Mr. Martin's older sister has come to tend to the infant. Since she has her own baby, she can act as a wet nurse, at least temporarily. Mrs. Weston can hardly do that at present," said Jane. "When Mr. Knightley stopped here yesterday on his way to London, he told us that a London physician would come to assess the situation."

"Yes," Emma said. "A Dr. Proctor. I expect he will be here before noon. Is there anything else we might do?"

"No," Jane replied. "We thank you for your offer and the help you have already given. Frank has taken his father out for a carriage ride. Mr. Weston is so distraught, he is in almost worse condition than his wife. He keeps repeating that he has been through this once in his life, and now perhaps must do so again. He has been quite inconsolable."

"I can only imagine," said Emma. "May I go up and see Mrs. Weston for only a moment? Would you like me to stay here with you until they return?"

"No," said Jane. "I've already turned Mrs. Elton away. My aunt is coming and given the solemn silence of the house at present, it will be good to have her here, with her good-natured chatter and willingness to see the best in everything. I do thank you, Miss Woodhouse—sorry—Mrs. Knightley. I am fine for the present. Do make your visit."

Emma thought Jane herself did not look good, but she decided not to press her company upon the house, and after a short visit with her old governess, walked back to Hartfield.

There, she found her father in his usual state of nervous apprehension waiting for the arrival of Isabella and, hopefully, the London physician. Traveling almost always meant disaster to Mr. Woodhouse, and he would not rest until they had safely arrived.

"You must keep little Emma here at Hartfield. We don't want her to catch whatever it is Mrs. Weston is suffering from," he said, watching from the front door for their arrival.

"Father, please come inside. Standing there won't help bring them any sooner. And I don't think what Mrs. Weston has is infectious, though we are surely not planning on bringing little Emma over there, given the situation. Where is Mr. Knightley?"

"He has walked over to Donwell to check on a few things with William Larkins. I told him I would be fine by myself for a while. And Emma, be sure to tell cook not to prepare anything too rich. Isabella always did have a weak stomach."

"Yes, Father, I'll see to the menu. Meanwhile, why don't you look through Mr. Knightley's collections again. He's brought them over just for you. I think he has arranged them in his study." Between settling her father, worrying about Mrs. Weston, wondering when Frank and his father would return, and waiting for Isabella's arrival, hopefully with the doctor, Emma was herself in a very nervous state. Here she was, nominally mistress of two great houses, now trying to help with a third.

The mention of Mr. Martin's sister reminded Emma she had not yet spoken to Harriet Smith since her wedding and had no idea of Harriet's mental condition, especially her thoughts about Emma's marriage. She hoped Harriet and her farmer husband were happy, though Mr. Knightley mentioned that Mr. Martin was pulling back a bit on his expansion scheme for the farm. Mrs. Elton had dropped a somewhat nasty comment about Harriet's rather immediate pregnancy. Since Mr. Martin's oldest sister was recently married and had left the farm, there would no doubt be extra room for the baby on the way. Emma wished she could find an opportunity to talk to Harriet, both about the embarrassing past they had shared, and the present. Her sense of guilt regarding her meddling in Harriet's love life remained undiminished. She must think of a way to meet Harriet alone. This anxiety about Mrs. Weston must put such plans on hold.

Fortunately, Jane seemed to have kept Mrs. Elton away from Randalls. She was sure Jane could not bear Mrs. Elton's officious offers of help, given so unwelcomely in the past. If something were really to go wrong, she wondered how present circumstances might affect Frank and Jane's wedding plans. Her thoughts returned to Milton's Paradise, which seemed far away this morning. Remembering the title, she only hoped it was not going to be Paradise Lost.

CHAPTER 8

Through the conversations that Mrs. Elton had with Miss Bates, the Coles, and others, news spread at Hartfield that all was not well at Randalls. Turned away at Randalls this morning by Jane Fairfax, Mrs. Elton decided to pay a visit to Emma to see what more she might learn of Mrs. Weston's condition. She knew, as did most, that the lady had given birth. But given the fragments gathered from Miss Bates, together with the news that Mr. Martin's sister was acting as a wet nurse for the new baby, she was sure something was amiss. As the vicar's wife, she felt she had a right to know what members of the congregation were doing or suffering. If she failed to get information from Emma, she would send her husband to Randalls. After all, no one would turn away a clergyman on a visit of mercy. She had not seen Emma since her return from her honeymoon and was also curious to see what the new living arrangements at Hartfield looked like. She and Mr. Elton both marveled at Mr. Knightley's removal to Hartfield. Quite shocking, they agreed. They knew of a couple who tried such an arrangement and separated. She was sure their friend Mr. Knightley could not bear it for long. Elegantly dressed, she arrived by carriage, appearing soon after Emma herself had just arrived from her early visit at Randalls.

Emma received her at the door and ushered her into the drawing-room.

"Mrs. Knightley," Mrs. Elton began, "I went over to Randalls this morning and was turned away. Obviously, something is amiss there. I wanted to find a time the vicar could visit. I don't think anyone realizes how busy and overworked he is, and yet he always is ready to be of help, should something be amiss. Perhaps you can apprise me of Mrs. Weston's condition."

"I really cannot," said Emma. "I paid but a brief visit. I think it would be best to leave them alone for the time being, until they ask for whatever help might be needed."

"Think how many buryings, marryings, and christenings Mr. Elton must perform every week. And then the sermons to write! I don't think anyone realizes all he does. And I must do so much too! Visits and teas! Bringing food to the poor! Every week something else! I have not touched my instrument for days! And still, my caro sposo is ready to pay more visits!"

Emma was astounded at the egos of this mutual admiration society. "Indeed, Mrs. Elton, I'm sure we are all grateful for his service. It's just that no visitors are wanted at present. And with all you say Mr. Elton has to do, perhaps he would be grateful to have some respite from his many labors."

She was glad her husband was away. This was almost too much for courtesy to stomach.

"I'm sure you know, Mrs. Knightley, how potentially dangerous the weeks after delivery might be. One learns almost every day of some unfortunate woman who has succumbed, even after giving birth. Indeed, your own mother is an example, as is Frank Churchill's—and Jane's as well."

What cheek the woman had! Bringing up private matters like this. Would there never be an end to Mrs. Elton's display of vulgarity!

"I did learn that Dr. Perry had been over there several days this week," said Mrs. Elton. "Perhaps Mr. Knightley knows more than you do."

"I cannot help you there, Mrs. Elton. My husband is away just now and I do not know when he is returning."

"I am sorry you cannot help me," said Mrs. Elton. "I will apply myself to Dr. Perry."

"Perhaps the rules and procedures of the medical establishment will prevent him from sharing with anyone outside the family the details of the patient's condition."

"So, she is still a patient of Dr. Perry. Indeed, there must be something wrong. We will see if the vicar can offer some spiritual assistance. Thank you, Mrs. Knightley." Mrs. Elton stood and with a great flourish of her skirts, made her exit.

Emma hardly knew what to do next. Her husband was gone by carriage to London to fetch the London doctor recommended by John. She hoped they would arrive soon. She was terribly worried. She knew that death and disease caused by childbirth were all too commonplace. In some cases, fever set in after a successful delivery, and then, no one knew why, pain, debility, and death followed within weeks.

Sometime after lunch, Mr. Knightley arrived, having first delivered Dr. Proctor to Randalls after their return.

"We've done all we can, Emma. Nothing to do but wait. I've asked Dr. Proctor to come by here later and give us a report before returning to London. On the way, he talked to me about current theories concerning this condition. The statistics indicate a dreadful mortality rate, especially in hospitals, of all places. He says there is talk that sanitizing the hands of doctors and midwives is the cure, but that there is great resistance to that practice at present. I know no more than that. But I'm satisfied that John has found a doctor who knows much about this condition."

"Mrs. Elton was just here," she began, "her usual officious and obnoxious self. She wants to have her husband admitted to see Mrs. Weston. That would be the last thing that is wanted, I think. Do you have any idea where Frank and his father could have gone today? I don't think leaving Mrs. Weston was a good idea, even for a short while."

"I know you think I don't like Frank Churchill—you are correct there—and I rather think that taking his father on these rides away is more for his own diversion than any help to Mr. Weston. I'm sorry Emma, but I continue to think of him as a scoundrel and a disgrace to the name of man! When I think of all he has put Jane through, it sickens me."

Her husband maintained his prejudices against Frank, somewhat unjustly, Emma still thought. "I only hope we can find them, should we need to call them back."

"After the doctor has concluded his examination, he may give us a better idea of the seriousness of the situation, and Jane might have some idea of where the men might have headed today. Meanwhile, let us not alarm your father as yet. I will go in and see him. Hopefully, he's still occupied with my collections."

Mr. Knightley gave his wife a quick embrace and went off in

search of Mr. Woodhouse.

"Ah, Mr. Knightley, you are back from your trip." Mr. Woodhouse was seated by the fireplace, wearing his usual indoors regalia, a thick shawl wound about his throat, and his feet in warm stockings, set on his footstool, insurance against 'the damp.' "How did you find Isabella and the children?"

"In good shape, as usual. I believe Isabella has made arrangements to visit very soon."

"That is wonderful. But it is very cold out. I hope you have not caught your death on your recent trip, being outside in such weather. I knew someone once, who went out to walk in such weather, and expired two days later. Are your feet damp, Mr. Knightley? One must be careful, even indoors. I must have one of the servants examine the window fastenings. One never knows when a draft will creep through!"

"Indeed. I've examined them myself, sir, and all is well. If you are well-settled, I'll go and join Emma." It was easier and easier for him to feel comfortable with Mr. Woodhouse. Over the years, he had come over to Hartfield almost every day for an hour or two. When he thought of it, he marveled that his motives for coming had never occurred to him. He remembered when he had walked over after returning from London and the birth of little Emma, that his father-in-law said it was good of him to visit after making such a big trip. He had replied that it was but a short walk and was fond of it. Then Emma commented, with one of her mischievous smiles, that she thought his daily walks weren't so much for his constitution, but because he wanted to scold her about something or other. He had certainly come to see Emma, he now realized, though his reasons had remained obscure to him until the moment he felt the stirrings of jealousy with the long-awaited arrival of Frank Churchill at Randalls for his first visit in twenty years. How different it all was now! These were memories to cherish, had all been well at Randalls.

A knock at the door interrupted his meditations. Dr. Proctor was back from Randalls. Mr. Knightley ushered the doctor into the drawing-room and went off to get Emma. She must hear whatever the doctor had to say.

"Can I get you some refreshment, Dr. Proctor," asked Mr. Knightley. "You have a journey ahead of you."

"Thank you, Mr. Knightley, but no, not now. As a matter of fact, what you could do is find me a place to sleep for tonight. I am going to stay at least another day. Your Mrs. Weston is not well at all," he said, taking a seat.

"Of course, you will stay with us," said Mr. Knightley. "Either here, or at Donwell, my other estate, a short distance away. Here comes my wife, Emma. May I introduce you."

The trio arranged themselves, Emma and Mr. Knightley more worried than ever at the Doctor's decision not to leave.

"I am afraid I do not have good news for you. Mrs. Weston is indeed in the throes of what looks very much like puerperal fever. Usually, it affects women within the first three days after childbirth and progresses rather rapidly. She already has severe abdominal pain and an increasing fever. In my opinion, it is sepsis that has been caused by some contamination during delivery. A controversy is raging just now on the continent about requiring improved hygiene during delivery. Here in England, we are taking the situation and its controversial diagnosis very seriously. Unfortunately, once the disease begins to manifest itself, there is little we can do to retard the progress of the infection. Some part depends on the age and stamina of the mother. Your Mrs. Weston is not young for giving birth for the first time, so she is at something of a disadvantage. Tomorrow I will meet with the doctor who delivered the baby, apprise him of the need for increased good hygiene in caring for her and do my best to alleviate the pain. But there is little to do beyond that. I think, Mr. Knightley, you should advise her husband and stepson not to venture forth again so they can be present if the worst occurs. I am sorry to deliver such bad news."

Emma was already in tears, and Mr. Knightley thanked Dr. Proctor for his help. He advised that it would be best if he stayed in one of the guest rooms at Hartfield. Emma would have it prepared, while he rode over to Randalls to inform Jane, Frank, and his father about the doctor's accommodation at Hartfield. Emma was to keep all this from Mr. Woodhouse, at least for the present. In a few minutes more, she was readying the guest room, and Mr. Knightley, having quickly saddled Bessie, was off for Randalls.

CHAPTER 9

The next day, Dr. Proctor stayed at Randalls through the early evening, but there was nothing further he could do. Mrs. Weston had taken a turn for the worse. The only good news was that Mr. Weston and Frank had returned and would not venture forth again.

It was fortunate indeed, for their remaining time with her turned out to be short before she left them forever. Now Mr. Weston faced the same situation he had faced so many years before. But he made one solemn resolution, a promise to his dying wife. This time, much better off financially, he would not send his infant daughter away. She would stay with him at Randalls, to grow up among her own people, with her father and those friends who would rally around him. She would be all he had left of the wife he greatly loved and with whom he finally found so much happiness.

When the news was brought back to Hartfield, Emma could hardly think or speak from grief. She had nearly wrecked Harriet Smith's life with her meddling. If, as she believed, she brought her dear Miss Taylor within the orbit of Mr. Weston—and that, at the very least, she had done—then she had surely destroyed her dear friend, someone who had been far more than a governess, nearly a mother to her. After Dr. Proctor delivered his bad news, she let out a gasp and ran upstairs to her room. All she could think of were her father's words when she first told him of her successful matchmaking efforts with Mr. Weston and Miss Taylor: 'You should not do any more matchmaking, Emma. Remember, mothers die. It's a fact.' Now those words rang in her ears as both prophecy and reproach.

Her husband did not immediately follow her upstairs. He knew she needed time to recover herself. And he had to manage Mr. Woodhouse who sat in an uncharacteristically stunned silence before the dwindling fire.

"Father-in-law, we must get you to bed. There is nothing any of us can say or do tonight. Emma is no doubt inconsolable, and I know your grief is great too. All we can do has been done. If you will sit here for a few moments, I will see Dr. Proctor out and call the carriage. James will take care of getting him back to London. His other patients need him now. Then I will get you settled upstairs. Tomorrow there will be time to talk."

After completing these tasks, and setting the household to rights, Mr. Knightley went slowly upstairs with Mr. Woodhouse, staying with him briefly until he was settled. Then he walked down the corridor to Emma. Words were going to be unnecessary tonight. Emma was already in bed. He undressed quickly, and lay down beside her, holding her tightly all through the night, until morning came.

The next day, news of Mrs. Weston's sudden passing was all over Highbury. Emma awoke to bleak thoughts. Her husband was standing beside the bed.

"You're awake," he said. "Your father is already downstairs at breakfast. Do you want to dress and go down? Or would you rather I brought something up for you here?"

"I really don't want anything just yet," she said.

"Do you want to talk, or would you like to be alone?"

"No, please don't leave me," she said, pulling him down beside her to sit on the bed. "I don't know what I want. I suppose with Frank and Jane there, and with Mr. Martin's sister caring for the baby, they will be all right, at least for a while. And what can anyone say, anyway?" She took his hand, clutching it as if for dear life. "What are you thinking?"

He considered carefully. "I know what you are thinking, and I'm afraid I must correct you. You are no more responsible for this than you were for their coming together in the first place."

"I did bring them together. And perhaps Father was right. She might have lived happily here with us even now, had I never meddled. Oh, I am so unhappy!" He was right about the direction of her thoughts, as her tears began to fall again.

"Emma. Let me tell you what I have told you before, when, so many years ago, you wanted to take credit for Isabella and John falling in love. People choose for themselves. They were not then, and are not now, anyone's playthings. Marriage is serious business, as we know ourselves. Even with the help of others, sometimes people make bad or empty marriages. Sometimes there is failed love, egotism, mere self-gratification." His thoughts went immediately to the proposed union of Frank and Jane. "We know how important it is to find a good marriage, no matter the obstacles. Consider how long I waited to find you, to achieve what we have together. As with everything in life, as your father has said many times, 'catastrophes happen.' Now they have, for the Westons. It is a black morning for us all, but the Westons did achieve married happiness. If you must accuse yourself of something, do so for helping them find the joy of love in one another, no matter how short their time together has been. It's a rare find, as I think we both know. Often, people miss it. We didn't." He paused. "Forgive me, if I'm lecturing you again, dear Emma." He waited for her to speak.

"I know you're not. It's just that, now that Mrs. Weston is gone, and Isabella so far away, you really must be all in all to me. Do you promise?"

"I did that when we stood at the altar. Of course, I promise. Remember what you once said, after we had disagreed about something. 'We always say just what we think to one another.' We will continue to be honest with one another, and each of us will help the other to be our best selves. But I see you have something more to tell me," he said, his steady grey eyes upon her in that searching way so peculiar to him.

"When I went to Randalls yesterday, I had a brief visit with dear Mrs. Weston. I had to see her, you know. She had been like a mother to me, and now I was sure I was about to lose her. When I lost my own mother, I was but a child, and hardly grasped what was happening. Now, I was about to lose a second mother. She took my hand and asked me to love her little one when she had left us. And take care of Mr. Weston. Of course, I nodded yes, and we wept together. Then, seeing her exhausted and in pain, I left. I could do no more." Emma looked near collapse. "When I came back downstairs, Jane embraced me and we held tight to one another. When I said goodbye, I felt as close to her as I have ever been," she said.

"I'm glad you were able to talk to Mrs. Weston and say goodbye to your beloved friend. But now, my dear Emma, please, if you can, come downstairs with me and have some breakfast. Your father also needs your help in coping with these new circumstances. And we must think about the Weston household. These two deaths, Frank's aunt, and now Mrs. Weston's, one after the other, will hit Frank and Jane very hard. They are not a very good prelude to a marriage celebration. There will be many decisions and further arrangements to be made." He stopped. "Perhaps they will need to wait even longer to marry."

"Oh, I fear Frank will not like that." She saw her husband frown. "But we won't talk of that now. You are always so good at knowing what to do," she said. "My very own Mr. Knightley. Is it any wonder I can't find a way to call you anything else?" She was changing what she saw could be a very unpleasant subject, and he was grateful that she had done so. The wedding of Frank and Jane, whenever it should take place, was a matter that lay completely out of their hands. Emma quickly dressed, going downstairs to meet the obligations of the day.

She was apprehensive of the problems that might await them in the coming days. It was a day she never thought would come.

CHAPTER 10

The grief-stricken Mr. Weston was unable to think, to talk to anyone, to make any plans other than to keep his baby daughter at Randalls. On that, he was determined. On every other subject, he had nothing to say. What would Jane Fairfax and Frank Churchill do now, given this new loss?

Frank had now resided at Randalls for several weeks, while Jane stayed in her old quarters with the Bates. Frank's restlessness was beginning to stir. About his aunt, he felt no terrible grief. She had been the instrument of his confinement so long that, were he to admit it, he was glad she was gone. In his mind, her loss should not in the least delay his long-anticipated marriage to Jane. Mrs. Weston's death was another story. Though he had known her only a short time, he liked her very much, found her younger, prettier, and more interesting than expected. She had been so much his advocate with Emma, though she had not in the least suspected his attachment to Jane. Surely, Frank told himself, she would not have wanted to impede the wedding plans. He knew he could manage Mr. Weston, at all times so amiable, pliable, and open to Frank's every suggestion. For his part, the wedding could not come too soon. He was eager to be away with Jane and off on his long-anticipated travels. Surely, no one would see it any other way.

But Jane felt bewildered, overwhelmed, and uneasy. She knew from the first that Frank was a different sort of person from herself—restless, volatile, a roving sort of creature, always eager for the next moment's adventure. While she suffered greatly under the secrecy necessary since their engagement, she sensed that for him it was, if anything, exciting, even a welcome diversion. Yet she loved him. Of that, she was sure. He loved her too, and of that, she was also sure. She was ready to marry him but to do so shortly after these two wrenching deaths, seemed wrong. Indeed, the secret engagement also seemed wrong, but he had demanded it, and she agreed, hoping it could be kept secret until such time as he could declare his love openly and honestly. Mrs. Churchill's recent death changed all that. She needed to talk to someone about Frank's wish to speed up their marriage plans. Not the Bates, of course. And though she and Emma bonded in the days after Mrs. Weston's death, she did not feel at ease talking about Frank with her, even though she was now happily converted into Mrs. Knightley. There was always Mrs. Elton, who earlier took up the task of finding her a governess position, forcibly and almost uncomfortably insisting on utilizing her Bath friends and connections. But she did not like her, or her caro sposo. She thought she would be able to talk to Mr. Knightley. She could trust him to listen to her concerns and truthfully advise her about her worries. But how to do this without including his wife?

She was resting in the Randalls drawing-room, watching Mr. Martin's sister feed the baby when Frank came in.

"I see you are enjoying these displays of domestic duties, my dear. But we are not there just yet. First comes the wedding and our honeymoon travels. Afterward, there will be time enough to think of babies. For now, we can do anything we want, go anywhere. Such freedom, after so long a confinement!"

"Yes. But let us think carefully first, let us take time to consider." He embraced and kissed her. Though she felt shy and unwilling, with the wet nurse and the baby there, she returned the kiss.

"I can't wait until we can be off and away, on our own for the first time in our lives!"

"But we need first to see about your father. Can we leave him alone just yet, after his unexpected great loss? I know you want to travel abroad, but perhaps, if we do have our wedding as planned, it might be better to take a short honeymoon at Weymouth, as I always wanted to do. We would be closer, and better able to return if needed." She saw him frown. This would not be easy, she saw.

"I've talked with Father. He has no objections to our marrying sooner and leaving for our honeymoon after. He understands."

"He knows what you want, to be sure. But does he understand

himself and how he will cope with his loss and the new baby in the months ahead?"

"Surely you don't think he expects us to stay here. He'll be fine. There are many good friends nearby who will help keep him company. The Woodhouses—excuse me, the Knightleys—are but a half-mile away. Taking care of my father will give Emma something to do. She's experienced at taking care of fathers, having looked after her own father for so many years. It will keep her out of trouble. Otherwise, she might find herself at loose ends. Mr. Knightley now has plenty to do with overseeing the finances of both houses, the farms, and his community duties. Harriet is busy at the Martin farm, and we know Emma doesn't like Mrs. Elton—so taking on my father is just the right thing for her."

Jane became uncomfortable at Frank's rather selfish analysis of Emma's new state. "Frank, it isn't Emma's job to care for your father. You have already used her rather badly, making her the cover for our attachment and engagement. We should leave her alone. You have not treated her well." Nor me, she thought, surprised at the judgment she had not yet let herself make.

"I didn't say it was her job, only that she was used to such tasks. She always says she loves Highbury, and would never leave it or her father. So, what is so reprehensible about temporarily adding my father to her landscape of responsibilities. She would enjoy it, I think."

"Frank. I don't want to discuss this just now. Let's go over to Hartfield for a walk. I need some fresh air. You don't have to come if you'd rather stay here, but I very much need a walk." She hoped she might find Mr. Knightley available for a talk.

Frank sensed himself in a dangerous place with Jane. He decided to let the matter rest for the present. "I'll get our coats and we'll be off. Father is resting. It's a good time to get out for a short while."

CHAPTER 11

Having only just relieved himself of one secret, Frank Churchill now faced another, one equally important to conceal. How very annoying had been his last conversation with Jane, and her insistence on spending their honeymoon in Weymouth. He had spent so many hours, some time ago, persuading his late aunt to let him have regular outings at Weymouth, it seemed ridiculous, now, to face the necessity of persuading yet another woman to stay away from the place! Strange how things turned out in life.

He liked Weymouth at first. It was a much smarter resort than Broadstairs, where the Knightleys spent their honeymoon. Many more parties, balls, and dances. Under other circumstances, he would have been happy enough to concede the point. But unfortunately, the presence there of a certain Miss Sharpe, a governess with an infant girl, made Weymouth a place he must now, at all costs, avoid. He had enjoyed some good times with Miss Sharpe, but she must understand they were over. The sooner he could marry Jane, the clearer his unavailability would be. It had been hard enough to convince Jane, elegant and principled as she was, to engage herself to him secretly. He had to act quickly to secure her love and attachment, and only a solemnly agreed upon engagement could do that, until he was free to marry her. Then, most accommodatingly, his aunt had died. He was a lucky man. The mourning period over, he could take Jane away from England and Highbury for a long trip on the Continent. And when his uncle died—as he would, no doubt soon—he would have all the rest of his uncle's fortune and the Enscombe estate as well. Then, he would do his duty and provide for Miss Sharpe's little girl. She claimed the child was his, and he had no reason to doubt her. But all that was over now, and he had to get away. He had announced to all, at the Box Hill excursion, that he was tired of England, and would leave as soon as he could book a ticket.

Now, Mrs. Weston's death threw his plans again into confusion. He hoped no one expected them to lengthen the period of mourning before the wedding. Indeed, he was determined to shorten it. Miss Sharpe might learn of his situation at Highbury and cause trouble.

His first concern was Mr. Weston. He hoped to persuade Emma to take care of him, as she always cared for her own father. He had enjoyed his adventure of keeping secrets from Emma. He deceived her once and was sure he could do it again. Mr. Knightley would be a bigger obstacle. But he had to do it. Everything depended upon it.

"Jane dear," he began. "I'll walk over to Hartfield with you. I'm sure Emma wants to know how we are coping with things here. Father is resting just now, and Mrs. Martin has taken the babies for a walk. I'll get your coat, and we'll be off." He bustled into the next room, informed the servants of their proposed outing, and was soon walking the half-mile to Hartfield with Jane.

"Frank, I know you are eager for us to be married and go away on our honeymoon, but I really think we must care for your father. You should also remember your uncle's lonely situation at Enscombe. Since Mr. Weston is hardly able to care for the little baby girl during these days so sorrowful and difficult for him, it will be good for me to stay here for a while to help care for the baby. I have never been around very young children before, and I want to learn. If you are tired of these occupations, you might visit Enscombe by yourself for a few days. Your uncle must be in need of the consolation of your company." She stopped and waited for his reaction to her suggestions.

"I hope you still want to marry me, Jane. It seems that all your thoughts are of helping others, I am the only one left out of your arrangements. Of course, I don't want to visit Enscombe without you. As for our honeymoon plans, Weymouth doesn't mean to me what it means to you. For me, it was an escape from my aunt, and I often indulged myself there in ways I want no longer to remember."

"But we met and fell in love there," she protested. "Surely that should obliterate any unpleasant associations you might have of the place. Yes, it might remind you of your aunt's partial release of her hold on you, so far as to permit your visits at Weymouth. But surely our time there together must weigh more heavily with you than any previous small escapades in which you might have participated. They don't matter to me. My life began when I met you there."

"Yes, of course. For me, too. It's just that I want to start our new life somewhere else, at a place that contains no past memories. Even though I learned to love you there, it was a time of worry and fear that we might never be allowed to marry. So, you see, my dear girl, I want to forget it. Think how beautiful Switzerland must be, with the romantic Alps reaching up to the sky. I want to go there. You must let me plan for us both." A wintry chill was in the air. Jane pulled her coat tightly about her.

They reached the front path leading to Hartfield. He made his case and hoped she would say no more about it.

They knocked and were admitted. Almost immediately, Emma appeared, followed by Mr. Knightley. It seemed Mr. Woodhouse was taking his afternoon nap, so the two couples went into the drawing-room and were seated.

"How is our dear Mr. Weston?" Emma began, "I can only imagine his sorrow and sense of disorientation."

Frank spoke first. "Oh, he is doing better than you would think. He is busy planning the funeral service and we are arranging for a lunch to follow the burial. And Mrs. Martin—it isn't Martin, is it? We really don't know her married name—but whatever it is, she is doing fine as well. She is being paid generously, of course, and has taken quite a liking to the baby. So, you see, all is better than you think."

He finished with one of his brightest smiles. While Emma had always liked him, calling him an amiable young man, she was a little put off by his cheerful good humor. During the time she was reviewing her feelings toward Frank, she had concluded he was not necessary to her happiness. She could not build upon his steadiness or constancy and imagined that his feelings could be rather changeable. He stood in stark contrast to her husband, even then. Mr. Knightley said nothing to Frank's depiction of the state of affairs at Randalls. In the silence following Frank's assessment, it was left up to her to reply, as Jane, too, said nothing.

Emma made a start. "Well, that is good to hear. I have not seen Mr. Weston since his wife's passing. We felt we should not intrude. But if, as you say, he is doing well, we should pay him a visit. Perhaps that is what you have come to suggest?" She looked at Frank and saw his face darken.

"Not just yet, of course. He still needs his rest. There is so much to do and to arrange. There is also the matter of our wedding plans to discuss. It is my idea, and I have not yet even had a chance to talk to Jane about this, that having the wedding occur a bit sooner would be good for my father and for all of us. I know my father very well, and he would not want us to delay our happiness on his account." He looked at Jane and took her hand. "Am I not right, my dear?"

Jane sat quietly and said nothing at first. "I must think about it, my dear. How much sooner?"

Emma was stunned. How could Frank and Jane discuss the details of their future arrangements with them and not first privately together. And marrying sooner, with Mrs. Weston only just gone, as well as his aunt! She waited for his reply to Jane's question.

Frank shrugged, unwilling to provide further details. "I don't know. But three months is certainly too long to wait," he said.

"We will have to talk about that when we get back to Randalls," said Jane, allowing the discussion to go no further. She was reddening. "We came over only to tell you that all is well, at least as well as can be expected, given our altered circumstances." She stood. "I think we must go back now. I do want to see how things progress. We will tell you when Mr. Weston is ready for a visit." For a short time, the ebb and flow of other conversation continued until Frank signaled that it was time for them to depart. He stood, joined Jane, and they left, rather abruptly, both Emma and Mr. Knightley felt. They returned to the drawing-room and sat down to discuss the visit.

Emma waited for her husband to begin, not yet trusting herself to speak.

Mr. Knightley was not pleased with what he had heard. "I believe you will find my thoughts impertinent, Emma, but when he talked of speeding up their marriage plans, all I could think of was Hamlet's remark, when, disgusted by his mother's hasty remarriage following her husband's death, he sarcastically said 'The funeral baked meats did coldly furnish forth the marriage tables.' Forgive me, but as you like to remind me, at least once a day, we always say to each other just what we think. And that is just what I thought. Sorry, my dear."

"I'll admit to being somewhat shocked as well." Then, as if to keep her own unpleasant thoughts to herself, she said, "Is *Hamlet* on our reading list, Mr. Knightley?"

"Now you are angry with me," he said, "I see you are."

"Not at all. I confess, it's an apt if a somewhat caustic comment. But surely Hamlet's situation was a little different from Frank's. There is no murder in this case."

"Of course not. But I think for Frank Churchill, it's all about putting his own needs and desires above all others. If you noticed, Jane did not seem to know about his plans to speed up the wedding date. I thought she looked not only surprised, but a little angered."

Emma had to agree. It was still hard for her to accept Jane's superiority in any way, but clearly, Jane's sense of what was morally right and even of the proper decorum surrounding matters of death was appropriate. Still, she found herself also sympathizing with Frank.

After all, she and Mr. Knightley married soon after his declaration of love. At first, she held back, fearful of even hinting to her father that marriage was in their plans. But her husband insisted that following her acceptance, her father be told at once. Of course, as she told her dear Mrs. Weston many times, when Mrs. Weston thought Mr. Knightley might have sent that mysterious piano to Jane, "Mr. Knightley would never do anything secretly." When she was honest with herself, she had to admit that was one of the things she loved about him most, even though it made moments like this challenging. After he had declared his love for her, and she had, surprised, almost gasped, "Can this be true?" he answered, "You will never get anything but the truth from me." She understood how another man might have let Frank's behavior pass, but knew that her husband could not.

Mr. Knightley looked at her closely. He was reading her thoughts, she knew. He too was recalling their own speedy union following his declaration of love. "I admit I was also eager to start our life together," said Mr. Knightley, as if picking up her thoughts. "But, as you said yourself, we had loved each other since you were ten! Frank and Jane have not known each other nearly that long, and perhaps it would be better for them not to rush. In any case, there is nothing we can do about it. So let us continue to say just what we think to each other and always be friends." He looked at her with his usual penetrating gaze, his steady gray eyes upon her.

Was he aware that she was withholding something from him?

Surely not her more forgiving attitude to Frank Churchill, which he probably suspected, or the remnants of her jealousy of Jane Fairfax. No, she thought he knew there was something else, for she had continued to keep this one secret from her husband—that Harriet Smith confessed she loved Mr. Knightley and thought he returned her affection. But it wasn't her secret only, and now that Harriet was transformed into Mrs. Robert Martin, Emma thought it best to keep it to herself. She knew how difficult it was to find perfection. She did not ever want to damage her perfect union with Mr. Knightley. And yet, she kept this one secret. Was that why she judged Frank less harshly?

CHAPTER 12

As Mrs. Robert Martin, Harriet Smith no longer resided at Mrs. Goddard's school. The tradesman who had been paying her board generously provided a small marriage settlement, as well as her modest wedding. Her life as a farmer's wife would be different now. Her leaving meant, of course, that Mrs. Goddard must find a replacement for her service in the near future. Then, as if in unexpected answer to this new situation, Mrs. Goddard received an interesting letter from a perfect stranger. Miss Sharpe, a governess in Weymouth, wrote with a request for employment at the school. She suggested she would also be qualified to initiate an infant school which could be attached to the premises. Her letter included a glowing reference from the family for whom she had worked and whom Mrs. Goddard knew quite well, and also one from Frank Churchill's uncle at Enscombe. Mrs. Goddard could hardly ignore the latter.

Without the reference from her old friend, Mrs. Parker, Mrs. Goddard might have dismissed the application and the unusual proposal out of hand. But the ties of friendship and previous professional collaboration, together with Mr. Churchill's letter, made Mrs. Goddard feel the need to respond with at least an invitation to the young lady so that she could explain her proposition in person. So, she wrote and prepared one of the guest rooms at the school to receive her visitor within a few days' time. In the meantime, in advance of the young woman's arrival, she wanted to talk to someone about the unusual proposal for an infant school. Given Mrs. Weston's recent passing, she knew Emma and Mr. Knightley would be busy helping at Randalls. It was then she thought of Mr. Elton. Surely the vicar would have good advice. Thus, on the morrow, she called at the vicarage and was cordially received by Mrs. Elton in the drawing-room. The vicarage was modest in size but had been well-furnished with pretty furniture. The wallpaper was a pleasant blue, the curtains a bright yellow, and a Scotch carpet lay on the floor. A small square piano stood at the far wall. No doubt all these improvements were Mrs. Elton's doing. The vicar soon joined them and, to Mrs. Goddard's surprise, his wife stayed to hear the business which had brought her.

Mr. Elton, noting Mrs. Goddard's reaction to his wife's continued presence, hurried to explain. "I am very busy with parish work, Mrs. Goddard, and Augusta has become so interested in all I do with the community at large, that I have included her in all matters concerning Highbury and its inhabitants. You may speak freely for, as she so often says herself, she is the very soul of discretion." From behind his desk, where he had seated himself, he smiled over at his wife who took a seat next to the one chosen by Mrs. Goddard, who had no choice but to begin.

"Thank you, Mr. Elton. You see, I've had an unusual request. A young woman who has worked successfully as a governess for an old friend of mine in Weymouth has written with a somewhat unusual proposal for my school. She is coming to see me in a few days to discuss an idea which she has suggested I might incorporate here at Highbury."

The Eltons sat silent and expectant.

Mrs. Goddard began. "She proposes to work at the school as a teacher, her abilities for which my friend and Frank Churchill's uncle write, she is most well qualified."

Mr. Elton seemed puzzled. "Surely that is something about which you yourself are qualified to judge."

"Indeed, Mr. Elton. It is her further proposal that is somewhat unusual. She suggests my adding a kind of nursery for very young children as an adjunct to the school and the ages we usually service. She would supervise the very young children, as well as teach in the school for older girls. She writes that she would bring with her a small child, the very young and natural daughter of her sister who, alas, has passed away. You may recall Harriet Smith and her very successful tenure at our school before her marriage to Mr. Robert

Martin. My friend writes that the girl's expenses have always been paid, and would continue to be, should she bring her to Highbury. She claims that what the presumed father of the girl remits would cover all the additional expenses. Of course, I would need to employ a nursemaid to cover the hours Miss Sharpe would teach the older girls."

Mr. Elton looked at his wife, seeking her reaction. "Of course, Mrs. Goddard, we must not appear to countenance the presence of illegitimacy in our midst." He continued to look at his wife for guidance.

Mrs. Elton now spoke. "Well Mrs. Goddard, reality is reality. On my own visits to the poor in these recent months, I have seen the presence of several children needing care and others in the situation you describe. It might illustrate our Christian benevolence, especially should the vicar consent to visit these children as they grew older and were able to absorb the important truths he always conveys."

Mrs. Goddard could see that Mrs. Elton was clearly the one in charge here.

Mr. Elton smiled benevolently at his wife. "Augusta is an example to us all, and most especially to me. Mrs. Goddard, I think you may entertain the young woman's proposal with no worry about scandal or gossip. I could myself make your small infant school a part of my regular parish visits, and even of my talks, should you go ahead with this idea."

The vicar stood, followed by his wife. Mrs. Goddard had her answer, if not from heaven itself, from its earthly representative and his spouse here in Highbury. Mrs. Goddard curtseyed and left. She wrote Miss Sharpe immediately on her return, setting a date for their interview.

As for the Eltons, they both wondered about this unusual proposal. Surely there was more here than met the eye. The child was illegitimate. And the coincidence of this woman applying at just the time when Mrs. Goddard needed a replacement was suspicious. Mrs. Elton resolved to keep her eyes on the matter. Now that they had been asked for their help, she would give it, of course, in her own way.

CHAPTER 13

Mrs. Elton was determined to visit Randalls and try to see Jane Fairfax again. She wanted to know what Mr. Weston was going to do, both with himself and his new baby daughter. She had some ideas of her own, friends in Bath, some of the ladies with 20,000 pounds, who would not be averse to a life with Mr. Weston, who was still a youthful-looking and agreeable man, well off, and with a fine house.

She made her plan. Claiming that she brought a message from Mrs. Smallridge, she thought she would not be refused entrance a second time. She knew that Jane still felt guilty about the withdrawal from her acceptance of a position as governess with the Smallridges upon notice of the death of Frank's aunt and his public announcement of their engagement.

"Hello, you dear girl," said Mrs. Elton with her widest smile and a warm handshake when the door was opened. "I've come to see you, of course, and the little newcomer, if possible." And before Jane could demur, she quickly added, "and I bring an important communication, a message from my friend, Mrs. Smallridge. May I come in?"

Of course, without discourtesy, this time there was no refusing her. "Come in, Mrs. Elton. How good of you to call again." They entered the drawing-room, and Mrs. Elton seated herself before the fireplace.

"And how is our dear Mr. Weston? Is he as yet quite recovered from his loss? Dear man. He is one of my favorites. He always likes to talk with me, you know. I've told him, time heals all wounds, they say."

Jane nodded, somewhat reluctantly, for Mr. Weston was indeed still in a deep depression, quite unable to be in company. Speaking very little, he was animated only in the presence of his new daughter. But none of this she communicated to Mrs. Elton. Of course, she thought, the woman means well, but she is difficult to tolerate sometimes. Jane was glad to be released from her obligations to her and Mrs. Smallridge. But she owed her and Mrs. Elton the courtesy of a listening ear.

"Mr. E. and I have been so busy with vicarage business that I haven't had any time for social visits. So busy always. Doing good everywhere. Everywhere! But I couldn't continue to ignore you and the current situation at Randalls."

Jane hoped to turn the talk away from herself and the future at Randalls. "I'm sure you are always very busy," she began.

"Totally! Just totally! Why only the other day, Mrs. Goddard came to us for advice and help with a new hiring at her school. Actually, it might be of some help to Mr. Weston. Can you imagine? She is thinking of adding an infant school to Goddard's. It is certainly a new idea."

"How will she manage, with all the students and boarders she already has to teach and care for? I suppose she would need to add extra staff."

"Yes. That's just what she came to see us about. It seems someone has coincidentally applied and is coming for an interview. A woman from Weymouth. Wasn't that where you first met Frank? Isn't it a small world? She also told us that Frank's uncle had written to recommend her."

"His uncle knows the person? I wonder if Frank does as well. He has been at Weymouth more than once. Do you know her name? Perhaps he met her there, or I have heard of her. At one point, as you know, I was thinking of a position as governess myself and made some inquiries at Weymouth."

"Mrs. Goddard didn't tell us the woman's name. Only that she has a small infant herself. Though I believe she said it is her sister's. Anyhow, so she says." Mrs. Elton gave Jane a knowing look. "I believe Mrs. Goddard is familiar with such anomalies. You recall Harriet Smith's situation there. She was very fortunate Robert Martin married her. Well, remember dear Jane, though you're no longer a sad girl, I am always here to help. If Mrs. Goddard goes ahead with this plan, it would certainly be a help to Mr. Weston. He would not be losing his daughter, as, I know, he lost Frank so many years ago. Why he could ride over and visit her every day! And not have the trouble of hiring someone to live at Randalls to assist him here. Mr. Elton and I are very supportive of the idea."

Jane listened quietly. She supposed good advice can sometimes come from a questionable source. She promised she would tell Mr. Weston about the idea when he was feeling better.

Mrs. Elton went on. "I also look forward to assisting you with your wedding plans. As a married woman myself, I will help you arrange everything. Everything! Special clothes are always necessary for a wedding—and the trousseau. We could make a special trip to London, to one of the warehouses that carry such things. Naturally, I know where the best ones are, being so recent a bride myself. You will need a white frock and a white ribband for your bonnet." When she saw that Jane remained silent, she went on. "Now don't forget to mention Mrs. Goddard's visitor to Frank. Perhaps he knows something of this young woman and could provide Mrs. Goddard with a recommendation, or not if that is the case."

Jane smiled and stood. It was time to end the visit. "I will let you know how the idea is received here when Mr. Weston is up to visitors. Did you not say you had a message for me from Mrs. Smallridge?"

"Oh yes," said Mrs. Elton. "She wanted me to say she quite understood your withdrawal from the position you had accepted, and bears you no ill will. She is so understanding! Of course, I did help in smoothing the way. That is all. Of course, you should invite her to your wedding."

Jane realized that Mrs. Elton had wanted only an excuse to be admitted. Putting her annoyance aside, she continued to ponder what Mrs. Elton said about Mr. Weston's need to find help with his new baby daughter. Many parents, looking for an environment that provided clean air and water, placed their youngest children with a wet nurse in a country setting for the infant or toddler years. But she thought it unlikely that Mr. Martin's sister wanted to make her work a lengthy or even permanent position. It might be helpful if Mrs. Goddard were to start this formal infant school. She herself had never been interested in caring for infants, but saw that such an institution might be helpful, especially to the newly widowed, like Mr.

Weston, if he could be convinced that in a few years his daughter would return to Randalls. Infants and children needed love, but also unlimited patience. In Mr. Weston's present state, she knew the little girl would have love, but patience might be harder to supply. She also was feeling the pressure from Frank about getting away. She would feel better, even about advancing the date of her nuptials, if she knew there were a solution for her father-in-law and his new infant daughter. She began to warm to the idea. Such a good coincidence, that someone had come to Highbury to suggest such an addition to Mrs. Goddard's at just this time! She wished she could find an opportunity to speak to Mr. Knightley about it. As the magistrate in the area, he would know about the possibilities of establishing such a school. In any case, she must talk to Frank about it at once. She wondered if he knew anything of a person from Weymouth seeking employment here. It was too bad Mrs. Elton didn't know the woman's name.

CHAPTER 14

Frank's uncle, Mr. Churchill, wrote to Highbury, sending his condolences to both Frank and his father, and enclosed a letter that had been directed to Frank at Enscombe. Frank recognized the identity of the sender immediately, for he had previously received several such letters there.

My very dear Frank,

I have learned of your step-mother's death and your current residence at Highbury. I admit to wondering not to have heard from you following the death of Mrs. Churchill. Surely, her passing makes you now free to choose your own way and, I would hope, to marry. I hope you will now do the right thing and make our life and that of our child legitimately united to your own. I am puzzled by your silence, and so have made arrangements to travel to Highbury. I realize there remains the difficulty of concealing the full extent of our previous relationship. I have thought about a way in which we could meet, become acquainted, and, as you have more than once declared your intention, eventually marry. I have secured an appointment with Mrs. Goddard to interview for a teaching position at her school, and have sent my good references ahead. Given the new thinking about the subject now called "Schooling the Innocents," and the success of several infant schools in Scotland, I have suggested to Mrs. Goddard that she add such a venture to her existing school and permit me to assist in it myself. Our child could board there, and surely, with the passing of your aunt, you will have not only additional freedom of movement but also more financial ability to help me offer payment for our child while working at the school myself.

As you can see, I have given this matter much thought and preparation and hope that you will concur. My interview will be next week. Mrs. Goddard has given me lodging at the school for a day or two while we discuss this potential arrangement. Please find a way we can see one another! Although I know we must be careful, as we used to be, in the old days at Enscombe and Weymouth, my feelings toward you remain unchanged, and I hope and anticipate yours are the same for me. I cannot imagine otherwise.

Yours devotedly, Anna Sharpe

Frank responded quickly.

My dear Anna,

Life here has been so very chaotic; I have hardly had the time to look about me and think of the future. You are no doubt unaware, but my step-mother has unexpectedly died, after giving birth to a child. My father is so grief-stricken, that he requires my company every waking moment of the day. The rest of the time is taken up by caring for his infant daughter. We have a wet nurse in the house, but she is clumsy and inefficient and has an infant of her own, so you can imagine how deeply I am suddenly mired in household duties and the care of my father. Thus, I have been as of yet unable to devise plans regarding any possible future for us.

I am surprised you have gone so far ahead on your own, but I suppose your idea is worth consideration. I could not meet with you now, as you must realize, as all eyes in Highbury—a small town full of gossiping wretches—are upon me, observing all I do, and criticizing me when I do not do enough. I am obliged to take my father out for walks and carriage rides, to manage the household, visit with distant relatives here and stay in touch with my uncle. My finances are not as yet settled, though, of course, I hope Uncle Churchill will eventually make a handsome settlement on me. But he has done nothing yet, and I must, at all costs, preserve my outward appearance as a grieving nephew, mourning not only my beloved aunt but now, a well-liked step-mother. So, you must understand that we cannot see each other, even after you arrive in Highbury. This town is a nest of spies! And all of them are watching me! So, dear Anna, we will not be able to meet next week.

Also, I do not think it advisable for you to direct any further communication to me, either care of my uncle at Enscombe, or here in Highbury. Going to the post office here is a social affair, and people actually watch to see who gets letters and from where! It's a far different locale from Weymouth, I assure you.

I know your Weymouth address and can write you there after your return from Highbury. I will arrange to have this letter hand-delivered to you on the day of your interview at Mrs. Goddard's. Our wet nurse, who, as I have said, is a farmer's daughter and quite illiterate, will deliver it into your hands. You can say that it comes from friends at Weymouth. Later, on your return there, I will write you further. I am not sure that your idea to find employment here is a good one. We must move carefully and slowly, for it will be impossible for us to meet here or reveal any kind of previous relationship. I plan shortly to make a trip to Enscombe, and will stop at Weymouth on the way so that we can talk together about the future. Please give me time to work things out. Should our relationship come to light, I might lose my uncle's money, and any ability I might have to regularize our relationship and provide for you and the child.

Meanwhile, I send my best love to you and yours,
Frank Churchill

CHAPTER 15

"Now that we are safely married, I wonder if you will continue to scold and lecture me," said Emma. "Actually, if you don't, I probably will miss it. Though I know now there are other ways of showing me your love."

She and her husband had completed their early dinner with Mr. Woodhouse, who was just finishing his own healthful repast of boiled eggs, soup, and his usual glass of wine.

He had heard his daughter's remark, and let it pass without comprehension. "Scold Emma?" he said. "Impossible! What could anyone want to scold Emma about?"

Mr. Knightley smiled in response. "Well, I don't know, Father-in-Law. We will have to wait and see what she has to confess tonight. Then we can decide together whether or not to absolve her from whatever she has done." Mr. Knightley's continued care of and conversation with Mr. Woodhouse had cemented his easy position at Hartfield. Mr. Woodhouse smiled and Mr. Knightley waited to hear what his wife might have to say.

"What makes you think I have some specific action for which I need absolution?" She rose to stoke the fire and arranged more carefully the woolen scarf around her father's neck. Cold weather had deepened its grasp on Highbury. "But I always did secretly like it when you scolded me. Nowadays, I must make things up, for I think you liked it too," she said, playfully.

"No Emma, you're wrong there. I'm not good at pretending. You should know that by now." Her husband looked serious.

"Well, I remember, not so long ago, you pretended you couldn't dance. Then, when you took Harriet to the floor, your secret was out! You danced better than anyone!" She could never forget that first dance with him, at the Crown Inn, and how, as she danced with him, she began to recognize her true feelings. Oh, how he looked at her when the steps brought them closer, face to face! Magical, it had been.

"Well, that was a special situation," said Mr. Knightley. "I said that, because I thought you would never dance with me anyway, with Frank Churchill whirling you around the room and taking the first two dances. Don't you remember, when you first mentioned the occasion to me, I said I was no good at dancing, and there was probably no room for me on your dance card anyway! There I spoke at least a partial truth, at least as I saw it then," said Mr. Knightley, with a loving look at his wife. "I gave you the chance to correct me," he said.

"You were quite right not to dance, Mr. Knightley," said Mr. Woodhouse. "Dancing is not good for people, especially people of your age. I'm surprised you finally asked Emma."

"Oh, I didn't. It was she who asked me, Father-in-Law. Let me set the record straight on that. I wouldn't have dared request it, on my own. All I said at the time was, 'Whom are you going to dance with?' I looked around the room for a potential partner for her. She didn't wait a moment, but replied at once, 'With you, if you will ask me.' So of course, I had to dance with her. As we continued, I found myself liking it much more than I had ever before in my life."

"So, who were your previous partners?" asked Emma. "Maybe Jane Fairfax? May I ask?"

"Oh, I've long forgotten. That one dance with you completely obliterated all memories of any previous encounters."

"Now you are a flatterer," she said, pleased at the way the conversation had taken a different direction from the one she had started. It would be far better to bring up a matter about which he might potentially lecture her when they were alone, and not with her father, who seemed actually to be enjoying this conversation.

But later, when they were in their own rooms, she knew she must make a start at telling him something which he wouldn't like.

"Mr. Knightley. You know I went over to Randalls today to visit with Mr. Weston. Well, Jane had gone over to see her aunt, and so Frank was the only one there. I was alone with him briefly. He seemed quite unsettled, and I asked him what was the matter. He told me he had received news from Enscombe that his uncle was ill, and feared he and Jane must travel there at once. He asked if I could fill in for them for a few days at most. Well, what was I to say?"

"That is a sudden request indeed. Did he give you any more details about his uncle? What is his complaint?"

"No, he did not. He said only that he and Jane must leave soon, preferably the day after tomorrow. I don't know that I would need to stay overnight, but I could go over mornings and return when all was well after dinner. I would actually like to see Mr. Weston, as I have not since his wife's passing. What do you say?"

"The question is, Emma, what did you say?" Mr. Knightley looked troubled.

"I said I would speak to you. And I am doing that now." She gave him one of her appealing looks.

"Is that why you brought up the subject of me scolding you?"

"I suppose I must admit it. I was surprised that Frank said he needed to bring Jane with him. And of course, she wasn't there for me to ask her about it."

"Are you seeking my advice, dear Emma?" he said.

"Well yes. I know you don't like Frank, and think he is a frivolous young man, but he seemed quite earnest about this request."

"I think he is quite capable of seeming to be in earnest, whenever it suits him. He managed that, to be sure, in keeping from everyone his attachment to Jane and his real reasons for visiting Highbury. Now, he tells you, he must leave again, giving you little specific information. Don't you think you should talk to Jane, get her feelings about leaving Mr. Weston and the baby at this time? I suspect she has been holding the household together, while Frank has been riding all around Highbury with his father."

"Is that fair? He has been trying to distract his father, I think."

"And himself," said Mr. Knightley. "But of course, you can't stop him from seeing to his uncle. However, bringing Jane with him doesn't make sense. Did you ask him why she had to go also?"

"No, I did not. But if you wish, I'll go over early tomorrow and try to talk with her. Actually, you might come with me too. You've always been better at talking to her, no matter how I try. I think she still can't stand the sight of me since my behavior at Box Hill," said Emma, regretfully.

"You must forget about that," he said. "We shall both go over tomorrow. That way, we may be able to get their perspectives on doing what is best, and necessary, for everyone. Do you agree, Emma?"

"That would be fine. I will bow to your superior wisdom, once again, my dear," she said.

"Not superior," he answered. "Merely more objective, in the case of Frank Churchill, if you will at least admit that much."

"I think you are still a little jealous of him," said Emma, moving closer to him and taking both his hands. "You must know, that is utter nonsense."

"I think I do. But ever since I have admitted my love to you and to myself, I find I am more prey to irrational feelings than ever before." He looked at her, almost as if he had admitted some terrible fault.

"I think love can go both ways, rational and irrational. But please know that you will always be all in all to me," she said, still holding his two hands and now placing them on her breast. "Remember what you said to me not so long ago—that your heart is here." Then, putting both their hands on his breast, she repeated, "You must always remember that my heart is here with you, and never to be removed." And so, it was. They spoke no more of Frank's request or of anything else that night.

CHAPTER 16

In the morning, immediately after breakfasting and settling Mr. Woodhouse in his chair with the day's newspaper, Emma and Mr. Knightley walked over to Randalls. It was a gray, late November day, with a heavy cloud cover threatening rain, reminding Emma of that happier day when Mr. Weston had supplied those prophetic umbrellas to Miss Taylor and herself. As the two had walked away, Emma overheard Mr. Weston inviting Miss Taylor to see the newly purchased Randalls, and her delighted acceptance of his invitation. Later, when she took credit for the subsequent marriage plans of the Westons, it precipitated one of those lovely scoldings from Mr. Knightley. How long ago it all seemed now.

Just as they approached Randalls, some drops of rain began to fall. The door was opened by a servant, and they entered the room of so many previous happy encounters—her first sight of Frank, the planning for Mr. Knightley's strawberry party, the many private chats with her old governess. All that lay now in the unrecoverable past.

In a few minutes, Frank and Jane came into the room, he with his usual broad smile, but she, if anything, more reserved and withdrawn than ever before.

Frank welcomed them briefly, while Emma enquired after Mr. Weston. Would his father be coming down to join them? They hadn't seen him for days now, and their mutual concern for his welfare began the conversation.

"How is your father, Mr. Churchill," said Mr. Knightley. "We hope he is gradually recovering and facing the many consequences and coming responsibilities of his terrible loss."

Her husband had made a start, Emma thought, in his usual careful and gracious way. How she admired him, more and more, every day she lived with him.

"Yes indeed," said Frank. "Unfortunately, not much better. But that's not what we want to talk to you about." He paused. Jane had not as yet said a word. "It's about my Uncle Churchill. He's not well. I had a letter from him to say that he's quite ill. I'm worried about him. He wants me to pay a quick visit to Enscombe."

"Well," said Emma, "While you're away, Jane will be here to take care of things." She hoped she was assisting him with all he had to say. Obviously, he was not finished.

"Actually, no, she won't. My uncle wants me to bring Jane with me. He's a little upset that we've stayed here so long. He says he has something important to say to both of us and is worried, lest he pass away before he has a chance to make certain arrangements. So, we both must go."

Mr. Knightley was silent. Emma wished he would say something, anything. And at last, he spoke.

"Are you asking for someone to fill in for you both while you are gone? Is that your request?"

"Yes," said Frank. "That's it. We'll make the trip as quickly as possible of course. We thought that Emma could come over to Randalls and stay. We could be to Enscombe and back in a day, and perhaps stay only one day with my uncle. Mr. Woodhouse could come over here to stay with Emma if that would make things easier."

Mr. Knightley interrupted. "Mr. Woodhouse would not be able to do that." He turned away from Frank and spoke to Jane directly. "Is this your request as well? It's a sudden plan, is it not? Is it necessary to accompany Frank on this trip? I don't think you have been looking well recently. Is such a long trip advisable? Yorkshire is a distance." He looked worried.

There was a brief pause, somewhat awkward. Finally, she answered. "I'm quite well, Mr. Knightley, really. I'm grateful for your concern, but we are already packed and have ordered the coach to be ready early tomorrow. But I do not think it necessary that Mrs. Knightley stay overnight at Randalls. It would be sufficient that she come over mornings, just to see that Mr. Weston is all right and that Mr. Martin's sister is still managing with the infant. I realize it is much to ask, but Mr. Churchill has been quite definite in his request that I accompany Frank."

Mr. Knightley turned to Frank. "If you find your uncle very ill, what will you do if he is unable to manage on his own?"

"In that case," said Frank, "I will make the necessary arrangements for his future care. I don't think he expects us to be there long. He has some formal legal arrangements to make for which he needs us both to be present."

Mr. Knightley had been answered. There was not much more to be said. However, he was not about to make a decision on the spot. "Emma and I will need some time to discuss what arrangements we need to make for us to do our part. Since you are determined on this course of action, we will return to Hartfield, and by this afternoon, will let you know the specifics of how we can assist you. We are still awaiting the arrival of Isabella from London. At the last moment, my brother had some commitments which required her presence at home. You will have a message from us as soon as possible." He turned to Emma. "Let's be off for Hartfield at once." It was clear he would go no further at the moment.

It was now raining in earnest, and Frank summoned the carriage to bring them back. They hurried out, climbed in, and were off. Neither of them said a word until they were home and able to find a private spot in which to discuss this sudden and unusual request.

Mr. Knightley began. "First, Emma, let me say that, of course, we will take charge of Randalls during their absence. Whether or not I think they both should go, is no longer our question to answer. In their absence, I will take care of Mr. Weston. You must stay here with your father and await the arrival of Isabella. I will go to Randalls every morning, and stay until evening, substituting that for my usual constitutionals to Donwell. When Isabella arrives, you can come over and visit me and Mr. Weston."

"My dear, are you sure? You always have business to transact, and my father is as comfortable with you as with me, these days. I am quite willing to go," she said. So far, nothing had been said about their opinions regarding this request.

"No, dear Emma. It will be far better for me to go. I can walk out with Mr. Weston when he wants to get some air and can take him on carriage rides when he wishes, without having to bother James or Mr. Weston's coachman. It will be much better for me to go. You can come over whenever you wish, I hope, to see me when you can. I am quite decided on this division of our labor."

"But why would Mr. Churchill have required Frank to bring Jane? It doesn't make sense. He is surely aware that there are needs here in Highbury as well," said Emma.

"As with most of Mr. Frank Churchill's doings, it will no doubt remain a mystery for the time being," said Mr. Knightley. "His explanation was vague, and Jane looked uncomfortable. Not being a master at deception myself, I confess I cannot figure it all out. But then, not so long ago, I was completely fooled by their secret engagement. Since Frank Churchill and I are so very different, it is hard for me to discern or even imagine the motives for his actions. At Box Hill, when he went on and on with his games to relieve boredom or his request that you choose a wife for him, I thought he was thinking only of you." Emma hoped he had forgotten all that, especially her part in it. But he obviously had not and, warming somewhat angrily to his topic, continued. "And with eyes just like yours! What nerve! It's what sent me to London, to learn indifference to you."

"I'm glad you never learned it," said Emma, taking her husband's arm, as if holding him back from an attack on Frank Churchill.

But he went on, a little differently, as if softening both to her touch and to the unforeseen event that had saved him. "Fortunately, Mrs. Churchill's death revealed the plot, and brought me back to Hartfield to claim you for my own."

Emma relaxed her hold on his arm and let herself drift back to those wonderful moments during their walk in the garden when she had realized, for the first time, Mr. Knightley's feelings for her. "I confess, I too was deceived," she admitted. "And I agree he was not entirely without fault. As I told you, he used me badly. But I forgave him, because he had not harmed me, and for the sake of the love he bore for Jane."

"For me, it was an odd way to show his love—flirting in an utterly merciless fashion with another woman while his intended had to sit closely by and watch his wonderful performance. I still repeat, he is a disgrace to the name of man!" His anger was flaring up again.

"As for me," said Emma, choosing to ignore his last remark, "I have forgiven him, and believe he is a new man, now that he has Jane by his side. Both Frank and I have been fortunate to ally ourselves with partners in marriage so much better than ourselves!"

"If you think to put me off with flattery, dearest Emma, you have almost succeeded. But I continue to regard Mr. Churchill as a man given to using deceit to gain his ends. However, now that he has won Jane, I will join you in thinking he is sincere in wishing to accede to his uncle's wishes. I will do what I can to make his visit to Enscombe quick and successful. Let us send word to Mr. Weston that I will be his daily visitor until they return." He looked at Emma with a look she knew was decisive. She took his hand and kissed it.

"Emma, that is for me to do, not you," he said, pulling her to him, more fully returning her kiss, and imprisoning her hands in his. "Let us be in agreement. We will help and not question further, at least until their return. Later, perhaps, they will tell us more. For the time being, I will join you in hoping he has become a new man."

Emma nodded. When the reason for Frank's request came to light, surely, they would both approve. But despite those old convictions that she was a master at understanding human motivation, with her growing maturity, her surety about such things had become less firm. She knew her husband still suspected there was something hidden about Frank's request. She knew that her dear husband was not so sure about the new man. Truth be told, neither was she.

CHAPTER 17

This part of Frank's complicated arrangements had concluded more easily than he had expected. While Jane went upstairs to finish their packing, he reviewed the events of the last few days. When Anna Sharpe's letter had come, he became alarmed and knew he had to act quickly. Having won Jane with such difficulty at Weymouth, he was not about to risk losing her now.

What he could not tell anyone was that his uncle knew all about Frank's relationship with Miss Sharpe, almost from the first. A man in a difficult and unhappy marriage himself, he had sometimes availed himself of feminine solace, often at Weymouth, where his wife had once or twice sent him to supervise Frank. Discovering their similar needs and tastes, they agreed to keep each other's secrets. His uncle had not, however, fathered children as a consequence. He seemed not to have that proclivity, hence, in the early years of his marriage, he concurred with his wife's desire to adopt Frank. And so it was, as Frank grew into maturity, they had almost become friends, as they shared their pleasures and stolen adventures.

After his wife had so mercifully passed on, Mr. Churchill envisioned enjoying more such dalliances in company with his nephew. But by then, Frank met Jane Fairfax, falling deeply in love with her. Well, these things happen, Mr. Churchill thought. Now, Frank wanted to marry Jane and appealed for help from his uncle. It was possible that Miss Sharpe might cause trouble. It looked like she had already begun, with her trip to Highbury and her application for work at Mrs. Goddard's school. So it was, that he and Frank hatched a plan.

He would recall Frank to Enscombe, pleading illness and a desire to have Frank's wedding take place there immediately, lest his illness prove fatal. Jane had already been told the story, and agreed reluctantly to marry Frank at Enscombe before the three-month period of mourning had elapsed. She paled at the thought of yet another secret marring the fulfillment of her happiness with Frank. But they had gone ahead. Mr. Churchill secured permission from the local clergyman for Mr. Elton, the Vicar of Highbury, to perform the ceremony. It was a favor to Mr. Churchill, as he was told that Mr. Elton and his wife were great friends of Frank and Jane. All was ready for their arrival at Enscombe. Mr. Churchill had also seen his lawyers and drawn up an agreement that the Churchill fortune would go only to Frank and the children of his marriage to Jane Fairfax. He had already given some financial support to Miss Sharpe and was ready to draw up an agreement with her, as well, for a sum to be paid for the support of her child, on condition that she did not bring any action against Frank.

For all his past entanglements, Frank was deeply in love with Jane and wanted her badly. To be sure, there would be some rough moments when they returned to Highbury, to face the surprise and questions of their friends there. But Mr. Weston was always an indulgent, easy-going man, inclined to see all his son's actions in a favorable light. The Bates would easily be won over, and Emma too, Frank thought, for she always thought the best of him, despite his many deceptions. Mr. Knightley would prove more difficult, but, as past experience told, even he could be deceived. The Eltons, especially Mrs. Elton, would revel in their new, self-important roles, in their patronizing friendship for Jane and her fashionable young man.

The next day, with the Knightleys in charge of Randalls, Frank and Jane were off to Enscombe. But Jane was not totally comfortable. "Frank dear, I do not think it right to keep our secret from the Knightleys and my aunt and her mother. Why could we not have told them why we are marrying in this way? They may think we have other reasons, and I cannot bear that our union be spoiled by unfounded suspicions and gossip."

"You must get used to people talking about us, Jane. When we are off on our honeymoon, traveling to the ends of the earth away from Highbury, they will forget about us and find some other topic for their gossip." Jane was difficult to convince, and he did not want to repeat their previous discussions. "We have made our decision, based on my respect for my uncle's wishes. Surely you can see that is the honorable course, despite what people may say or think."

"I do understand you must think of your uncle. He has been through so much. But so has Mr. Weston."

"My father is in complete agreement with our plans. He even talked happily to me of the future celebration at the Crown Inn, as something to which he is now looking forward. My uncle was so desirous of having the ceremony at Enscombe, the family estate. I really could not say no to his wishes. He has already seen to everything, including the public posting and the marriage license, which will be issued after the ceremony."

"Yes, but none of our friends will be there," said Jane.

"Your friends will be present at our reception at the Crown," said Frank, "And for our wedding day itself, the Eltons will be present. I know you suffered some difficult times with Mrs. Elton, but you must agree she always had your best interests at heart and was a better friend to you than some others in Highbury. She will provide the necessary female companionship on the night before our wedding. Conveniently, Mr. Elton is an authorized person for marriages and will perform the ceremony. Enscombe has a small chapel, which will serve the purpose beautifully. They are both more than willing to do this for us."

Jane was not completely satisfied. "I wish my relatives and the Knightleys could have been present. Of course, Mrs. Knightley might not wish to be present. I don't blame her for keeping her distance from me. She told me she still blushed at things she did and said during the time we were keeping our engagement secret."

"She'll get past it," said Frank.

"Still," said Jane, "You used her rather badly."

"It was all for love of you, dear Jane, even though it didn't look that way at the time. Even now, I recall the delight I felt in tricking all our friends. But let's stop talking about that and think of what remains ahead. Tomorrow we will be married! You are an angel sent down from heaven just for me."

"I'm afraid I'm becoming a fallen angel, what with these lies and deceptions," said Jane, sadly.

"I thought we were finished talking about the past. Think of tomorrow, when you will finally become Mrs. Churchill. Despite the absence of some Highbury residents, our wedding will be a fine occasion. Mrs. Elton will delight in comparing our service to the Knightley wedding—a poor affair—shabby, I think she called it, with not much finery, white satin, or veils. We will change all that. I want you to wear as many of my aunt's jewels as possible. And you have your beautiful wedding dress, thanks to your shopping trip with Mrs. Elton before we left. Oh Jane, when I look at you, soon to be mine, I can't believe your beauty, your skin, so smooth, so delicate, your dark eyelashes and hair. The turn of your throat, your eyes—and you will be all mine tomorrow!"

"Frank. I am all yours right now. My beauty, as you call it, is bound to fade one day. I hope you love me for my mind, my disposition, my soul."

"Yes, yes, my dear, but men seldom fall in love only with well-informed minds instead of handsome faces. You are so lovely. Of course, I treasure your sweetness of manner and temper and all your accomplishments, but I think you don't understand what men desire—how could you?" he concluded.

"As for me, my true happiness will begin only when we have finally put away our life of deceit. I thought we were finished with concealment when we revealed our engagement. Now, it seems, we are again living in the shadows. I hope and pray that in a short time, all can be in the open."

"Yes, of course, my dear. But make no mistake, my uncle will be delighted that I have chosen so lovely a wife. He loves feminine beauty almost as much as I do. He is ready to make a handsome settlement on us. I remember my father and his wife wondering how we would satisfy the claims of Enscombe, and now we are on the way to accomplishing everything we have ever wished." He drew her to him and sank back in the carriage as they completed the last miles before reaching Enscombe.

The Eltons made the journey separately, Mr. Churchill having provided their carriage, and there was to be a festive dinner tonight at Enscombe. Frank's uncle had the hall decorated and ordered a rich and rare menu for dinner. Jane brought with her the wedding clothes, but nothing to match Mrs. Elton's elegant wardrobe at dinner.

They were all a little tired, but conversation must be made, and so talk turned to their only common subject—Highbury, and how things were progressing there. Of most interest was Mr. Weston's situation and how he would fare without his deceased wife and with the care of their new child.

"Frank," began Jane, "I heard in passing at my aunt's, that Mrs. Goddard was thinking of adding an infant school to her establishment. She was interviewing a replacement for Harriet Smith at the school. Apparently, the woman comes from Weymouth. Perhaps you or your father knew her? She had good references, I'm told." She turned to Frank's uncle. "Mr. Churchill, I was also told she had worked here at Enscombe." Frank's uncle darted a quick look at Frank.

"My dear, we can't be expected to remember all the servants here at the estate, especially not those who have left us. Uncle, do you recall such a person?" asked Frank, looking directly at Mr. Churchill.

"My dear Jane," he said. "There were some abigails who waited on my wife whose names I can't remember. But neither of them could be expected to qualify as a teacher in a school."

"It's so important that Mr. Weston have the right person to help care for his child, whether at Mrs. Goddard's or at home. I don't know that I could embark on a wedding journey unless I felt satisfied on that point. I will investigate further when we return." Jane had spoken quite deliberately.

Mrs. Elton now weighed on. "If needed, I have many contacts in Bath. If the new person coming to see Mrs. Goddard does not work out, I'm sure I can find a suitable substitute. I will look into it on our return."

"As always, Mrs. Elton, we are so grateful for your help on Jane's behalf," said Frank. "But after the wedding festivities are completed and we return to Highbury, I plan to go to Mrs. Goddard's myself and review the qualifications of this new person. Now, I'm concentrated on tomorrow, our marriage, and our new life, which is about to begin."

Jane was silent. She would not let so important a matter rest only with Frank. Certainly not with Mrs. Elton. She would do her own looking into this new woman's qualifications. On their return to Highbury, she too would try to meet her. A paper application, no matter how good the references, can tell only so much. There was also the matter of whether Mrs. Goddard would add an infant school to her establishment. If the woman to be in charge were suitable, only then would she agree to leave Mr. Weston and his infant daughter for two months. She too looked forward to a new life. But what exactly that new life looked like might be different in the thoughts she and Frank entertained as they finished eating their sumptuous dinner and retired to their separate rooms, ready to rest before tomorrow's wedding.

CHAPTER 18

So, at last, Frank and Jane were pronounced man and wife. A note had been sent ahead, informing the Knightleys of their marriage and expressing their gratitude for Mr. Knightley's solicitude for Mr. Weston in their absence. By the time they received it, Frank and Jane would be back at Randalls, and there was no further need for Mr. Knightley's attendance at Randalls.

Out for a walk in the Hartfield gardens, Emma and Mr. Knightley were exchanging their opinions of the news Frank and Jane had brought back.

"Well," said Emma. "They are married. It's surely a surprise and not the way we thought or wished things to be done, but at least they are together at last." She waited for her husband to speak, suspecting that he might take another view of the recent news.

"Had they told us this was their plan, would you have agreed, Emma? Would you have been part of this latest subterfuge?" Mr. Knightley could not but speak the truth of his feelings.

"I don't know. We shouldn't judge them. We had no such obstacles in our way, beyond those we made for ourselves. We only had to discover our feelings for each other. They had done that more quickly, months ago at Weymouth, apparently. Our story is very different, my dear."

"Indeed. But no less difficult, in my opinion. After all, here I was, visiting you and your father almost every day since you were born, a part of your life, but in a brotherly sort of way, to be sure. As the years went on, my brother John would tell me, especially after he married Isabella, that I needed to find a mistress for Donwell. On one occasion, he ventured an opinion that my problem was that I spent far too much time at Hartfield. Told me, that my interest in Emma was a little unusual. Too much, for a man of my age, he thought. After all, he said to me one night, after dinner, she's still just a child, don't you realize that? I was quite annoyed with him then and almost lost my temper. Said I had always been interested in Emma, and what would become of her. That my interest in her had nothing to do with any future marital plans. That I was only a mentor to her. That we were only friends. We almost had one of our rare quarrels after that. John gave me one of his knowing looks and turned away, and so we let the subject end. It's always hard when your younger sibling seems to know more than you do."

"So, let's not criticize Frank for doing whatever he could to marry Jane. When you love someone, you can act somewhat irrationally, you know," she said, holding his hand tightly. "I thought I told you that."

He did not think he had ever acted irrationally. But in recent months, he had let his feelings color his actions, that was certain. Dancing with Emma at the Crown started it. He had not planned or expected to dance that night. His one venture onto the floor was merely an act of polite heroism, to rescue poor Harriet Smith from Mr. Elton's pointed snub. Then Emma came over to talk, and soon he was dancing again. In all the years since she had grown into a lovely young woman, he had never held her in his arms or faced her so closely. The music, her presence so near, warmed him with completely new sensations. He felt a different kind of interest in her. As the music went on, they circled, holding hands, and one of the steps permitted him to hold her tightly around the waist. Then, when the various bows and approaches brought them so close, their faces almost touching, for the first time he thought they might have been approaching each other as lovers. All at once, he found himself wanting to hold and kiss her.

After the game at the Donwell Strawberry party, when the words 'blunder' and 'Dixon' caused Jane so much pain, he was once again baffled. That evening, he went to Hartfield to see Emma. He needed to understand what was going on between her and Frank. Then, her defense of Frank's actions confused him. Perhaps she really was in love with the man, and he should forget her. Not because she was a child, but because she was now a young woman about whom he had discovered feelings he might need to control, perhaps put aside. When she invited him for dinner after that heated exchange, he declined, pleading that the fire was too hot for him to stay. Indeed, it was. Too hot, everything had become. Finally, at the disastrous Box Hill outing, when she insulted Miss Bates, he reprimanded her sharply, almost as if she belonged to him. He had to remind himself that she did not. His solution then, was to leave Highbury, go to London to forget her. Yet when he realized she had made a penitential visit to Miss Bates, he almost kissed her hand before he left. Perhaps he needed to give Frank Churchill some sympathetic understanding. He would try his best.

When Jane and Frank came over to Hartfield later that day, congratulations were in order. Mr. Woodhouse had been his usual admonishing self, reminding the new Mrs. Churchill that he always said: "people should not marry!" Of course, that brought smiles to everyone's face, especially when he turned to Mr. Knightley for confirmation of his words.

"Well, Father-in-Law," said Mr. Knightley. "I suppose we will have to make exceptions in certain cases. Let us toast the new married couple, and wish them well."

A decanter of Mr. Woodhouse's finest wine was put on the table in the drawing-room, together with the best glasses and some biscuits.

Mr. Woodhouse accepted his glass graciously, but could not stop himself from cautioning his guests about the biscuits. They looked suspiciously like cake, he thought, though Emma assured him they were quite healthy and good for everyone.

"Of course, we will give you and Frank a dinner here," said Emma to Jane. "I'd like to wait until John and Isabella can attend. We will invite the Eltons and your aunt, Miss Bates. Perhaps Mrs. Goddard can come, to make an even number."

"That is so kind of you," said Jane. "We will look forward to it. If you'd like, I can mention it to Mrs. Goddard, as I plan on going over to see her. I'm still concerned about Mr. Weston's plans for taking care of his new daughter."

"You don't need to bother yourself, my dear," said Frank, rather quickly. "I've arranged to go over there myself tomorrow. You will best stay at home with my father and the child."

Jane made no reply. Then, after some brief further discussion, the

Churchills left for Randalls.

When they had gone, Mr. Knightley added another suggestion about the dinner party. "What about asking Harriet and Robert Martin," he said. "Don't you think it would be a good idea?"

Emma had almost forgotten about Harriet. They had not met since her wedding. Then, Mr. Martin called her away quickly, and Emma hadn't time to voice more than brief congratulations. She wondered if Harriet told her new husband that her first refusal of him had been at Emma's prompting. She would surely have needed to explain that refusal and eventual acceptance.

"Yes, of course, it's a good idea," she said, both surprised by his suggestion and unsure how it would be received by the Martins. "I wonder if they will accept, given all the nasty things I said to Harriet about Mr. Martin. I fear she has shared them with her husband. If so, she might be unwilling to accept an invitation to the Knightleys at Hartfield, don't you think?" Oh, how her past meddling actions came back to haunt her! She seemed never to be rid of her old mistakes! She certainly could not accuse Frank of deception when she had been so willing a partner in his game and was still in possession of Harriet's confidences.

"Robert Martin is sturdy enough, Emma, to come here as our invited guest. I told you once, he is a man without vanity. And since he has now been happily accepted by your friend, I think you need have no worries on that score," said Mr. Knightley.

She would make the invitations, of course, but she would try, if somehow, she could find an opportunity to talk with Harriet before the dinner party. More importantly, she needed to decide herself whether or not it was necessary or even advisable to reveal Harriet's old secret to her husband. About that subject, she remained conflicted and confused.

Changing the topic, she made one last addition to her list. "I think we should also invite Mr. Weston. Of course, he may understandably decline, but perhaps a social outing in honor of his son will bring him to the table."

Mr. Knightley agreed. He said nothing further to Emma about the party. But her curious reluctance to add the Martins to their guest list puzzled him. He found it odd that Emma, at first so eager to bring Harriet to all social occasions at Hartfield, now appeared to draw back from his suggestion. He thought she would be pleased, and saw she was not. Was it the old snobbery returning? He hoped not. And Jane had seemed uncomfortable with Frank's perfectly rational suggestion that he be the one to see Mrs. Goddard.

Well, he thought, there was no understanding the female mind. He would keep trying, though he knew a long path lay ahead of him. For the time being, he resolved to keep his thoughts to himself. If Emma was withholding something, he was sure she would tell him in the end. They always told each other just what they thought. That had been their old way with one another. He was content to wait until she was ready.

CHAPTER 19

Everyone in Highbury had now heard the news that Jane and Frank were married. Frank sent word that Mr. Weston was feeling much better, as was his Uncle Churchill. Still, the sadness of Mrs. Weston's passing hung heavy over Highbury and Hartfield, as Emma completed her invitation list for their proposed dinner in honor of Frank and Jane. She had invited Mr. Weston. After all, it was a party in honor of his son. Her husband suggested inviting the Martins and she was prepared to welcome them to the table at Hartfield. These matters of the heart can be so difficult!

At last, Emma determined what she must do. She would get her husband's advice, albeit without revealing Harriet's old secret. So, a day or two before the group was to assemble, Emma asked Mr. Knightley to take a walk with her in the garden. Mr. Woodhouse was settled in the drawing-room before the fire. Mr. Knightley had been reading in his library.

"Of course, dear Emma. I always like to take walks with you, now that I am certain that my proposal is not going to be refused," he said, smiling. "But it's quite cold outside. Not the usual kind of weather for an outing."

"It's always good to be walking when one has something difficult to say," she replied.

"Oh," he replied. "Perhaps we had better stay indoors. Are you afraid I might lecture you about something you haven't told me? I can't think what you might have done to merit one of my scoldings."

They donned coats and hats and set out. At first, she was silent, then took his arm, and began. "I'd like to give you a hypothetical case and ask your opinion if you'd be so kind."

"I am all yours. I hope it's not about Frank Churchill. We should be finished with that topic," he said.

"Yet, as you told me yourself, he was quite serviceable to you once. You said your love for me began when Frank Churchill returned to Highbury. Remember?" she asked, with one of her prettiest smiles.

"Indeed, I do, though it's not something I find pleasant to remember."

"That's because you did not want to confess to an emotion as unpleasant as jealousy. I did not scold you for feeling it. Indeed, I was happy to hear your confession," said Emma.

"So, your hypothetical case is about Frank Churchill," he said, with resignation.

"No, not at all. It's about someone else who confessed to a friend of mine that she loved the same man her friend loved—well at least, her friend hadn't recognized her own heart until she heard the man's name. Just as you began to recognize your feelings for me when Frank Churchill returned to Highbury, this confession made my friend realize she herself had always loved the very same man."

Mr. Knightley turned to his wife. "This is a complicated story, Emma. It sounds like it comes from one of your novels."

"Not at all. I just wonder what you will think when I tell you what happened. As I already said, the confession prompted my friend to discover her own feelings for the man. My friend has since married the person her friend had loved. Her friend's confession was told to her as a secret. Do you think my friend owes some kind of apology to the woman? Or should she just let it all pass? After all, the other woman has since married, and my friend thinks she is happy." Oh dear, this is awfully complicated. Emma had tied herself in knots and began to be unhappy she had started this conversation at all.

"I am getting cold. Maybe we should go back inside," she said.

Mr. Knightley soon realized this situation was not hypothetical. "No, Emma. Let's finish your story. I think you are still talking of Frank Churchill. Did the woman who made the confession love Frank Churchill? And Jane Fairfax is the woman who ultimately married him? Are you confessing to another of your Harriet Smith efforts? Since they are all coming to dinner, you are worried that it will be embarrassing for them? Emma, please tell me straightforwardly what you have to say. You know I hate this kind of secret."

"I swear it isn't about Frank Churchill." She paused. She had gone too far to stop now. "It's about Harriet Smith all right. But the man isn't Frank. It's you."

Mr. Knightley looked perplexed. "Me? Harriet Smith thought of me? Impossible. I never gave her any reason to imagine I had any feelings for her, of that, I am sure. But then"—he looked even more confused—"That would make 'the friend' you, Emma. Please unravel all this for me. I can decipher Milton all right, but this plot eludes me."

Thus prompted, she told him all. A man totally without vanity, he found the story hard to believe.

"I concede that Harriet might have mistaken my small kindnesses as meaning something more. But they were all for your sake, Emma, of course. I'd already suffered Mr. Cole's supposition that I cared for Jane Fairfax and had sent the mysterious piano. Now, I'm accused of giving Harriet Smith cause to think I cared for her. Matters of love are indeed beyond me," he said. Well, hadn't he himself supposed Emma loved Frank Churchill, especially after Box Hill?

"So do you think I should say something to Harriet before our dinner party?" asked Emma.

"No, I do not, unless you want to apologize for marrying me. No, dear Emma. I think that your Harriet is happily married to Mr. Martin, and wants no more reminders of the mistakes and false suppositions of the past. You should not mention anything unless she does. And I believe she will not."

They turned back toward the house. "Managing some of the awkwardness surrounding Frank and Jane will give us quite enough to do for one dinner party. Let me hear the guest list once more." He was determined to speak no more about Harriet and these old fantasies.

"Well," replied Emma. "Jane and Frank, of course, the Eltons, the Martins, John and Isabella—and I think we should add Miss Bates. To make an even number, I'll ask Mrs. Goddard as well. And Mr. Weston."

"I suspect he won't come," said Mr. Knightley." Emma was not as sure.

They had returned to Hartfield. The sun had come down lower in the sky, illuminating the red brick of the house as they walked past the carefully trimmed shrubberies and went into the rather grand entrance hall. Emma was satisfied with their conversation and would mention Harriet's secret no more. She was glad to be rid of it and, to be once again, totally truthful with her husband. With such a man as Mr. Knightley, even keeping someone else's secrets from him felt like a kind of betrayal. She turned, took his face in her hands, and kissed him.

"Well, I like that," he said, holding her tightly. "Do you have any more stories to share with me? If that is the kind of punctuation at the end, I will always be ready for another. Please, though, no more about Harriet. She is now Mrs. Martin, the wife of a hard-working, intelligent farmer and mistress of Abbey Mill Farm. That is surely the end of her story. There is no further room for the charms of your imagination on that subject!"

CHAPTER 20

The Knightleys received regrets from one invited guest: Mrs. Goddard had a previous invitation from the parents of one of her boarders. Emma received acceptances from the Eltons, the John Knightleys, the Martins, Miss Bates, and surprisingly, from Mr. Weston, who asked to bring along a Miss Sharpe, at Mrs. Goddard's suggestion. Since Mrs. Goddard was considering hiring the woman at the proposed infant school, she thought it might be helpful to introduce her to his friends at Highbury. Of course, Mr. Weston was not in a festive mood, he had written, but with Frank and Jane headed on their honeymoon journey, the matter of future arrangements weighed heavily on his mind. He needed the support and advice of his dearest friends and family at this time. Miss Sharpe was scheduled to return to Weymouth very soon, so the dinner party, although primarily for Frank and Jane, of course, also allowed him to see Miss Sharpe in the social context of Highbury where, should she be engaged, she would function.

Both Emma and her husband found Mr. Weston's request unusual. Nevertheless, Emma went ahead, planned the meal, ordered new candles for the table, as well as two fruit centerpieces. The evening should be as celebratory as possible, though the grief of Mrs. Weston's death still hung over her, as well as her surprise at the hasty nuptials of Frank and Jane. All in all, she had to confess she was not looking forward to this gathering. John and Isabella came up from London the day before with all the children. That at least brought some joyfulness into the house.

But her dinner party guests made an ill-assorted group, Emma thought, especially with Mr. Weston bringing a total stranger. Well, he always was a social animal, sometimes annoyingly so, as in the days he had included the Eltons to the Box Hill outing, despite Emma's hope that they would invite just those whom they liked. But she understood. It was no doubt difficult for him to contemplate the long days alone now, especially with Frank and Jane departing. She must be as understanding and helpful as she could.

She spoke to John Knightley in private, explaining the presence of a newcomer, and begging him, as she often did, to 'be nice,' a caution that always perplexed him. Assisted by his wife's unwavering adoration, he continued to believe he was the best-natured man in the world. Emma remembered being annoyed with John's warnings about Mr. Elton's intentions before that terrible Christmas party at the Weston's. Until her disastrous ride home in the carriage, she had not realized that Mr. Elton would propose marriage to her, with never a thought of Harriet at all. It was another of the humbling experiences of the last months and always made her feel terrible guilt at having nearly wrecked Harriet's life. In any case, all had turned out for the best, she hoped, and surely Harriet had forgotten all that misery.

But she was sure Mr. Elton had not. He and his new wife deliberately snubbed her whenever possible. She was a little surprised they so readily accepted her dinner invitation. She supposed they saw themselves as superior to her now since Frank and Jane owed them so much for helping arrange the wedding at Enscombe. Emma wondered how Frank was so quickly able to procure a marriage license, and discovered that Mr. Elton had facilitated that. She would have to endure their company this evening. But it would be a long time, she vowed, before they would be guests at Hartfield—or Donwell—again.

In the afternoon, Mr. Knightley took the older children to Donwell for a long walk and some games, while Isabella and Emma entertained baby Emma, hoping to tire her out so that she would sleep well in the evening. Isabella brought one of her nursemaids to help care for the children.

Isabella was glad of the time to be with her sister alone. She was curious about the Churchill marriage. There was so much talk in the days following their Christmas visit, of a possible attachment between Frank and Emma, that she and John were astonished at Frank and

Jane's secret engagement and Mr. Knightley's proposal of marriage to Emma. In short order, Emma filled her sister in on the sudden revelation of deep feeling between herself and Mr. Knightley. She always loved telling that story.

"I am so happy for you, dear Emma," said Isabella. "George Knightley has always had a special place in my heart. Now we can be closer than ever, married to two brothers!"

"Though devoted to one another, yet they are very different, I think," said Emma.

"Yes indeed. I remember being surprised when George asked to come and stay with us for a long visit. He never liked London very much or stayed away from Donwell very long. He was so difficult at first—refusing to join us at any dinner invitation and not playing as joyfully with the boys as usual. He wanted only to sit with little Emma, cuddling her and jogging her on his knee. I think it was her name he liked to hear himself saying," said Isabella with a smile.

"I hope he didn't scold her," teased Emma, her eyes twinkling.

"Not at all. When we received the news of Frank and Jane's engagement, he left so abruptly, giving no explanation! John told me to ask no questions and let him go. I think George confided his purpose to his brother, but you know those two: they keep their communications with each other to themselves. Anyway, he was off, almost as soon as I had finished reading the last words of the letter."

"He came to console me for having been misled by Frank Churchill," said Emma. "And yet, he found another purpose."

"You have been lucky. More than one woman would have gladly taken your place as mistress of Donwell," said Isabella.

Emma smiled. She knew exactly how great had been her good fortune. "It's time to dress for dinner, Isabella. We must wear our best, for no doubt, Mrs. Elton will shine in some new frock or other."

So, the sisters ended their conversation, and several hours later, all the house was in order. The guests arrived in a timely fashion and were briefly seated in the drawing-room. Emma wanted to be sure there would be no pointed comments about the hour of dinner at Bath. And the butler promptly made his announcement, ushering the guests to the table. Candles glowed, illuminating Hartfield's Crown Derby china and making the fine cut-glass goblets sparkle.

Mr. Woodhouse, dressed in his best, and without his usual array of scarves, seated himself at the head of the table. Mr. Knightley, in a black frock coat with silver buttons, was at the other end, directing their guests to their seats. Emma sat on her husband's right, dressed in the palest pink gauze over an underdress of white satin. She had given the places of honor to Frank and Jane, who sat on either side of her father. The vicar wore his usual somber colors, but his wife provided all the necessary decoration. Mrs. Elton displayed her pearls prominently on her bright mauve, open-necked, and short-sleeved evening dress. Still, Emma was confident that her own outfit, modestly cut, with long gauze sleeves, was more appropriate for the occasion.

The first course was brought out and served.

Mr. Knightley gave Emma a knowing smile. He was thinking of the first time Harriet Smith had been invited to Hartfield when he watched Emma directing her where to place her napkin and how to use her soup spoon. There seemed no need of that now.

Emma began by introducing the newcomer, Miss Sharpe, as having a connection to Mrs. Goddard and the school. Before she could elaborate, Mrs. Elton spoke up.

"Yes," she said. "We know all about the plans. Of course. Mrs. Goddard came first to us for advice. The vicar and I thought the idea for an infant school at Highbury a good one. We gave our approval." Smiles followed all around the table, though no one said anything further. Help was needed in continuing the conversation. Surprisingly, it was Mr. Woodhouse who spoke next.

"I always miss not having poor Miss Taylor at our table. She was with us so many years, it is hard for me to comprehend that she will never come again."

"Mrs. Weston, father. You always did want to call her by her maiden name." Mr. Weston bowed his head, while Emma smiled, but there was little joy in her eyes. "We understand how much you miss her."

"Oh yes," her father said, touching his forehead, as though he were only just remembering her passing. "It is a great loss. And, of course," he added as if remembering all that had happened, "for Mr. Weston too."

"We must offer a toast to the newly married couple," said Mr. Knightley, moving quickly away from that sorrowful subject. "We raise our glasses to you both and wish you a long and happy life together."

Everyone drank the toast, after which the first course was taken away. "We are very happy already, Mr. Knightley," said Frank. "And my uncle Churchill sends his best to all. He was quite ill, you know, but has recovered nicely. And we are grateful to the Eltons, especially our vicar, who did the ecclesiastical paperwork which made it possible for my uncle to see us wed at Enscombe."

"Quite so, but it was nothing at all," said Mr. Elton, looking appropriately self-important. "When true love and family togetherness are the issues, I am always at your service." He looked across the table at his wife. "It was so important that Augusta came with me, to be one of the witnesses at the ceremony and a welcome companion for Jane. Augusta and I salute you both with another toast." He raised his glass, and the others followed, though it was odd, to say the least, since the dinner party had already congratulated Frank and Jane.

Emma found herself disliking the Eltons as much, or even more than she ever had before.

Mrs. Elton spoke again. "I know you will all want to hear about the wedding. We were the only ones there, of course, except for Frank's uncle. It was glorious! Jane was simply bedecked—yes, bedecked—with Mrs. Churchill's jewels. I think she may be wearing some of them right now! Even though it was a private wedding, it was a grand affair. Frank wore a satin waistcoat and a full frock coat. Jane wore white silk brocade, which, of course, showed off her jewels. I helped her choose it. I wore my best gray paisley, with matching ribbons. Flowers, too, filled the place. And what a splendid wedding dinner we had after the ceremony! Pheasant, and duck, and I don't know how many courses. Far grander than any dinner I have ever seen served at Highbury."

Emma almost gasped at the woman's vulgarity. But she nodded, and let Mrs. Elton continue with her detailed descriptions of the wedding clothes and the food.

The conversation went on with no particular hindrances, although Jane had not yet said a single word. Miss Sharpe, head bowed, was also silent, looking uncomfortable. Mr. Martin had also not yet spoken. Mr. Knightley thought to engage him and his wife in conversation.

"It seems Abbey Mill Farm is going on well, now that you have somewhat expanded its borders."

"Very well indeed, sir," replied Mr. Martin. "The additional space has permitted me to add livestock and increase our productivity. We now can do stall-feeding, and we have added sheep as well." He was almost ready to talk about his increased stock of manure when he thought better of it. "We have been able to add Mrs. Goddard's school to our list of patrons. Just yesterday, Harriet went over to discuss future orders with the headmistress." He turned to his wife, an invitation, he thought, for her to speak.

"Oh yes, indeed. And it was lovely to see the old place again. Mrs. Goddard was so very civil. She invited me to stay for tea. I've already met Miss Sharpe there." She smiled at the newcomer, who nodded lightly. "I told her all about what I did at the school when I was there." Harriet smiled again, speaking directly to Miss Sharpe. "Of course, you would do some teaching, should Mrs. Goddard have the new school," she said. "I was only a boarder who helped the girls with their clothes, letters, and homework." Harriet spoke somewhat bashfully.

Miss Sharpe spoke for the first time. "At a school, everything is important. I'm sure you were a valuable asset," she finished, offering a brief nod to Harriet.

"How interesting," said Mrs. Elton. "As I said, we already knew all about this idea. We thought an infant school would surely be a help to Mr. Weston, with his new daughter. Many families in the neighborhood could use such assistance. I know all about such things, of course, for I make weekly visits to the poor." She gave her husband a knowing glance.

"Brava," said Mr. Elton, saluting his wife. "Augusta has quite taken over that ministry. She hopes that Jane might help, whenever she is here at Highbury. She means to start a club, a group of women dedicated to watching over the poor. I commend her! Bravissima!"

"Oh, my caro sposo! It's the least I can do."

They had quite departed from Harriet's remarks.

Mr. Weston, speaking for the first time, now weighed in. "Miss Sharpe was a governess at Weymouth. I think she knew some people here. That's why she wanted to settle in Highbury," he added, drawing another slight nod from Miss Sharpe. He looked, Emma thought, as if he had aged in the days following his wife's passing. Still, he had dressed himself elegantly in his old style, the only hint of color in his appearance one of his paisley waistcoats.

Harriet, pleased at having something more to add to the table talk, resumed her subject. "Mrs. Goddard is quite enthusiastic about the school." Again she addressed Miss Sharpe. "I hope you liked Mrs. Goddard's. I always loved being there, even when I was a small child. Your little daughter is so pretty! How good of you to take care of your sister's child, after she died. I sometimes help my husband's older sister with her baby when she comes to nurse Mr. Weston's little girl. I know it can also be quite a care."

Emma began to notice Frank Churchill's somewhat darkened expression. What could be bothering him? Now that he had gotten everything he wanted, one would think he should look happier. Maybe Mr. Knightley was right to find him a frivolous young man.

At least Harriet seemed to have recovered from her year of falling in love with three men. Emma stopped herself. That was an unkind thought. After all, she was the instigator in two of the three.

"That's interesting, Harriet," said Emma. "The idea of an infant school is an intriguing and novel one. I've heard educators believe that children acquire much in temper and disposition even before the age of two." She looked over at Mr. Weston. "I'm sure Isabella and I are grateful to your late wife for helping us develop whatever good temper we have enjoyed in later life." She smiled at her husband who gave her one of his knowing nods of approval.

"Indeed," said Mrs. Elton, interjecting herself. "Even at six or twelve months, I have heard."

"Yes," added her husband. "A philosopher named Pestalozzi has advanced just such theories. I have thought of making regular visits to the infant school. Augusta might make it a stop on her visits to the poor. We are always in the midst when help is needed."

"Yes, perhaps Jane would come with me." She turned to Jane. "Now that the governess trade is no longer in your future plans, you might like to make some visits to the infant school. As for me, I simply dote on children! Yes, dote!"

She looked expectantly at Jane, who spoke for almost the first time. "Yes, when we return from our wedding journey, I will come along." Jane was dressed in her usual blue, but with the addition of an emerald necklace that had come from Uncle Churchill. She had fingered it lightly throughout dinner as if she were still unaccustomed to such finery.

"I would like to do that," she added. "Perhaps Miss Sharpe would tell us more about the plans," and seemed ready to say more when Frank interrupted. "That would be interesting, but I think my wife needs to recover her full health before taking on any additional responsibilities," he said. "In fact, I think she looks tired already. There has been so much to do at my father's, and the journey has been tiring for both of us."

Miss Bates, who had been uncharacteristically silent, began to talk. "Oh, dear Jane. Are you tired? I have some of Mrs. Knightley's arrowroot at home. Or Mr. Churchill could stop at our home on the way and get it. So good it is for everything! Mother swears by it. Or perhaps there is some here? I always believe it helps headaches. Dear Jane, you look like you might be suffering from one right now," she said.

Here, Mr. Woodhouse nodded vigorously. "Health must come first! Though I do enjoy seeing you all here at the table, sometimes sitting in these hard chairs can strain the back. We should start to think about the evening's rest."

"We can withdraw from the table, and congregate in the drawing-room, sir. You are quite correct to suggest a move. It is much more comfortable there, and warm, with the fire," said Mr. Knightley. "We'll get something for Jane to drink."

Emma was about to fetch the arrowroot when Frank stopped her. "Thank you very much, but I don't think so. We must get back to Randalls. I don't like leaving your sister alone in the evening, Mr. Martin. We have enjoyed ourselves greatly, have we not, Jane?"

Jane did look pale. She nodded, smiled, and rose next to her husband. Emma had never been able to get close to her, and she felt further away from her than ever. Now married, and the secret of her engagement out, she continued to be a sphinx.

Their abrupt departure seemed almost rude to Emma. But she resolved to take no offense. "Mrs. Churchill—I must call you that now, of course—may I come over tomorrow to visit? I could walk over in the afternoon. I would like to see the baby, as well."

Jane nodded, though without much enthusiasm. "As you wish Mrs. Knightley. Early afternoon would be the best. Thank you again for a very lovely dinner." Then, without further conversation, they were away, followed closely by the Eltons, who offered to take Miss Bates back in their carriage.

John and Isabella excused themselves to go upstairs to see how the children were faring, leaving Emma, Mr. Knightley, Mr. Woodhouse, Mr. Weston and Miss Sharpe, and Harriet and Robert Martin in the drawing-room. After more agricultural talk, and some discussion about the Martin experiments at the farm, they too took their leave.

Last to depart, as always, was Mr. Weston, who offered to take Miss Sharpe back to Mrs. Goddard's in his carriage.

"Thank you so much for including me," said Miss Sharpe. "It has been a good opportunity for me to meet the community, should I be able to join it."

While their guests donned their coats, Emma had the opportunity to look at the newcomer with greater attention. She was attractive in her way, to be sure. Not pretty or beautiful, but intelligent-looking, and quite in command of herself, entering as she had, into a group of total strangers. She had not said much, nor put herself forward in any way. There was an air of mystery about her, something intensely private, Emma thought. She wondered whether Mr. Weston would be comfortable with her in charge of his new daughter, should she be chosen by Mrs. Goddard for a position. Yet he seemed at ease. Quiet, as he often was, but quietly sociable. He thanked Emma and said he would see her tomorrow, as he settled Miss Sharpe's cloak around her shoulders and prepared for the ride back to Mrs. Goddard's.

"Well," said Mr. Knightley. "Have you been satisfied with our party, the food, and the guests dear Emma?"

Mr. Woodhouse thought there had been too much meat. "Scandalous," he said. "What a waste. We didn't eat it all, I'm sure. And the vegetables were a bit under-cooked."

"Father-in-Law! Surely you don't want to criticize dear Emma's first dinner party as a married lady," said Mr. Knightley, with a smile.

"Oh no, of course not. Any faults I just mentioned were the doing of the cook. Dear Emma could never have done anything wrong, Mr. Knightley."

"I quite agree, sir. No scoldings from me tonight." He paused for a moment. "I did think that Mr. Churchill might have provided the transport for our new visitor. But then," he added, with a glance at his wife, "I'm always finding his actions falling a bit short of my expectations." He turned to his father-in-law. "Now, sir, shall we make our way upstairs? It has surely been a long evening for you."

Giving his arm to Mr. Knightley as usual, Mr. Woodhouse led the way, with Emma just behind. She looked forward to a more in-depth discussion with her husband once they were safely in their own rooms. She loved their evening talks, always so frank and open, and without the social restrictions of everyday life at Hartfield. She went up, eager to share her own thoughts about the Hartfield wedding dinner for Frank and Jane Churchill, confident that her husband would have much to say. He always did, and she was always glad of it.

CHAPTER 21

Emma had always been curious about Jane. Her history was somewhat similar to Frank's. She had been taken away from her Highbury family by one Colonel Campbell who sought to fulfill an old debt to Jane's father for saving his life. Thus, rescued from the straightened circumstances of the Bates, she had been well-educated by the Campbells. But having a daughter of their own, their circumstances did not permit them to do more for her after Jane came of age. Thus, like many young women in her situation, she was destined to become a governess.

When Jane made visits back to Highbury, Emma never took the initiative and sought her friendship. Harriet Smith was an easier companion for Emma to patronize. Indeed, some thought Jane to be Emma's superior. Mr. Knightley always admired Jane as a charming young woman, but it seems only Frank Churchill had really known and appreciated her.

Yet he had brought her conflict and trouble, pressing her into a secret engagement, forcing her to watch him play-act with Emma so that everyone's eyes would be turned away from the truth. Mr. Knightley came closest to fathoming the depth of Jane's relationship with Frank. Yet in the end, even he was surprised and perplexed at her choosing Frank Churchill, a man, in Mr. Knightley's opinion, hardly worthy of Jane. As he told Emma of the relationship, "I feel sorry for her."

Throughout their dinner, Emma watched Jane closely, seeking some clues to her relationship with Frank. She knew that Jane had broken off their engagement after Box Hill, deciding then to take the governess position procured for her by Mrs. Elton. While writing her acceptance letter, Jane cried all night, and even the dull-witted Miss Bates knew that people did not often cry for joy. The Box Hill fiasco resulted also in the sensible Mr. Knightley leaving suddenly for an extended stay at Brunswick Square with John and Isabella.

But then came that unexpected release, the fortunate decease of Mrs. Churchill, opening the way for both Jane and Emma to find their true loves. One would think Jane would be less guarded now, more open, more joyful. Yet, Emma felt, she was the same reserved Jane. She offered no details about her wedding in Enscombe, nor any information about their immediate plans.

There was, however, a moment when Emma thought that Jane showed emotion, during Harriet's description of her meeting with the newly arrived Miss Sharpe at the Goddard School. What could be the reason?

Emma stopped herself. She must be careful not to weave some new kind of fantasy about Jane. It was bad enough, having concocted a relationship for Jane with Mr. Dixon, the son-in-law of the Campbells. Mr. Knightley would surely scold her, were she to start that kind of thing again. But that Jane had shown a definite reaction to Harriet's information about Miss Sharpe, Emma was sure. She hesitated to tell Mr. Knightley. He might think she was looking for another protégé. Heaven forbid! Still, she wished to know more about this lady who had dropped into Highbury so suddenly with her interesting and progressive plans for a school for infants. Why had she not taken the opportunity of the dinner party to further promote her idea? She had said nothing about the school, leaving the floor to the Eltons on the matter. It was a mystery. Tomorrow, Emma might take a walk over to visit Mrs. Goddard and find out a bit more. It wasn't every day that an interesting newcomer appeared in Highbury!

When her husband returned to their rooms and they were finally alone together, Emma began, "So, what did you think of our party?"

Pulling off his jacket and then his boots, he stopped and paused to look at her. "It went off as well as could be expected, I suppose. As for the dinner, it was a model of correctness. All the dishes were excellent, and placed exactly right on the table."

"I wasn't interested in your opinions about the food or the table settings, my dear. It was the people I wanted to hear you talk about," she said.

"There's not much to say. Without some precipitating event, people don't change much, Emma. We haven't had the Martins here before and while I think they were uncomfortable at first, they warmed up. I saw that Harriet needed no hints about table manners," he added, smiling with his usual thoughtful expression.

"You never let me forget my past sins, do you," she replied, but also with a smile. "I thought she did well in drawing Miss Sharpe into the conversation, perhaps best of us all."

"She had already met her," he said, "and so had an advantage. And she had some common ground, with Mrs. Goddard's school. As for Miss Sharpe herself, she seems a well-bred sort, quiet and pleasant. One couldn't expect she'd have much to say, the only so-called 'outsider' present. Considering how disruptive our two previous outsiders were—Frank and Mrs. Elton—I think she did rather well. And Mr. Weston continues always the same. He's a man who takes things as he finds them."

"I thought Jane looked uncomfortable, though I can't think why. She was fingering those emeralds as if they were a rope to hang onto for dear life," she added, her imagination firing up. "And of course, our Mrs. Elton and her cara sposo lived up to all my expectations," Emma concluded.

"They can be counted on always to provide a quantity of disruptive force," he agreed, his brow darkening. "But overall, Emma, we learned very little new about our guests. Your father did well, although his reference to Mrs. Weston was an awkward moment. Indeed, my overall impression was that Frank and Jane were the most uncomfortable persons present, though why, I cannot say, nor do I intend to speculate." He continued to undress.

Emma saw that her husband would add no more. As for herself, she continued to wonder if Frank and Jane harbored any more secrets. They were as tantalizing as ever. But she would not share that thought with her husband at present. She would see what awaited her tomorrow, during her proposed visit to Randalls.

As for the newly married Churchills, when they returned to Randalls after their dinner with the Knightleys, Jane began to question her husband about Miss Sharpe. She thought she remembered being introduced to her on one of the walks Frank and she used to take along the seaside at Weymouth. She asked Frank if he remembered the lady.

"I think not, my dear. Why do you ask?"

"One day when we were out walking by the seaside, a woman passed by and greeted you. She asked very pointedly, I thought, to be introduced to me, and I'm almost sure she said her name was Sharpe. You were a bit short with her, I recall. You bowed and walked on rather quickly. Do you think the woman who has come to Mrs. Goddard's is the same lady? She looks as if she might be, though I can't be sure. She was dressed so differently and spoke so little. But surely you would have recognized her." She waited for her husband to reply.

"It's quite possible she's the same woman," said Frank. "I told you I knew several ladies there before I ever saw or met you. You said you understood all that. And I swear, after meeting you, I have forgotten all of them. If it is the same woman, it's of no consequence. We have more to think of than some past acquaintances at Weymouth. I'm through with Weymouth now, eager to be off on our honeymoon trip. There is really no reason to wait further. My father has encouraged me to take you away from the sadness at Randalls. I have already ordered the tickets. I was told that Mr. Knightley kept their honeymoon destination a mystery from Emma. I'm going to follow in his footsteps. We will be leaving quite soon, so please make yourself ready."

"This is very sudden, Frank. I need time to prepare, to get my wardrobe ready." Jane was uneasy.

"You're not usually one to be concerned about organizing your wardrobe," he said, with a question in his expression.

"Frank, I am finished with secrets. If you have any more, I beg you to tell them now, so we can be done with all subterfuge."

Frank took her in his arms. "I told you the truth about my past at Weymouth. Before I knew you, I had several dalliances there. You said that didn't matter to you. Now, I want to start our life together with no more thoughts of the past, of my troubles with my aunt, my necessary releases from her domination at Weymouth, the frivolous pleasures I relieved myself with before I met you. You are my beautiful, elegant Jane, my angel sent from heaven, and for the first time in our lives, we can do anything we want. And what I want is to travel. With you. Now." He kissed her before she could reply.

She felt herself unable to question him further. It was all so difficult. She had not yet completely forgotten his attentions to

Emma. Even though she knew his actions were born of the need to conceal his love for her, it had been torture for her to watch. But because it had not been real, a kind of play-acting, she tolerated it for the most part, though she had several times been quite angry. Then, Mrs. Churchill died, and all that was over. Mr. Weston had forgiven them on the spot, and Emma surely had forgotten all that, so she put it all behind her. So, she had intended. But the presence of a lady come here from Weymouth, perhaps the very person, she thought, who had so pointedly spoken to them during that walk at Weymouth, made her again wonder about Frank. He told her once, that he could not always be serious. But that's what she was, in her way. Always serious, especially about him, the man she loved with all her heart.

And so it was that she resolved upon an action of which she knew Frank would not approve. She would walk over to Mrs. Goddard's tomorrow. If the woman was still there, she would ask to see her. She would not tell Frank of her plan but would go after he left for tomorrow's trip to London to pick up the tickets for their honeymoon trip.

Then Frank surprised her by suggesting she accompany him to London. They could take the carriage, he said. But Jane protested that "Emma—Mrs. Knightley—was coming over to see Mr. Weston tomorrow," and she promised to be at home. It was to be for an early tea. He should go alone, she told him. And he agreed.

Though she wanted no more secrets, she prepared some excellent excuses for her visit, should Frank find it out. She wanted to talk to Mrs. Goddard about the plans for the infant school, to see if Mr. Weston's new infant daughter might, at least part of the time, be cared for there. Then she would feel better about going away. There was a truth in that. When Frank returned, if necessary, she would have her explanations ready.

Even before the sun had risen, Jane was awake and at the breakfast table with her husband, who immediately after, left for London by horseback to arrange for their upcoming travels. Uneasy with herself, she bid him an affectionate goodbye.

Since the carriage was available, as soon as she had seen him off, she called for it to be made ready. She was uneasy about her actions. Wasn't she doing what she said she wanted no more of from him? No more secrets, no more subterfuges? But perhaps, as their love had bound them ever more closely together, she was fated to take on to herself some of his being, as well. She always thought that people in love could benefit from the moral character of the person they marry. Perhaps the opposite was also true. Perhaps a wife's character could be worsened by that of her husband.

She must stop thinking this way. Still, she felt there was something mysterious about this woman. She was determined to find out if this Miss Sharpe was one of Frank's former loves, or dalliances, as he liked to call these relationships. Then, she told herself, she would be ready to put it all behind her. But first, she had to know. And even as she prepared to take these uncharacteristic steps, she feared they might change their life forever, before it had even begun.

CHAPTER 22

Mrs. Goddard was surprised by Jane's visit. She had never come there before, though they met previously at Randalls. After greeting her with congratulations and regrets that she had been unable to attend the festive dinner in her honor at Hartfield, she waited for Jane to state the purpose of her unusual visit.

"Mrs. Goddard. Thank you for receiving me so courteously. I am here on a very private matter, one which I hope you will keep to yourself."

Mrs. Goddard nodded. As Miss Fairfax, Jane was always reserved. But now that all the secrets were out, and she was safely married to Frank Churchill, here she was asking for confidence about a communication yet to be delivered. Always alive to the need for respectability in all matters concerning young ladies, Mrs. Goddard reluctantly nodded acquiescence.

"Last night at the Knightleys, I met a Miss Sharpe of Weymouth, who, I learned, has come with the proposal to teach and perhaps begin an infant school here," said Jane.

"Yes indeed," said Mrs. Goddard. "And very good references she has brought with her from Weymouth, where she has been a governess. She also comes with a high recommendation from Mr. Churchill's uncle. I have been impressed by her, and am in the way of seriously considering both her employment and her proposal. So, you know her as well?" Mrs. Goddard thought it best to state her intentions before Mrs. Churchill began the subject of whatever brought her here on this early morning visit.

"Oh, I know very little of her," said Jane, nervously. "I believe I met her briefly at Weymouth. After seeing her again last evening, and learning that she was staying at your school, I wondered if you would be so kind as to let me have the opportunity to speak with her, if possible. I come because of my interest in Mr. Weston's future arrangements for his daughter." She hoped her manner betrayed none of the agitations in her heart.

"Yes indeed. She has come seeking employment here, which I am considering." She paused. "I do not know if she has risen as yet, but if you will give me a moment, I will go and check in the breakfast room, to see if she is there. If you will excuse me." Mrs. Goddard had been her polite self. If she was uncomfortable or curious about Jane's visit, she did not show it.

Jane sat quietly, and before long, Mrs. Goddard returned.

"Miss Sharpe will be with you shortly. I presume you would like to talk with her alone?"

"If you would be so kind, Mrs. Goddard." Jane looked pale and now betrayed her uneasiness.

"I will leave you both here. No one will disturb you. I will see to it."

Mrs. Goddard left Jane to await Miss Sharpe's arrival.

Before too long, the lady entered. She was dressed in a modest brown dress, high-necked and long-sleeved, quite plain and devoid of decoration, and was clearly as nervous as Jane. She was attractive and youthful-looking.

"Good morning," Jane began, inhaling deeply. "We met last evening at the Knightley residence at Hartfield. But I think we saw each other once before, at Weymouth." She shifted in her seat. "It was when I was out walking with my husband, Frank Churchill. We hardly had time to speak then. A dinner party is also not the best place to renew our acquaintance. So, hearing that you were still in the vicinity, I came over so that we might have the chance to talk further." It was awkward, but it was a start.

"Yes, I do remember the previous occasion," Miss Sharpe replied, quite in command of herself. "Indeed, Mr. Churchill and I knew one another at Weymouth and met on several occasions over the past years. I have not seen him since his wedding."

"You must think it odd, my coming here and asking to see you. Since you and Frank had been friends at Weymouth, I hoped perhaps to invite you to visit us at Randalls," continued Jane. "But alas, we will soon be off on our honeymoon journey, and I will not have the opportunity to entertain you. So, I did not want to miss the chance to meet and talk with you."

Miss Sharpe remained silent. How could this woman want to meet her? What purpose could she have with her? She hardly knew what she could say. After all, she had wanted to see Frank, but surely not his wife. Now that she learned of his marriage, she was not sure she wanted to see him at all. At least not with her previous purpose. It was not necessary for her to explain herself to his new wife. She waited for Jane to speak.

"You must excuse my boldness in approaching you in this fashion, but at Weymouth, this past October, Frank and I became secretly engaged. You may have heard of Aunt Churchill, who would not have permitted Frank to have an alliance with anyone but a great heiress. I was surely not, as I was about to begin seeking a position as a governess to support myself. I understand that has been your profession, as well."

"Yes. I came here to seek a position in a school, a better fate, by far."

"Indeed. I myself narrowly missed the governess trade, as some call it."

Recovering herself somewhat, Miss Sharpe spoke. "What do you want with me, Mrs. Churchill? I cannot imagine." She kept her eyes steadily on Jane.

"I think you may have been close to Frank in the past." She paused, hardly able to believe herself speaking these words. "Before I married him, I asked him about his past life, and he has confessed to previous relationships." Again, she stopped as if to catch her breath. "Since I love him, I have said they mean nothing to me, as long as they are over. When I heard you had come to Highbury, I confess I thought that perhaps you were seeking to continue some kind of further relationship with Frank. If that is so, I need to know and hope you will be truthful with me. I bear you no ill will, but if you and Frank wish to continue your previous relationship, of course, that will be important for me and him." Jane finished and felt she could not say another word. And yet, she added one more sentence. "He does not know of my visit here."

Miss Sharpe continued to look at her, taking in Jane's state of emotion, what it must have cost her to come. She found herself admiring the woman, despite herself.

"When I decided to come to Highbury, I did not yet know of your marriage. Hearing of Mrs. Churchill's death, and Frank's lengthy visit to his father, I did hope to renew our relationship. It had faltered a bit last October, which I now realize was caused by his meeting you. I see now that things have changed. I hope you have not come to prevent me from securing a position at Mrs. Goddard's."

Jane remained silent. Indeed, now that Miss Sharpe admitted to her previous relationship with Frank, there was little more for her to say.

"I have already given up my governess position at Weymouth, which had been very unpleasant. I am actively seeking another and better one. I also have a child whom I must support." She paused, not sure, but deciding to go on. "Frank's child, though he may not admit it—and therefore this opportunity is crucial for me. So, if you have come to ask me to go away, I will not. I have no obligation either to Frank or to you."

Jane was feeling faint and confused thoughts flooded her mind, making it difficult for her even to hear Miss Sharpe. The blood rushed to her face and she sat silent for a few minutes. She was shocked at the woman's bold announcement and found herself wondering at the aggressiveness of her actions. To come here in her situation, not knowing what she would find. To have given up an existing position. If she found nothing at Mrs. Goddard's, what would she do next? Would she throw herself at Frank and require his assistance? A child? If that were so, surely, he owed her something. Jane felt completely at sea in this conversation. She had sought it out. Yet, what she found now threw her into confusion.

Miss Sharpe saw that she held the upper hand in this discussion. Though elegant and well-educated, Frank's new wife had not experienced the life she had. She had not been forced to make her own way, clawing a path into respectability. She had staked much on this trip to Highbury.

On Jane's part, she found herself reluctantly feeling sympathy for the woman. Though she was secure in being possessed of Frank's love, she thought it must have taken much for this woman to tell her story.

In the silence that now remained between them, Miss Sharpe determined what she would say. "I assure you, at the moment, I seek no further relationship with Frank. Though as you see, I have not been a completely blameless woman. But renewing my old relationship with a man now married to someone else is not what I want. I need to earn my living. More than that, I cannot tell you. If you need any further assurances, you should seek them from your husband." She had finished and stood.

Jane stood as well, recovering herself. "I am sorry to have troubled you, Miss Sharpe, but I thank you most sincerely for what you have told me. Should you procure this position, and we meet again in the course of time, I will not refer to the past. I will tell Frank of my visit and what you have told me. Should you secure a position at Mrs. Goddard's, we will probably see one another again, as I am sure Frank's father will want to bring his infant daughter to the school. As you may know, Mr. Weston is newly widowed and has been left with a little girl. He knows nothing of my real purpose in this visit, beyond meeting you as a possible teacher in the infant school. My engagement to Frank was a secret one, and it cost me much pain to keep it from my friends at Highbury. If asked, please do tell Mrs. Goddard that I came over to meet you on Mr. Weston's behalf and that of his infant daughter. That is at least partially true." She stopped. "Please believe me when I say I wish you well, Miss Sharpe." Jane turned toward the door.

Anna Sharpe was surprised. Perhaps this woman was not as weak and helpless as she thought. She had thus far been unexpectedly generous. "I wish you well too, Mrs. Churchill. I hope your marriage to Frank may be all that you desire. At the present moment, I have no plans to disturb either of you. I will let you know in advance if and when I propose doing otherwise." She watched Jane leave, fully aware of what the visit had cost the woman. For the time being, at least, she would do her no harm.

CHAPTER 23

Emma and Mr. Knightley sat in the breakfast room, having just finished some of Serle's boiled eggs and the dry toast ordered by Mr. Woodhouse.

"You don't really like your eggs that way," said Emma, after Mr. Woodhouse had left them to sit by the fire in the drawing-room. "I know you don't. I will order some more to your liking if you wish."

"I can eat any kind of eggs," he replied. "All I need is something for breakfast before getting underway. Don't fuss. I've told James I want Bessie this morning for a ride over to Mr. Martin's farm. He wishes to show me one of his experiments."

"I can always tell when something is not your favorite," she continued, persisting. "I know you don't like the eggs that way."

"Emma. Did I not tell you when I came to live at Hartfield that I was prepared to live here and do far more without a second thought? How my eggs are cooked is the least of the sacrifices I was prepared to make." He looked at her with the hint of a smile in his gray eyes.

"What were your other sacrifices?" she asked with an engaging twinkle in her eyes.

"I can't name one right now. Give me a few minutes to think." He took her hand, pulling her near enough to kiss her. "Well, that isn't one. But I'll keep trying to think. So, you are going over to see Mr. Weston today?" he added.

"Yes. Jane said I could come in the afternoon for tea. We really haven't talked since—well, you know since what." She still could hardly speak of the passing of her dear old governess. "But I do want to see the little girl. What do you think of the idea mentioned at dinner, about an infant school at Mrs. Goddard's?"

"I should think it might help if the persons taking care of the infants were the right sort."

"I'm glad you feel that way. That's why I want to know more about this new woman who has proposed the school. I would have thought Frank and Jane would have tried to draw her out at the dinner party a bit more. After all, they are the ones going away. They ought to take care of Mr. Weston first, I think," said Emma.

"Quite correct, my dear. So, we must let them do that. You wouldn't want to step in front of them in this matter, would you?"

"Of course not. But I felt some hesitation in both of them when the idea was mentioned at the dinner. Didn't you?"

"I think it was only Jane's natural reserve. I'm sure she will be at Randalls this afternoon when you go over. Why not talk privately to her about your concerns. Perhaps get her to voice her thoughts on Miss Sharpe and the infant school. Why not broach the subject this afternoon?"

Of course, he was right. Always so sensible. Thoughtful and careful. She did love that about him, although she sometimes felt he was a bit too deferential in matters concerning Jane. Well, she didn't want to sound jealous. Or become another Mrs. Elton, arranging things for everyone, pushing herself forward. Mrs. Elton always knew best how to do everything. Find a governess position for Jane. Make the invitations to Donwell for Mr. Knightley's strawberry party. But she would talk to Jane in the afternoon, perhaps offering to visit Mrs. Goddard's with her—or at least stay with Mr. Weston while Jane went over. Her memories of Mrs. Elton would be a cautionary tale against too much interference.

And so, she stayed at Hartfield with her father in the morning, even playing a game of backgammon with him before she left in the afternoon for Randalls, sent off with his usual cautions about getting chilled or, as it happened, overheated. She decided to walk, not wanting to trouble James about the carriage.

When she arrived, she found Jane with her father-in-law, downstairs, in front of the fire. Jane discreetly left them alone for several minutes, and without company to inhibit them, they both cried a little until Jane returned with the tea things.

"It's no use asking how you all are," said Emma, drying her eyes. "But I do want to see little Adelaide. Is the nursemaid still here?"

"No, but Jane can bring the little one in," he answered. "The Martin woman will be back later to put her to bed. How different things are now, dear Emma, are they not? For years, I was so accustomed to being alone and then, after I bought Randalls and married my dear Anne, life became so comfortable and lovely. Of course, Frank and Jane have been very attentive, but I cannot ask them to stay here and not take their wedding travels. Frank has gone to London today to make arrangements, and early this morning dear Jane went over to Mrs. Goddard's to see about plans for the infant school there. I'll let her tell you what she found out."

Jane put a tray of tea and biscuits in front of them.

"So, you have gone over to Mrs. Goddard's already today?" asked Emma. "I was going to suggest accompanying you if you wanted. Did you speak to Mrs. Goddard?"

Jane poured the tea, and then sat back on the sofa next to her father-in-law. "Yes, but more importantly, I saw and spoke with Miss Sharpe, who wishes to be engaged for the proposed infant school. She said so little at your dinner, that I wanted to talk to her in more detail."

"Was your talk satisfactory?" asked Emma.

"We had a conversation, yes, and I think she is suitable. I believe she is ready to start almost immediately. She was a governess at Weymouth and looks forward to a different sort of employment at a school. I can certainly sympathize with that desire."

"Did she seem likely to be calm and patient with infants?" asked Emma, wanting more information than had been forthcoming.

"How she will manage with infant care I cannot really say. There are few external demonstrations of patience or kindness in conversation. They have to be observed in practice." Jane's tone, though not unfriendly, was a bit admonitory.

Emma felt herself reprimanded. "Of course, but sometimes one has a sense about people."

"Yes, and sometimes people are right about their sense, and sometimes wrong. We will have to wait and see." She turned to Mr. Weston. "But it is a solution you wish to try, do you not, Father-in-Law?"

"Yes, most especially since Frank is eager to be away. I would like such an arrangement. I could bring the child over to Mrs. Goddard's every morning and fetch her back before the dinner hour. That way, I wouldn't feel I was totally abandoning her to the care of others, the way I abandoned Frank." He looked sadly at them both.

Emma felt that tears were not far from coming. "You didn't abandon him, Mr. Weston. You gave him to the care of a family member better equipped to care for him," said Emma, though she had been grateful that her own father, in spite of his valetudinarian habits, and general fearfulness about life, had kept Isabella and herself at Hartfield, in their own home. She always told him so, together with her promise that she would never leave him. She hardly knew how he managed in the very early years before dear Miss Taylor came and virtually mothered them. She doubted anyone, as capable as she might be, could ever be what Miss Taylor had been to her and Isabella.

"Do you think Mrs. Goddard has definitely decided on adding the infant school?" asked Emma, continuing the subject in a more positive direction.

"I don't know. But I hope she will decide before Frank and I leave." She looked troubled. "Indeed, I do not want to leave until Mr. Weston's situation is settled."

"You must be understanding of your new husband, my dear," said Mr. Weston. "Frank is his father's son. Very impetuous, loving to be off, to travel, to see the world. He must have his chance. After all, you may soon start a family of your own, and then travel such as Frank proposes will not be possible. I will be fine here at Randalls, even should the school not work out."

Mr. Weston was being his comfortable, easy-going self. Emma was not so sure he could manage an infant alone. She knew or thought she did, that his financial situation was secure. But if left alone, he would need assistance. Well, she was not going to learn any more here today. It was time to go back to Hartfield and see what her husband could make of what she heard.

Jane saw her out. Frank had not yet returned, and Jane made his excuses.

"I'll come back tomorrow to see Mr. Weston again," said Emma, "if that is all right."

Jane looked pleased with the suggestion. "Yes," she said. "That would be helpful. Frank and I might take that time to prepare our next steps. Thank you very much," said Jane. "Goodbye."

Emma left feeling somewhat puzzled. It seemed no agreement

had as of yet been reached about what those next steps would be. She hoped her husband was back from his day at the Martin farm. The house did not feel the same without him. She knew her feelings, indescribable as they were. She knew now what being in love meant. How lucky she was, to have Mr. Knightley for her very own! Tomorrow she would see to it he had his eggs prepared just the way he liked them!

CHAPTER 24

The next day, Emma walked again to Randalls to visit Mr. Weston. Jane opened the door and, before leading her into the drawing-room, stopped her.

"Mrs. Knightley, I must prepare you for another visitor. Miss Sharpe has come wishing to speak directly to Mr. Weston. I could not get word to you in time, so I decided to go ahead with your visit as planned."

Emma thought Jane's manner rather stiff and formal, but she supposed she must get used to it. She thought it was the residue of her discomfort about the secret engagement, but perhaps it was merely an integral part of her personality. Emma nodded, smiled, and entered.

In the drawing-room, Miss Sharpe sat across from Mr. Weston. Jane led Emma to a chair next to the woman. After greetings were exchanged, Jane left to assemble the tea things, giving Emma a few moments to assess the situation.

Miss Sharpe seemed more at her ease than she had at the Knightleys' party. She looked neat and was fashionably dressed in a dark-colored gown of what looked like muslin, with a neckerchief tucked into the bodice. She wore no other ornaments, save a shawl over her shoulders and a bit of velvet around her head, holding her hair back. All in all, Emma thought her quite respectable looking and even more attractive than she had looked in candlelight at their dinner table.

Jane returned, set the cups on the table, poured the tea, and spoke.

"Miss Sharpe has come to tell us that Mrs. Goddard has decided against the addition of an infant school to her present enterprise. She already has over forty girls, together with several boarders, and thus feels she is not ready for the additional work and responsibility such an addition would require."

Emma was surprised at the quick decision. "I am sorry to hear it," she said. "I was hoping it might be a resource for Mr. Weston. I suppose you will have to look elsewhere for a solution."

"Indeed, I was also disappointed, but Miss Sharpe has come here with a proposal of her own." Again, Emma could find no hint in Jane's demeanor of either approval or disapproval with whatever Miss Sharpe was going to say. And why was Frank not here?

"I am most grateful, Mr. Weston, that you will consider my proposal," said Miss Sharpe. "As I have already told you, I am the caretaker of my sister's infant child, a girl of almost a year. Though I have some financial assistance, it is not much, and have found it necessary to work as a governess in Weymouth, a position I did not enjoy. I became the teacher of three little girls, all much spoiled by their mother, who allowed no discipline from me to be visited on her children. There were, of course, servants who helped with my little charges when necessary, and for that reason, I stayed with the position for almost a year. It was while I was there that I heard of these newly developed infant schools. Mrs. Goddard's school was well known and of good reputation, and I hoped to prevail upon her to add the care of infants to her establishment. She has considered it, but in the end, has decided against it."

"I'm sorry to hear that," repeated Emma, "for your sake, but also because I think Mr. Weston was planning on having his young daughter placed there, for at least part of the time."

"Yes. But Mrs. Goddard has made another suggestion," added Miss Sharpe. "It is that Mr. Weston consider engaging me to care for his infant girl, as a kind of governess here at his home. It would be quite different from the situation at Weymouth. I would, of course, need to bring my sister's infant with me as well. But that would provide companionship for Mr. Weston's daughter, as she grows in years. Mrs. Goddard told me about Mr. Weston's deceased wife, who had been so beloved a governess to the two little girls of the widowed Mr. Woodhouse. I decided to propose a trial—of perhaps a month or two—to see whether Mr. Weston would be satisfied with the care I could provide to his daughter. I am here today to suggest such an arrangement." She stopped talking and focused her eyes on Mr. Weston.

In the silence, Jane spoke first. "My husband, Mr. Frank Churchill, has purchased tickets for our protracted honeymoon journey. We plan to be away for at least two months. Sometime after that, his uncle Churchill strongly desires we make our home at Enscombe. Hence, my feeling that an arrangement such as Miss Sharpe suggests, should at least be tried. We could not ask you, Mrs. Knightley, to make Randalls part of your daily affairs. You have your own domestic responsibilities at Hartfield. But we would rely on you to communicate to us, during our travels, how things at Randalls were progressing."

Emma was surprised at these plans, so quickly proposed and possibly imminent.

She spoke first to Miss Sharpe. "I am one of the two little girls Mrs. Weston cared for so lovingly. So, I am indebted to her for my and my sister's upbringing here in our home in Highbury. But it is Mr. Weston who must tell us what he thinks about such an arrangement."

She turned to face him. "You know how we loved your dear wife, our beloved Miss Taylor, for so many years before you even thought of her. You must surely be the one to decide whether or not you wish to proceed with this rather sudden proposal."

Mr. Weston shifted in his chair. "As I have told both Frank and Jane, one of the great disappointments of my life, something I regretted from the first, and ever after, was sending young Frank to live with his Aunt Churchill. The scene of his departure, on a bitter cold and rainy day, still haunts me. Of course, his adoption at Enscombe gave him a splendid education and now seems to have made his fortune. But twenty years of his life were lost to me. After he grew to manhood, I saw him every year for a day or two in London, but it wasn't the same as if he had lived here with me after his mother's death. I am determined not to repeat my mistake. Little Adelaide must stay here with me, though I am hardly capable of taking care of her myself. Mr. Martin's sister has told me she cannot stay away from her own home much longer. This proposal from Miss Sharpe, who comes highly recommended from her Weymouth employers, from Frank's uncle, and even, after an only short acquaintance, by Mrs. Goddard, has disposed me to accept this trial offer. It will be a relief to know little Adelaide will have a caretaker, even as little Isabella and Emma had the motherly care of my beloved Anne so many years ago now. I am ready to employ Miss Sharpe under these conditions. I do have a cook, butler, and housekeeper here at Randalls. Miss Sharpe must care only for my daughter, and of course, for her niece as well. The house is so situated, that we can turn the two guest rooms into a suite for Miss Sharpe and her niece, and little Adelaide will stay in her own room, nearby. Well, dear Emma, I have so many times turned to you for advice—will this plan do, at least for a time?" He looked rather imploringly at Emma, whose heart melted in sympathy for him.

"Of course, Mr. Weston. It is certainly worth trying. I will do all I can to help, of course, and will visit you more than you wish, I think. What do you think, Jane? Have you and Frank had time to discuss this plan?"

Jane nodded. "We received a note from Miss Sharpe, suggesting her plan. Mrs. Goddard has spoken approvingly of her interactions with Miss Sharpe. Given Frank's plans for our journey, we will have to leave almost at once. But first, Father-in-Law must approve."

"Is Frank not here?" asked Emma. "Surely he should have a voice in all this."

Jane spoke quickly in response. "Frank has gone into town to do some last-minute business. He has left to me the final decision regarding Miss Sharpe. Given our conversations today, I wish to go ahead, and quickly too, if all is to be put in order before we leave."

Emma thought Jane had a strained look. But she was never good at understanding Jane. She wanted to ask if Mr. Knightley should be consulted as well when she realized the others might not think so. She was eager to return to Hartfield, so she could tell him everything. Even priding herself on her ability at understanding human relations—which she had, of course, resolved to give up—she was perplexed by the suddenness of these monumental decisions. She wondered if it was Frank's idea, so eager to get away that he hardly considered how this change might affect his father. Emma could not imagine herself having put her own interests so far in front of her father's. She remembered the happy day when she and Mr. Knightley finally declared their love for one another. But the next day, with thoughts of her father alone at Hartfield, she ran over to Donwell to tell her beloved that, although she loved him, and always would, they could never marry! It was then that he also put Mr. Woodhouse's needs first, and declared his intention to live at Hartfield, because, as he so lovingly said, putting their clasped hands on her breast, 'that was where his heart was.' She found herself wondering, where was Frank Churchill's heart in all this? Though she had not always recognized it, her husband had always been the moral compass of her life. How suited was Frank Churchill to be anybody's moral compass? Mr. Knightley had called him 'a scoundrel,' and 'a disgrace to the name of man.' She feared her husband would raise more questions than she could answer.

It was time for Emma to leave. "I will leave you both to make arrangements and will go back to Hartfield. I want to tell Mr. Knightley of the plan." She turned to Miss Sharpe. "My husband and I always talk things over together. He usually has good advice to offer."

Miss Sharpe watched her closely. "How fortunate you are, Mrs. Knightley. Some of us must face our decision-making alone." Emma made a bow, gave Mr. Weston a kiss goodbye, and left Jane to make their preparations for new arrangements at Randalls, while she walked slowly home. She knew Mr. Knightley would have more than a little to say about this new plan, and not all of it positive. Though she was always grateful for his wisdom, it was not always easy to receive.

CHAPTER 25

Upon her return, Emma found Mr. Knightley at the drawing-room desk, going over some Donwell accounts. Mr. Woodhouse had fallen asleep in his chair by the fire. Even indoors, he wore one of his many scarves around his neck. She entered quietly, kissing her husband lightly on his head, until he turned and caught her around the waist, applying her kiss to his lips. Mr. Woodhouse slept through it all, quietly and peacefully.

Emma sat down in a chair beside the desk waiting for her husband to finish his business.

Mr. Knightley put down his pen and papers and turned to her. "So. What news from Randalls? Has anything been settled there? How is Mr. Weston? Any better, do you think? Was Frank Churchill there too?"

"Actually, only Jane. Frank was in town doing some last-minute business."

"I see." Mr. Knightley seemed reluctant to say more about the young man.

"You will be surprised when I tell you that Miss Sharpe, the woman from Weymouth who has come to Mrs. Goddard's about the infant school idea, was there."

"Now you have surprised me. Miss Sharpe visiting? There are several of Mr. Weston's friends in Highbury who have not yet paid their respects. Did you not find that odd, Emma?"

"Indeed, I did. But I was told that she had written, asking for the visit, and that Mrs. Goddard recommended Mr. Weston see her. So, it seems Jane was prepared for her coming. Yes, it was unusual, to be sure. But she came with a new idea, a proposal for Mr. Weston."

"What is to happen about the infant school?"

"Mrs. Goddard has declined. She feels it is too much at the present time, what with the number of students and boarders she already has."

"So, what was the purpose of the woman's visit?" Mr. Knightley seemed impatient to get to the point.

Emma decided to waste no more time. "Miss Sharpe has proposed herself as a governess to Mr. Weston's infant daughter."

"Governess to the infant girl?"

"I suppose it's no different from an infant school, except that Mr. Weston's daughter would be the only enrollee. Oh, and the infant daughter of Miss Sharpe's sister as well. And before you say more, I must tell you that I believe her suggestion may already have been accepted. They were talking about a two-month trial period. Comparisons were made with Miss Taylor's coming to Hartfield to care for me and Isabella. Now, I know we were a bit older—three and seven, was it? I'm not exactly sure."

"What did Jane say to the idea?" asked Mr. Knightley.

"She seemed relieved to get something settled. She also mentioned that on their return, Frank's uncle expected them to visit and eventually live at Enscombe. It seemed as though some kind of decision has already been made. And Mr. Weston—you know how accommodating he always is—will probably accept the arrangement, at least as a two-month trial."

Mr. Knightley sat silent, a dark look about his eyes. "Then there is nothing for me to say, is there, since the decision has already been taken."

"You can at least tell me what you think," said Emma.

"I think it is a reckless decision, much in Frank's style, like riding to London and buying a piano for a woman about to be a governess and leaving it in her aunt's small apartment, where there is no room for it. It would have been better had he merely gotten the haircut he said he went for. Emma, more time is surely needed to consider the hiring of a total stranger."

"I believe, though I'm not totally sure, that Frank was acquainted with the woman in Weymouth. And she brought very good references." Emma was trying to make the best of it.

"It's all about what Frank wants. I'm not sure that even Jane has been included in his deliberations. I thought she did not look well at our dinner party. Taking her off now, on an extended trip, when his father is still in mourning, and she has not yet recovered her health, and trying to decide how to care for the child left behind—to me, Emma, it is inconceivable. Of course, his father would agree with the proposal. He always agrees with everything Frank says or does. He is still consumed by the guilt he feels for giving his son up to the Churchills in the first place."

"I wish you would go over to Randalls and talk with Mr. Weston—and Frank, too, if he is there. Perhaps there are aspects to this decision about which we as yet know nothing."

Mr. Woodhouse had begun to awaken, and Emma went over to check the fire. "Did you have a good nap, Father," she said, stirring the coals.

"I think I did. Would you rearrange my scarf a bit, my dear? And how did you find Mr. Weston? And the infant? How I wish poor Miss Taylor were still alive and could help."

Emma nodded. "Yes indeed. But as she is not, Mr. Weston must think of other arrangements for now. Are you ready for your dinner? I'm afraid it's earlier than usual today."

Mr. Woodhouse gave Emma his order, suggesting that perhaps she and Mr. Knightley would like the same.

"No, Father. We've just come from tea and we will wait for a more suitable time to have our regular dinner. Mr. Knightley is just starting to review your accounts, as you see. I'll order your dinner and be right back."

She thought of how her father always referred to Mrs. Weston as poor Miss Taylor. Poor, indeed. Certainly, in this case, her father had been right. 'People should not marry. Mothers die.' No, she would not think such thoughts. She hoped herself one day to be a mother. Surely, if Isabella could be safely delivered of five children, she might hope for one or two herself!

After Mr. Woodhouse had eaten and expressed himself ready to retire, Mr. Knightley went up the stairs with him, returning soon after. "Your father seems quite tired tonight, Emma. I hope he is feeling all right."

"I think all this talk of change, does him no good. You know how he is. He likes things to remain the same. I'm still surprised that he has adjusted so well to your presence, my dear. He has not sent you home to Donwell for at least several weeks now. And he asks for you whenever you are out and about. You are a charmer, you know," she said, pulling him away from his usual chair to sit beside her on the sofa. "You know, when you left for London, after Box Hill, I couldn't bear the sight of that empty chair. I was ready to reupholster it, so it wouldn't keep reminding me of you."

"It is rather worn, I think," he said. "But it always was my favorite spot, across from your father, but looking at you all the while."

"After we announced our engagement, my dear Mrs. Weston told me that you and she frequently had little spats about me."

"Let us just call our talks, the presentation of different points of view, especially on your friendship with Harriet."

"She told me—and I admit I was delighted to hear it—that you said once, 'I love to look at her.' Do you still?" she asked, drawing quite close to him.

"And more. In those days, I only looked, still unconscious perhaps of my growing desire for you. Now I can take your hand and kiss it—like this—and lead you upstairs to our room to express my love more fully," he said. "But you know I don't like to talk about such things, Emma. I told you when I proposed that I cannot make speeches," he said, reddening somewhat.

"I think you are the best speech-maker, and the best dancer, I ever met," she said, her eyes twinkling.

"You are getting us off the topic, dear Emma, of Mr. Weston and what's to be done about arrangements at Randalls, if anything."

"I propose that you go over tomorrow and tell him what you think. But first, try to listen to him, and see whether this idea should be tried. You and your brother are such forthright types, you both speak your mind so forcefully that others often don't have a chance to reply. You must try to see it from his standpoint, and then give your best advice, although I fear it may be too late."

"I will do as you ask. I hope that his son will be out and about elsewhere. Maybe he is in need of a haircut."

"Please be fair. I'm sure he and Jane are quite busy. Mr. Weston will be glad to have your visit. Please do try."

And so it was, that the next morning, Mr. Knightley took his usual constitutional in the direction of Randalls to see if he could be of any assistance in Mr. Weston's future plans.

CHAPTER 26

Mr. Knightley reached Randalls quickly, his long strides carrying him on a direct route across the fields and finally onto the curving gravel path leading to the front door. The house stood in a rural setting, a modest estate adjoining Highbury. Its purchase had represented a step up for Mr. Weston, who now became a landed proprietor. Though small, the house was constructed of handsome red brick and featured a few mullioned windows and several turrets. It was surrounded by attractive shrubbery which opened on to a large garden in the back. It was after purchasing the place, that Mr. Weston had asked for Miss Taylor's hand. Thus, in Mr. Knightley's mind, Randalls was always associated with the beginnings of that happy relationship. Dispelling such thoughts, he was admitted almost at once to the drawing-room, where he took a seat. Before long, Mr. Weston walked in and greeted him.

"Mr. Weston. I've been wanting to come over but didn't want to intrude on your time with family. I have thought of you often, and want, once again, to offer my sincere condolences on your loss. As you no doubt know, your late wife was one of my favorite people," said Mr. Knightley, shaking Mr. Weston's hand with some warmth.

"I know that, my friend, and am glad to see you." Mr. Weston took a seat nearby.

"I have so many memories of my talks with her, mainly about Emma, I think, as we both loved her very much from the start. It just took me longer to discover my true feelings for my wife." It cost him much to speak about those days now, but he wanted to be truthful. Mrs. Weston had meant much to him, and, as always, it was difficult for him to speak his feelings in words.

"It is very lonely here now," Mr. Weston confessed. "I had lived so many years alone, I thought I was accustomed to it. But Anne so enlivened my home and everything in it, that it has been hard for me to reconcile myself to this new loss."

"You do have Frank and Jane here, which must be helpful," said Mr. Knightley, making a start into the discussion he wanted to have. "But I understand they will be away very soon on a long honeymoon journey. Am I correct?"

"Yes, indeed. They have had to wait for each other so long, that I could not in good conscience make any objection to their plans. And they have been so good to me, suggesting that I engage Miss Sharpe to care for little Adelaide at least until they return. I really don't know how I would have managed without help, though I never said that to them. Fortunately, Miss Sharpe, whom I brought to your dinner for Frank, had only just come to Highbury to seek a position at Mrs. Goddard's. He knew her at Weymouth, you see, and she has good references, so I felt quite fortunate to have found this solution, however temporary it may be."

"Is it a temporary solution?" asked Mr. Knightley. "Has Miss Sharpe employment elsewhere?"

"Well, she had, but was unhappy in it, and is glad to give this position a trial. If she likes it here, and things work out, it may turn into something more permanent. But for the moment, Frank says it will be a two-month trial. Miss Sharpe has come over today to meet little Adelaide. I will ring for her."

Mr. Knightley nodded, and shortly, the woman entered.

"Thank you for joining us so promptly, Miss Sharpe. Your recent dinner party host is here for a visit. You met Mr. Knightley at Hartfield the other night," said Mr. Weston.

Miss Sharpe made a bow and said she was glad to see him. "Mr. Weston has told me that the late Mrs. Weston had been a governess to your wife for many years. I am learning that in Highbury, everyone seems to have some connection with everyone else. It is so different from Weymouth, with its largely transient population."

"Yes indeed," said Mr. Knightley. "We are all in some way or another family. Certainly, the Westons have always been family to us."

"Would you like to join us, Miss Sharpe," offered Mr. Weston.

"Thank you, but just now the children are awake and shouldn't be left alone. Unless there is something else you might want, Mr. Weston?" When he nodded no, she made a curtsey and left the room quickly.

"She is a very nice and proper young lady, Mr. Knightley. I think she will do fine, for the foreseeable future. Mr. Martin's sister has left her service here, and my little Adelaide has been weaned to cow's milk, so she was not needed any further. She has been longing to return to her family. Miss Sharpe is glad to leave her position as governess in Weymouth. Jane has told me much about the problems of governessing. She likens it, even, to the slave trade, though how she can know much of that is not clear to me. She was almost made ill when she had to face leaving Highbury to take that position at Bath, found for her by Mrs. Elton, who, I know meant well. Mrs. Elton always means well. Miss Sharpe is equally grateful for her release from her prior duties."

"But what about after the two months of trial. What then? What if she leaves then? What will you do? She will again be without a position. Do you contemplate keeping her here on a permanent basis? Have you discussed that possibility with her?"

"No, of course, not yet. I have to see how we get on. But I do have the example of your father-in-law on my mind. He was so very fond of my wife. At the start of our marriage, he actually had trouble calling her Mrs. Weston, so much did he love his Miss Taylor. So, it is possible I will feel the same way about Miss Sharpe—but it is too early to tell."

Mr. Knightley thought but did not say, that Mr. Weston was younger than Mr. Woodhouse when he had been widowed. Mr. Woodhouse had married very late, and so Miss Taylor was more like a daughter to him. Miss Sharpe had a different look about her. He did not think anyone would mistake her for Mr. Weston's daughter. Was he aware that some women might regard him as an eligible marriage partner?

Well, there was nothing more for him to say at present. He could not find fault with Mr. Weston's decision for a two-month trial employment. He hoped, should his friend decide to terminate the position, that Miss Sharpe would be equally amenable to a parting of the ways. Something told him that when Frank and Jane returned, it might not be easy to send this lady away. She had something quite steely about her. Emma said that Frank's uncle wanted them to live at Enscombe on their return. Who would then stay at Randalls? This two-month trial seemed only a partial and imperfect solution to him. But with Frank and Jane going away, what was the alternative?

Mr. Knightley said his goodbyes and walked back to Hartfield, this time more slowly, trying out his thoughts this way and that. By the time he reached the house, he had formulated no definite conclusions.

He found his wife in the kitchen with Serle, busy making up the menu for dinner.

"We will have chicken and scalloped oysters," she said. "Father enjoys that. So, how did you get on with Mr. Weston? Is the plan with Miss Sharpe all set?"

"Emma, let us go into the drawing-room and sit, and I will tell you all I know," said Mr. Knightley. "Miss Sharpe was there."

"Do you think she will do?"

"Emma, let me get started in my own way," he said, pulling his wife down on the sofa beside him. "First, it is clear to me that this plan has already been decided upon. She will stay at Randalls for two months, while Frank and Jane are abroad. At the end of that time, I think, there will have to be an assessment and a decision."

"So, she might stay?"

"Yes, I think that is clear. Certainly, Weston will continue to need help, as Frank and Jane, upon their return and after staying at Randalls for a bit, will have to go to his uncle at Enscombe where, I believe, they will reside. So, this arrangement with Miss Sharpe, not at present permanent, might become so, if the trial period works out well."

"So, what did you think?" asked Emma. "Will she do?"

"It is hard to say. While I was there, she stayed not even five minutes with us, and seemed anxious to get back to the children."

"Well, that would be a good sign," said Emma.

"Yes," he said, somewhat hesitantly. "If that was her reason for excusing herself so quickly. But I had a feeling she also wanted to get away and not be examined, certainly not by me. She knew that Mr. Weston's late wife had been your governess for many years and brought that up during her brief stay. Perhaps she thought I would be making comparisons. I don't know, but something in her manner seemed overly guarded. Otherwise, as you saw for yourself the other night, she seems a comely, well-mannered young lady. Nothing of Mrs. Elton's vulgarity about her, but also, nothing of Jane's elegance. And nothing of your high-spirited openness, or your beauty. I saw nothing negative about her. I would need longer acquaintance to decide if she could be another Miss Taylor to Baby Adelaide. Perhaps you will be able to tell. You have always prided yourself on your talent at human relations."

"Now you are making fun of me," Emma said. "Me? With a talent at human relations? Have you forgotten my many blunders of the past?"

"They occurred only when you were match-making. You won't be match-making here. If you try to see her only as a potential Miss Taylor, you will come up with the proper assessment."

"You forget, don't you, that Miss Taylor married Mr. Weston."

"Yes, but not Mr. Woodhouse. Let's keep these comparisons straight."

"Very well, I will try to talk further with her when next I visit Randalls. Though I am much more cautious these days about detecting or predicting people's feelings and motives. You are the only one whose feelings and motives I care to understand. And, of course, Father's."

"And I yours, dear Emma, as well also as my dear father-in-law's." He was finished with the subject for now. His business duties awaited him. "I must be off to Donwell for the afternoon and will be back just before dinner. Mr. Martin has some more plans for me to see. That kind of thing is more in my line of work," he said, kissing his wife's hand before leaving.

She watched him move vigorously up the hill in his top-boots, striding out into the meadows until she couldn't see him anymore. How many times had she waited for him to come and enliven the atmosphere at Hartfield, and how often she hated it when he left, especially after one of their quarrels. Now he was here to stay. Marriage was much more pleasant than she ever expected in those days when she so confidently declared she would never marry!

CHAPTER 27

It was a dreary February afternoon, not much sun, and rain threatening. Emma was not feeling well. Her stomach was churning again, and she contemplated ordering some gruel for supper. But she knew her husband needed something more substantial, and told Serle to prepare a separate meal for Mr. Knightley. She was about to go up to her room to rest when a visitor came to the door. Jane Fairfax, of all people! There she was, just like her father, always calling Mrs. Weston 'poor Miss Taylor.' Well, at least she had not applied a similar adjective to Mrs. Churchill. But indeed, she did look poorly, Emma thought, not as blooming as a woman just returned from her honeymoon should look. She welcomed her and led her into the drawing-room.

"So, you are back from the honeymoon and your tour of foreign parts! We want to hear all about it. You must have seen so many wonderful places!" Emma seated herself in what she always called Mr. Knightley's Chair, and indicated the sofa for Jane. "Frank always talked about visiting Switzerland. I hope you got to see the Alps." She went over to stoke the fire. Jane looked chilled.

"Oh yes, indeed. Very tall, white, and forbidding," Jane said, with a half-smile. "They quite overwhelmed me. I am glad to be back here in the Highbury landscape for a while. I like the human scale of this gentle countryside much better."

"Can I order some tea?" asked Emma. "Or perhaps something else?"

"No. I need nothing just now." She paused. "Is Mr. Knightley not at home? I want to thank you both for all your help at Randalls while we were away. Frank has gone to town, catching up on some business. We found Mr. Weston looking much better. I am pleased to say for myself that the arrangement with Miss Sharpe seems to have worked very well. I am glad, because, unfortunately, we must be away again, perhaps even by the day after tomorrow. Frank's uncle is very keen to see us as soon as possible."

"It seems he has become as demanding as his late wife," said Emma. "But I agree that all has gone well at Randalls. I have been a regular visitor, as has my husband, and though nothing can ever be the same, life is much better there than it was two months ago, it is easy to see." Emma said no more, waiting for Jane to give her impressions if she would.

"Yes. Father-in-Law has included Miss Sharpe in all his activities, and it seems to do them both good. Baby Adelaide is thriving, as is little Edith, Miss Sharpe's niece."

"We have had Mr. Weston here for dinner several times. He seems to like being with my father, and they have spent more than several pleasant evenings together. Of late, Mr. Weston has asked us to include Miss Sharpe for dinner invitations, and of course, we have done so. We find her always very quiet, but pleasant. She improves upon acquaintance, I think," said Emma.

Jane made no comment on Miss Sharpe but went on with her thanks to Emma. "I'm grateful for all you have done. I also wanted you to know that we will be leaving for Enscombe soon. Frank will tell me exactly when after he returns." Jane paused, folding her hands together tightly as if summoning up the strength to continue. "But there is something else I must tell you. I confess that Frank and I are not of the same opinion regarding the future situation at Randalls." She paused again. "I am not sure if you have noticed how much Mr. Weston has come to rely on Miss Sharpe. Frank thinks it too much."

"Well, of course, that would be natural, would it not?" asked Emma, at first oblivious to what Jane was hinting. "When Mrs. Weston was Miss Taylor, she quite became part of our family. When she and Mr. Weston married, the celebration was at Hartfield, which had become as much her home as ours."

"Let me be completely clear. I am satisfied with Miss Sharpe's service at Randalls, but Frank believes his father may have a growing attachment to the lady, and wishes that she be terminated at once. He says the trial period has elapsed, and now is the best time to make other arrangements."

Emma was somewhat shocked. "I do think Miss Sharpe and Mr. Weston have become good friends. After all, she is caring for his child and, by extension, his household as well. Surely men and women can be friends without anything inappropriate occurring." Though as soon as she spoke, she remembered how many times she and Mr. Knightley had resolved 'always to be friends.' Transferring this memory to the arrangements at Randalls was a new thought.

"Frank finds that Miss Sharpe is rather too friendly with his father. He wants another person sought as soon as possible."

"Does he mean to take over the task of finding a replacement?" Emma was really not feeling well, and this discussion was making her stomach worse. "Then you should not leave for Enscombe, but rather stay here while Mr. Churchill himself seeks to find a replacement. As for me and my husband, we have found no fault with Miss Sharpe, and have not seen any untoward behavior, either on her part, or Mr. Weston's. If you are to change things, your husband needs to discuss his decision with his father and stay here longer to find someone else. Perhaps Mrs. Goddard could suggest one of her boarders?" Emma did not want this task to fall to her, when she was not feeling well and did not see any reason to make a change.

"I do not want to terminate the lady's service. And I must tell you, there are other reasons why it is important that Miss Sharpe must stay at Randalls. Sending her away at this time might cause much trouble."

"What reasons?" asked Emma. "I mean beyond the obvious ones, that she has done very well with the babes and that Mr. Weston likes her. What kind of trouble?"

"I don't have the time to talk about the situation now," said Jane, who stood up to leave. Suddenly, the visit had turned very formal and even unfriendly. Jane did not find Emma's suggestion about finding a replacement at Goddard's welcome.

"Perhaps you will tell me a little more when you have time. Meanwhile, I'll inform my husband about this decision when he returns," said Emma, a note of interrogation in her voice. She wondered if Jane had hoped rather to speak with Mr. Knightley, than with her. It was clear she had come over with some purpose and left without realizing it. It must have been to see her husband.

Jane said no more.

Emma showed her visitor to the door, and went into the drawing-room to rest herself and think. Clearly, Jane had something else to tell, though she could not imagine what. If anything, she had become more reserved than ever. Her marriage had not changed either that or her unwillingness to regard Emma as her friend.

In a short while, her husband returned. "You had a visitor?" he asked.

"Yes, it was Jane, and a very strange visit indeed. I think she wanted to see you, not me. That was clear. But she did tell me her main point—that Frank wishes to terminate Miss Sharpe's service at Randalls."

Mr. Knightley was surprised. "What is the reason?" he asked. "That is rather sudden, is it not? Evidently, his married state has not decreased his tendency to act impetuously."

For once, Emma did not feel able to take his part. "He thinks his father is growing too friendly with the lady and wants to hire someone else as soon as possible."

"Have you noticed anything, Emma, which might have caused Frank to have this impression? You have stopped there almost on a daily basis." Mr. Knightley looked troubled. "Perhaps Frank has not given up concocting romantic plots."

Emma reflected. "Perhaps not. But although I'm also good at that kind of thing, I've seen nothing like that. The children are flourishing. Mr. Weston seems happy. You have seen Miss Sharpe's behavior when invited here for dinner. I am completely in the dark." She felt herself feeling a little dizzy, and the pitch of her voice was rising. "I told Jane that Frank needed to explain himself further. After all, if he plans on leaving again, he cannot go without putting Randalls in order. Why does he want to make this change so suddenly?"

"He is not a man whose actions I have ever understood. He cannot leave without seeing his father's situation settled. After all, without Miss Sharpe in charge, all the responsibility would fall upon you—and our household—should Mr. Weston again be left to himself, with the young infant to care for and the household to be run. I do not want that to happen, especially when you are not feeling well." Mr. Knightley said no more.

"And there's more. At the end of our conversation, Jane said there were other reasons why Miss Sharpe should not be terminated. She said it would cause trouble. But she was unwilling to tell me what the reasons were. She's always so mysterious!" Emma was frustrated. "I'm sure she wanted to talk with you. I think you should try to see her. She was tired today, having only just returned from her travels. Even though I haven't a similar excuse, as you say, I am myself not quite well at present." She stopped. "Why don't you go over to Randalls and talk to her. I will try to be only a little jealous," she added, making a joke, but feeling a bit vulnerable, nevertheless.

"It seems there is always a mystery when dealing with Mr. Churchill. Perhaps you could send a note telling Jane I would like to visit as soon as possible. Then I will try to discover what these 'other reasons' might be. I will do my best, dear Emma. For now, I want you to go upstairs and have a brief nap before it's time for dinner. And if you mention being jealous again, I shall surely scold you." He kissed both her hands and she obeyed so readily that he felt somewhat alarmed. He must ask Dr. Perry to visit without further delay. He would send a message, hoping only that Mr. Woodhouse would not be unduly upset when he learned the call was to see Emma. Sometimes, he had to concede, openness was not always the best medicine. Marriage was giving him a new perspective on that aspect of life.

CHAPTER 28

Mr. Knightley always enjoyed his daily constitutionals, walking most mornings from Hartfield to Donwell. As he always explained to Emma and her father, when arriving from Donwell for his usual visits, 'It is a short walk, and I am fond of it.' After his marriage, and resettlement at Hartfield, he continued this practice. This morning he headed in the direction of Donwell and Abbey Mill Farm. He had arranged to meet with William Larkins and the servants at Donwell. After, he would extend his progress down a short avenue of lime trees, which led past a low stone wall, then further on to Abbey Mill Farm. Donwell did not stand on an eminence, as later houses always did, but was in a low and sheltered area, which had all the old neglect of prospect favored by a former generation of owners. This made the path a particularly private place.

On this day, after the return of Frank and Jane from their honeymoon, and his conversation with Emma, he set out early, pondering his wife's information regarding Frank's decision to terminate Miss Sharpe's employment at Randalls. They had sent a message to Jane but had not yet received an answer. Both he and Emma were perplexed by this unexpected turn of events. He was thinking about these matters, as he set out on his usual route. At the point on the rambling and irregular path to where the old stone wall stood, he found Miss Sharpe seated. Despite being startled to see her on the Donwell grounds, he bowed a polite hello.

She rose quickly. "You are surprised to see me, Mr. Knightley, I am sure. I am sorry to trouble you, but I fear I must intrude upon you, for I am in need of help." She seemed to be summoning her strength. "I learned yesterday that Mr. Churchill has decided to seek a replacement for me as governess to Mr. Weston's little girl." Then she stopped, as though weighing what she would say next.

In the pause, he motioned her to be seated again. "Indeed, I was myself surprised to learn of it, as I thought both you and Mr. Weston were well satisfied with your position and life at Randalls. Please be seated again. It is strange that you appeared just now, as I was only just thinking about Randalls and Mr. Weston. I was planning to talk to Mrs. Churchill and her husband about this sudden decision. Are you also wishing to leave your work here? Or is this Mr. Churchill's idea only?" Mr. Knightley watched as she sat and lowered her head at his questions. Then, she looked up at him, somewhat searchingly, he thought.

At first, she made no reply. Her decision to talk to Mr. Knightley had been reached only with difficulty, after reviewing the wisdom of such a step. After learning of Frank's intention to dismiss her, she had not slept well. She had spoken briefly to his wife, and, somewhat reluctantly, was contemplating whether or not to make good her threat—to tell Mr. Weston all about her relationship with Frank and most especially, of the child which was his.

During the past two months, her life at Randalls had become more complicated. She had grown to love little Adelaide and her position there. If, as she had threatened, she told about the affair with Frank and the child, that would surely destroy everything. And yet, it was her last weapon.

On more than a few evenings over the past two months, she had enjoyed dinner engagements at Hartfield. Mr. Weston had thoughtfully engaged a woman to come to Randalls in the evenings when he wanted her to accompany him to Emma's invitations. At these meetings, she felt sure she learned more of Mr. Knightley's character, closely observed during that time. She saw the way he looked at his wife. How deeply he loved her. She watched him treat the servants and other guests with attention and respect. She felt his courtesy toward her and his friendly compassion toward Mr. Weston. He listened attentively to the always talkative Miss Bates, never losing patience no matter how long or irrelevantly she might go on with a subject. Most of all, she observed his loving care and tact when handling Mr. Woodhouse, who obviously had come to love and rely upon his son-in-law. Mr. Knightley's behavior was not the result of mere surface courtesy but came from an upright and unblemished character. She supposed his name told it all. Looking now, into his direct and not unkind glance, she knew she was right in taking this chance to tell him her story. He was a man unlike Frank, she thought, a man to be relied upon, steady and true. She would confide in him, for she had no other choice. They were both quiet now, she, sitting on the stone wall, and he, standing tall and directly in front of her. Then, he sat down beside her. He realized this was no chance encounter; she had been waiting for him.

She began. "I have decided to tell you my history, Mr. Knightley, though I confess I am ashamed of it." She paused as if to find breath and strength for what she had to say. "For almost a year before Mr. Churchill met and fell in love with Miss Fairfax, he and I had a brief relationship which, he warned me, could never end in marriage, for his aunt would oppose any alliance with a woman who brought neither station nor money into the relationship. So, against my better judgement I acceded to an illicit relationship. The little girl I call my niece is Frank's child." She waited for some reaction, but he continued to listen, the expression on his face inscrutable.

"Naturally, I had to leave my position at Enscombe, so I subsequently engaged as a governess in Weymouth, and saw Frank whenever he came there. When I heard of his aunt's passing and his departure from Enscombe for Highbury, I followed, thinking he had gone to see his father, hoping, for the sake of my child, to regularize our relationship. You might perhaps judge my actions as unladylike and bold. But I hoped he would marry me. Then, at Highbury, I found that he had already married Miss Fairfax. Afterward, I met her at Mrs. Goddard's. She asked me for the truth, and I told her everything. Despite all, she kindly did not prevent me from gaining the position at Randalls. I assured her I had no further interest in Frank, as he was now a married man, and that I would cause neither of them any trouble. I did, however, threaten that should I be dismissed at the end of the two months, I would tell Mr. Weston that he is the grandfather of my child. I asked her to help me in convincing Frank not to terminate my service. If she did, I would keep my secret forever."

"His secret too, surely," said Mr. Knightley, frowning. No wonder Jane did not look well. This was far worse than the flirting Frank engaged in with Emma when he first came to Highbury.

"I am ashamed of making that threat now when I see how revealing Edith's parentage would not help me or my child and would destroy Mr. Weston. I fear I have given Mrs. Churchill a somewhat wretched honeymoon. At any rate, when they came back, Frank told me it was time for me to leave Randalls. If I did not go, he would himself tell Mr. Weston the truth about my past and his. Of course, if he does that, I must leave. But he and his wife are going to live at Enscombe now, not at Randalls. I need never see him again, or at least, not very often. I very much want to stay. I am fond of little Adelaide, and of Mr. Weston, who has been very good to me. Nevertheless, I am ready to leave if Frank dismisses me. I will not have Mr. Weston destroyed with my information. I have grown too fond of him to want him to endure such unsavory revelations. I don't know if Frank can be dissuaded. I have formed the opinion that only you can help me."

Mr. Knightley was doubly shocked. First, about Miss Sharpe's unexpected revelations. And then, all over again at Frank's decision to terminate her service at Randalls. He was indignant. And angry. "Miss Sharpe, thank you for your confidence in telling me all of this. You must give me time to think carefully. Please say nothing to anyone else until I contact you again. Be assured I will do my best to help. Now, if you will excuse me, I must finish my business at Donwell, before returning to Hartfield. Thank you for your honesty. I will consider all you have told me, and see whether or not a solution can be found. I am indeed very sorry for the situation in which you find yourself." He bowed briefly to her, and she rose and stood motionless, looking flushed. He turned away and walked on, pondering the substance of Miss Sharpe's sad story and wondering what he could do about it if anything.

CHAPTER 29

Mr. Knightley could hardly believe what he had just been told. When he first learned of Frank and Jane's secret engagement, fearing Emma had been wounded, he easily found words to describe Frank— 'abominable scoundrel.' Frank was a disgrace to the name of man. But he could find no words to describe him now.

Back at Hartfield, he faced the task of telling his wife all he had heard. Emma waited for him to speak. "You look troubled. What has happened?" she asked.

He was learning more each day about marriage and what it meant to him. It meant everything. He knew that he must tell his wife all. That old phrase they had used so often must still be true. "We always tell each other just what we think." Yes. He must tell her. He hoped she would see it in the way he had. It was, to be sure, a shocking story, and he was unsure how Emma would react. Her life before their marriage had been a sheltered one. Box Hill was the furthest she ever traveled from Hartfield until he took her to the seaside at Broadstairs. And although she conjured up fantasies about Frank Churchill in the past, he was sure no such scenario as he had just heard would have entered Emma's wildest thoughts. And he knew she was not feeling well. Still, he had no choice. He and his wife were equal partners in their marriage. He would withhold nothing from her. While he was not a man who condoned secrets, it seemed he was fated to live among them.

"Please let's sit in the drawing-room for a few moments. I have had a surprising morning. On the path over by Donwell, Miss Sharpe was waiting to see me."

"Waiting to see you there? Why not here? What's the matter," she cried, fearing that something was wrong at Randalls. "Is it something about Mr. Weston?" she asked, worry creasing her forehead.

"No, dear Emma. You must let me tell you all slowly, and in my own way."

"Is it the children? Has something happened to them?"

"Please let me speak, my dear. No one is in any physical harm at Randalls. But there are severe problems, and I have been asked to help." And so, slowly, gradually, he told her all of Miss Sharpe's sad story, watching her closely as he continued. Her eyes, always so beautiful whenever he looked into them, were wide open with disbelief and shock.

"What can we do to help them?" she asked her husband.

In that brief moment, how much he loved her all over again. Her response had been instinctive, generous, not one of condemnation or judgment, but of willingness to be of service. With those simple words, Emma took the weight of this problem from his shoulders alone. Yes indeed, surely something must be done, if not for Miss Sharpe, then certainly for poor Mr. Weston. And together they would seek whatever solution could be found.

"We must talk to Jane first," said her husband. "You say Frank has ridden over to Mrs. Goddard's to see if there could be a replacement for Miss Sharpe there?"

"Yes," she answered, "That was the answer Jane gave to my note."

"Then I will ride there now, and find him. He must be brought back here first, so we can both talk to him. Since Jane appears to know all, we will leave her at Randalls with Mr. Weston, the children, and Miss Sharpe, for the time being." He stopped. "But first, you must see to your father, and get him to eat his dinner early, and go up to bed. By that time, I should be back, hopefully with Mr. Churchill, and we can talk with him. But perhaps you would rather not?" He did not know how she would feel about seeing that so-called 'amiable young man' in this new light.

"Of course, I will be ready for you. First, I will have something to eat with Father and await your return." She went into the other room and found her father lightly dozing before the fire. She awakened him and directed Serle to bring them dinner, two orders of gruel. She set up one of the usual Pembroke tables near the fire.

"What about Mr. Knightley," her father asked. "Why is he not here with us?"

"He had an errand to run, and will eat when he returns," she answered. "I will order something for him later."

"It's not good to eat too late," he said. "Dr. Perry says it isn't good for the digestion."

"He won't be too late. He will be back soon."

"I don't like him to be riding out after sundown," Mr. Woodhouse continued. "It isn't safe, you know."

"He'll be back before that." Emma never ceased to wonder how completely her father had become accustomed to her husband's presence. Indeed, as now, he treated him much in the same manner as he had always treated her and was uncomfortable if he was not present.

"I'll get you upstairs tonight," she said.

"No, dear Emma. That is the task of my son-in-law. He wouldn't like it if I were not to wait for him."

"As you wish, Father. But you mustn't stay up too late, you know. It wouldn't be good for your health."

Mr. Woodhouse settled back in his chair. "Perhaps tonight, my dear, I will have another small glass of wine. And maybe you would read to me a bit."

She took up her copy of Milton which was near at hand and was in the middle of the council in Pandemonium when she heard the sound of horses on the gravel path outside. "He's here Father. Are you ready to go up?"

Mr. Knightley entered, saw that his father-in-law was still at his dining table, and strode over. "I am sorry I have kept you waiting, sir."

"I couldn't go up without you," he replied. "You know what a creature of habit I am," he said. "I do apologize. Dear Emma offered to take me upstairs, but I have become so accustomed to leaning on you, even more heavily of late, I think. And Emma is not feeling well, she tells me. She has been reading Milton to me, and I confess, I can't make it all out. I thought the angels resided in Heaven."

"Father-in-Law they do, except for our dear Emma whom we are lucky enough to have here on earth. I hurried back, as I myself do not like to miss our evening rituals. I am sorry I could not have joined you for dinner."

"Be sure to eat at once, as soon as you come back down. You know what Dr. Perry says."

"Indeed, I do. Let us go up and I will fill you in on the situation in heaven on the way. I'll eat dinner as soon as I come back down."

He turned to his wife and spoke quietly. "Emma, Mr. Churchill is waiting outside. Please have him brought into the drawing-room. I'll be with you shortly."

She complied, asking her serving-man to escort Mr. Churchill in. Thankfully, Mr. Knightley was back quickly. He bowed briefly and motioned Frank to take a seat.

"Your husband has interrupted my visit to Mrs. Goddard. He says there is something urgent we need to discuss. I am at your disposal. Mr. Knightley gave me no hint of what it is." Frank looked pleasant, but there was a wariness about his eyes. Emma was sure he had guessed the subject.

Mr. Knightley began. "Miss Sharpe paid me a visit today."

"Oh, I see," said Frank. "Has she been telling stories about me?"

"Let us not make any more pretenses, Mr. Churchill. Miss Sharpe has told me about your previous relationship with her."

"Jane knows all about that, so you will not be revealing anything to her that she does not know already," said Frank. "So, if that is all, I would like to leave, as Jane and my father will be expecting me." He rose and made as if to depart. "My angel Jane has forgiven everything. Indeed, she has gone so far as to forgive Miss Sharpe as well. Under the present circumstances, father has not, obviously, been told."

Emma felt herself becoming angry. "Indeed, Miss Sharpe is more to be pitied than forgiven. Women always bear the brunt of the shame in these matters. When I told you to treat Jane well at the Martin's wedding, I had no idea it was already too late!"

"The reason I wish to terminate Miss Sharpe's employment has to do with any future attempts she might make to draw my father into an unsuitable relationship. Let me remind you how damaging it might be to my father to discover one day that he has my former lover under his roof and his grandchild as well. I have tolerated the arrangement for a while, but my wife's poor health—she is in the early stages of pregnancy—and my father's somewhat precarious state have determined me to take action. You had better think twice before approaching my father with any allegations."

Emma turned to her husband. She looked almost ready to faint.

"What I want to say, Mr. Churchill," said Mr. Knightley, "is that more discussion is needed on this matter. I gather that your wife is not in favor of your resolution to terminate Miss Sharpe. Though I do not like interfering in business that is not mine, since you plan on leaving very soon, we must all agree on future arrangements at Randalls before you depart."

Frank nodded curtly. "Very well. I must get back to Randalls. We will continue this discussion tomorrow." They parted with bows, but without words.

When they were again alone, Emma began. "I feel sorry for Miss Sharpe, dear. Don't you?"

"Yes, I do, and not just because I have never really liked Mr. Churchill. Meanwhile, we must keep Mr. Weston out of this, as nearly as possible. What to do about it all, I cannot at present imagine. I have never before been so reluctant to reveal the truth about a situation."

"You have always told me the truth, indeed," said Emma. "But it was always the truth about ourselves. This is something quite different, is it not? This is telling the truth about someone else, a truth that may upset their entire life. It is not something to be done lightly. You lectured me once on showing compassion to those in need of it."

"Indeed, I remember. And hopefully, Miss Sharpe cannot be dismissed at once. I don't know if Mrs. Goddard will suggest someone else to help at Randalls. A complicated situation, dear Emma. We must go slowly, and try our best to hurt no one, if possible. On second thought, I think you should go over to Randalls alone tomorrow to see Jane."

"But I'm sure she would rather see you," said Emma.

"I think it better that you talk with her. Mrs. Weston often told me that women needed the company of other women. She will be more able to share her intimate feelings with you. Please do give it a try."

Emma left the room to order his dinner. She had not yet told her husband of her own physical condition. She resolved to see Dr. Perry, but that would have to wait. This task had to come first, of that, she was sure.

CHAPTER 30

The carriage ride from Hartfield to Randalls was not long. Emma remembered the day Miss Taylor's engagement was announced, and Mr. Woodhouse was in one of his dark moods. He could not understand why Miss Taylor wanted to leave Hartfield. 'She might have stayed with us until she died!' he had exclaimed. Mr. Knightley, taking a seat in his usual chair, reasoned that Randalls was but a half-mile away, and only a short walk. By carriage, he joked, they could visit there several times a day. Well, today's ride over was indeed short, but there was no Mrs. Weston to greet her, and no anticipation of pleasant times shared when she arrived. Jane met Emma at the door as if she were waiting for her.

Emma was at Randalls once again, the site of so many pleasant visits and confidential chats, but its recent mistress was no longer there.

"Mrs. Churchill," Emma began. "Thank you for receiving me. I realize my visit is perhaps too early."

"Not at all, But will you please call me Jane," she answered. "We must begin with that, at least."

Emma nodded, they went into the drawing-room and she seated herself. "Then you must call me Emma." A small fire burned in the grate, and the room felt comfortably warm. How to begin? She might as well be direct. "Your husband told us yesterday about his resolve to terminate Miss Sharpe's appointment here at Randalls. I know you have a different view about that decision. I thought it might help if I described my impressions of the last two months when I frequently visited your father-in-law and Miss Sharpe and the children. They often came to Hartfield as well. We do believe we have good knowledge of the situation."

Jane raised one hand as if to stop her. "Emma—I may call you that? I know you have a right to speak about these things. Frank and I are both very grateful for all you have done to make our wedding journey possible."

She paused, almost as if to take a deep breath. "Frank has informed me that he told your husband everything about his past life at Weymouth. He has confessed everything to me as well. It was not easy to hear, as you might imagine, but as you have also recently married the man you love, perhaps you will understand that I have forgiven it all and wish only to put it in the past."

Emma thought but did not say, how different were these two men. How true had been her own Mr. Knightley, and how false Jane's Mr. Churchill. But she had not come to judge, but to help, if possible.

Jane continued almost at once. "As for Miss Sharpe, I know too well what it is to love and to be unguarded. To make mistakes. She has made many. But I too have done wrong. I was persuaded by my love for Frank, and my wish not to lose him, to form a secret engagement which caused distress to ourselves and to others. When I think of that, I believe that Miss Sharpe must be forgiven for her mistakes, arising out of love as well. How can I judge her, when I might also have fallen, had not Mrs. Churchill's death occurred, releasing us from our false position. I do not know whether I might have gone deeper into our relationship, had that death not occurred."

For the moment, Emma was speechless.

"Yes, you might well stare at such an admission. But your great love, your Mr. Knightley, would never have asked such a capitulation from you. Of that, I am sure. But Frank is a different sort of man. I do not know what I might have done had he asked of me a further demonstration of my love. I can be honest about that. I do not know."

Silence fell between them. Emma thought now of the differences in their situations. She always had the security of Hartfield, the protection of her father. Most of all, when she first felt the stirrings of mature desire, even of a sexual response, she had the security of being loved by a totally honorable man. What did Jane have? Brought up by strangers, albeit loving ones, meeting Frank in a place like

Weymouth, where people sought their pleasures, escaping the roots and restrictions of family and friends. And Frank—he surely was an amiable man, as she herself defended him once to Mr. Knightley— but honorable? No. Turned out of his home at an early age, brought up by a demanding, proud, luxurious, and selfish aunt, his father so distant, always compliant, unwilling to discipline him—how could he have grown to be a man like her husband. She saw it all, in one blinding moment of understanding.

Jane was continuing. "Miss Sharpe has assured me that she respects my marriage and will never interfere with us. How can I deny her the chance she has found here, to earn respectability? It would be most unchristian, I think. I am not afraid of her presence. I am quite secure in Frank's love for me."

She had completed her statement with an expression of some relief before her face darkened again. "Unfortunately, on this subject, Frank and I have differed, and he thinks Miss Sharpe should go. He believes her presence here is annoying to me and potentially damaging for his father. I have disagreed with him, and we are at an impasse. There, I have told you the whole of it."

For the first time in her life, Emma caught sight of the real Jane Fairfax. She was not the cold, reserved, superior young woman whom she always resented and disliked. Yes, she played the piano far better than Emma and was always more kind and patient with Miss Bates. But she was also a passionate, open, and, yes, truly superior woman ready to face a world she had not chosen for herself, but reluctant, indeed unwilling, to charge another with a sin she might herself have committed. Emma found herself speechless in admiration.

"What does your Mr. Knightley think?" asked Jane. "I confess, I have long admired him for his upright nature and truthfulness. I remember the day he was called into my aunt's apartment to view the piano Frank had so romantically but foolishly sent. He stepped out of my aunt's hearing, but I heard him turn to you and say, 'It is a reckless gift! She is about to become a governess. Where will they put it?' Fortunately, then, attention was taken away from his comment by my aunt's gratitude for the barrel of apples he sent. I was grateful that no one heard his earlier comment, but he could not even then resist telling the truth. Is it not so? What will Mr. Knightley do now? If Frank terminates Miss Sharpe, will he tell all to Mr. Weston? That is what I fear, and what it would do to my father-in-law. He so admires Frank! In the midst of his most recent loss, I do not know that he could survive knowing these truths!" She was close to tears. "And if Frank goes through with the termination, Miss Sharpe may tell my father-in-law about the child."

Emma also felt overwhelmed by emotion. "I think she has regretted her threat about taking such a step. Still, will it not be an extraordinary effort for Miss Sharpe to remain here without recalling the deception?" asked Emma. Though she had imagined many scenarios for others, she had no success imagining herself either in Jane's or Miss Sharpe's position.

"I suppose when your very life depends upon it, you could. I know keeping my secret—trivial by comparison, to be sure—almost cost me my health," said Jane. "But I can tell you, without reservation, that I am prepared to keep all aspects of Frank's relationship with Miss Sharpe as secret as if they had never happened. I believe she will be too. If you and Mr. Knightley could support me in this, Frank might be won over. After all, we are removing to Enscombe, and will not be living here at Randalls. What can be gained by turning away this woman who has done so much good here already? And what harm can it be to Mr. Weston for his house and the children to be cared for? You, above all, should understand that. Your father having found such a person enabled you to grow up safely, here at Hartfield."

Emma could say nothing to the contrary. "You find me on your side, Jane. We must both put our efforts toward a good solution. Frank will need to be convinced. And, as we both know, my husband finds keeping secrets difficult and inadvisable. I appreciate your frankness with me. I will do all I can to help. In any case, Mr. Weston must never know all of this. There is no need, and it would be devastating to him, do you not agree?"

"In part. But he has been so forgiving to both Frank and me already, I can imagine him ready to forgive even something greater."

"You may be correct, but that must be faced later, if necessary. Let us work first on keeping Miss Sharpe in her position now and the secrets kept. I must return home and talk to my husband. Thank you for your confidence and the goodness of your nature. I have so wanted us to be friends and that moment seems to have arrived." She paused to take a breath. "It is no wonder that Frank loves you. I fear mine has loved me in spite of my faults."

"You do yourself an injustice," said Jane, taking Emma's hand. "You also have a lovely and good nature. But no more of this. Let us make a start."

After pressing her hand in return, Emma stepped back and made Jane a deep curtsy. The two women had completed their deliberations. Emma's carriage was waiting to bring her back to Hartfield and Mr. Knightley.

CHAPTER 31

When Emma returned to Hartfield from Randalls, Mr. Knightley was not at home, having walked over to Donwell at the request of William Larkins, still his faithful business manager at the Abbey. Emma was almost glad, for she had not yet formulated her approach. While they were equals now, she never could shake off those sixteen years of difference. She had been wrong so many times and yet he loved her still. He had even won her father's heart. But this situation was not a case of love. Years make little difference in all things moral. This was a case of trying to right a wrong, but in so doing, entering again into the world of secrets. She wondered if he would countenance that.

She heard the door open and shut. He was there.

"Emma? Are you home?" He removed his coat and hat, came into her, kissed her hand, and looked at her. "Come, tell me how your visit went." He led her into the drawing-room and they sat together on the sofa before the fire. Mr. Woodhouse was still upstairs, and there was some time before dinner was to be served.

"Jane was very honest and open with me. She is truly a remarkable person." Best to start with the main point, she thought. "She wishes Miss Sharpe to stay. She knows all, forgives all, thinks it is best for Mr. Weston to know nothing of the truth of it, and for things to go on as they are." There. She was out with it.

Mr. Knightley was silent, considering. "She knows everything?"

"Yes. She says she made mistakes too and was saved from them being worse by Mrs. Churchill's death. How things might have gone on otherwise, she is not sure. She is so forgiving and generous. She says she knows Frank loves her, and she fears nothing from Miss Sharpe. She is ready to remove to Enscombe and leave all at Randalls as is." She paused. "A remarkable woman, to be sure."

"And what did you say, Emma?" He looked at her earnestly. "Did you agree?"

"I fear I did. What would be the harm? The sins are committed, the woman needs work and a home. Who is Frank to deny it to her? He was the cause. Now he wants to undo what cannot be undone. Yes, I confess, I do agree with Jane. She thinks that if you would agree and talk to Frank, he would relent."

"I fear my opinions mean little to Mr. Churchill. He has never cared for anyone's, other than his own. He played false with Jane, with you, and with Miss Sharpe. I wonder if he can be trusted to judge unselfishly here."

"We must think of Mr. Weston. Even if Miss Sharpe goes away, might he not eventually learn the whole story anyway? You once said, when remonstrating with me about my interference with Harriet and Mr. Martin, 'People are not your playthings, Emma. They are real flesh and blood.' You were right then. The words can be applied here. These people are flesh and blood, and we must think of them that way."

"Emma, if we are to be recalling my past words and using them against me, I also once told you that Frank Churchill was a fortunate man. I repeat that now. Here are three women, each of whom he has harmed, albeit in different ways, and each one willing to forgive and forget. I repeat: I envy him."

"Are you angry with me?" she asked, his words bringing back that moment in the garden when he spoke those words to her.

He looked at her. "No, of course not. I admire you more than ever. In this matter, you are correct, my dear Emma. There is wisdom in what you say. But we must think carefully about how to proceed." He rose. "I will go and get your father so he can have his dinner. We will talk more later."

In a few minutes, he was back with Mr. Woodhouse, and they seated themselves together at the table. "After visiting Donwell today, I went over to Abbey Farm. I must tell you all how wonderfully well Mr. Martin's expansion project is going on. He has become quite the enterprising farmer. He tells me he plans to add on to his house. It makes me wonder if they are expecting," said Mr.

Knightley.

Emma was brought up short by these words. She must see Dr. Perry, and soon. Though it would not be necessary to add space to Hartfield should her suspicions be correct, there were alterations that needed to be made. Her most momentous task would be telling her father. But Mr. Knightley would help Mr. Woodhouse through the anxieties she knew would follow the announcement. It would be a welcome change of subject, yet she could not forget the situation at Randalls.

When all was quiet, Mr. Woodhouse long in bed and asleep, she and her husband also in bed, Emma waited for her husband to speak.

"Would you like to do some reading in Milton tonight?" he asked, not looking her directly in the eye.

"You know I would not," she answered. "I would rather speak about Randalls and Mr. Weston."

"My very dearest and most beloved Emma, will you let us go to sleep without talking? Then I will return the favor by not subjecting you to Milton tonight. We know everything we need to know. Right now, I need some quiet time. You have done your part in visiting with Jane. I will do mine and visit Mr. Churchill in the morning."

Emma looked at him. He looked so tired, and troubled, that she could not bear to ask him for further talk. She gave him a long kiss and lay back down in his arms. In some strange way, she reasoned that she had brought all this down upon him. Had he stayed at Donwell, with his books and library, happy with reading Milton and tending to his estate responsibilities, and had she not fostered the attachment between Mr. Weston and Miss Taylor, none of this problem would have been theirs to solve. She almost told him as much, when she remembered she had promised him some quiet time. She needed sleep herself, as her symptoms of nausea had returned after dinner. She would soon have other matters to attend to, she told herself. She resolved to call Dr. Perry in the morning.

CHAPTER 32

Both Emma and her husband were up early and seated at the breakfast table by eight. Mr. Woodhouse had enjoyed his eggs and was settled in his usual seat by the fire with his newspaper.

"I'm sorry," said Emma. "These eggs again. I forgot to tell Serle. I'll go in and order some others."

But Mr. Knightley stopped her. "Actually, I was looking forward to them this morning. It promises to be a somewhat difficult day, and in such cases, boiled eggs are just the thing for the stomach."

Emma was not convinced. "You're making that up," she said.

"No, I am not, I assure you. And you said your stomach hasn't been right either. I think they are just the thing for us both." He began attacking his eggs with vigor.

"I don't believe a word you are saying," she said. "You're just delaying talking about the situation at Randalls. And I have kept my part of the bargain by staying quiet last night. Now you must keep yours and talk to me."

He put his utensils down and turned to her with a look she recognized.

"You aren't going to talk to me," she said, with a frown. "I see it."

"I am," he answered. "And here is what I am going to say." He paused and took her hand and kissed it.

"Yes, you know how I like that. But I still want to hear something from you," she said.

"As soon as I finish these excellent eggs, I am riding over to Randalls to talk to Mr. Churchill. When I return, I promise to tell you exactly what Mr. Churchill has to say. For the moment, I know no more than I did last night." Still holding her hand, he kissed it again.

She took his hand and kissed it back. "You know I love you and I always will. I will wait for our talk until you return."

Before much longer, he saddled Bessie up and was on his way to Randalls where, upon admission, he asked to speak to Mr. Churchill. Frank ushered him into the drawing-room. And so, for the first time since Frank Churchill had returned to Highbury, upsetting so many lives, Mr. Knightley and Frank Churchill were alone.

Mr. Knightley began. "I realize you may think I am interfering in matters which are none of my business, and I apologize in advance. But we have been somewhat involved in your affairs, ever since your return to Highbury."

"There is no need to apologize, Mr. Knightley. Of course, I have thought about what you have said, though I believe you can have no particularly friendly feelings toward me."

"In the past, that was true. But whatever my feelings were at that time, they are different now. My wife had a great devotion to the late Mrs. Weston, and to Mr. Weston as well. She felt toward your mother-in-law as toward the mother she never knew. And so, we hope you will make the right decisions about Mr. Weston's future and that of his child."

Frank was about to speak, but Mr. Knightley stopped him. "May I add just one more thing. My wife and I are aware of your previous relationship with Miss Sharpe, as well as of the paternity of her child. I believe your wife knows as well. I also know of Miss Sharpe's threat, which I believe she now regrets. We all understand that Miss Sharpe has performed her duties very well here and that she wishes to stay on after you and your wife remove to Enscombe. I remain in favor of continuing Miss Sharpe's employment, as does my wife and, I believe, Mrs. Churchill." He paused. "Now that I have told you everything I know, would you share with me your view of the situation?" Mr. Knightley folded his hands and sat back, telling himself to be as fair as possible to Frank. It was not an easy situation, he could only imagine. Yet Frank had crafted it for himself. Now he had the task of doing something about it.

After a pause, Frank spoke. "I know you have never thought very much of me. And to be truthful, I cannot blame you. I was toying with your Emma, and for all you knew, I might have taken her away from you. Admit it. Is that not true?"

Mr. Knightley felt in no mood to make confessions of his feelings to this man who had nearly stolen his happiness from him. He had treated Jane so very badly, she, a woman whom he respected and admired. He had taken advantage of another woman in a very vulnerable position. His conduct with Miss Sharpe—for him, it was unimaginable. And what of the child he was so ready to abandon? Mr. Knightley felt himself becoming angry and hoped he could restrain his emotions.

"Mr. Churchill, may I remind you that this situation and its solution is not about me, or anything I have done, but is solely about you and the people whose lives you have meddled with or harmed. So let us rather focus on that, and not on me. May I add, you overestimate any success you might have had with my wife. She has made clear to me that while she at first found you an interesting outsider, she never loved you. Fortunately, she also told me that though you used her badly, you did her no harm, else I might be much rougher with you. But as I said, this other situation is one of your creation, not mine. Nor could it ever have been. So let us continue with a view to your problems, not mine."

"How can I leave Miss Sharpe here so that she can one day tell my father all about me and my many sins? How can I trust that she will keep silent? And about the child. She says she will, and Jane and your wife seem to believe her. But how can I? You are telling me that they can keep all the truth about my previous relationship with Miss Sharpe secret. How could you keep it, no matter what the others say?"

"I can imagine you would find it difficult to believe that people can act honorably and keep their word," said Mr. Knightley, his anger starting again to display itself. He stopped. "I apologize. I have not come here to judge you and do not wish to. But the two women we love have favorably assessed the situation and the likelihood of Miss Sharpe keeping your secret. And what of your child? Do you wish her to be thrown out along with her mother?"

"But Jane is also with child, and I do not wish to have another take its place. Can you not understand that?" said Frank, passionately.

"What I can understand is that you must make what amends you can to those you have damaged, without worrying about harm to yourself. It remains for you to be a man and take responsibility. As for myself, I hate duplicity and secrets, but reluctantly recognize a need here that is, at least for the time, greater than the truth. I hope that Miss Sharpe can stay on at Randalls. You also owe this support to your child. As for your wife, I seem to recall your very brief words of apology to my Emma at the Martins' wedding. What she told you then referred to Jane: 'Treat her well,' were, I think, the words. Do the same with Miss Sharpe. That is all the advice I have to give, though you have asked me for none."

Mr. Knightley paused. "I assure you, all your secrets are safe with me. When you come to a decision, you can send word by letter to Hartfield. Thank you for your time, Mr. Churchill. Please believe me when I say I wish you well." Mr. Knightley bowed slightly and left. He did not want to see Frank Churchill ever again.

CHAPTER 33

On the following day, Mr. Knightley received a brief note from Frank Churchill. It was written in Frank's careful handwriting, though it was not as long as some of his earlier missives—What a letter the man writes! Nor did it contain any of the flourishes of style previously criticized by Mr. Knightley. For once, Frank was brief, and, one hoped, sincere:

Sir,
I have decided to take the advice you have given me, and at the present time will not disturb Miss Sharpe's position as governess at Randalls. Thousands of thanks to you and your wife for your interest and efforts to assist me in setting my affairs to rights. My wife's aunt will keep us appraised of how things at Randalls are going along. We depart for Enscombe tomorrow.
Your most obliging
F. C. Weston Churchill

"Well at least it's a short letter, but he still cannot stop himself with his 'thousands of thanks.' In any case, he did not raise his sum to the ten thousands," said Mr. Knightley.

"It is surely not your style, my dear," said Emma. "But he has not gone forward with his plan to dismiss Miss Sharpe. For that, we must be thankful. It seems your visit with him was successful."

Emma tried to see Jane before they left, but she was given the message that Mrs. Churchill was not at home, and the next day, Frank and Jane left before any further meeting could take place.

"I don't think she has ever really forgiven me," said Emma.

"They had to leave early to make the trip to Enscombe in a day. Uncle Churchill was eager for their arrival and looking forward to the forthcoming birth of his first grandchild," said Mr. Knightley.

"How do you know that?" asked Emma.

"I happened to meet Jane in town at Ford's when she was purchasing some items for their residence at Enscombe," he replied. "We had a brief moment to talk. That's all."

Some old feelings of jealousy arose in Emma, but she put them aside as best she could. "She will never be my friend," she said. "And It is somewhat difficult to understand. She has forgiven and accepted Miss Sharpe, who had a real relationship with Frank. But me, who only played and flirted, and who never really loved him, nor him me, I cannot be forgiven, I see."

"Emma, my dear. You and Jane are now both mistresses of great estates and in possession of the men you love. You must take Jane as she is. She will come to see you as you are, in time. Let us be grateful that Mr. Weston and his infant will be well cared for and that Miss Sharpe and her child are not turned out. That, after all, was our object, was it not?"

"Of course," she said. "And the man I love is the best man in all the world!"

"You do know how to make good speeches, my dear Emma!" said Mr. Knightley.

A few months after leaving Highbury, and after a very difficult delivery, Jane gave birth to a son. The weeks following were filled with anxiety, given the so recent memory of Mrs. Weston's untimely death of childbed fever. But in spite of her frail condition, no such affliction visited Jane, and soon she was downstairs with her husband, father-in-law, and child, eating fairly well, and even receiving a few visitors. No more had been said about the arrangements at Randalls, but letters back and forth with Miss Bates kept them apprised of all the doings in Highbury, where Mr. Weston and Adelaide seemed to be doing well.

Putting all this behind her, Emma saw Dr. Perry and ascertained what she had suspected. She was pregnant and expecting their first child.

Fortunately, she soon began to feel better, for now, it was Mr. Woodhouse who was in need of care. His condition was nothing physical, but his nerves were on terrible edge. Having so wonderfully and easily accommodated himself to her marriage, he now was thrown back into a constant state of apprehension when he learned she was with child. He could not stop himself from recalling the fate of 'poor Miss Taylor' almost every day, and it took much patience and careful tending on the part of Emma and her husband to keep him in relatively good spirits. Cure there was none, but they set about employing various distractions.

"Perhaps we should try reading to him," suggested Emma. "But I fear he did not like Milton. And I have to agree, there are some very dark parts in that work. I did not like Satan at all, and Father did not either."

"No, dear Emma. Milton will not do. Perhaps some Shakespeare? Or something comical? I will search in the Donwell library to find something suitable," said Mr. Knightley.

"He prefers his newspaper to books, but there are always your collections," she offered. "Still, I suspect he has been through almost all of them several times."

Mr. Knightley tried to interest him in Abbey Mill Farm and its various expansions but in vain. Farming was not one of his interests, neither cows nor crop rotation. His passion was for possible catastrophes, mostly of a medical kind. Oddly enough, in spite of bundling himself up at every opportunity, his solicitude was always for others: for Miss Taylor, after she married Mr. Weston, for James the coachman and the danger of overtiring the horses, about Mr. Knightley catching a cold from being too much outdoors, about Frank Churchill having to cross a road in Highbury where there might be a puddle, about Jane Fairfax not changing her stockings after she had been to the post office in the rain, about Mrs. Bates' digestion, in fact, about the digestion of everybody who refused gruel, and primarily about the colds people could catch in draughts, especially when dancing in rooms with open windows. For all these things, Dr. Perry was the best remedy, and Mr. Knightley soon decided that a daily visit from Dr. Perry to Hartfield was just the thing to relieve his father-in-law from his multitude of anxieties.

Fortunately, Emma's first confinement, though long, ended with the successful delivery of a healthy boy. And the following weeks, anxiously monitored by Mr. Woodhouse, brought no further problems. Emma wrote of the situation in a note to her sister, 'Thank God, the baby has finally appeared. My labors are over, and my husband has been released from his own labors with Father.'

Spring had come to Highbury and the happiness of the Knightleys only increased after the birth of this firstborn son. Since Isabella had already named her first son Henry, after Mr. Woodhouse, Emma was free to name her son George, after her husband. Though she continued to use his title when addressing him, Mr. Knightley loved to hear his Christian name pronounced by Emma and his father-in-law with great regularity. Mr. Woodhouse worried and fussed over his new grandson even more than he had over Isabella and Emma. As soon as she was up and about, Emma made a visit to Mr. Weston at Randalls, and stayed to chat with Miss Sharpe, who brought the two little girls to visit with 'Aunt Emma.'

"Mrs. Knightley, I am so glad to see you looking so well," said Miss Sharpe. "You know how grateful I am to you and your husband for all you have done for us here at Randalls."

Mr. Weston nodded his agreement. "Yes, indeed. I do not know how we could have managed without your assistance, and of course, without Miss Sharpe herself. She is a marvel of good sense and organization, you know. She will be caring for the whole place in a week or so, while I go up to Enscombe to visit with Frank and Jane to see my new grandson. I am quite happily occupied with my family and friends these days."

Some evenings, Mr. Knightley, having not given up Milton with his wife, continued to read aloud to Emma, though her father often dozed off from time to time. But Milton was still not a favorite with Emma. Though pleased to see Satan get his just desserts, she was not sure she liked Milton's God. "I think Adam and Eve's ejection from Eden was too harsh a penalty for their transgressions. I don't like punishments. Sometimes I think God scolds too much."

"Like me, dear Emma?" asked Mr. Knightley.

"No. He's not at all like you, my dear. You always give me something good to think about after the scoldings. Like how Adam and Eve's new state of being is almost better than their first. I hope that was true," she said. "I think so, for though I have made so many mistakes, look how happily everything has turned out."

For Emma and Mr. Knightley, the perfect happiness of their union continued. One of Emma's favorite walks was on the path near the shrubbery where her husband had finally declared his love for her. Unprepared for his declaration, she had asked, "Can this be true?" and he answered with his customary forthright directness, 'You'll get nothing but the truth from me." Then, when he asked what she thought, she had been almost speechless. She hoped she had answered him more fully and completely as his wife, ever since she had first loved him when she was ten years old, no matter what he or anyone said to the contrary.

EPILOGUE

Given Jane's always somewhat fragile condition, she and Frank Churchill made no subsequent trips to Randalls. Frank resumed the practice of meeting his father in London fairly regularly, and on some of those occasions, Jane went with him. Sometimes, she took the carriage and visited Randalls alone. Some Highbury residents thought these traveling habits odd, though the Knightleys understood the reasons for them. While Jane lived only nine years after becoming the mistress of Enscombe, Frank remained a faithful and loving husband to the end. After his wife's passing, he began the practice of inviting his father for regular visits to Enscombe. He wanted his young son to know his grandfather. He avoided visits to Highbury, claiming pressing obstacles of various sorts. Miss Sharpe, however, continued to be a valued presence at Randalls. No further mention of her past connections disturbed Mr. Weston, who enjoyed her company and grew to love the two little girls as if they had both been his own.

Mr. Elton received the good news of a promotion to a larger parish in the vicinity of Enscombe. It was thought that Frank's uncle had something of a hand in recommending the position. Mrs. Elton informed the entire community of her husband's elevation and planned a festive celebration in his honor. As she told everyone who would listen, 'The Sucklings were sure to come, Selina so delighted and proud, even Mrs. Smallridge making the effort, the Barouche-Landau carriage to be at everyone's disposal.' Emma secretly hoped that Mr. Elton's departure might coincide with one of her confinements so that finding excuses to miss the event would be easy.

The Martins continued to be happy with their growing family, and with the extension of their farm. The addition to their house was almost complete, which they hoped would be ready in time for the arrival of their third child. There had been no need for any further explanations or apologies to Harriet, who was busy and totally occupied with her domestic duties and her eventual brood of six children.

After a few years, Mrs. Bates passed away at a great age, happy to have seen the marriage and elevation of her granddaughter as mistress of the great estate at Enscombe. After her mother's death, Miss Bates was invited to join the Churchills there, but declined, as she had been so long connected with Highbury society and her many friends there. She did accept Jane's offer of a better residence—'so kind, so generous, so thoughtful'—and moved away from the small rooms above the butcher shop with its dark, narrow stairway, to a pleasant cottage near the Weston residence at Randalls. She made frequent visits to Enscombe and continued to be a great talker, regularly regaling Emma and Mr. Knightley with detailed accounts of all Jane's happiness and many accomplishments. "At her piano every day, almost finished with her reading list of 100 books, and her needlework quite remarkable." In Highbury, Miss Bates was invited to Hartfield at least once a week for dinner and a backgammon game with Mr. Woodhouse— "Mrs. Knightley always so thoughtful, so kind, the dinners so elegant, the company so pleasant."

In the two years following Emma's marriage to Mr. Knightley, Mr. Woodhouse finally succumbed to a bad cold that went to his lungs. He was much mourned by his family, most especially by Emma. Mr. Knightley also mourned his father-in-law, of whom he had always been fond, and even more so, during his marriage when his wife told him, she believed her father had grown to love him as much as his daughters. He greatly enjoyed having a grandchild in the house. The presence of little George had somehow made his life complete, finally healing the old wound left by the passing of Mrs. Weston. Those like Mr. Elton, who expressed the opinion that Mr. Knightley would find his residence at Hartfield difficult— 'Rather he, than I'—or his wife— 'Shocking plan living together. It would never do'—were proven wrong. Indeed, for months after Mr. Woodhouse's death, Mr. Knightley told his wife he missed his father-in-law's hand on his arm when, each night, he walked up the stairs without him. On many a morning, he most especially directed that his eggs be cooked just as Mr. Woodhouse had always ordered them, telling his wife with a tender look that "Serle understands boiling an egg better than anybody."

After the proper mourning period, Emma and her husband removed to Donwell, and Emma, vowing to practice more often, brought from Hartfield her piano, her favorite Turner painting of Broadstairs Bay, and her copy of Milton's *Paradise Lost*. Mr. Knightley restored all his books and papers to his Donwell Library. Emma also insisted on bringing over what she always called 'Mr. Knightley's Chair' which, after her engagement, she never had reupholstered, as she had once threatened to do when he unexpectedly left for London to achieve indifference or at least relief from his love for her. She also brought the small sofa and the fireplace implements which reminded her of so many evenings preparing for visits with Mr. Knightley. Her father had just been kindling the fire with them when she and Mr. Knightley came to tell him of their engagement. There were further changes made at Donwell Abbey, as rooms were fitted up for another child, soon to follow.

Mr. John Knightley eventually received the main reward to which a hardworking lawyer could look forward, having been appointed to a judgeship. This was a position of great distinction (there were only about fifteen in all England at the time), so there was no longer any need for him to reside permanently in London. He and Isabella and their five children had been rather crowded in their Brunswick Square home, so they made Hartfield their principal residence, now Isabella's inheritance. Once again there was an almost daily close connection between the two principal houses of the neighborhood.

There were innumerable family dinners and get-togethers among the Highbury families, with Mr. Weston, young Adelaide, Miss Sharpe, her daughter Edith, and the George and John Knightley families. When little Adelaide Weston was about ten, and young Henry Knightley had reached the age of sixteen, they became special friends; Henry taking the role of older brother. There were times when watching them together, it seemed to Emma that they might be preparing to repeat the fate of their Uncle George and Aunt Emma, most especially when young Henry could be heard lecturing Adelaide about something or other. When she mentioned her observation to her husband, he gave her one of his old scolding looks and said, "Emma, you are mistaken. They are but children. Please, no more matchmaking!" It was then she would think to herself that she now had a whole new cast of characters over whom she would have, of course, 'only a little influence.'

Emma Redux

Happily Ever After

Part II

CHAPTER 1

His wife had just brought Mr. Knightley some disturbing news. She thought she had become aware of a growing attraction between their eldest son George and Miss Sharpe's girl Edith. She saw nothing amiss during family dinners. But—to use a phrase once employed by her dear husband—she detected certain 'secret looks' between them at dances or at some of the family picnics and outings that were always such enjoyable amusements, shared by their community of friends.

Of course, Emma always had a fertile imagination, Mr. Knightley thought. She was probably wrong. He hoped she was. Yet she brought him her tale, and now he must pay attention to it himself, though neither she nor her husband was very good at detecting romantic attachments. Here was a subject likely to ruin what had promised to be a lovely afternoon at Donwell Abbey.

The young folks were all occupied elsewhere—the boys out riding, the girls visiting some friends at Mrs. Goddard's School. He and Emma had been blissfully left to themselves. Now she brought him news that was indeed deeply troubling. He always regretted keeping Frank Churchill's secrets from Mr. Weston, the worst of which was that Frank had fathered Edith, the girl Miss Sharpe claimed was her sister's child. Mr. Knightley would never permit the marriage.

"Emma, my dear. Are you quite sure about your suspicions that

George may be attracted to Edith Sharpe?" he said, with a darkling look.

"One can't be sure about something like that. It's just an observation that has grown on me in recent months. George always seems to make himself available when Edith is present. He has loaned her books from your library. And I'm sure they have exchanged looks. Of course, I have been wrong so many times, and may be again."

Mr. Knightley was silent. "I seem fated never to be rid of Frank Churchill and his baneful influence in my life. I confess, I hoped never to see him again after he and Jane removed to Enscombe to live with his uncle. Poor Jane. She deserved better," he said. "And dying so soon."

"She loved him, my dear. And he loved her too, and was faithful to her."

"As far as we know. Perhaps he has fathered some other brood somewhere in Enscombe," he said bitterly.

"Please try to be fair. It is hardly the fault of Edith, that her father once strayed."

"Sometimes, when I look at her, I have imagined I see traces of Frank in her countenance," he said.

"Now that is unfair. The girl can't help how she looks. Besides, I think you're wrong. True, she has Frank's dark eyes, but she is so quiet and self-effacing. You can't find much of Frank in that kind of behavior," said Emma.

"Mr. Weston has treated her as if she were his own daughter. Imagine if he knew the truth!"

"I don't know," answered Emma. "He's such a pliable man, so accepting of everything, so easy. I sometimes wonder if it had been better to have told him the truth years ago."

"Now you say that. It wasn't your opinion when Frank and Jane came back from their honeymoon and he wanted to terminate Miss Sharpe's employment at Randalls."

"No, it wasn't. At that point, I thought it might have destroyed Mr. Weston to know the truth. I think you did too."

"It still might, if the whole story of her parentage were to come out now," he said with some bitterness.

She wasn't sure of that.

"So, instead of enjoying the day with you, I must go and find

George and try to talk with him."

"You aren't going to tell him," she said with alarm.

"Of course not. I will merely have a fatherly conversation with him on the subject of his future plans. I've been meaning to do that. His Oxford degree is finished, and he has not yet declared himself for any profession. Of course, he is the heir to Donwell, and there will be plenty for him to do in that way, as the years go on. But I'll try to move on to other subjects." He frowned. "You know I dislike subterfuge, Emma. Sometimes you don't like to hear me say that."

"That is certainly untrue. I have always listened to you, to your opinions and thoughts. We have never disagreed on anything of consequence. I have conceded your superiority of years many times. That is why I have brought these observations to you. If you still remember, I once told you, at a particularly difficult moment for me, that I will listen to anything you have to say. You didn't like it when I qualified with, "as your friend." Now, I repeat, adding only the important words, "as your wife." Then, as always, I will tell you exactly what I think. Isn't that how we have come so far together, and so successfully?"

He pulled her to him. "Yes, my dear Emma. But it seems we are about to enter a new phase of our marriage. Now, we must include in our thoughts and deliberations, these delightful, if troublesome, young people who are in our care and charge. I must try to find out what our George is thinking. He is, after all, just short of twenty-one."

"Your intelligent Robert Martin made his addresses to Harriet Smith when he was but twenty-four. And I have loved you since I was ten," answered Emma. "Just because you had to wait so long for me to grow up, doesn't mean that your sons will do the same. Indeed, I've noticed John's son, Henry, following in your footsteps. I told you how he's always lecturing little Adelaide Weston."

"Emma, let us not worry about the progeny of your sister and my brother."

"I'm not worrying—just making an observation."

"It has the sound of your old match-making self."

"Be assured I'm certainly not match-making for our son."

"With that assurance, I'll be off. Let us hope that this time, at least, you have been wrong in your observations."

CHAPTER 2

George Knightley was a well-made, good-looking young man. He loved to ride, and was a good handler of horses, exhibiting his gracefulness indoors as well, for he loved going to dances. He would never have said, as had his father in the old days, somewhat untruthfully, 'I do not like dancing, and am not good at it.' Though not exactly a ladies' man, he had an endearing smile, which he exhibited much more than did his father who, he sometimes observed, reserved his tender smiles almost exclusively for his wife. He had the good manners and intelligent conversation of his father, and the charm and impulsiveness of his mother. He had begun his life at Donwell Abbey as a well-beloved child of his parents, and, not losing either of them as he attained his young manhood, continued to have little to disturb him during his almost twenty-one years of life.

He was the presumptive heir of Donwell, and had, upon returning from Oxford, assisted his father with some of the duties attendant on the owner of that magnificent estate and properties. Upon taking up residence at Donwell, he renewed his acquaintance with his Knightley cousins and with the two young women residing at Randalls, Adelaide Weston and Edith Sharpe. He liked them both and enjoyed going out for rides with them and taking walks. At first, he had not himself realized that what was growing in him was a decided preference for Edith. She was much quieter than Adelaide, who was always bustling with projects and opinions on all sorts of things. Edith often held back and needed to be drawn out, which he found he was quite good at doing. He started by bringing her books from the large Donwell Library, sharing with her his own recent interest in subjects like geology and history, but most particularly his love of the great novelist of the age, Charles Dickens. Adelaide too listened to his talk about the great man and took home with her one of Donwell's collections of Dickens novels, *David Copperfield,* one which he and Edith greatly enjoyed. George read the storm scene to both young women, telling them that Dickens wrote it in Broadstairs. Edith had actually wept when Steerforth drowned. Adelaide was unmoved, and returned the novel in short order, with her pronouncement, "too many words," telling him she much preferred the romances of Maria Edgeworth.

But Edith loved to read and talk about Dickens with George. She noticed in Mr. Weston's papers that the great man was giving charitable public readings of his works in Birmingham, and especially *The Christmas Carol.* She wished he might have come to Highbury, she had said—but of course, that could hardly be expected, for they had no great halls or large audiences for the man who, she had read, called himself 'the Inimitable.'

"Indeed, he is that," said George. "My mother told me once, that Father had taken her to Broadstairs on their honeymoon in part because the great Dickens used to summer there." Edith widened her eyes in some astonishment.

"Yes," he said. "I was surprised to hear it too, for I never dreamed my father had either a literary or romantic side."

"I suppose," Edith said, "we never really know the secrets of our parents. As for me, since I never knew either of them, their secrets will never be divulged. You are so fortunate to have both your parents—and to be granted these glimpses into their lives. How I wish—but that's silly. I just will have to make up some stories about mine," she said, somewhat shyly. "My aunt never talks to me about either my mother or my father, even when I ask her to tell me about them. I suppose it's a painful subject to her, but it wouldn't be to me. Maybe that's why I like Dickens so much. So many of his orphans come successfully through all their trials."

Imagine, Edith was able to identify with these characters, he thought, just the way he did. George always found she had something interesting to say. Unlike most of the other girls he knew at Oxford, she was never boring. That's why he liked her so much. He enjoyed being with her and talking with her in ways he never did with his parents, though he loved them very much. But his father was a bit formidable. He respected him and even admired him greatly. But he was not a man given to small talk. George supposed he shared his thoughts with his mother, but that was always after hours and when they went upstairs to their rooms. He knew his parents loved him and the others, but it wasn't the kind of love he was sure his father expressed to his mother behind those closed doors. He could understand that. He couldn't talk about his feelings with them, the way he could with Edith. That was different.

His brother Charles was a very different sort than himself, loving to sport his Hessian boots and Beaver hats. A bit of a dandy, he thought. Like Adelaide, he had not found Dickens to his liking—or any prolonged reading of any sort. Of course, George would do anything for his brother—who had already gotten into some scrapes at school, from which his older brother had saved him—but he couldn't say he enjoyed his company and conversation as much as he did that of Edith Sharpe.

In the midst of these reflections, he saw his father riding toward him on old Bessie. He thought his father should have gotten himself a new mount, but he said he preferred Bessie. He wondered what brought him out on this day when he could well have stayed with his mother. He waved at George, and it looked like he had come expressly to see him. George drew his mount up and waited for the arrival of his father. He hoped it wasn't more talk about him getting some more educational training, perhaps in the law, a subject his father had broached on a few previous occasions after his return from Oxford. Well, whatever it was, he would listen respectfully, as he always did. He did like to see his father. Maybe this would be one of their good conversations.

CHAPTER 3

Mr. Knightley dismounted, tying Bessie to a nearby tree. He approached his son with a smile and they shook hands.

"Hello sir," said George brightly. "What brings you here, and without Mother?"

"You know your mother is not a fan of horseback riding. If she wanted to come along and see you, she'd no doubt have made me bring the coach," he said, somewhat humorously. "No, she's busy up at the house, and I decided to take a ride for myself, hoping to catch you somewhere in the vicinity." He still had not decided how he was to begin this difficult subject with his son and was awaiting an opportunity to make a start without being too obvious. He was never good at round-about actions and knew he would eventually have to make a blunt beginning.

"It's good to see you, sir. Would you like to take a gallop together? It's a fine day for such sport," offered George.

"No, my boy. I think I'd rather just find a cool spot to sit and talk for a bit," said Mr. Knightley.

George knew at once he was going to be in for something, but he could hardly imagine what. He and his father had already had one difficult conversation about getting a law degree, and he hoped he had put that idea to rest. After all, his father managed very well in fulfilling his many duties at Donwell, in estate management, farming, and as Justice of the Peace and official of the parish, all without such a degree. He thought in time, and with practice, he would do as well.

"Do you have something specific you want to talk about?" asked

George.

Mr. Knightley was not glad to recognize in his son his own directness in getting to the point. "Nothing very specific," he said, unconvincingly. "I was only wondering how you were enjoying it here at Donwell, after the intellectual stimulation of Oxford. No doubt you are missing the company of your accomplished fellow students and graduates."

George continued to wonder at the odd direction of the conversation. "Well, I always have Charles to talk with, and Henry, over at Hartfield, has been a good chum. I've even had a few interesting meetings with our new vicar, Reverend Rufus Brewer."

"Do you not miss female company? Did you make some lady friends at Oxford? Though I cannot recall your speaking of them to me or your mother."

He could not follow his father's thoughts at all. Did the governor think he had made some missteps with a young woman at Oxford? "As for that, sir, I had little time for such amusements. And now, if I want female company, there are always my sisters and cousins here." He stopped himself short. He began to suspect that Edith Sharpe was going to be the subject of their conversation. Better to get it out in the open. "And I have been enjoying the company of Adelaide Weston and Edith Sharpe. Indeed, I have invaded your library in attempts to introduce them to the works of the great Dickens." There, that should do it. If his father wanted more, he would have to go after it himself.

"Yes, I have enjoyed the novels of Dickens myself," said Mr. Knightley. "I've read some of them serially, of course, and have always ordered the three-volume set when it was ready. I've been interested in his work since the start of his career, beginning with *Boz* and *Pickwick*. Though I'm not sure the ladies would enjoy those as much as some of his later works."

"Indeed. I've been reading *David Copperfield* with them. We enjoyed the storm scene, and I told them that you and mother had honeymooned in Broadstairs, where he wrote large parts of that novel looking out at the sea. Have you read that one, sir?"

How on earth had he been diverted into a literary discussion? Now it would be difficult for him to get back to his point.

"Yes, I have. And I'm glad they enjoyed the book. You're welcome to whatever others you want to read yourself or lend to them. So, the ladies enjoy Dickens?"

"Oh yes, sir, greatly. Though I must say Adelaide is not as enthusiastic about the author as Edith." There it was. He had made a fatal slip towards the subject he suspected his father of wanting to introduce. He knew he would now seize his moment. Well, he would face it as best he could.

"Oh, Edith is another enthusiastic fan of the great man? Do you find her an adequate conversationalist on the subject? Of course, ladies cannot have the benefit of your educational background. But her mother, being a governess, must have given her some knowledge of the subject. Does she ever talk about her education at her mother's hands?" Mr. Knightley had at least made a beginning, even if, in his own judgment, it was a clumsy one.

"It's odd you mention that. Edith and I were just talking about parents and children the other day, and she mentioned how little, if anything, she knew of her parents. I think it makes her a little sad, watching Mr. Weston's fond fatherhood of Adelaide, and your and mother's care of us. It makes a difference, sir, doesn't it, to grow up with loving parents."

Mr. Knightley was now at the point to get closer to his subject. "You realize, George, do you not, that a girl like Edith, a delightful and pleasant friend though she may be, would not be a suitable wife for a young man of family and property, the heir to a great estate and fortune." There, he had said it.

"What are you implying, sir?" said George, coloring slightly and heating up. "I do not recall mentioning any marital intentions to you, I believe, or to mother. Do you suspect me of harboring secrets from you? I know how much you despise secrets and double-dealing. I remember your talk about the secret engagement between Frank Churchill and Jane Fairfax and how inappropriate it was. You can be sure I would never conceal such serious intentions from you or mother. Edith and I are only good friends." But as soon as he spoke the words, George knew he was not being totally truthful with his father. He had only lately realized how much he enjoyed being with Edith. He had not thought beyond that and now realized that perhaps he needed to do so.

Were Mr. Knightley privy to his son's thoughts, he would have realized how complete a failure his talk with George had been. Instead of turning his son away from any possible relationship with

Edith, he had quite unintentionally started his son thinking about his feelings toward the girl. He was dissatisfied with the conversation he and his son had shared. Though he was not ready to accuse his son of duplicity, he felt an undercurrent of strong feeling when George spoke of Edith.

"Indeed, sir," continued George. "You may be quite sure, and at rest, to know that when I have marital intentions, I will not hide them from you or from mother. I know that when you first began to realize your own feelings for mother, you had neither mother nor father with whom you could have talked. I do not know if you shared any of your feelings then with Uncle John. Somehow, I suspect you did not. I think men don't, as a rule. You probably kept your innermost feelings to yourself, living alone so many years at Donwell, and being your own master. But be of good cheer, sir. I promise you that when I am ready to declare myself to the woman I intend to take as my wife, you and mother will be the first to know." He smiled encouragingly at his father, opening wide those bright blue eyes which always reminded Mr. Knightley of Emma. He was disarmed and felt conquered by his son. He could bring back to his wife no assurances about the possible attraction and "secret looks" she had suspected. Well, if another try was to be made, he would tell her she must be the one to do it. He had done his best, and it had proven to be not good enough.

With shared handshakes and farewells, Mr. Knightley untied Bessie and rode her slowly back to Donwell. As they trotted along, he voiced his thoughts and fears to his mount. It was so much easier to talk to his old friend Bessie than almost anyone—except, of course, his dear Emma. She would be waiting for his report and he would have to give it.

CHAPTER 4

When Mr. Knightley returned to Donwell, he was informed by their servants that his wife had taken the carriage to visit the Martin farm. He went inside the library, to await her return.

He was glad to see that Emma had reestablished cordial relations with Harriet. In recent years, the Martins had been financially successful. In 1851, at the time of the Great Exhibition, Robert had been invited to display several of his inventions. There was a new interest in all kinds of machinery which had the wonderful power of shortening human labor, though some of the novelists, especially the great Dickens, had written negatively about these developments in his novel *Hard Times*.

Mr. Martin had been interested especially in agricultural matters. He had done well with his sheep, selling their wool at a premium in a market for the manufacture of woolens which was in the first stages of industrialization. His specialty, however, was in the area of agricultural machinery. He had been appalled to know that in some parts of England, farmers were still using the scythe!

A special section of the Great Exhibition was dedicated to agricultural machines and implements. Those competing for recognition in this area had been invited to demonstrate their wares on the property of a Mr. Philip Pusey, a member of Parliament. Among the most successful was a steam plough, which worked two ploughs at once, on the principle of the funicular railway and Mr. Martin's four-wheeled seed drill, calculated to decrease manual labor and increase output.

These practical exhibits shared space with more fanciful ones, like a Gothic bookcase from Austria (which much appealed to Mr. Knightley, on the family's one trip to the exhibit) and a sportsman's knife with 80 blades, the mother-of-pearl handles representing various subjects, like Windsor Castle and Osborne House, which was the boys' favorite. Emma found the most interesting section the one focusing on carriages—gigs, curricles, traps, broughams, landaus, barouches, buggies, coaches, and jaunting cars in a glorious medley of extravagance and elegance, gleaming with paint and leather and chintz. Emma always loved her carriage rides, though her husband still preferred to travel with his old saddle on the back of Bessie.

In this area of the new developments in agriculture, Robert Martin had made his mark. The attitudes of farmers toward mechanization were changing, and Robert Martin was at the forefront of the new procedures and inventions. He was prospering greatly from his many inventions. It was a good thing, for he was now the father of six children, and it had been necessary to expand their farmhouse a number of times. The two oldest Martins were boys—Robert and William—and the other were four girls. The boys were tall and, Knightley thought, promised to be as intelligent and hard-working as their father. The girls had inherited Harriet's soft blonde beauty. Robert's sisters had all married and moved away from Highbury.

Emma and Harriet had never referred to the old match-making endeavors. That was so long in the past now, Emma hoped they were long forgotten. The Knightleys had included the Martins in their dinner parties over the years, and the young Martins joined her children in picnics and other festivities.

Today, Emma went over to Abbey Mill Farm to extend several future invitations to some special events to be held at Donwell.

"You are very good to pay us a visit," said Harriet. "We are always so busy here, I rarely get out except for our visits to you and Mr. Knightley."

"We are going to have a celebration to welcome the new vicar," said Emma. "I hear he is an older man, a widower with a son and daughter." At last, the community of Highbury had been able to engage a permanent replacement for Mr. Elton, who abruptly left some years earlier, leaving the church hierarchy to scramble for replacements. For her, Mr. Elton was no loss. "The new vicar's name is the Reverend Rufus Brewer. He has not yet established himself at the vicarage, but is to be there soon."

Emma asked if Harriet would like to take a ride in the carriage, it being a lovely day, but her friend declined. And so, Mrs. Knightley rode back to Donwell alone, to find her husband in his usual spot, the library.

"So," she said. "How did your visit with George go?" Emma was still wearing her cloak. "Were you successful? Did you learn anything?"

He turned away from the book he had been reading. "Let us go into the drawing-room," he said. "It's more comfortable to talk there." He was assembling his thoughts. He had not been successful, nor had he learned anything that would dispel Emma's observations.

"I'm afraid, dear Emma, I did not do well at all. In fact, I may have actually made him think more deeply on the matter of his attraction to Edith Sharpe." He told her all, not sparing himself and what he thought to be the clumsiness of his approach to the subject. "Talking to George is not at all like talking to you. With him, I find myself always at a disadvantage, though the boy is always courteous and respectful. It's just that when I start, a wall seems to come up between us, and everything I say, at least today, comes out awkward and intrusive."

"Are you sure? Sometimes you don't acknowledge your own successes, my dear."

"No Emma. Today was not a success. I am turning the matter over to you now. But this I will say—when I blundered into mentioning Edith's unsuitability as a wife to a man with a large estate and a fortune, I could see he reddened, and thought I was speaking out of turn."

"Did you say that? Oh dear, yes, that was bad. You know, my dearest, I always rather liked your scolding of me. Deep down inside me, I really never wanted it to stop, but I think children are different. They don't like scolding. It doesn't light them up inside as it did me. For them, I suspect, scolding turns the lights off. I must think on this. I will try, in my way, to engage him. But we must let a few days go by, don't you think?"

"Indeed. I don't want to touch the matter again. But Emma. To you, I can say this: the girl is not right for him, and I will never permit an alliance between them." He spoke in a tone that betrayed an anger she knew would do no good.

"Of course. I understand. Let us talk no more about it today. There is still some light outside, and we can take a walk together. Let's go out to our favorite spot, the place you told me you loved me. And then, we'll go up and sit on the bench, it's one of my sacred spots, you know," she said, taking his face in her hands and moving toward him for a kiss. "It will make us both feel better."

"One always wants children, doesn't one," he asked. "We did. And for a long time, they were quite wonderful. And then, they started to move away from us, disagreeing with our plans, and suddenly, it isn't so wonderful anymore."

"Put it out of your mind for today." She pulled him up from the sofa, and went into the front hall still wearing her cloak. "The rest of the day is just for us," she said. "No intruders will be allowed."

She took his arm, and they went out into the garden which held those many memories for them both. So many loved ones had gone away now—her father, Mrs. Weston, Jane. Even Miss and Mrs. Bates had departed from Highbury. It was a good thing, she thought, although often difficult, that these young people had come to take their place. He was wrong, of course. It was still wonderful.

CHAPTER 5

For the time being, Emma's projected talk with her son would have to wait. There was much to be done to prepare the welcoming party for the new Vicar of Highbury, to be celebrated at Donwell Abbey. Ever since the Eltons left, Highbury had been treated to an assortment of temporary clergymen. Now, it seemed, there was to be a permanent appointment. She thought that giving a party to welcome him was a good idea. When she first proposed it, the party seemed also a wonderful way to share the house and grounds of the large property with the community.

In earlier years, she had not embarked on such community projects, as she was much preoccupied with her young, growing family. Imagine! Four children! Though she had not outdone Isabella with her five, she had entered with formidable swiftness into the realm of motherhood, which she had once declined to consider, claiming to have found sufficient satisfaction in her nieces and nephews. Indeed, she had not attended her sister in London for any of her five birthings—for how could she have left her father? But she was present with her dear Mrs. Weston, though the memory of that tragic conclusion to motherhood had made her fearful of her own entry to that unknown world. But she had borne her deliveries well, with her dear husband's assistance. He had, after all, been present for the birth of all of Isabella's five, and so could not in conscience absent himself from the first appearances of his own progeny. Indeed, his greatest task for the first had been delivering Mr. Woodhouse of his terrible fears that Emma might die like her old governess, either in or after childbirth! It cost Mr. Knightley many hours of backgammon, carriage rides, and examinations of his many collections with his father-in-law until their first son and heir was safely delivered and Emma out of danger from the dreaded threat of childbirth fever, a specter which haunted many bedsides of recent mothers in those days. But all had been well, and now the four were hale and healthy youngsters—George soon to attain his maturity in a few months, the two girls still young, Hetta, in her late teens, and her sister Caroline, close in age, the last his brother Charles.

Thus, occupied with the upcoming celebration, Emma had to delay her encounter with her son George to investigate his possible attraction for Edith Sharpe. Now there were Donwell's grounds to make ready, though that was her husband's charge. She had to arrange menus and make space in the house for the many guests sure to come to meet and greet the new vicar, the Reverend Rufus Brewer, and his son Saul and daughter Susan. She spent an afternoon writing out the invitation cards from her list:

Mr. Weston and Adelaide
Miss Sharpe and Edith
The Coles
Dr. Perry and family
The Martins, Robert and Harriet, and family
Mrs. Goddard and older girls

She debated about sending an invitation to Enscombe, to Frank and his son Weston. In the end, she decided not to do it. She was sure he would not make his first trip since he had left Highbury for such an event. Of course, he might make the journey just to see his father and display his young son Weston, who, like his father in the old days, had not yet been formally introduced to Highbury society. But she would not send an invitation. He would not come in any case.

When she had persuaded her husband to keep Frank's secrets, she had not, she conceded, anticipated how difficult it would be seeing the fruit of that deception emerge as a young woman ignorant of the burden of her parentage. She did not contemplate seeing Frank's son being introduced to the girl who was, did he know it, his half-sister. Oh dear, life was more complicated than she had dreamed. But Enscombe seemed as far away as the moon, Frank removed there as if transported on an air balloon, far above her small Highbury orbit.

Meanwhile, preparations went on apace. It was early spring, and the weather was turning warmer. She would order tents for the outside, reminding her of the celebration of her dear Mrs. Weston's wedding. Such a time of great happiness, followed by great sadness. Would her celebration be the same? She must stop herself from such imaginings. But when she was ordering the cake, her father's admonitions came back to her—'No, Emma. No cake. Cake is not good for children!' She smiled. Why was it so many things brought him back? Mr. Knightley's insistence on ordering boiled eggs, 'just the way that Serle makes them.'

Fortunately, her husband stood by her side, awakening her from these reveries.

"Emma? You seem to be somewhere else? What are you thinking of?" he asked, solicitously.

"Oh, I'm fine. I was just thinking of the party and the food orders."

"Surely that wouldn't put such a faraway look into your eyes," he said. "It's something else. You can never conceal anything from me for long, you know," he said, with his steady gray eyes upon her.

She debated with herself for a moment and decided to tell him the truth. "Well, I was thinking of the past. Of Father, of course. But also, I must admit I had thought of inviting Frank and his son to the celebration." She saw him frown. "But I decided against it."

"I should hope you did. What interest could Frank Churchill have in meeting the new Vicar of Highbury? And if he brought his son along, he would be together with his half-sister under our roof."

Emma was upset. "I told you I did not invite him," she said, tears starting at her eyes.

He immediately regretted his severity. "Let's talk of other things. Let us leave what is past in the past." But even as he spoke, he felt uneasy. He would speak no more of it to his wife. Mention of Frank Churchill always brought out his bad temper. He would try to banish the situation from his thoughts, though the matter of George and his possible attraction to Edith remained a trouble to him. As soon as this celebration was over, he must speak with Emma again.

CHAPTER 6

Within a few days, the invited guests began to receive their invitations. The Martins were delighted to accept. Mr. Knightley had always been more to Robert Martin than merely the landlord of his rented farm. Indeed, he felt there existed something almost like a friendship between them. Mrs. Knightley, of course, was another matter, though she had softened much over time, a change he attributed almost entirely to her husband's influence. Mr. Knightley had never treated him as anything other than an equal in all their dealings together.

But changes in the world also played a part, as Robert Martin passed from farmer to gentleman-farmer and now, given the financial successes of his agricultural inventions and innovations, almost to bona fide gentleman. He and Harriet were often invited to the dinner table of the Knightleys, and he felt increasingly at ease there—though Robert rarely conversed with Mrs. Knightley except on the most trivial of subjects. He much preferred his after-dinner visits to Mr. Knightley's library, where they discussed the newest political and agricultural matters. He also knew that it was Mr. Knightley who had contrived to send him on a mission to deliver some papers to John Knightley, precisely because Harriet was staying there. It had been a conspiracy of the Knightley brothers that, in the end, helped him to find the opportunity to once again make an offer of marriage to the young woman he had loved so long. Indeed, the Martins would be happy to attend the celebration at Donwell in honor of the new Vicar of Highbury.

The Coles and the Perrys also sent immediate acceptance of the invitation. Gone were the days when Emma hesitated to accept an invitation to the Coles because their financial prosperity had come from their being 'in trade.' This kind of progress was now increasingly acceptable, and upward mobility was evident everywhere.

At Randalls, however, there was considerable discussion about the invitation. Mr. Weston himself, of course, was ready to send his immediate acceptance together with that of the residents at Randalls. He was eagerly looking forward to the event, for he had received a note from his son Frank that he was coming with Weston and the Eltons to the celebration. The Eltons knew the Reverend Brewer from his Enscombe days. When he shared this information with Miss Sharpe, he was surprised that she declined the invitation for herself and her niece, expressing a wish to stay at home. He could not fathom it. After all, she had visited the Knightley residence many times, since she first came as governess to Adelaide. What could possess her to refuse this opportunity to join with the community to meet the new vicar? But when he attempted to raise the subject with her, she simply said she would not attend. When he offered, in any case, to take Edith with him, she was similarly adamant that Edith would stay behind at Randalls with her. When Mr. Weston pressed her for a reason, she gave none, only repeated that she would not be persuaded to attend. He knew her well enough to recognize that she would not change her mind. She was mostly a delightful companion, but she had not the sweet submissiveness of his dear Anne. Women were different, nowadays, he thought. He noticed it in his own daughter. She too had about her a certain stubbornness, something quite unfeminine, he thought. He could not understand Miss Sharpe's behavior. He wondered if he should talk to Mr. Knightley about it. He knew she liked Mr. Knightley and respected him greatly.

What he could not have known, was that Anna Sharpe was already acquainted with the Reverend Rufus Brewer, whose last clerical appointment had been in Yorkshire, in the area of Enscombe. It was he to whom she had gone for assistance when she first realized she was to bear Frank's child and must leave her position at Enscombe. It was he who persuaded Frank's uncle to help in writing a reference for a position at Weymouth and making her a financial settlement. It was he who helped her survive those terrible early days. Now, she had built a new life for herself and did not want to meet him at the Donwell celebration. It would never do for them to meet unprepared, perhaps on the streets of Highbury, by chance, even worse, at the Knightleys' dinner table! She had put her old life behind her, and conquered Frank's determination to end her employment at Randalls. Now the past had come back to trouble her again. She never wanted to bother the good vicar again. Her secrets mustn't be revealed. Now, however, she would have to find a way of explaining to Edith why she could not go to the celebration. That was harder, she thought, as Adelaide would certainly attend with her father. But if Edith went, surely the Reverend Brewer would not recognize her. But the name, if they were introduced. Perhaps she could visit the vicar before the party. Oh, what a terrible dilemma she was in.

At this very moment, Mrs. Goddard was in the midst of accepting her invitation to the event and deciding which of the older girls to bring with her when she was told she had visitors. Going to the door, she was surprised to see Mr. and Mrs. Elton, greeting her most effusively.

"I am so glad to see you again, Mrs. Goddard," said Mr. Elton. "It has been so long since we have visited Highbury, I wondered if you would no longer recognize us."

There was no danger in that, thought Mrs. Goddard. Mrs. Elton was still her fashionable self, older of course, but outfitted in a very youthful manner, her hair high-dressed, a hat trimmed with a variety of feathers, ribbons, and flowers, a scarf-like cape drawn about her shoulders. Mr. Elton was, as usual, dressed in black, though his Hessian boots had a brown top with tassels, and his cravat was of silk brocade.

"Of course, I do. Won't you please come in," she said, recovering from her initial surprise at seeing them.

"We have come for the celebration in honor of the Reverend Brewer," said Mrs. Elton. "We knew him in Enscombe, and he was kind enough to tell us of this party in his honor. We knew we would not need an invitation. Mr. Churchill and his son have also come, so we decided to make quite an expedition of it," she said, in her usual flourishing manner. "Mr. Churchill has engaged rooms for us at the Crown, as we knew there would be no room for us, either at the vicarage or Randalls. Oh, what a pleasure it will be to see everyone again, after all these years. We understand you did not, after all, go ahead with the infant school."

"No, I did not, Mrs. Elton. It would have been entirely too much for me. The school has grown so large, and I not getting any younger," she said, with some regret.

"Whatever happened to the young woman who had come here to propose it to you?" asked Mrs. Elton.

"That was quite fortuitous," said Mrs. Goddard. "Since Mr. Weston at that time was so much in need of assistance with his own infant daughter, Miss Sharpe was engaged at Randalls as a governess. Indeed, it has turned out so very well, that she is still there. Young Miss Weston is eighteen now, and Miss Sharpe's girl is a year older. They all reside at Randalls, of course."

Mrs. Elton and her husband exchanged knowing looks. Finally, Mr. Elton spoke. "I am glad they have found a home. As I recall, Miss Sharpe's girl was the natural daughter of her sister. Does she enter into all Highbury's doings, as does Mr. Weston's girl?"

"Indeed yes," said Mrs. Goddard. "Mr. Weston treats the girl as if she were Adelaide's sister. But you may recall, he always was a generous-hearted man, very social and outgoing. Young Edith could not have found a better foster-father, for that is almost what he has been to her."

"Is that so?" said Mrs. Elton. "It will be our pleasure to meet them all again. I understand the Knightleys have been removed to Donwell for several years now, and have quite a large family of young people. I must admit, I am surprised that Knightley managed to endure his years at Hartfield. They must have been a great trial to him."

"I believe not at all," said Mrs. Goddard. "Whenever I was invited to dine there, I found him even more solicitous than his wife about Mr. Woodhouse. I think they became great friends. It is too bad Mr. Woodhouse caught that dreadful cold, which went straight to his lungs. Both the Knightleys mourned him greatly."

Mrs. Elton gave an ironic glance at her husband. "I wonder," she said. "But I'm sure you know better, as we left Highbury so soon after Miss Woodhouse married Knightley. We always were much closer to him, than to his wife. He and my cara sposo were great friends," she concluded.

Mrs. Goddard was not sure, but she nodded agreeably. "Mr. Knightley is everyone's friend here in Highbury," she said. "He is always the first to help if anyone is in need. Quite the gentleman, I always say."

"Well, it has been good to see you, Mrs. Goddard. We must be on our way to the Crown. Mr. Churchill will be waiting for us. We bid you good day. Until the party!" With bows and handshakes, the Eltons were away, leaving Mrs. Goddard to reflect on how little they had changed over the years. She couldn't say she liked them, and still remembered Mr. Elton's unkind snub of poor Harriet Smith at the Crown Inn's dance party. Then, of course, Mr. Knightley had stepped in, inviting the girl to the floor with him. Yes, he was ever the first to help. That is what he always did. She had been very happy to see him dance with Miss Smith. But after supper, when he led Miss Woodhouse out to dance, a veritable glow came over him. Perhaps she had imagined it, but they both seemed enveloped in a light that outshone all the other dancers on the floor. They still do bring that light with them, whenever I see them together, she thought. How happily that all turned out! And Harriet has found a good life as Mrs. Robert Martin, as well. Well satisfied with her thoughts, Mrs. Goddard went back into the school. She could only hope that her pupils and boarders could find a life as pleasant and fruitful as that found by Emma and her friend Harriet Smith.

CHAPTER 7

There had been no more talk between Mr. Weston and Miss Sharpe about the celebration at Donwell. But when Adelaide came to sit beside him after dinner the next night, he knew the subject was not over. And he was not wrong. His daughter demanded to know why Edith was not coming, and Miss Sharpe as well.

"Father," she began. "We always go everywhere together. And it would be such a treat to see everyone at Donwell. It isn't every day Mrs. Knightley opens up for visitors. Edith said her mother told her they wouldn't be going. Were they not invited? That's not like the Knightleys, I think. There must be some reason behind such a snub. I don't like it," she said, with spirit. "If Edith isn't going, I won't go either." Had she been standing, she would have stamped her foot, a practice with which her father was well acquainted.

"Believe me, my dear, I have no idea. But I don't think you need to blame the Knightleys. It's our dear Miss Sharpe who made the decision. When she proclaimed it, of course, I couldn't argue with her. You know I never do contradict her."

"All right, then. I will go and ask her myself," she said, now free to stamp that foot, arising to go upstairs to the rooms of her governess.

"I think you had better beware, Addy. Be careful of yourself. You know she can cut up pretty hard," he said, somewhat sheepishly. "When she says no, she usually means it."

"That's all right, Father. I'm not afraid of her. She can discipline me when I don't do my reading, or practice the piano. But I'm not going to be muzzled when I have a legitimate question to ask. I'll be back," she said, on her way upstairs.

Mr. Weston decided it was time for a walk. He did not want to be present for what promised to be fireworks. He donned his coat and headed for Donwell. He would talk to Mr. Knightley about it. At least his old friend would not stamp his foot!

When he arrived and was welcomed inside, he headed for the drawing-room to await Mr. Knightley's appearance. But it was Emma who came in to greet him.

"Mr. Weston! How good to see you! You've had a fine walk, I hope? It is a lovely day for an outing," she said, realizing that her friend was not coming to see her. "You want Mr. Knightley, I see. Unfortunately, he has just left for town to attend to some magistrate's business. I fear he won't be back soon. Let me get you something to drink and we'll sit and visit for a bit. Surely, you don't want to walk back right away." She bustled about, calling one of the servants to bring tea. "Or perhaps you'd like something cold?"

"Anything is fine with me," he said. "I did hope to find your husband at home, but perhaps you can help me as well." Mr. Weston was very fond of Emma and her matchmaking attempts in the old days.

"It's about your party, my dear Emma. Adelaide and I are so looking forward to it. It's not every day such a festival takes place in Highbury. But Miss Sharpe and Edith have declined to attend. And you know Adelaide. She wants to know why and has gone to see Miss Sharpe about it. She can be quite a spitfire, you know. Hence, I debarked for Donwell. I wonder if you know why Miss Sharpe would decline such a lovely invitation?"

She didn't know. She and her husband had faithfully kept the old secret of Miss Sharpe's previous relationship with Frank and Edith's parentage, she was sure of that. Jane had also known, but she was gone now. Then, with Mr. Weston's next remark, Emma knew the reason.

"Something else, dear Emma. Frank has written to tell me and let you know he and young Weston are coming. The Eltons convinced him, as they knew about it from the Reverend Brewer. They will be attending too. It will be a great reunion!"

Emma was stunned. Frank was coming to the party—to Donwell. He had had sense enough to stay away for years, most circumspect about visits to Randalls, only fetching his father and Adelaide away for visits to Enscombe. Of that, she was sure. Why would he come now?

Indeed, thought Emma, trying to divert the conversation. "Perhaps Miss Sharpe doesn't like such large gatherings. You know, she's a very private person. She doesn't go out very often. Just our small family dinners, and such," offered Emma.

"That's all right for her, my dear. But what about Edith? She so enjoys being with the young Knightleys, I have observed," said Mr. Weston."

Indeed, thought Emma. She had observed that too. Now, she felt herself at a loss. No doubt it wouldn't be long before young George would appear, asking the same questions. She would not be able to handle him as easily as she had Mr. Weston. She needed to talk to her husband about this. And soon.

CHAPTER 8

Having received no enlightenment from a stern-faced Miss Sharpe, Adelaide returned downstairs, only to find her father had fled, gone out for a walk. To escape from more questions, she thought. Well, it wouldn't do. She called upstairs to tell Miss Sharpe she was going out to look for her father.

But she was not looking for him. Instead, having donned a shawl, she was headed for Hartfield to see Henry Knightley. He might know something. If he did, he would tell her, she was sure. But she must make up an excuse. It wouldn't do for a young lady to call upon a gentleman, she knew—ask to see Henry? Aunt Isabella would be scandalized, she knew. So, she would say her father had sent her because he needed help with something at Randalls. She didn't know exactly what, but it was Henry he wanted.

And so, she arrived with her story, but since Aunt Isabella was out, it was easy. The servants located Henry and he headed out with her for Randalls.

"What does Mr. Weston need, Addy?" he asked, following her on the familiar path through the shrubbery and garden and out onto the open road.

"He doesn't want you," she said. "I do."

He stopped, looking at her somewhat reprovingly. "Why did you say that," he asked.

"Don't start lecturing me, please. I knew I'd be taken to task coming to ask for you on my own. Had I known Aunt Isabella was out, I wouldn't have bothered."

"Addy. I don't like it when you tell tales," he said.

"It's not a tale. It was only a diversion so I could get you out and away with me. It's not considered ladylike to be direct, I think," she said.

He said no more. There was a part of him that very much liked her spirit. She wasn't calm and docile, like his mother. But he also didn't like her making up stories. In that, she reminded him of his Aunt Emma. Still, part of him liked that too. "Well, all right then, what is it you want?" he asked, overcome by curiosity and deciding for the moment to suppress his lecturing self.

"My father tells me that Miss Sharpe has refused the invitation to the Donwell party for the vicar, and Edith won't be coming either. What can be the cause? He says the Knightleys invited them, so it isn't their fault. No one will tell me. I think your mother might get the truth from Aunt Emma. I want you to ask her to find out." She looked at him with appeal in her eyes.

He liked her large, luminous eyes, especially when she was smiling at him. Often, when they quarreled about something, they sparkled with fire. At those moments, he liked them even more. "What makes you think my mother will do that on my say so? I'd have to give a reason for asking her."

"Make something up," she said. "Say I told you Mr. Weston was upset about it. Or Edith was upset."

"Didn't I just now say that I don't like it when you tell tales. And now you want me to tell some."

"It's not your tale, it's mine. You will only be relating what I told you."

"Addy, it's the same thing. You're the one who wants to know. It's got nothing to do with Mr. Weston."

"But it is true that he's upset. Only he won't dare ask Miss Sharpe. What's the difference if, through me, he's asking your mother to find out. I am telling you the truth."

"You certainly know how to twist things, Addy."

She looked at him again, her eyes wide and expectant. He felt himself disarmed. "All right, I'll do it. But I don't like it," he said.

"You are a dear," she said, holding out her hand to him. He would liked to have kissed it, but pressed it hard instead.

"You can kiss it later if you wish," she said, smiling and pulling her hand away. "When you have found out what I want to know."

Those eyes again, this time twinkling.

"Your father has spoiled you badly," he said.

"That is certainly true. But you don't spoil me, do you? When you come back and tell me everything, you can scold me, if you wish. I give you permission in advance," she said, drawing her hand back. "I must go home now. Be sure to work on this without delay. It's just two days before the party." She turned and fairly ran down the path back to Randalls.

She certainly is a pretty girl, he thought, if in need of some discipline. He wished he would be the one to give her some, though he hardly knew what he meant by that himself. He always was the one to scold her in the old days, when she was a child. But she wasn't anymore.

Recovering himself from these thoughts, he went in to see his mother, recently returned from town. Best get this out of the way at once, he thought.

"Have you had a good shop, mother?" he asked, making his beginning.

"Yes, I did, dear. And what have you been up to this afternoon?" Isabella asked. "You're usually out and about at this time of day. Is your father back from London?"

"I don't think so," he said. "Actually, Adelaide Weston came over to see you just now. It's too bad you missed her," he said. That wasn't exactly true, he thought, but it was a beginning.

"Really? What did she want with me? Was Edith with her?"

"No. She came by herself."

"That's unusual. Those two are usually inseparable. I'm surprised Miss Sharpe let her come alone. Young ladies don't usually walk the paths alone, at least they didn't when I was a girl. Years ago, Harriet Smith—Mrs. Martin now—was attacked by gypsies very near where Adelaide was walking."

"Oh, Adelaide often goes walking alone," he said. "She says there's nothing wrong with that," he said, consoling himself that thus far he had told the truth. Henry idolized his Uncle George, who, he was sure, never told anything other than the truth. How was he to get through this with at least a vestige of the truth? "Addy says that Mr. Weston is upset that Miss Sharpe and Edith will not be coming to Aunt Emma's big party for the vicar."

"Quite probable," his mother said. "I wonder why not. Why

doesn't he ask her?"

"Well yes, mother," he said, sensing his opening. "He probably did and was not given an answer. Maybe you could ask Aunt Emma if she knows anything. I think Mr. Weston worries that something is wrong. Do you think you could find out if there is?" He was staying just this side of the truth.

"What makes you think Aunt Emma would know?" she asked. "Is that why Adelaide came?"

"You know how fond Addy is of Edith, and probably will miss her company. If anyone knows about such things, it would be Aunt Emma." There, he had evaded her question and waited for her reply.

"I don't know that it is my business," she said. "But when I see her, I will ask. With all of Highbury coming, it would be a little odd of them to stay away."

"If anything's to be done about it," he said, "you had better talk to her quickly. The party is only two days away."

She gave him a long look. "I don't know why you are so interested. What else did Adelaide have to say?"

"That was all, mother. It was only a short visit," he said. "Maybe you could go over to Donwell today and offer to help Aunt Emma with preparations. Then you could ask her about it."

"Henry. If it were Adelaide not going, I could understand better your concern. I don't think you've ever given much thought to Edith Sharpe."

"No, I haven't, mother. It's just that Addy was saying that Mr. Weston was concerned." What was it about parents, anyway? They always seemed to see through one, just when they shouldn't. It was so hard to continue with this conversation without getting himself further entangled. "Would you like me to walk over to Donwell with you? I'm sure I could also be of some help over there."

Isabella gave him a quizzical look. "All right, my dear. I can see this visit is somehow important to you, though I can't think why. Since your father is not yet back from London, I can spare an hour or so. And I do always enjoy a walk with you."

Henry helped his mother get her coat back on, and they set out for Donwell. Though his mother suspected him of something, he could at least tell his conscience that he had not told her an out-and-out lie. And maybe she could get an answer. Then he would remind Adelaide that she owed him her hand for that kiss.

CHAPTER 9

Isabella and her son set out for Donwell. It was a sunny afternoon, perfect for a walk. Henry was still uncomfortable about the deception he had performed upon his mother. He was even more uncomfortable about the feelings that Adelaide Weston was beginning to stir in him. He was a serious young man, just turned thirty, and in the midst of deciding upon a career for himself. His mother once told him, in the days before Aunt Emma and Uncle George had married, that he had always been referred to as the probable heir of the Donwell property. Thus it was, he had taken a degree in law, and was now expected to follow in his father's footsteps. He should be thinking about his professional future, he told himself, and not about kissing Adelaide Weston's hand. And yet, some thoughts were hard to entirely dispel.

He liked Addy and enjoyed being with her. Of her feelings toward him, he was not certain. Aunt Emma told him once that he and Adelaide reminded her of her relationship with her husband.

"When she was a little girl, you were like an older brother to her, telling her what to do a bit too much, we thought. Your Uncle George also had a tendency to scold and lecture. But," she added, "we finally found our way past that and discovered other feelings."

He wondered if he was making a similar discovery. About Adelaide's feelings, he was not so sure. But there were certainly similarities between her and Aunt Emma, not the least of which was great devotion to their fathers. He was eight when his grandfather Woodhouse passed away and remembered him as a stuffy old gentleman who was fanatical about food and health. He could still remember a dinner party when for the first time he had been permitted to join his elders at the table. As nearly as he could recall, they spent the whole time arguing about the seaside, whether or not it was good for you, what was the best place to visit, and so on. His father had nearly lost his temper, and Uncle George saved the day by changing the subject. It had been then, at that early age, he decided he would grow up to be a man like Uncle George. Always calm, always courteous, and always fun to be with. He loved it when his uncle came to London, and would take him and his brother out to search for frogs in the park ponds, or rough-housed with him, tossing him over his shoulder, and carrying him out of the room for some more adventures.

"What are you thinking about, Henry," asked his mother. "You look like you're in a trance. Here we are at Donwell."

"You know, mother, I think you will do better to talk with Aunt Emma alone. I'll go over to the stables and see if I can get a quick ride on George's mount. Or maybe he's there. I'll come back for you in about an hour." He did not want to play any further part in this visit.

"But you are the one who got the message from Adelaide," she said protesting. He was already striding away from her. Oh well, she thought, I'm here and I might as well go in and see what I can find out.

Emma welcomed her warmly and brought her into the sitting room, which had now many more feminine touches than in the days when her husband lived a more masculine life here, alone.

"How are things going on for the party," Isabella asked. "Is there anything I can help with? I'd be glad to. You know I love parties."

"No, all is proceeding in good order. All the acceptances have come in. But Isabella, I admit I was surprised to hear from Mr. Weston that Frank Churchill, his son, and the Eltons are coming, even though I did not invite them. It seems they were friendly with the Reverend Brewer up in Enscombe."

"It's odd, isn't it. After Frank and Jane left for Enscombe, he spent little or no time here in Highbury. It will be almost twenty years since I have laid eyes on him," said Isabella.

"The same for me. You know, Isabella, when they left, after returning from their honeymoon, we were not on very good terms.

You were fortunately not privy to our outrageous flirting at the Box Hill picnic. It was why Mr. Knightley went to stay with you in London. Oh, I really don't want to talk about it. But I was very ashamed of my conduct. It was a lucky thing that old Aunt Churchill died, and Frank and Jane could reveal their engagement."

"I can understand you might not be looking forward to seeing him. But to change the subject, Mr. Weston is upset that Miss Sharpe and Edith will not be coming to your party. Could that have anything to do with the return of Frank Churchill and the Eltons?"

Emma paused. Isabella was not usually very penetrating. It had been said that Emma could do Math problems at ten, that her sister could not at seventeen. And yet, Isabella had now come alarmingly close to the truth. She could not enlighten her about the situation.

"I don't really know, Isabella. Perhaps Miss Sharpe doesn't like large gatherings," offered Emma.

"But Edith is a very sociable girl. Why hold her back from attending," pursued Isabella.

"I do not wish to speculate."

"Emma. For some reason, Henry seems quite keen to find out the reason. It was his suggestion that I come over and ask if you knew anything. I was surprised myself that he would concern himself with something that could be of no interest to him. Perhaps I should send him back to Mr. Weston to see what he knows."

"Please do not disturb Mr. Weston with questions of this kind. There may be no further reason other than what I said originally— Miss Sharpe doesn't like big parties." Emma was growing uncomfortable. "I wish you would tell Henry to drop the subject. It's not important."

Isabella could see, however, that it was, at least to Emma. What had she stumbled on, she wondered. Well, it was none of her business.

There was a knock at the door, and Henry was back, ready to escort his mother back to Hartfield. Nothing more was said about the subject until they left, and Isabella relayed her conversation with her sister.

"So, you see, I didn't get much information. But it made your aunt uncomfortable," she said. "I think you had better drop it. It isn't really that important, you know. Not as if Miss Sharpe and Edith's absence will even be missed by most."

But Henry was not satisfied. He now was determined to ask his Uncle George. He would surely get help and perhaps even the truth from him if he knew it. He should have gone to him first. If there were any hidden reasons behind the action of Miss Sharpe, he was confident his uncle would either know them or help find them out.

CHAPTER 10

In a rational sense, Henry agreed with his mother. This was none of his business. Still—there was always Adelaide's specific request of him. He was headed back to Hartfield, his mission not accomplished. He thought of the legal work that lay in his future now. What if Addy had been a client who came with a request—weren't the requests of clients always his business? He should look upon this situation, trivial though it seemed to his mother, and even himself, if he were to be honest, as the business of a client. He had already learned nothing by relying on either of the two women he had asked. And his mother had been distinctly told not to bother Mr. Weston. Of course, his Uncle George was his last resort.

He had always had a good, one might almost say, special relationship with him. During the years of his childhood, visits from his Uncle George to Brunswick Square had always been great times for him. Afterwards, he had been away at college and law study at Lincoln's Inn for over ten years. He had hardly seen his uncle in those days, except at holidays, when there was no chance to be alone with him. And though he loved his own father dearly, John Knightley had become even more short-tempered as he aged and took on the heavy responsibilities of his judgeship. Maybe that's why Henry always felt 'on trial' during his various conversations with his father. They had recently had a number of difficult encounters, and Henry knew his father would have no patience with a matter as trivial as this one. He was at present only concerned with Henry's annoyingly slow approach to finding a legal apprenticeship, a necessary start for a career in the law.

When he went over to the stables at Donwell, he noticed that Bessie was not there. Since Mr. Knightley never rode her very far these days, he conjectured that he was on one of his trips to Abbey Mill Farm. After depositing his mother at Hartfield, he hurried back to Donwell. His uncle would soon be back, he thought.

He did not have to wait long before he saw him trotting along on Bessie.

"Henry," he called. "How good to see you! Are you looking to find George?"

"Actually, sir, it was you I was hoping to find."

Mr. Knightley dismounted. One of the stable boys took Bessie's reins. "Give her some water, and rub her down, if you please. I think I've rather tired the old girl out today," he said, with a smile and his usual pat of the mare. "Let's go down to the house, my boy. It's more comfortable there. Though I think your Aunt is in the midst of all the preparations for the big celebration." He began removing his riding gloves.

"Actually, sir, I've already paid a visit to Donwell today and would rather take a brief walk outside with you, if you were not too tired by your ride."

Mr. Knightley looked more closely at his nephew. So, this was to be one of those outdoor walks Emma sometimes took him on, for the discussion of difficult things. He hoped he was wrong.

"Certainly. There's a path on the way to Abbey Mill where a stone wall will give us a place to sit and talk." In a flash, the place and its old associations came back. It was where, so many years back, Anna Sharpe unburdened herself of her sad story. Well, that had all come to rights, he thought. Perhaps whatever is bothering his nephew can also be resolved there. Henry had always been his favorite—though he would have denied it if asked, for his rational self did not encourage favorites. Yet he sometimes wondered how Henry would have functioned as master of Donwell Abbey, had Emma not come between him and the inheritance many thought he would one day receive. Foolish thoughts, he reproved himself. Why is it that the mere mention of his dear wife's name so often softened him and brought him away from that rational self he so prided himself on.

They walked on, talking of the day and the weather and the

endurance of Bessie until they reached the wall.

"Here we are," said Mr. Knightley. "We can sit here undisturbed." Always direct, he began at once. "Are you in any trouble or distress, Henry? How can I help?" He directed his steady gray eyes on his nephew's face.

"No, nothing like that at all, sir. Though I admit my father is becoming a bit restive about my delay in finding a firm to take me on as an apprentice."

"I fear I cannot help you there. I'm not a London man, as you must know. My associations are all here in the country. Your own father would be of much better assistance in legal matters."

Henry shook his head. "It's not a legal matter. I'm afraid you'll think it a bit silly, sir. I mean, for me to concern myself with acceptances to your upcoming celebration for the new vicar. But I've been asked by someone to find out why Miss Sharpe and Edith have declined to attend. And despite having asked my mother to ask Aunt Emma, I've gotten nowhere." He stopped, as he watched Mr. Knightley begin to frown.

"Henry. May I know who is the person who asked you to embark on this investigation?" He wondered. Could Frank Churchill be the person? He learned only this morning from his wife that Frank, his son, and the Eltons, were to attend the celebration for the vicar. He knew at once, of course, why Miss Sharpe might not be inclined to see Frank, and why she wanted her daughter kept away from him.

He looked closely at his nephew. "I'm afraid you must tell me who it was asked you before I can begin to consider the matter." Mr. Knightley was looking stern, and Henry began to think his idea of asking his uncle to help had not been a good one.

Henry considered. He had come to the family truth-teller, and ought not to be surprised at being asked for the whole story. He would have to identify Adelaide. Though why it could be important to Mr. Knightley, he could not fathom.

"Sir, it was Adelaide Weston who came to me, quite upset and threatening not to attend herself. She asked me to find out Miss Sharpe's reasons, and I have failed. So, I came to you, in hopes you could tell me something to bring back to her."

Mr. Knightley relaxed a bit from his frowns. He even had the hint of a smile in his eyes. "And you must do whatever Miss Adelaide Weston asks of you?"

"Of course not, sir. Especially when I now see how much trouble her request is causing. I wish I had told her it was none of her business. But she's a very persistent young woman, very spirited, and not one to take no for an answer easily."

"I can imagine, Henry." He smiled, more in his old way. "I am glad you've come to me with your questions. Quite right. I will undertake to look into it. But it's still two days until the celebration. I will need a day on my own to investigate. You can tell Miss Adelaide she will have to wait for an answer and must keep any further questions to herself until then. She must especially not bother her father. Can you manage this much for me?"

Henry felt relief. "Of course, sir. I'll go see her now. I am so sorry to have troubled you."

"No trouble at all. Come to see me at this spot, day after next, in the morning. I will try to have some answer for you. No need to mention my involvement to Miss Adelaide. Just tell her that getting an answer requires that she keep still for another day. And now, I must get back to Donwell," he said, rising.

They walked back quickly, silent again. Henry felt, if anything, more puzzled than ever. He would, of course, follow his uncle's directions.

CHAPTER 11

Mr. Knightley walked slowly back to Donwell. What Henry had brought him was a dilemma indeed. It was clear why Miss Sharpe wished to stay at home with Edith during the festivities for the vicar. As he approached Donwell, he resolved to talk frankly with his wife. Miss Sharpe surely had no further interest in Frank Churchill. Yet absenting herself and her daughter would raise questions. He wondered. Was it time to end Mr. Weston's ignorance of these secrets?

What would Mr. Weston do if he were told now? Given Anna's past relationship with his son, would he regret having employed Anna in his household? Frank feared Mr. Weston might have married her, but that had not happened. Such a marriage would be unthinkable.

He went in and called to his wife. "Emma. Where are you, my dear? I need to talk with you."

She answered, "Here I am," her bright face shining at him as it always did. Then, seeing his expression, she knew there was trouble somewhere ahead. This morning they had already regretted the news of Frank Churchill's impending visit. Later, she had endured the questioning of Isabella. Now, it seemed, there was more to come. She went up close to him, took his face in her hands, and kissed him. Whatever the problems, they could wait until they connected as they always had. He drew her to him and held her tightly in his arms. "My beloved Emma," he said. "As you always were and always will be." Thus calmed, they entered the drawing-room and sat on the sofa before the fire. Much of the furniture had been moved out to make room for the many guests expected. But the sofa and Mr. Knightley's chair remained in their places, reminders of the old days at Hartfield. Emma could not put them away, even for a few days.

"So," she began. "What is the matter?"

"I have just come from a meeting with Henry," he said. "He told me that Adelaide is upset about Miss Sharpe's decision to stay away from the celebration for the vicar. She wants him to find out why. Of course, we know the answer. The question is what to do about it, if anything."

"That must be why Isabella visited today with the same questions. No doubt Henry asked her to come." Oh dear. She didn't want these young people involved in that old story. "I thought we had put all that behind us," she said.

"I think, my dear, one never puts the past completely behind one."

"But I don't want the children to know, to become involved. To know how we were part of it."

"It doesn't seem as if we can avoid this."

"What did you tell him?"

"I told him to give me a day to look into it, and to find an answer he can bring back to Adelaide."

"But how can you?" she asked.

"I wonder if it's time we told the truth. But of course, we can't without Anna Sharpe's consent."

"She will never consent to that," said Emma. "How could she? It would be too terrible for Mr. Weston and for her daughter." She paused for a moment, her thoughts racing, a look he recognized coming to her face. "Have you never wondered if Mr. Weston ever proposed marriage to Anna Sharpe?" she asked. "I confess that I have, more than a few times. They get on so well together. And he has always asked that she accompany him to our dinners. Of course, there is an age difference, but that never bothered you."

"That is a whole different story," he interrupted. Staring at her, he went on. "Are you suggesting Mr. Weston would marry her even if he knew the truth?"

"I do not know," she said, thoughtfully. "But I have come to know the great power of love."

"Yes," he said, "as I have too. But what would Edith say to

knowing her parentage?"

"I don't know. But if Mr. Weston married Anna, and adopted Edith, knowing the whole truth——"

"Emma. I'm afraid I detect signs of your old matchmaking self. You forget. Even if he married her, there would still be a secret to be kept from Edith."

"A secret is already being kept from her, no?"

He was quiet, thinking.

"I'm going to say something which may not please you," she said. "If Edith were adopted by Mr. Weston—and if our son George did want to marry her—would you consent? I remember you said just a few days ago, when we suspected an attraction, that you would never permit it. Would you, if things were thus altered?"

His face darkened. "I don't know," he said. "Of course, I wouldn't want it. But George is a very strong character. He'll attain his maturity very soon now. I wonder if I could stop him, even if he knew the present circumstances. Young people think so differently now." He paused again. "I would not have been hindered by my father, once I had made my mind up. Not that there was a reason like this for him to have objected. Besides, my father had passed away long before I began to love you. And I was considerably older than George when I married you."

Emma widened her eyes. "That is a change from your previous position. Don't you remember," she added, "we agreed you loved me since I was ten and you were twenty-six. George is older than that," she said, with her mischievous smile.

"Perhaps I'm getting old, my dear. I don't know myself, at the moment, what I would do. But what I suggest, is that either you or I visit Miss Sharpe tomorrow and make her see that she must attend the celebration. That we will watch out for her, and for Edith. But I must tell you, I have been wondering if the best solution might be telling Mr. Weston the whole truth. You once said you thought he would be able to bear the news of Frank's transgressions. It is so long ago now, it should be easier."

"Perhaps you could ask Mr. Weston if he had ever proposed to Miss Sharpe. Then we might at least set some things to rights."

"Emma. I could not do that. Absolutely not."

Emma was silent. "Well, the first thing, is to convince Miss Sharpe to attend," she said. "I will go to Randalls and tell Anna that you very much want her to attend. She will not refuse you, I suspect. After the party, we can think about the difficult rest of things."

She rose from the sofa. "Meanwhile, I will return to the kitchen and start ordering the refreshments: some fresh fruits, slices of cold meat, cheese, custards and jellies and, of course, wine and champagne. It will all be laid out beautifully on tables for our guests to browse and pick from. Will we have enough space in front of Donwell for all the carriages?"

"Yes, my dear. You are right to concentrate on such distractions. These aspects of life over which we are at present in control." He took her close to him. "But for now, dear Emma. Please go no further with any matchmaking maneuvers."

"I'm a matron now, with children old enough to think of marriage. It's more appropriate, you must admit, than the days I set myself to arranging alliances before I had reached the magic age of twenty-one." She smiled up at him, the old twinkle back in her eyes.

"You always were a dangerous woman," he said, smiling back, almost against his will. "I couldn't control you when you were ten. How can I expect to do that now?"

CHAPTER 12

Emma did not wait for the next morning. She completed her food orders and left for Randalls, stopping briefly at the library to tell her husband she was off. He made no objection, ordering the carriage to be made ready.

She had made the trip to Randalls so many times, she wanted to walk. But her husband, recalling her father's frequent admonition 'not to be out driving after sunset,' over-ruled her.

"I have some work to do here," he said. "I'll tell Serle to prepare dinner a little later." He escorted her out, helped her into the carriage, and went back inside to await her return.

At Randalls, Miss Sharpe opened the door. "Mrs. Knightley. Please come in. It's always a pleasure to see you. I'll call Mr. Weston."

"No, please do not. It's you I have come to see," said Emma quickly, bringing a look of some apprehension to Miss Sharpe's face. "Please tell the servant not to disturb him. I have come to talk to you about the upcoming celebration." She had decided to be as forthright as her husband. "May we talk together privately for a moment?" she asked.

"Of course. Both the girls are out for the afternoon, on a visit to Mrs. Goddard's for a late tea. We won't be disturbed in my rooms," she said, leading Emma up the stairs.

Emma had never visited Miss Sharpe's upstairs suite. It was large and sunny, the windows looking out over the front gardens. Tastefully furnished, a space at once friendly and livable, stylish and even somewhat elegant, a lovely Chippendale chair in one corner near the window, a Pembroke table at its side, laden with books. There was also a small sofa, and Emma took a seat there.

"Forgive me for disturbing you like this, but I am on an errand for my husband, who sends his compliments and best regards."

"Thank you, Mrs. Knightley. Please return mine to him. But tell me, is there anything he wishes me to do? As you know, I am always at your service and that of your husband." She sat rather stiffly in the chair, leaning forward as if in expectation of a request.

"It's about our celebration for the vicar. We have been told that you and Edith have declined our invitation, and both Mr. Knightley and I are most desirous that you attend. Mr. Weston and Adelaide have already accepted. We think we know why you have declined. Mr. Knightley has requested that you do him the special favor of attending. He will make sure that you will not be disturbed in any way while there. He thinks that your absence may raise questions. Indeed, it already has with Adelaide, who has come to Donwell asking that your potential absence be explained."

Miss Sharpe looked troubled. "Adelaide has been my pupil for many years now, Mrs. Knightley. She is respectful and attentive to her schooling in every way." She paused and sighed. "However, she is very willful about other matters. Not in a bad or rude way, you understand. But she will make up her own mind about matters outside my control. I am sorry she has troubled you."

"No. It is good that she has come to Donwell with her questions. Better there, than anywhere else. My husband has promised that he will help, and he now asks you to attend the party. We have said your reluctance is perhaps because you do not like large gatherings. Though we think we know why you do not want to come. Will you please do Mr. Knightley and myself this favor? Believe me, it will be far more natural for you and Edith to be present. Indeed, I fear my son George, who much enjoys your daughter's company, will be next at our door with his own questions if you do not come. We have a rebellion of the young on our hands!" she said, trying to smile and joke a bit.

Miss Sharpe remained quiet. "It will be difficult for me, and I will have to find a corner in which to hide myself and Edith, but you know, I cannot refuse either of you whatever you might ask. I will come, of course, with Edith, and tell Mr. Weston tonight that I have changed my mind. He may ask me why, and I will tell him of your visit and request on behalf of the young people, who do enjoy being together. But I admit, I do not look forward to seeing Mr. Churchill again."

"I can imagine. I do not either, Miss Sharpe. Nor do I relish being again in the company of the Eltons. But we must suffer it, I fear."

"Mrs. Knightley. Now that we have these private moments together, I must tell you that I have been thinking about leaving Mr. Weston's employ. After all, Adelaide is nineteen now, and Edith twenty. There is really no reason for either of them to have a governess."

Emma put up her hand as if to stop her. "Our Miss Taylor stayed with us until I was nearly twenty-one. And we would never have let her leave after that, even had she not married Mr. Weston. She had become a member of our family. Has it not been like that for you, Miss Sharpe?"

Emma noticed the woman's face darken, and her hands tightened on one another in her lap. "Yes, of course," she said. "But I could hardly stay on here after Adelaide marries. In fact, I have been thinking about perhaps teaching at Mrs. Goddard's. Edith is educated enough to also be a teacher in her own right. I don't think it would be good or proper for me to remain here much longer." She reddened and seemed agitated.

For the first time, Emma realized that perhaps Miss Sharpe was right. It would be odd, at best, for a single woman to live at Randalls with Mr. Weston. Why had she not thought of it before? And what of her suspicion that perhaps Mr. Weston had proposed marriage to Anna, and been refused, for obvious reasons. She decided quickly to seize the moment that lay open before her.

"May I presume to ask you, Miss Sharpe, if Mr. Weston, perhaps seeing the situation which lay in the future, might have made you an offer of marriage?" There, she was out with it.

"Mrs. Knightley. Because you ask, I must answer, though I do so reluctantly. "Yes, he has. Several times. And, as you can imagine, I have had to refuse him. I see it saddens him, but there is no way but to refuse."

"If circumstances were different, would you have accepted him?" asked Emma, determined to carry this conversation to a conclusion.

"How can you ask that? One cannot change what has happened.

There is no way to alter the circumstances of my past. I must continue to pay for what I have done, and only to hope that I do not harm this man who has been so good to me. Or harm my daughter, who suspects nothing, of course. But it has become clear to me, of late, that I must leave his house and employ." She looked Emma steadily in the eye. "About that, I have become sure. I am only making him sad by staying, without the true explanation for my refusals which I cannot give him."

"I must admit that I have suspected as much. Mr. Weston is such a sociable man, so happy of company, so obviously delighting in your presence at Randalls, that I thought such might have been the case. Oh dear, I do not know what to advise you," said Emma.

"I need no advice, Mrs. Knightley. You must see that yourself. I cannot stay at Randalls forever. Mrs. Goddard and I have talked, and she will be quite willing to take me on as a teacher. I have also spoken to her about Edith, but that is another matter altogether. Please, you must allow me to find my own way. For now, I think we had better end our talk, lest Mr. Weston be looking for me. I thank you for your concern and for your help and that of your husband. Please relay my gratitude to him. For now, I will tell Mr. Weston that Edith and I have decided to accompany him to your party." She extended a hand to Emma. "You are both so very good and kind," she said softly. "I shall never forget it."

That was all, as she led the way downstairs and to the front door. Emma's carriage stood outside, ready to bring her back to Donwell with her news. She felt uneasy and unsettled. She had solved the immediate problem but saw that other issues remained. Whether she and her husband could help with those, she was not sure.

CHAPTER 13

The visit from Mrs. Knightley had thrown Anna Sharpe back into the past she had, for years, tried to forget. Of course, many times she was so occupied with domestic cares at Randalls, she imagined herself a different person from the young woman who had unfortunately succumbed to the advances of Frank Churchill. At first, in the rush of duties with a newborn infant, Mr. Weston's daughter, and the caretaking of her own young child, then barely a year old, she almost forgot him and the Enscombe and Weymouth days. Then, too, there had been other responsibilities at Randalls. In those early years, she functioned as more than a mere governess, working with the housekeeper on menus, and with the other servants on household tasks.

Then, when her duties became somewhat lighter, she accepted Mr. Weston's kind invitations to join him for dinners with the Knightleys. The older Martin sister still lived in the vicinity of Highbury and was happy to earn extra monies for evening sit-ins with the children. Often, she and Mr. Weston sat up a bit later afterwards talking about a variety of Highbury doings. He was always a kind and pleasant man, easy-going and so different from his son, she thought. Frank never had much time for casual talk. Her encounters with him were always brief and furtive. It wasn't until she was installed at Randalls, during that two-month honeymoon absence of Frank and his new wife, that she began to learn the pleasures of quiet companionship. In those days, Mr. Weston was a sad and lonely man, and she was glad to provide a companion with whom he could talk and sometimes, unburden himself of his sorrows.

He told her of his first marriage—not a happy one, he said, for his wife longed for comforts and pleasures he could not provide. They had married for love, but their love did not last amid the privations of a narrow income. Then, she sickened and died, and her sister came and took Frank away. He had agreed, and afterward, bitterly regretted his decision.

His happiness with Miss Taylor had been great and brief. He loved to talk about her, and how they enjoyed their life together and looked forward to the birth of a child. Then, so suddenly, he was once again bereft. Anna Sharpe felt his sadness, for she too had been left bereft, albeit in a very different way. Still, they were each granted a child, who brought relief and a future. Often, they talked of their young daughters, though she felt terrible guilt at the secret that she kept. Still, she loved Edith as he loved Adelaide, and they were happy watching the two little girls bond together as if they were sisters. Indeed, she often thought, with an even greater pang of guilt, if he only knew how closely they were related.

After a time, their relationship began imperceptibly to change. His enjoyment of being with her became obvious. Often, he looked for her company, suggested outings with the two girls. Yes, if she were honest with herself, she had seen it coming but knew not how to stop it, for she too enjoyed his company, finding him all goodness and kindness. She liked him very much. More, indeed, than she had ever really liked his son. Yet, she could not permit this to go on. One evening, when they had been sitting by the fire after the girls had gone upstairs, he asked her to marry him. She could not say she was surprised. But she could not marry him, and could not tell him why. She said she had no thoughts of marriage, and preferred to remain a single woman. She saw she hurt him and knew then she would have to leave, though, at that moment, she knew not how.

Later that same evening, when she had withdrawn to her rooms, she set herself to thinking. She should tell him that now the girls were coming of age, she could no longer remain at Randalls. It would be improper. No doubt, she would say, he had seen that too, and hence his offer. She would tell him she wanted to again find a teaching position. She would, of course, take Edith with her. But first, she would have to see Mrs. Goddard, who was growing older and might welcome not only the services of another teacher but perhaps an assistant in her administrative work at the school. Yes, that was the best plan for the present.

He remained silent, but she was not prepared for what followed. A week or so later, before she had been able to see Mrs. Goddard, Mr. Weston spoke again. He pleaded with her to reconsider. He spoke of his growing feelings for her. He did not propose because he feared compromising her. He loved her. He asked that she take some more time to think. She agreed, asking him only not to renew his offer until she had an answer.

Then came the visit from Mrs. Knightley, with her questions. She almost wished she had not told her the truth. Several months had passed since Mr. Weston's second offer. She knew he was waiting only to ask again. She must find some arrangement at Goddard's. Now, this unexpected visit from Frank Churchill threw her into further confusion. What a muddle she had made of things, letting time pass without acting. She could not refuse the Knightleys her attendance at the celebration. She would have to endure seeing Frank again. But she vowed she would visit Mrs. Goddard as soon as all was over at Donwell.

CHAPTER 14

The next day, informed by his uncle that Miss Sharpe and Edith would be attending the celebration at Donwell, Henry Knightley donned his walking coat and lost no time in finding Adelaide and delivering his message. No details had been given, but Henry was satisfied his mission had been accomplished. Always a welcome visitor at Randalls, he was invited inside and asked Adelaide if she would take a walk with him. Pulling on a bonnet and pelisse, she led the way outside, where he told her his news and was surprised at her reaction.

"Is that all?" she said, raising her eyes reproachfully. "Were you told nothing about why the refusal and why the reversal?"

"I didn't ask for any reasons. It's none of my business or yours, for that matter. You wanted them to attend, and they are coming, and that is the end of it," he said with some impatience at her reaction.

"It isn't the end of it!" she said, stamping her foot as she did when angry. "There must be something behind this, something we don't know. Aren't you the least bit curious?"

"No, I'm not," he said. "And neither should you be. I've succeeded in securing you Edith's company at the celebration, and as far as I'm concerned, I'm finished."

"Don't you think it's odd? Even a little bit? First Miss Sharpe absolutely refuses, and then, with a word from your uncle—or aunt—she makes a sudden turnaround and changes her mind. I heard her tone of voice when she told my father she wasn't going and that was that. Once she makes up her mind to something, she doesn't change. I know her better than you do."

"If you know her so well, why don't you ask her yourself?" he said.

"That would show her that I was involved in going to you. I can't let her know that. She would consider it very improper—or some such nonsense," she fumed. "Well, I'm not satisfied. I'm going to talk to Edith, see if she knows anything."

"You will be interfering in something that is not your business, Adelaide."

"If you thought it was none of my business, you shouldn't have gone to your uncle in the first place."

She was the most maddening girl he had ever met. He wanted to shake her. Years ago, he sometimes did that, but it was hardly the thing to do now. They were too old for that. But he was getting angry and didn't like it. He had never seen Uncle George lose his temper, and he resolved not to lose his now. Still, Adelaide could be so irritating!

"You are simply being nonsensical. Why can't you just say thank you to me—which you have not, by the way, said as yet—and leave well enough alone."

"Because I think something is brewing. You don't live at Randalls and can't see what I have seen. For one thing, I heard Father and Miss Sharpe speaking in an agitated way over this. And also, I think my father and Miss Sharpe like one another."

"Of course, they like each other. They are old friends now, after having lived together so many years," said Henry.

"No, silly. I mean they really like each other."

"Adelaide, if they do, it has nothing to do with you and you should not even be talking about such fantasies."

"Who says they are fantasies? You have been away so much, so occupied with your legal studies, you haven't been able to watch as I have." She looked up at him. "Sometimes you don't see things that are right in front of you," she said, opening wide her large blue eyes.

"I can certainly see you, Miss Adelaide," he said, taking her arm impulsively. "More than that, at the moment, I do not see." He had spoken without his usual reserve.

"And when you see me, what do you see?" she said, looking up at him mischievously.

"I see a spoiled young woman who always gets everything her

own way," he answered, flustered, but trying to recover himself.

"There's more to me than that," she answered. "But I think we should stop talking about this. I'm going to do some investigating on my own and when I find the reasons I'm looking for, I'll tell you."

"I'm not interested," he said. "But I think it's a good idea for us to stop talking about this." He continued to hold her arm. "Let's just walk," he said. "It's a lovely day. I'm looking forward to the big celebration. Before long, I'll be headed to London to be a drudge in some law office or other. I'll miss being here," he added.

"I'll miss seeing you," she said. "Who will I argue with when you're gone? Edith never disagrees with me, nor does father. I suppose Miss Sharpe will have to take your place until you return. Are you leaving after the celebration? Will you come back and forth, or will you have to stay in London?"

"I don't know. It depends on the work I will have to do. When I look at my father, he's always occupied with some casework or other. I'm not sure I want a life like that," he said.

"What kind of life do you want?" she asked.

He found himself unable to answer. "I could ask you the same question. What kind of life do you want?" he replied.

"Oh, for women, there's really only one choice. Matrimony, I suppose. I'm not really sure I'm ready for that," she said. "I like being on my own, making my own decisions, my own choices."

"Choosing a husband for yourself will be your biggest decision," he said. "It's more important than choosing the right law office to work in."

"I suppose it is. But Highbury doesn't offer a wide variety of choices." She gave him an unnerving smile. "Fortunately, I hear that Mr. Churchill is bringing his son to the celebration. We'll get to meet him for the first time. At least he'll be a new face in town."

"Are you so tired of the old faces?" he asked.

She still looked up at him. "I'm never tired of your face, Henry. I rather like it, except when you are lecturing me about something or other."

"You are often in need of lecturing, my girl. And if no one else except Miss Sharpe will do it, I reluctantly accept my responsibility to keep you in good order." He grinned but felt himself uncomfortably on the brink of saying something she might not like.

"You've been trying to do that for years," she said. "But you can keep it up. I give you permission. I really don't mind. There are even times I rather like it." She paused. "But this isn't one. I intend to find out more about Miss Sharpe's change of mind. We'd better turn back. Father will be looking for me."

He was still holding her arm, and she did not take it away from him. Together, they walked toward Randalls, neither of them completely happy with their conversation, yet happy enough to continue arm in arm all the way back to the house, where he bid her goodbye.

CHAPTER 15

George Knightley was thinking about Edith Sharpe. Yesterday, he had been in the library at Donwell when his Aunt Isabella came to visit his mother. He had been about to finish what he had been reading and come to say hello when he began to be interested in the conversation they were having in the kitchen. Their voices were loud enough for him to understand the whole. It was about the festival for the new vicar. It seemed that Edith and Miss Sharpe would not be coming. Like Aunt Isabella, he would also have asked his mother why, but seeing how she had simply shut the conversation down, he supposed she would do the same with him, were he to ask. It was odd. Everyone at Randalls always came to doings at Donwell. What was so different about this party?

The next day, he decided to ask Edith. But he could hardly go over and ask to see her without some legitimate purpose. Perhaps Hetta could lure her out for a walk. He sought out his sister, at the moment in her room. When he asked her to help him, she quickly agreed. She had a romantic side, like her mother, and thought she noticed George and Edith's preference for each other's company.

So it was, in the afternoon, George told his mother that he and Hetta were going up to the stables for a ride. Instead, they headed for Randalls, and Hetta, after performing her task admirably, left her brother and Edith walking on the paths between her home and Donwell.

"I hope you will forgive me for getting your company under false pretenses," he began.

Edith was silent for a moment. "Of course," she said. "Is there something I can help you with?" She seemed a bit flustered.

"I wanted to talk to you about the celebration for the vicar. Why aren't you and your aunt coming? It seems a bit odd, doesn't it?" he began.

"Oh, but I am coming," she said. "We weren't, but I have only just been told we are."

"But I heard you were not," he said, surprised.

"There has been a change of plans. I'm glad, for I was looking forward to it."

"Well, I'm glad too. It will be quite the bash, don't you think, what with all of Highbury coming, and even, I've heard, the Enscombe Churchills and the previous vicar and his wife."

"Oh yes," she said. "Is that what you have come to talk about with me?" she asked, somewhat quizzically.

"No, now that I know you will be there," he said, "I'm satisfied." Without thinking, he added, "I would have been disappointed had you not been there."

She lowered her head and made no reply. There was something quite bold about his behavior, she thought, and she did not know exactly how to react to his words.

"Would you have been disappointed not to come?" he asked, pursuing the point. "I mean, disappointed at not seeing me?" Then, when she said nothing, he added, "I mean, missing all the fun," realizing that he had perhaps said too much.

"I like small gatherings better," she said. "But I am glad to be going." She was feeling increasingly embarrassed at his words.

"You don't sound glad. In any case, I'll be sure to seek you out, and maybe we'll find a quiet spot to sit and talk." Looking for a subject to continue the conversation, he recalled that last week he gave Edith a collection of Shakespeare's sonnets from the Donwell library. "We can talk about what we have been reading. Our recent favorites. I like the sonnets very much, myself. That's why I suggested you read them too. Sometimes, I've heard people say Shakespeare's language is too flowery, but I disagree. He's very direct, in my view. Would you like to know which one I like best?"

She nodded yes. How could she not, she thought.

"It's the one that starts with a rather bold and forceful statement. I like that kind of direct language. It's almost like he's giving an order:

'Let me not to the marriage of true minds admit impediments.' Have you read that one?" he asked.

She had, she replied.

"It seems to me the poet is talking about being prevented from continuing a relationship that he desires, that he treasures. What do you think he means?" He had started and resolved to continue with this, even if she remained silent. "All right, I'll answer my own question. It's because he has found someone with whom he enjoys an honest and true relationship and he won't be prevented from it. He's describing a certain kind of companionship. You see, he says very specifically, 'the marriage of true minds.' There should be no impediments to that kind of relationship."

She was very red now and was still silent.

"Don't you wonder what the marriage of true minds is like?" he asked.

"George," she said, finally speaking, "I think it means two people who understand each other and speak the truth to each other."

"Yes, that's what I think too. But that word 'impediment' is interesting. It's used in the marriage ceremony when the priest asks if anyone in the congregation knows whether or not there are any impediments to the union. So, you see, the marriage of true minds is serious. Maybe even more serious than the marriage contract itself. Do you know what? I think it describes our relationship, don't you? I mean, there's no one I'd rather talk to or be with than you, though you're awfully quiet just now. So unlike, it seems, your usual self, that you force me to continue on my own." He paused, and then went on. "How do you feel about being with me?" he asked, pressing her directly now, though he could see she was agitated.

"Yes, of course, I like being with you and talking with you. You know that," she answered softly.

"I also like looking at you," he added, "And holding your hand, whenever I do. I intend to tell my father just how I feel about you, Edith. Of course, if you don't feel the same way and don't want me to make a proposal, I will obey your wishes." He had not come over here intending to do this, but as they had walked together, like a lightning flash, the conviction came over him that it was time for him to declare himself.

She looked at him with some wonder and disbelief. "You can't be serious," she said. "You must realize that there is a vast difference in our condition. You will be master of the Donwell estate one day."

"Yes, and I will be ready for that. I intend to follow in my father's footsteps and I continue to take an active interest in the management of the estate. When I'm in charge, I'll see to it that the tenants are cared for and appropriate improvements made. I'll be as interested as my father in farmer Martin's new crops and methods of farming. But you've gotten me off my subject. I'm not thinking about the future of Donwell, just now."

"But you must think of it. You are the heir, and you forget my position, relative to yours. I am the niece of a governess who has charitably brought me up. I have nothing to offer you," she said.

"Just yourself," he said. "I care for nothing else, and need nothing else."

"I doubt your father will agree," she said. "He is the principal person in the whole county, and I am nobody. You had better think again of any such idea before daring to approach him. I wish you would not bother him at the present moment when he and your mother are preparing for this grand celebration."

"So, are you saying you don't mind my speaking to him afterwards?" he said, seizing his advantage.

"No, that is not exactly what I meant. I really don't know what I mean at the moment," she said, flustered and her thoughts in a muddle.

He took her hand and kissed it. "I won't do anything you don't want," he said. "But I do mean to offer for you. We don't need to tell anyone immediately if you want to wait. But I think my father would want me to tell him the truth of my feelings now. He is not a man who likes secrets, I have often heard him say." He looked at her closely and thought he saw in her eyes a return of his feelings.

"I'll say no more for a week, if you wish. But I must tell him and quickly if you accept my offer."

"I can't accept you now. Wouldn't that be a secret engagement?" she asked. "We have heard so much of the secret engagement between Mr. Churchill and his wife, and how wrong it was. If I accepted your offer today, we would be engaged, would we not?" she said, looking into his eyes directly for the first time.

"I suppose we would. All right. But take notice. I do not withdraw my offer. Let us say, I will come back to you after I have spoken to my father. And I will delay that conversation with him until after the vicar's celebration." He looked back into her eyes, now most directly. "I would very much like to kiss you, Edith, but I will wait until you accept me. I can see you want me to do everything properly, and I will."

They said no more and turned on the path heading back for Randalls. Something momentous had occurred between them, which neither had anticipated when they began their walk. But he had spoken. And George Knightley was determined that he would have what he wanted.

CHAPTER 16

Donwell Abbey was undergoing yet another transformation. After Emma's move there following the death of her father, she brought over various treasured items from Hartfield, making room for them fairly easily. But as the years went on, she made even more changes, turning Mr. Knightley's old residence lighter and brighter and a bit more modern, though he had not always been happy with all her alterations. The one room she was never permitted to change was his library, his inner sanctum, his holy spot ever since the days when he had first come into his inheritance.

Mr. Knightley loved the old library, with its precious leather-bound volumes, its spacious reading table, his comfortable if unfashionable chair. It was the place where, during his young manhood, he came to read and reflect. It is also where he usually met with William Larkins, his estate manager, informing himself about conditions on his many properties and working on his accounts. In short, it was in some sense a visible incarnation of himself—a careful landowner, a thoroughly traditional and well-educated man, appreciating the best that had been said and thought and bound in books.

He included some modern authors on his shelves, most prominently, his favorite, Charles Dickens. Dickens always held a special place in his heart, for it was the great man himself who led him to choose Broadstairs for the honeymoon which had been such a magical time for him and for Emma. It was, as she herself said, the best gift he could have given her. It was there, at what is now called the Royal Albion Hotel, that they began to forge their indelible and permanent bond of love. And so, the great Dickens, 'the Inimitable,' enjoyed a prominent place on shelves reserved for his works. Mr. Knightley was pleased to see that young George was a frequent visitor to the library, and also an avid reader of Dickens. He sometimes thought he should talk to his son more about their common intellectual interests, but somehow, life always got in the way. That brought to his mind the mention his son had made of reading *David Copperfield* with Edith Sharpe. Yes, that matter had yet to be fully resolved.

Meanwhile, Emma and the servants were decorating the downstairs, the drawing-room, and entranceway. Most of the furniture had been moved out, and tables set up along the walls for refreshments, and further tables positioned outside, under tents. The tables were ornamented with festoons and wreaths of flowers, and some fruits of the season. The overall effect was pleasant and festive. Many lamps were set in place, ready to be lit, should the day grow dark. Emma had engaged a performer on the harp, one Wiepart, whose name Emma was told was famous, though unknown to her. The festivities were to start in the afternoon, with food laid out on the tables later, while the performer played. Then, the Reverend Brewer would be asked to say a few words, after which the party would gradually break up.

The day opened fine and bright, and by two o'clock, the time given on invitations, guests started to arrive. Emma and her husband stood ready to greet them, with Isabella and John not far behind. The young people eagerly awaited their friends from Randalls and Hartfield, and soon many other Highbury residents followed. The Reverend Brewer was already inside, with his son and daughter by his side. And before too much longer, Frank Churchill, his son Weston, and the Eltons arrived.

Emma was almost shocked at the first sight of Frank. He had aged, to the point where she thought her husband looked the younger of the two. But he maintained his old dashing aspect, and his son was almost an image of the younger Frank. The Eltons also looked a bit the worse for the years that had passed, though she came heavily adorned with her usual feathers and ribbons and pearls. The Martins arrived next, with the eldest two of their children, and soon, there was a large crowd, some going inside, others staying outside, where the sun shone brightly on the proceedings. She noticed her son George coming forward to welcome Mr. Weston, Miss Sharpe, and the two girls. He was followed closely by Henry, who did the same. But with so much going on, it was impossible for her to watch as closely as she would have liked. Mr. Knightley went to talk with the Martins, and Frank Churchill headed straight for her. Well, she would make the best of it.

"Hello my dear Mrs. Knightley," he began with a flourish and a bow. "So good to see you after all these years. You are looking as charming as ever. I hope we were not discourteous in coming along without an invitation. But I thought you would be glad to see me and my son Weston, whom you have not yet met." The young man also made a bow. "I've told Weston so much about Highbury, he was eager to see for himself. So many memories here," he said, somewhat sadly.

"I am most sorry for your loss, Mr. Churchill," Emma said. "It is not very recent, I know, but such losses remain with one, do they not?"

"Indeed. As you can see, I have resigned myself to the single life. For me, there will never be another Jane." He looked as sad as his words. "But I mustn't put a damper on this party. The Eltons first introduced me to the Reverend Brewer in Enscombe, so I thought it proper to come and give him my congratulations on his appointment. I was a little surprised that he would leave his important appointment in Enscombe for one in a small village like Highbury. But perhaps he was growing tired of those larger duties."

Emma thought his remark somewhat pompous but merely nodded. "I must greet our other guests," she said. "Are you staying long in Highbury?" she asked.

"I don't think so," he said. "Now that my uncle has passed away, I am now master of Enscombe. There are many duties I must attend to there, and cannot stay here very long. Give my very best to your husband, should I not have the opportunity to talk with him myself. I'm sure he will be much engaged with all these guests."

Once again, she nodded, without comment. She was certain her husband would avoid Mr. Churchill, if possible. For now, she was looking for Anna Sharpe. She hoped Frank would stay away from her.

The Weston group was still outside, and Mr. Knightley went to greet them. "Mr. Weston, it's good to see you out and about," he said. "And Miss Sharpe. You too. Very good of you to come to our party." She gave him a curtsy and smiled. He looked at the two girls, and most particularly at Edith, who had also curtsied and retreated behind her aunt, almost as if she wished to hide herself. Mr. Knightley noticed that, as he usually noticed everything. "Hello Adelaide," he said. "Good to see you too. How are your studies coming along? I trust Miss Sharpe is working you and Edith hard."

"Indeed, sir," answered Adelaide. "She always does. A bit too much, in my opinion," she said with an arch look at her governess. "But we can take it, can't we Edith," she said, hoping to draw her friend into the conversation. But the girl merely nodded and moved even further back.

Then Henry Knightley joined them. "Adelaide. Good to see you." She gave him a look hard to interpret. "And you, Mr. Knightley," she said.

"Since when am I Mr. Knightley to you?" he asked.

"On social occasions. I follow the instructions of Miss Sharpe about such matters. Don't I?" she asked, turning to Anna. "I must be proper, especially on such a grand occasion."

"Oh, don't be such a goose," said Henry. "Come on inside with me, and I'll show you around all Aunt Emma's decorations. She's been working on them for days." He took Adelaide's arm and drew her away, leaving Edith exposed to Mr. Knightley's glances, which she thought were hard upon her.

Thus finding a place in the party around Mr. Weston, George moved over, making his greetings to the group.

But Mr. Knightley continued to talk, and now he directed a question directly to Edith. "I understand you like the works of the great Mr. Dickens," he said. "I do too. He continues to be the favorite of all England, at the moment. Do you have some preferences among his works?" he asked.

She was much unnerved, but answered, "We have been reading *David Copperfield*. I like that one the best just now, but of course, I have not read all his works as yet."

"Yes. I like it too. What is it you particularly like about it?" he persisted.

George was feeling uncomfortable and somewhat annoyed with his father. He could think of no way to help.

Edith was determined not to falter under this questioning. "Well, I admire David—the way he makes his way in the world, even after losing both father and mother. I thought it quite wonderful when he bit Mr. Murdstone's hand."

Mr. Knightley was taken aback. "It does not seem an action of which a young lady would approve. Rather violent."

George entered the conversation. "Not at all, father," he said. "I think it was positively heroic, just the kind of action that would appeal to a certain kind of right-minded young lady."

"I do hope Miss Sharpe will be safe from her students," he said with an enigmatic smile. With one more look, Mr. Knightley nodded and excused himself to greet another guest who had come up to him at that moment. He had seen enough to know that his son's feelings for Edith Sharpe were indeed real.

CHAPTER 17

Anna Sharpe saw Frank Churchill enter with his son and go over to speak with Emma. She still stood next to Mr. Weston, after Adelaide left with Henry Knightley to view the inside decorations. She heard Mr. Knightley's brief talk with Edith and understood his purpose. He must know or have been told, of his son's growing interest in her daughter. It was one more reason why she must soon leave this place, happy as she had been here. Mr. Knightley, good as he was and had been to her from the start, would never approve of a relationship between Edith and his eldest son and heir. Of that, she was sure. And Mr. Weston's proposals of marriage to her still hung in the air, unresolved. Everything was against her staying in Highbury. Despite Mrs. Goddard's favorable response to her teaching, what she would really like was to leave Highbury altogether and perhaps start a boarding school herself. She still had some money from Frank Churchill's uncle and had saved quite a bit during her stay at Randalls. But relocating to Mrs. Goddard's might not be far enough, now that she saw the situation with Edith. In the midst of these thoughts, Dr. Perry came over and greeted Mr. Weston. She moved away, for she knew they might be talking of the old times and the death of Mrs. Weston.

"Edith," she said, after exchanging some pleasantries with Dr. Perry, "Let us go and view the decoration of the house. I think Adelaide is inside." As she moved away, she saw that George was following them. "Mr. Knightley," said Miss Sharpe. "Do not let us keep you from your guests. You are part of the hosting family."

But he was not to be deterred. "Not at all. I'm afraid I must confess I have done nothing toward the celebration, and I would rather accompany you and Edith into the house. Mother has indeed done herself proud with decorations." He led the way, and there was nothing to do but follow him.

Mrs. Goddard had now arrived and was heading toward Mr. Weston, just as Anna, Edith, and George Knightley had left. "How do you do," said Mr. Weston. "I trust I find you well."

"Indeed," said Mrs. Goddard. "Very well. I was just coming over to talk to Miss Sharpe. You see, she has visited me and suggested coming to the school to teach. With the girls grown now, she thinks her governessing days are over. I trust you have found her a satisfactory guide for your daughter."

"The very best. I am surprised to hear from you that she thinks of leaving us. Even grown girls can use education and training, I believe. Especially my Adelaide. I fear I spoil her, and Miss Sharpe is a good antidote to my permissiveness with her. I am glad you have told me this. I hope to persuade her to stay with us a while longer." He looked somewhat discomposed, and Mrs. Goddard feared that she had spoken out of turn.

"Well, Mr. Weston, you know how young women are nowadays, and Miss Sharpe is one of the more modern types, you know, the independent sort, who want to be on their own. Yet the world still offers them little opportunity outside of teaching or governessing. She did mention that she also thought of starting a boarding school of her own. Of course, not here, as Goddard's enrolls all the young girls in the neighborhood. She asked me to investigate other areas where such a school might thrive. But, I'm going on and on about matters that perhaps I should not disclose."

Mr. Weston bowed to Mrs. Goddard and moved to where Mr. Knightley was talking to a group of Highbury people including the Coles. He was upset, and would not talk to Anna about this here, but would wait until their return home.

Seeing him alone, Emma went over. "Mr. Weston. It is so good to see you here at Donwell. It's not like our friendly dinner parties, is it, with so many people around."

"Oh, I like to see lots of people," he said. "I saw you talking with my Frank. I confess I do not like the look of him. He seems a bit worn, don't you think?"

"I fear I must agree. I think he still suffers from the loss of Jane. Some losses, perhaps, are hard to recover from." As soon as she said this, she regretted it. Since she knew that Mr. Weston had proposed to Anna Sharpe, it was an inappropriate comment.

"Indeed, you are right. But sometimes, you are fortunate, and a person comes along who fills the void. Frank has not been fortunate enough to meet such a person, I think. All his care now is for his son. He is really a delightful boy. I'm thinking of asking him to stay on for a bit at Randalls. There are so many young people here of his age and station. It would be good for him. I have asked Frank to stay too, but he says he must return tomorrow. He is now in charge at Enscombe, and as you no doubt are aware, there are many duties connected with running a large estate. But Frank seems quite reluctant to leave young Weston here with me."

Emma felt, but could not say, she could readily imagine why he did not want his son mixing with the young people at Highbury, one of whom was, if he knew it, his half-sister. Frank had not approached Edith, for which she was grateful. Nor had he tried to speak to Miss Sharpe. He seemed another person now, not the gay, reckless, devil-may-care man who rode to London to purchase a piano for his love and longed only to dance and flirt. He looked an old man now, one tired of life, even. She imagined that he still mourned Jane. She felt his loss and could not herself conceive of life without her Mr. Knightley. She looked across the lawn and went to rescue her husband.

"I haven't yet spoken to the Eltons," she said. "Will you join me in going over to greet them?"

Together with Mr. Weston, Emma walked across the lawn to where they stood in conversation with her husband. Although Mrs. Elton, as usual, was doing most of the talking.

"Hello, Mrs. Knightley. How good to see you again! I was just about to come over to you. Isn't this a splendid gathering! Such a treat! Of course, Reverend Brewer would not hear of it if we did not attend. He absolutely would not! I feared he would not come at all if we did not join in the festivities. So, we simply had to attend. I knew you would approve, rather than suffer the loss of your guest of honor! Am I not right, Mr. Elton? Of course, my caro sposo is too modest to admit it, but he has almost been Reverend Brewer's right hand in Enscombe." As she rambled on, much in her old manner, she twirled a small parasol above her head.

Emma made no reply. There was simply nothing she could say that would be in the least polite, so silence was better. Any reply seemed unnecessary. Mr. Elton smiled at his wife, nodding in agreement with everything she said.

"John," called Emma to her brother-in-law. "Here are the Eltons, come all the way from Yorkshire. I'm sure you remember them." It was cruel, but she had to get away. Then she decided to make a remark she knew would be cutting. "So long ago, that Christmas dinner at the Westons. You must remember, John. Mr. Elton shared our carriage, both there and back." At last, they were silenced. She left them with John, who threw her a dark look. She would hear from him later, she had no doubt.

Emma went to join her sister. "Where are the young people gone?" she asked. "I think if we can find Adelaide, Henry will be somewhere in the vicinity."

"Indeed, you are right. They are over there with Mr. Churchill's son," said Isabella. "Henry is probably not happy that Adelaide is chatting in so animated a way with young Mr. Churchill. I think it is Adelaide who is keeping Henry here in Highbury. His father wants him to go to London and work with a law firm. He's finally finished with all his education. Imagine! Twelve years of study! And nothing yet to show for it!"

Emma nodded. "Mr. Knightley is also a bit troubled about George's obvious interest in Edith Sharpe. But there's no moving him to London. He insists he wants to work with his father on estate matters. It's not really a bad idea. As he grows older and the duties seem to increase, my dear husband does need the help."

"Is he looking for his son to find a woman with the 30,000 pounds we each brought to our marriages?"

"That is a bit unfair, Isabella. Mr. Knightley is never one to decide a relationship on the basis of money. There are other factors to consider in choosing a marital partner."

"I'm sure there are. I think people know themselves when they have met the right one. I knew very quickly. You took longer."

"Not really. I loved Mr. Knightley since I was ten. It just took longer for me to grow up, you see."

"You mean you had first to experiment with your matchmaking disasters?"

"Don't be so superior. I was the one who assisted you and John to find each other. And the Westons, too. You want to stress my mistakes, but I did have some successes," Emma said, tartly.

Isabella gave her sister a knowing look. "Well, with all those successes behind you, are you at work on facilitating any other relationships?"

"To tell the truth, I have told Mr. Knightley several times that your Henry and Mr. Weston's Adelaide remind me of our courtship days. Don't you recall how often my husband came over to Hartfield and wound up scolding me?"

Isabella shook her head.

"Maybe you don't, because you had married and left by then. But the two of them seem to make a good couple, don't you think?"

"Emma, I never indulge myself in such fancies. I'm too busy with my household and husband. I leave all that to you," she said with a smile.

CHAPTER 18

Frank Churchill knew that his presence at the celebration for the new vicar would not be welcome. Probably the only person glad to see him was his father. That was all right with him. It was his father he had come to see. Ever since he and Jane settled at Enscombe, he had carefully arranged his visits with his father so that he would not bother either Anna or little Edith. While he was satisfied with not seeing Anna, he did often wonder what his little daughter looked like, even more now, that Jane was gone from him forever. How short had been their time together. He could hardly think of that without anger. Emma and her Mr. Knightley had been together since she was a young girl, and even now, continued to enjoy their mutual love. He and Jane had so short a time—the stolen afternoons and evenings at Weymouth, the brief, hidden visits at Highbury. At the Crown Inn dance, he could not even ask her to stand up with him, for he knew Mr. Knightley suspected from the first, he thought. To give him credit, he was a man who knew what love looked like. It did not always show itself obviously, in kisses or hand clasps, but shone in the eyes. Yes, he had known.

Well, he was paying the price for everything now. For what he had done to Anna and little Edith, and to Jane, whose health, he feared, he contributed to ruining. She was gone now, only Weston left to him. But now, his situation was changed. He was the sole master of Enscombe. He had money and plenty of it. But he was alone and with no one save Weston with whom to share it. Weston was a curious boy. Somewhat like himself, but as Jane's son, also quite different. Wealth meant little to him, he saw that. But there were some who could use some of his wealth, like his daughter. She was portionless, and he had promised Jane, just before she left him forever, to attend to that. He had let more years pass than he should. Given this opportunity, 'he sent word that he was coming to Highbury to the celebration for the vicar. He knew Rufus Brewer well, in fact. In the days following Jane's death, he was so bowed down with grief, that for the first time he found himself seeking clerical help from the Reverend Brewer. In one of those coincidences of life that never ceased to amaze him, he discovered that Anna Sharpe had also sought his help, in those terrible early days when he and his uncle offered her monetary help, but little else. Indeed, neither his uncle nor his aunt had given him much by way of strength of character. Well, it was time now to put as much to rights as he could.

He also regretted his conduct to Anna Sharpe, their brief affair, and his wish to terminate her at Randalls, fearing exposure. Well, the Knightleys had remedied that. And his dear Jane. What a generous soul she was. He often called her his angel come down from heaven. Indeed, so she had been. She wanted him to take care of Anna as well. He must try to use his immense wealth for some good.

After the celebration, he arranged to fetch his father and take him for a carriage ride. Weston was glad to be told he could stay back and visit with the young ladies at Randalls while his father and grandfather were out.

As they rode along the old familiar paths, Frank readied himself to explain to his father the purpose for which he had come.

"Father, I must tell you that I have important reasons for coming uninvited to the Knightleys' celebration. Perhaps you have already guessed why," he began, hesitantly. Mr. Weston merely smiled and turned to his son expectantly.

"Why else could it be, my son? To see me and to bring Weston to visit Randalls, instead of my always journeying to Enscombe or London to see you," his father replied. "I was sure that was why you have come."

"No. I fear I have rather an unhappy story to tell."

Mr. Weston looked alarmed. "Is this something financial? Or some issue about Weston?" He knew of nothing else to suggest. "Surely not some further sadness concerning your loss of dear Jane?"

"No father. None of that. But I could not tell you before. For years after my stepmother's passing, you were grieving so, that I could not add to your sorry state. But now, after many years, you look so well, even so happy, that I'm encouraged to make a start. Finally, I am ready to unburden myself. Though I fear in so doing, I will add again to your sadness."

Mr. Weston waited. "Just to be with you Frank is such a source of joy for me, I think nothing you could tell me would disturb me."

Frank held up a hand as if to stop his father. So, he started, haltingly at first. "I must tell you first, that I knew Miss Sharpe at Enscombe and Weymouth." He stopped. His father's eyes were upon him. "I confess, there was a brief affair, between us, Father." Mr. Weston said nothing. "It went on for a bit. But soon we realized we were unsuited to one another. By then, I had met Jane, and loved her deeply."

"Surely you ended it, then," said Mr. Weston. "Nothing so terribly wrong with that. I understand."

"No. That's not all. In a short while, Miss Sharpe and I parted company, without regrets. But then, alas, we found it could not be over. She was with child, and had to leave Enscombe and procured a governess's position at Weymouth."

His father looked at him steadily, but not unkindly.

"There was no hope of marriage. You know, my aunt had great plans for me. So, Anna removed to Weymouth. Then, after my aunt's death, she came to Highbury, to Mrs. Goddard's, seeking a position there, hoping we could marry. It wasn't because she loved me, you understand. It was for the child's sake. But by then, I had met Jane and engaged myself to her. I could not give her up. I feared Anna might tell Jane, and so to forestall any trouble, pleading my uncle's ill health, I convinced Jane to marry me at Enscombe. Once Anna learned I was married, she had no further interest in me. It was then Mrs. Goddard suggested she care for little Adelaide while Jane and I went away for our two-month honeymoon. What I reproach myself with most, is intending to send Anna away upon our return. I had no right to do that. But my Jane and the Knightleys intervened, so she stayed on, and I left things as they were."

His father was still silent.

"You see, I also feared that since you and she had gotten along so well during our absence, you might think of marrying her. Then she might tell you everything."

"I must stop you there, my son. Indeed, I did grow fond of Anna Sharpe, but not so quickly as you suggest. In the first years after my dear Anne's death, I depended on her so heavily, that I could not do without her services. She did so well with the children. It gave me time to grieve in private, during those first years when I was not myself. Gradually, her presence began to mean more to me than her service to the girls. I started asking her to accompany me to the Knightleys for dinners, and such events. Recently, as Adelaide and Edith have grown into young women, I realized she might be thinking of leaving my employ. And I proposed marriage to her. Sadly, she has refused me. Now I see she has reasons why."

"You must realize, Father, that Edith is your granddaughter, do you not?"

"Yes, I see that. But I have come to love the girl, almost as much as I love Adelaide. Frank, all that you have told me is now long in the past. It means nothing to me when measured against what Anna's companionship has given me. I must tell you that I will propose again, informing her that I know the secrets of her past."

Frank went on. "There is more. Before her death, in her last illness, my beloved Jane asked that I promise to take care of my daughter and Miss Sharpe. I have now done what she asked. Through a London law firm, I have arranged an endowment of 20,000 pounds for Edith. She will no longer be a portionless girl. With that, she can make a good marriage for herself. I have arranged a similar sum to be put at Miss Sharpe's disposal. Mrs. Goddard said she was looking to establish a boarding school. That would help her do that. Neither of them must know that the money comes from me. In a letter arriving today, a lawyer will inform them that the bequests come from the estate of a distant relative, now deceased. There is some truth in that, father. It is really Jane's gift to them."

"I think you have done right, my son. That is all that matters."

"No one must know that the bequest comes from me. In some way that I cannot fully explain to you, it has come from my dear Jane."

So, with more talk and much mutual understanding, Mr. Weston forgave his son all. Thus reconciled, father and son now focused on a new future. "Weston wants to stay on a bit with you, father," said Frank. "But with the two girls and Miss Sharpe in the house, I think I had better put him up at the Crown during his stay. Yes, I think that might be better."

"Indeed. We have but two guest rooms at Randalls, and years ago, I converted them to house Anna and the two girls. The Crown is a good idea. You know, I can arrange a dance there, while Weston is with us. The young people would like that. It would be a bit like the old days, don't you think?"

Yes, Frank agreed, remembering how much he had wanted to dance with Jane that night so many years ago. Well, that was all past now. He hoped he had set things right. He thought of telling Emma the real reason for his visit, but in the end, could not. Perhaps his father would tell her. He wanted the Knightleys to know he had made what amends he could.

He recalled his last conversation with Mr. Knightley, who, despite hating secrets, had agreed to keep his. Well, it was clear, one was never done with them. He wondered—though he was far from a spiritual man—if Jane, wherever she was, would know that he had done what she wished. No matter how happy they had been—and they had been very happy together—he knew the old secrets had taken their toll on her.

It was time for him to return to the great estate and all his possessions, which no longer brought him happiness. Hopefully, young Weston would find a different kind of life for himself. He, of course, knew nothing of the past. Frank was glad of that. He had tried to be a good man at Enscombe, far better than when he was under the care of his aunt and uncle. A better father to Weston. An unknown benefactor now to Edith and Anna, if only financially. These amends for his past actions, at least, he hoped, he had accomplished. This last visit to Highbury must remedy all the rest.

CHAPTER 19

The Knightley family was at breakfast the day after the big celebration. Charles was not yet present. He seemed unable to rise before eleven these days, a fact which never ceased to annoy his father who was often the first downstairs. But George, Hetta, and Caroline were there, so he had to be content with the presence of a majority of his progeny.

"Well, dear Emma, I think you did us proud yesterday! I heard nothing but compliments about the decor, the food, and the new vicar's remarks. He seems a modest, unassuming man, and I feel sure we will like him, even upon longer acquaintance," said Mr. Knightley, facing his usual plate of boiled eggs and toast. George, of course, was digging into the ham and kidneys. His father wondered how anyone could eat that much food before noon! He certainly could not. And the eggs were fried. But he had long ago given up recommending Serle's healthier presentations.

"Thank you, my dear. All went well, I agree, despite our various apprehensions," she said, corroborating his opinion. "I gather that young Mr. Weston Churchill will be staying on at Highbury for a few extra days. He is putting up at the Crown, and Mr. Weston is planning a dance evening before he returns to Enscombe."

"Oh, how wonderful," said Hetta. "I did think him a fine-looking young gentleman. So very polite, and interesting, too. Might we have him and the girls over to dinner one of the next nights, Mama?" she asked.

Though it was his wife who had been asked, Mr. Knightley

answered in a voice that had something of an edge to it. "We will have to see, Hetta. I'm sure he will be fully occupied with other things. He is staying on to see his grandfather, not to socialize with us."

Her mother agreed. "We don't want to take his time away from visiting his grandfather, you know."

Hetta politely disagreed. "He told me he was enormously glad to be in the company of young people. There is absolutely no one for him at Enscombe, he said. I'm sure he would accept an invitation if you sent one. You could ask his grandfather Weston too if that's what's bothering you about asking him."

Mr. Knightley felt himself increasingly unable to handle these children of his. And before he could supply some assistance to his wife in these deliberations, his son George spoke out.

"I think it's a great idea, Mama. I'm sure Miss Sharpe and Edith would love to come as well. Might as well make a party of it," he said with a look at his father both watchful and defiant.

Mr. Knightley fumed inwardly. Would he never be finished with the results of that old secret he so long ago reluctantly agreed to keep? "It will be up to your mother, George. She has had quite a bit of work on this big party. She may well need a rest."

Emma said nothing, not wanting to prolong the discussion while the children were present. "Your father and I will think on it, George. For now, he has promised me a walk on the grounds. It is a fine day, and I am in need of a different sort of exercise and some time alone with him. Hetta, I think you need to prepare your lessons. Mrs. Goddard said your teacher is still awaiting your latest essay. And George, do try to rout your brother from bed before all the breakfast things are put away. I'm going to don my best shawl and head outside with your father. How I do love my walks in the garden."

She rose, putting an end to further discussion. She could see her husband's face and knew he needed an outside airing.

He rose, joining her at once. "Your mother is right. We're off," he added, in a voice that put an end to further talk.

They walked out through the garden doors, and she took his arm. "Well, that was a timely escape, wasn't it," she said, looking archly up at him. "I'm getting good at it."

"Good at what?" he asked.

"Getting you away from discussions with your children before you say something you will regret."

"Emma. Am I never to be free of that old secret? I can't imagine why Mr. Churchill left his son here. He's probably already on his way to Randalls to see Mr. Weston, and of course, Edith will be there."

"My dear. We must make ourselves free of it, else we will perpetuate it into the next generation. There must be an end sometime."

"You can't return to what things were before Frank Churchill began this train of events, beginning with his affair with Anna Sharpe. Getting back to Milton, our first parents couldn't return to Eden, you know."

"And you mean to be the angel with the flaming sword guarding the gate?" she asked, with a provoking look.

"I think I should never have let you finish your Milton. You've become a dangerous scholar." He smiled a bit. "But they couldn't go back, you know, angel or no angel, and I am hardly one."

"Yes, but you pointed out to me—making me go on reading that dreadful book—that their lives became better, even after their sin."

"Emma, if you are determined to give in and have a dinner for all of them, so be it."

She could not allow him to win the argument that way. "No. You must agree that it would be for the best. Unfriendly, to be sure, otherwise. And the good thing about dinner parties is that etiquette prevails. No one can say anything untoward. It will be using up an evening during which the young people are prevented from congregating elsewhere without us."

"You always were a good plotter. Very well, invite them all over. I will be a good host, and lead the talk in safe directions. I don't want Hetta getting involved with Weston."

"I thought all his attention at the celebration was for Adelaide Weston. Did you not notice Henry's dark looks?"

"I told you, I won't be involved with my brother's progeny, on top of mine. Poor John has been trying to pry him loose from Hartfield for months now. The boy needs to get going on his law career."

"He's not a boy any longer, my dear. He's nearing thirty, and I suspect he won't leave if he's not ready. But I agree, it's not our problem, though it's interesting to observe." said Emma. "It's time to go back. I need to write a note of invitation to Randalls and start thinking about returning the house to order and deciding on new menus." She gave her husband's arm a strong squeeze. "Will you still kiss me the way you did here, so many years ago now?" she asked, looking up at him in the old inviting way.

"You took the first steps toward me then," he said, softly. "I admit to having been shocked."

"Not for long, I think," she said, drawing him to her. "You answered my unladylike invitation rather quickly."

"Indeed," he said, answering it once again.

"We will have to walk out here more often," she said, replacing her shawl to her shoulders. "It's positively restorative."

When they returned, they found a visitor waiting for them in the drawing-room.

"Mr. Weston," said Mr. Knightley. "How good to see you. But you come very early indeed. Is anything wrong? I hope not."

"No, indeed. Something has, on the contrary, been put right. I wanted to tell the two of you at once."

Emma and her husband sat down on the sofa to listen to Mr. Weston's news. "Yesterday, Frank and I had a good talk. Perhaps the best we have ever had. He told me all about his past, about Anna and Edith. Of course, I forgave him all. It is so long ago now."

Mr. Knightley was about to speak when Mr. Weston stopped him. "I have come here because he told me that both of you, and dear Jane, knew it all, and also forgave, and kept the secret. I have come to thank you for your friendship and care for me."

Emma could see her husband wrestling with this new idea. It was perhaps not quite correct to say that he had forgiven Frank all. Tried to forget, and not to harm further, would be closer to the truth. But fortunately, he remained silent.

"What about Edith and young Weston," he finally said. "Are they to be told as well? And everyone else?"

"No, I think not. It is time to bury the secret forever and go on with life as if it had never happened. Someone the other day used an expression I think pertains here— "It's time to bury the hatchet.""

Mr. Knightley frowned. "Hatchets have edges. Can they ever be buried deep enough?" he demanded.

"We can try," said Emma.

"There. I have finished with all my news. For now, I must get back to Randalls. I have taken the carriage over, as I have left everyone and Weston at the breakfast table." He took Emma's hand. "I thank you so much, my dear Mrs. Knightley. I once hoped you would be Frank's choice. But how much better you choose for yourself. I think women always do. I hope my dear Anna will consider me a worthy choice. Mr. Knightley, I thank you too, knowing how much more difficult all this is has been for you. I have always trusted to your goodness and kindness and wisdom." With that, he made a deep bow to Mr. Knightley, turned, and let himself out.

CHAPTER 20

"What wonderful news!" Adelaide had cried, when Edith told her of the letter outlining the bequests to her and Miss Sharpe. "Imagine! Getting an inheritance from a relative you never knew about! It's like the happy ending of a novel, Father, don't you think? When did you find out? Who told you?" Adelaide was bursting with questions.

Edith gave her the letter. "My aunt has received one too! I can hardly believe this. It is like a novel, you are quite right," she said.

"My dear Adelaide. Quiet yourself down," said Miss Sharpe. "You look as excited as if all this was about yourself!"

"I've always known that I'll have a handsome settlement from father whenever I wish to marry. But now Edith has one too!"

The conversation dominated breakfast at Randalls. Anna said no more. She would talk to Mr. Weston later when they were alone.

Edith went up to her room, wanting to be alone to think. She felt like a princess, just visited by a fairy godmother, but who it was, she could not imagine.

Lacking Edith's company, it wasn't long before Adelaide walked over to Hartfield and relayed the good news to Henry Knightley. Since Hetta was present when she delivered the story with her usual embellishments, the news was quickly received by the other young folk at Donwell Abbey. When George heard of it, he had to see Edith immediately. He decided to take a copy of *Dombey and Son* from his father's library, insert a small note inside, and deliver the package to Randalls for Edith.

When Miss Sharpe came to the door, she told him Edith had not yet come downstairs.

"That's all right," he said. "I've just brought the usual kind of thing for Edith. She's been asking for the next Dickens novel." He handed her the volume, which he had wrapped in brown paper.

Miss Sharpe took the book, thanked him, and went upstairs to Edith.

"Mr. George Knightley has just been here and has brought another book for you, Edith."

"Which one is it, aunt?" she asked.

"I can't tell, for it is wrapped up tightly and sealed. He said it was one very new, perhaps even with the pages not yet cut."

"Thank you. I'll open it carefully, and we'll see which one it is."

"He said it was from your favorite, Dickens," said Anna, curious to see the book.

Just then, there was a commotion downstairs in the kitchen. "I'll be right back, dear," she said, leaving quickly.

Edith took scissors to the wrapping and saw Volume One of *Dombey and Son,* bound in maroon leather, with gold-tipped pages. As she carefully opened it, a small paper fell out to the floor. It was a note, sealed with a wafer. Opening it, she read:

My dear Edith,

I must speak with you today if you can get away. Can you meet me at the stables at Donwell—At two this afternoon? I will be there.

Yours, George

What could it mean? For the second time today, a mysterious communication. First, and most shocking of all, this strange letter telling of a recently received inheritance. Her mother received a bequest as well, but knew nothing more, she said. And now this urgent note from George Knightley. Does he, perhaps, know about the bequest? She pondered it, almost too much to take in at once. Of course, she would try to meet him. She would tell Adelaide and ask her to accompany her this afternoon. She slipped the note under the pillow of her bed. When her aunt returned, she showed her the book, and said nothing of the note, though she was not comfortable with the deception. Nevertheless, when Adelaide was back, she showed her the note and asked for her company on an afternoon walk.

Just a little before two, the girls set out.

"I think it's exciting, Edith," said Adelaide. "I love things like that. George is so romantic! I sometimes wish Henry would send me such a note. But then, what would I do when I met him? I think he likes me, Edith. And I like him too. At least I think so. Do you like George? I think he's very handsome. Like his father, tall and commanding. Edith, answer me."

"I can't just now. I'm too confused about everything. Will you stay with me when we meet him?"

Adelaide bristled, then laughed. "Of course, I shan't. He didn't send a note asking to meet me. I'll just walk on a bit, to that place on the path beyond Donwell, where there's an old stone wall. I can sit there and wait for you."

"I don't like it, Adelaide. I don't think either my aunt or Mr. Knightley would like me meeting him alone like this," said Edith.

"Of course, they wouldn't, you silly goose. That's why you have to do it," replied Adelaide. "Here we are, at the stables, and there is your George, brushing down one of his horses."

"Hello George," sang out Adelaide, watching a slight frown come to his handsome face. "Don't worry. I'm not staying. Just a chaperone for the walk. Didn't want Edith to run into any gypsies!"

The expression on his face relaxed into a smile. "Well, if you do, just give me a shout," he said.

He took Edith's arm and guided her to a place behind the stables where a bench was placed.

"I have only just heard of your good fortune," he began, direct as always, just like his father.

"I too. I hardly know what to make of it. Or what to think."

"Well, when one receives a handsome inheritance, I think the idea is to be grateful. No great thinking involved."

"Yes, if I only knew more about where it comes from. I have told you, my aunt never talks to me about my parentage, and now, it seems, there was considerable wealth there. Do you think it could have come from ill-gotten gains?" she asked.

"What a question. Of course not. Are you thinking of Oliver Twist's discovery? That's fiction, my girl."

"Then why am I told nothing about the people who possessed the wealth? There was also a considerable bequest to my aunt. It's all so mysterious. "

"Life is mysterious, dear Edith. Maybe even more than our

novels. I can think of several reasons why such a bequest was delayed. There might have been a stipulation as to your age. Perhaps Miss Sharpe's is for gratitude for rearing you when her sister died. You could ask Henry. He knows a lot about wills and such. What I want to talk about is how it removes at least one of the objections you made to my making a proposal of marriage. You are no longer a portionless girl. Indeed, you are rich. Or perhaps you wish to seek a husband with rank? A penniless duke or viscount?"

"George. Do not talk like that. This inheritance will make no difference of that kind to me."

"So, you will accept me?"

"Have you spoken to your father?"

"No, of course not. There hasn't been time. The celebration was but yesterday. If he agrees, will you accept me?"

She looked up at him, transfixed by his startlingly blue eyes, hard and shining upon her. Then, before she could say anything or think otherwise, he took her in his arms and kissed her.

"There. That's how I feel about you." He stood back and looked at her with a penetrating glance. "And do you deny you returned my kiss?"

She stepped back from him further and was silent, quite overcome by emotion and the excitement of the day. "How could I not?" she said, her cheeks reddening. "But you must talk to Mr. Knightley before I can accept you. Let's go find Adelaide," she said. "It's time for me to go back, I think." He pressed her hand reassuringly and kissed it.

"That's better," she said softly. "Much better, at least for now."

CHAPTER 21

The Reverend Rufus Brewer had settled into the vicarage. It was a little prettified, he thought, for a vicarage. But he did like the yellow curtains.

He had long been a widower and was glad to have arrived in a congenial place where his son and daughter might have the enjoyment of some pleasant young company. What a surprise it had been when Anna Sharpe came to see him soon after he arrived in Highbury, and now yesterday, Mr. Churchill. He had often spoken in his sermons of the coincidences of life, wondering whether or not they were part of some larger divine plan. No way to know, of course. But he always thought so. Of course, one needed faith to be sure, but he always had that. Yet even he found this convergence of paths truly remarkable.

Anna Sharpe wanted to see him before the grand celebration at Donwell Abbey. He was glad to learn she had so happily situated herself here in the community of Highbury. Yet as she spoke, he saw she still carried her troubles with her, especially after she told him the details of her situation at Randalls.

"You see, Revered Brewer, I have managed to make a home for myself here, and do good work, taking care of Mr. Weston's daughter and my own Edith. But it cannot go on much further. Mr. Weston has made me an offer of marriage, and though I do have feelings for him, I cannot accept. Consider my past, which you well know."

The vicar was for a moment silent. How hard was sin, he thought. One never got quite rid of it, though he was also sure one must get past it, if possible. All this was so long ago. His heart ached for her. "Indeed, I do know, my dear Miss Sharpe. But for every fault, there is forgiveness, especially when it has been so richly earned as in your case. Have you ever contemplated telling the truth to your Mr. Weston? You say he is a kind and good man. Perhaps you need to give him the chance to know all that has been kept from him so many years now. You may be surprised by his generosity in this matter, as in so many other ways, as you have told me." He told her to come again for a talk. He wished he could help, but he had come so recently to Highbury and knew nothing more of Mr. Weston than what she had told him.

For her part, Anna had left her meeting with Reverend Brewer more confused and uncertain than before. Then had come this surprising bequest. An unwelcome thought followed. Had it come from Frank, who wanted to make amends to Edith and her? That would make her angry. No. He was not that sort of man. Thinking further, she reasoned that the gift made it possible for her to leave Randalls on her own terms, to start a boarding school elsewhere, to live, at long last, as an independent woman. Mr. Weston need never know the whole story. With this money, she could depart from Randalls and leave him to continue to love and think the world of his erring son. Of course, he would again be alone. She was sorry for that. She did have feelings for him. But it was all too complicated for any simple resolution.

At the celebration for the vicar, she feared Frank would approach her or Edith, but he had not. At least he had that much decency, she thought. But then, the next day, news of the bequests threw her again into turmoil.

But she had made up her mind. She would tell Mr. Weston she was leaving. That must be done. She hoped Mrs. Goddard could recommend a likely location where she might advertise a boarding school for young ladies. Then, the lawyer's letter had been delivered at Randalls. She went to find Mr. Weston.

"I have received a letter with rather astonishing news. Do you know anything of this," she said, handing him the letter.

"Well. Very good news, indeed," he said.

"I don't think I have any wealthy relatives," she said. "I cannot fathom it."

"Good news for Edith, surely. Now she may look around her for an eligible marriage someday. And you? What plans do you have for your inheritance?"

"I can hardly think," she said. She saw that the money gave her the chance to leave Highbury altogether and start a school of her own. It was time to tell Mr. Weston that she planned to leave his employ. But when she started, Mr. Weston stopped her.

"My dear Anna," he said. "I believe it is time to renew my offer of marriage to you. Now, before you speak, I must tell you that Frank has made me aware of everything. Your brief time with him, the parentage of Edith. Before you say anything I must tell you none of that means anything to me. I already love young Edith, as though she were my own—and now, in a sense, I have found that she is. If you have refused me because you feared my learning all this—well, I have, and it makes no difference to me. I still want you to be my wife. Now, say nothing at this moment. You have much to think about. I will say no more, other than, I await your answer with renewed hope." He stopped, took hold of her hand, kissed it, and rose to leave the room.

"You are all kindness and goodness," she began to say. "But you cannot marry me knowing—"

He interrupted her. "No more just now. Think on all this—and give me your answer when you are ready, if you can. Meanwhile, I am going out for a walk." He bowed and was gone.

Anna sat down to think. Even if she accepted him, there was something that would still be unresolved. She had not been unaware of the growing attachment between Edith and George Knightley. Now that Edith had a fortune, there might have been hope, though she was sure money would not have meant anything to the Knightleys. No. Her new fortune would make no difference. Edith was still illegitimate and Frank's daughter. It would be better the sooner she got Edith safely away from Highbury. She owed that much to Mr. Knightley. Now, this visit of Frank's son was making things more difficult. They had received an invitation for dinner at Donwell, and Mr. Weston had arranged for supper and dance at the Crown to introduce young Weston to the community. The young people were invited to everything. She would have to go through these further obstacles before any removal was possible. She did not look forward to the stay of Weston Churchill. She must wait until he left before she told Mr. Weston of her decision. How she would get through it all, she did not know. But get through it, she must.

Just then, the door opened, and the two girls returned from their walk. She gave a concerned look at Edith, who seemed flushed.

"Are all right, Edith?" she asked. "Where have you and Adelaide been walking? I hope not too far," she said.

"Oh no, Miss Sharpe," answered Adelaide. "She's fine. Just a bit out of breath, I think. There's a wind coming up, and we were walking right into it."

"Did you have a look at the book Mr. George Knightley sent over for you? What was it?" asked Anna.

"Another Dickens novel," she said. "I had only time to read the first chapter. It starts off rather sadly, I think, with the death of a mother after bearing a child. I don't like it much," she said. "I think I'll ask him to make a better choice. Actually, I am a bit winded by our walk. I think I'll lie down for a bit."

"Me too, Miss Sharpe, if you don't mind. No more lessons or reading for today, for either of us, I think."

On their way back, Edith had told her what happened in her meeting. As usual, Adelaide was all enthusiasm, even while she suspected George would have hard work ahead with his father.

Once in Adelaide's room, their talk together continued. "And he actually kissed you? How thrilling! I haven't been kissed yet. Did you like it?"

Edith continued red-faced. "Adelaide! How can you ask me that?"

"Well, did you? I want to know. I'm actually thinking about kissing Henry one of these days. Though I think Weston is very nice too."

"Stop talking like a flirt! You know you don't mean it," said Edith.

"Don't I? I'm not sure. Henry is older, though, and may make a fuss if I tried it. I do like him though. Every time we quarrel, he takes my hand, presses it, and says, 'Let's be friends.' Next time I may surprise him and tell him only a kiss will heal the wound."

Edith could not help laughing. "You're just trying to cheer me up, I know. You'd never do anything like that."

"Well, you didn't ask George to kiss you, or even give your permission, did you? Why can't a girl start such things up? I think men have much the better of it in these matters." An irrepressible twinkle sparkled in her eyes. "I may try it. Wait and see if I don't. If you won't tell me what it's like, I will just have to experiment myself."

CHAPTER 22

Why is the time for action never right? George Knightley left Edith yesterday after kissing her. He had done it, almost without thinking. He was sure she returned his feelings. It was time to tell his father his intentions. He would do so the next morning. His father was always at his best early. Then, when he had just finished his breakfast and was about to ask his father to see him alone for a few minutes, his mother ruined his plan.

"Glad to see you all at the table this morning," she said. "Even Charles. I have an announcement: we are hosting dinner for all the Westons and John Knightleys this evening. Because young Weston is staying only a week, we must move quickly. Mr. Weston has already arranged an evening for dancing and supper at the Crown the following night. So you see, we must be busy!" She looked around the table. The girls were delighted, she could see, though Charles, as usual, seemed still half asleep. It was George whose reaction was strange. One would have thought he'd be delighted with the chance to see Edith Sharpe on two consecutive days. And without plotting to deliver books to her! Instead, he did not look pleased. She knew him well enough to see that. She mused. Perhaps he and Edith had quarreled. Maybe that was all over. Her husband's face was inscrutable. Well, nothing for it but to start getting the house and menu ready.

The rest of the day was filled with domestic activity. Emma started drawing up the menu with three courses. Soup would be placed on the four corners of the table, ready for serving, the entrees in lines along the sides. "Our guests can select their food from the dishes nearest to them, though passing will also work. The second course will be just a goose, with French beans, asparagus, and then, a basket of pastries for dessert. All very simple. Of course, we must also have some savories and sauces. We'll use our best linen, crystal, china, and silverware."

"Emma. This is sounding altogether a bit grand," said Mr. Knightley with a smile.

Ignoring this, she went on. "We will eat early, at five or six, so that we can have a little visiting after. Or perhaps some music. Oh dear, I fear I have let my piano-playing languish. But Hetta, you have been taking lessons. We'll have a little music. We'll need the piano repositioned. I fear it has been relegated to a corner. I'll alert the Westons so that perhaps Adelaide or Edith can perform a song. For drinks, we will have wine—Madeira or Burgundy should do. We'll have a punch for the young ones or lemonade. Orgeat is also a refreshing drink."

How on earth could he tell his father what was on his mind in the midst of all this annoying menu-planning? He must wait, though he was somewhat apprehensive about seeing Edith for the first time since he had so boldly taken her in his arms and kissed her. Well, there was nothing for it at present. He went with his brother to see to furniture rearrangement and the other preparations not left to the servants.

The rest of the day passed quickly. An hour before their guests' arrival, the family went upstairs to dress for dinner. Frock coats for the men of the family, boots well-polished, neckcloths carefully tied. George was always a bit careless about his cravat, which to be perfectly tied required both patience and considerable skill. Usually, he did not bother, though tonight he made it right. The women donned their best lawn and muslin dresses, and some jewelry. All was in readiness when family and friends arrived promptly at five.

They were a large group: Emma, Mr. Knightley, George, Charles, and Hetta, John, Isabella, Henry, William, Mr. Weston, Miss Sharpe, Adelaide and Edith, and Weston. Although the table usually sat twelve at the most, with some ingenious place-setting, fourteen were accommodated. The younger children were served at Hartfield, attended by the servants there.

At dinner, the conversation began slowly at first. Mr. Knightley and Emma sat at the two heads of the table, and the others filled in around. The Knightleys had devised no seating plan, preferring to let their guests seat themselves as they wished. As it turned out, the family groups took seats together.

George tried several times to catch Edith's eye, but unsuccessfully. Mr. Weston was uncharacteristically quiet, as was Anna Sharpe. Emma made a start. "Weston, it is good to meet you after all these years. How do you like Highbury? I fear it is a much smaller community than the one to which you are accustomed in Enscombe."

"Not at all, Mrs. Knightley. It's only my father and me at Enscombe. We have little to do with our nearest neighbors. And I have been away at school quite a bit, so it is pleasant for me to enjoy the company of ladies my own age." He smiled over at Hetta, who smiled back, bringing a pang of pain to Mr. Knightley. How he wished he could be anywhere but at this table!

"You'll enjoy the dance, then, Mr. Churchill," said Adelaide. "We will too since it has been a long time since we've had something like that at Highbury. Do you like to dance?" she asked, smiling brightly.

"Well, I know how to dance, though I have never thought of it as an enjoyable activity," he answered. "More like a chore, remembering all the steps and bows and such."

"I'm not a fan of it either," offered John Knightley. "Seems a waste of time, when one could be out walking or riding."

"Do you like dancing, Edith?" asked George. He was determined to have her look at him.

She looked up. "I suppose I do," she said. "Learning the steps is part of the curriculum at Mrs. Goddard's."

"Indeed, dancing, sketching, the ability to play an instrument are essential skills for young ladies," said Isabella. "Dancing is so popular because it is one of the few social activities in which men and women can participate together."

"But the steps are quite intricate," offered Hetta. "Will there be waltzes tomorrow night, Mr. Weston?"

"I'm sure there will be. Along with the quadrille, of course."

Mr. Knightley remembered that dance at the Crown with Emma, two lines, facing each other, when he had first realized his feelings for her. Magical, it had been.

"In London, there are places which provide directions for the correct execution of the various figures and changes," said Isabella.

"We won't need that at the Crown," laughed Mr. Weston. "We will all have to take our chances." He glanced at Miss Sharpe, who, like Edith, had been almost silent throughout.

"We can practice tomorrow morning," said Hetta. "Caroline can play for us."

"I don't think we should have waltzes," said John Knightley. "They are too intimate and strenuous for our young ladies."

"I will see what our musicians plan to offer," said Mr. Weston. "But I think our young ladies will be up to anything."

Mr. Knightley was torn away from his own pleasant recollections to the dangers of tomorrow night. Mr. Weston is a good man, he was sure, but entirely too accommodating. A good thing, in some cases, he conceded to himself, but not in others. Emma was looking across the long table at him, smiling with a look that told him all would be well. But would it?

The dinner party broke up early. Though Emma asked Hetta to sing a piece, and she did, there were no others who offered. Weston Churchill paid her a compliment—"The best song I ever heard!"— and then the coats and carriages were called for. Mr. Knightley gave a sigh of relief. But the dangers were not over. There was still Mr. Weston's dance party tomorrow. As they climbed the stairs to their rooms, Emma tried to cheer her husband away from his worries. "Are you going to tell me you will not dance and are not good at it?" she asked, mischievously.

"I was thinking of it," he said, taking her hand. "Must I dance?" he asked.

"You must," she said. "And then we will see what comes of it all." She continued. "Since, as I told you so long ago, you dance better than anybody. We must dance. If you will ask me," she said, drawing close to him.

As the old memories flooded back, he felt himself weakened. "Will you dance, dear Emma," he said, leading her to their bedroom.

CHAPTER 23

At Randalls the next day, everyone anticipated the evening's entertainment at the Crown. Breakfast passed quickly, amid servings of chocolate, coffee and tea, hot rolls, and bread and butter. As soon as they finished, the girls eagerly excused themselves, wanting to go upstairs to examine their wardrobes. Adelaide reviewed her dresses, selecting one, deciding whether or not it needed new or extra ribbons or a silk sash. Edith was quieter, wondering if George had spoken to his father and if he had, how she would face him and his parents at the dance. Even though she was now an heiress with 20,000 pounds, that circumstance was not foremost in her thoughts. Mr. Weston informed his grandson Weston, who had joined them, that they would not meet again until evening, as the ladies had much to do to make themselves ready.

With the young people all gone from the table, Anna Sharpe and Mr. Weston remained alone. At first, they continued the conversational topics begun at breakfast. But finally, both fell silent. As Miss Sharpe rose to leave, Mr. Weston began to speak.

"Please stay a while, my dear Anna. May I ask if you have had sufficient time to consider my renewed proposal—or will you want still more time? I will do whatever you wish, of course. It's only that I have been thinking about this for quite a while now, so need no further time myself to consider—or reconsider, as the case may be."

"Indeed," she replied. "Reconsider is the word, I think. Now that you know all, now that Frank has told you everything, surely you must reconsider your offer. You are quite right that my initial refusal to you sprang from a desire to keep these old secrets buried, and to leave you to your life here, and with Frank and Weston at Enscombe. I am sorry you have had to know it all. I am sure that upon careful consideration, you will not wish to renew your offer. And I assure you, I understand it all." She sat with her eyes averted from him, her hands folded tightly in her lap.

He, on the other hand, continued to look directly at her. "Of course, I realize there are issues that need to be considered. At present, none of the younger generation know anything of this past. And I ask you, why should they? Why should their young lives be burdened by old actions, now almost forgotten, now certainly all forgiven? I do not wish such to be their inheritance." Then, displaying more emotion than he had yet shown, he added, "I forbid it!" Quickly, bringing a hand across his temple, as if to erase his outburst, he became his old self, smiling apologetically. "Forgive me, dear Anna. I did not mean to speak so sharply. But I have been through so many sad moments in my life. The death of my first wife was a terrible blow, though I admit our marriage had been a troubled one. My abandonment of young Frank to my wife's sister was a terrible mistake and a great loss. Then after finding happiness with my dear Anne, she left me so quickly I was almost dazed. Whatever new happiness I have been able to find, after all these losses, has been with my dear Adelaide, and with you and Edith. I hope you are not going to take that happiness away with you." He paused. "I am finished now. I await only your answer." He looked at her with a pleading expression.

"I hardly know what to say," she began. "You have been so very good and kind to me. Unlike what I have ever experienced at the hands of anyone. I have been very happy here at Randalls. I am ever indebted to the Knightleys and Jane Fairfax, before she married Frank. To you, most of all. I love Adelaide as you do, and of course, my dear Edith. It will be very hard for me to leave you, and Adelaide." She stopped, struggling with herself, he saw. "But if you think it possible to go forward, ignoring the sins of the past, I will try. I cannot promise that I can ever completely put all of it behind me. Keeping her true parentage from Edith will always be my burden. You see, she will never call me mother. But, I suppose, I gave that up long ago. Still, if you wish to do this—for me—I will embark on this new journey in your company. Yes, I accept your proposal."

No more needed to be said. She gave her hand to Mr. Weston and he kissed it. "Then come, let us tell the girls," he said, smiling. "They must be the first to know."

And so, all was settled. The only question was whether they would make their engagement known that very night, at the supper-party at the Crown.

Afterwards, when Adelaide and Edith had kissed both Mr. Weston and Miss Sharpe and said how happy they were, they returned their rooms. When the girls were alone again, Adelaide as usual, bubbled over with excitement at the news. "Imagine that! Did you ever suspect?" she asked. "I confess I did. I saw it coming. I can't believe you saw nothing. Well, you know, I'm good at that sort of thing. I can always tell about people, how they feel about each other. I knew you and George would be a match, long before you did. Now that he's kissed you like that, it's settled, isn't it?"

"Adelaide. Of course, it's not settled. Stop talking like that."

"Of course, it must be. You now have a big marriage settlement to offer. You're almost an heiress!"

"That will mean nothing to the Knightleys. They're not that sort of people. I'm still rather a nobody, when it comes to it. I'm sure they want something more for the woman who will become the mistress of Donwell Abbey."

Adelaide laughed, an irrepressible twinkle in her eyes. "It will be what George Knightley wants, mark my word. Don't you think he's just the image of his father? Can you imagine anyone talking Mr. Knightley out of anything he wanted to do? I can't. Oh, I hope George will have talked to his father before tonight's party."

"He won't, I assure you," said Edith. "I know him better than that. He will wait until all the visiting and partying is over before he does. Oh, I do wish we didn't have to go tonight."

"Don't be ridiculous. The big news will be about my father and your aunt. I hope they tell everyone tonight. That will be the greatest!"

Edith spoke no more on the subject. She would know, with one look at George and his father, whether her prospective lover had raised the subject, and, even more, what Mr. Knightley's reaction had been. She would know if it had been a negative response. If so, she knew not how she would get through the evening. She thought she would know, when she saw him tonight.

CHAPTER 24

Once again, the Crown Inn blazed with light, torches set afire outside, and inside, candles everywhere. Flowers festooned the mantelpiece above a bright fire in the large room, and in the gallery overlooking the dance floor, three musicians were tuning up—a fiddler, a flutist, and a drummer. Benches had been set around the room. In the side parlor, supper would be laid out in the interval between dances. Mr. Weston had spared no expense. Soon after five o'clock, the guests started to drift in, with many exclamations of delight at the decorations. "Magical," said Mrs. Cole. "A fairyland indeed," said Emma, entering on the arm of her husband. "Almost just as it looked years ago." She was smiling broadly, her husband bowing to Mr. Weston. Soon the room was full of noise and chatter, as Mr. Weston called for quiet. "Before we begin dancing, Miss Sharpe and I have an announcement to make. She has agreed to become my wife." There was more noise, applause, smiles all around. "We will lead the first dance. I've asked our musicians to play some of the tunes that were last heard here so many years ago. They will begin with *Ship's Cook.*"

Couples took their places on the floor, Mr. Weston and Anna Sharpe at the head. Emma pulled Mr. Knightley out to the floor, and others began to form a line ready to begin. The young people stood around the edges, waiting for the gentlemen to choose their partners. Young Weston went over to Adelaide and she curtsied, joining him in the line of dancers. Henry Knightley watched from the sidelines, his face expressionless until he strode over to Hetta and took her hand. George tried to catch Edith's eye, and when he could not, walked to her side, and led her onto the floor. Others joined in, and the music began.

There was little opportunity for conversation, for it was a lively dance, one with intricate steps, requiring concentration. These were dancers who had not had practice in a long while. Edith looked once or twice into her partner's eyes but could discern nothing. Why did he not signal something to her! She could not imagine what he was thinking!

The dancing went on, with partners mixing in other configurations. George did not come near her again. Adelaide was asked for a dance by Henry Knightley, and Hetta danced with Weston. Charles mixed with some of the older girls from Mrs. Goddard's, and the son and daughter of the Reverend Brewer danced with some of the older Perrys.

Finally, it was time for the supper break. Food was laid out on tables, cold meats and fruits, and pastries. Still, George did not come near Edith. She was nearly ready to faint with dread of what could have happened. Adelaide came to her.

"What is wrong with you?" she asked quietly. "You look positively ill. Has George said something to you?"

"No. He has said nothing. That's just it. I don't know how to behave, what to think. I wish I could just disappear!"

"Well, you can't. So, you can't look and act like that! Eat something, and perk yourself up. He may not have spoken to his father yet and wishes to be cautious."

"I don't know. He might have just given me a sentence during our dance."

"Here he comes. I'm going to leave you," said Adelaide, with a smile.

George approached Edith and looked at her with those penetrating eyes. "Are you enjoying the dance?" he asked.

What can he be thinking? Enjoy the dance? "George, tell me if you have spoken to your father."

He smiled at her. "Let's just say that the discussion has begun. One never has a brief discussion with father on important matters. I've made a start. Now, stop looking as if I'm about to murder you! The music is starting up again. A gentleman is permitted two dances with a lady if she will accept him. It's a waltz. I was waiting for that.

At last, I don't have to move in a line but can actually hold you by the waist. Come. Let's go. And please, don't look as if you're going to faint in my arms. That would cause a scandal, to be sure." He smiled at her and led her out to the floor.

The other young people joined in. Then, when the music began again, Weston Churchill offered his hand to Edith.

"But you look a bit tired," he said. "I think that waltz wore you out. Perhaps you'd rather sit this one out. We could have a chat instead."

Edith was relieved. "That would be fine. I think it's become a bit hot in here."

"Indeed," He led her to one of the side benches. "I'm so glad to meet you. After all, you must know my grandfather much better than I do. Do you like living at Randalls?" he asked. "Don't you find it a bit quiet here in Highbury?"

"Oh, not at all. I like quiet, actually. And Mr. Weston is so very kind and obliging. Sometimes I forget that I'm not his daughter, like Adelaide, for he treats us just the same," she said, her soft eyes lighting up as she spoke.

"Adelaide's quite a hornet, isn't she?" asked Weston. "Quite full of spunk. How do you get on with her?"

Edith smiled. "Oh, Addy's a grand girl. She's never at a loss for things to do, though sometimes she says the most shocking things. But just in fun, of course."

"I've noticed that," he said with a grin. "I like it. I should like to know you both better, but here comes George Knightley who looks to claim you again for the next dance. I'll call on you tomorrow," he said, rising with a bow to both. "I'm going to dance with Adelaide for the next!"

It seemed as though only the younger generation was going to attempt the waltz. That's when Emma pulled Mr. Knightley into the dance.

"Come, my dear. We mustn't let these young people have the whole room to themselves for the waltz. I know you can dance it."

"How do you know, Emma?" asked Mr. Knightley, taking her hand.

"Because. As I told you, you dance better than anyone," she said smiling. "Come. Now's not the time to think about problems. It's time to dance." She knew he had been watching the tête-à-tête between Weston and Edith.

He followed her, obeying her wishes, as he always had. His brief talk with George, before leaving, had unsettled him. He was so much a man used to getting what he wanted, that these independent-minded children were a trouble to him. Emma said that George was just like him. Yes, that was the problem. Knowing that, made it more difficult. He supposed, that even if George were to know the truth about Edith's parentage and status, it would not deter him. It was hard to think about all this while waltzing with Emma. Holding her, looking into her large eyes, considering her beauty and love for him made it almost impossible to consider his parental problems. Holding her close brought him back to that first dance with her. He wondered. Did George feel this kind of thing about the girl he was whirling about the floor just now? And if he did, could he stop his son in his desires?

"Mr. Knightley! You almost stepped on my foot," said Emma. "And these, my best blue leather shoes. My best! Stop thinking about George or Edith. I know you are. Look at me, instead," she said, an irrepressible twinkle in her eyes.

He faced her and held her a bit more tightly. "I am thinking of you just now," he said, finishing the dance in good style.

"That's better," she said. "Tomorrow is another day. Let's enjoy this evening."

"And there's Hetta, going around with Weston Churchill. I think he's asked her twice. It's almost too much for me to bear, Emma."

"You will bear it, my dear. I will too. Isn't it great news about Mr. Weston and Miss Sharpe," she said.

"Yes, I suppose it is. But tonight, I'm afraid, I feel the presence of Frank Churchill all around me."

"He's gone back to Enscombe. He's not here any longer. You must forget about him, my dear. More important, you must learn to forgive him, and stop imagining him present in his children. They will be different. Even as our children will be different from us. If you could only remember that. We are not copies of our parents. A little, perhaps, but not all."

"I will obey you," he said.

"If only you could. But at least do try. You will have time for a good talk with George tomorrow. He's just bringing Edith back to the benches now. Do you see how he looks at her? How do you plan to stop that, my dear? Do you really want to?"

He went back into the supper-room. He thought he did want to stop it. But could he?

CHAPTER 25

Not long after the celebration for the vicar and Frank Churchill's return to Enscombe, he fell suddenly ill with a nagging fever. A doctor was summoned, and though the ailment remained undiagnosed, he was told to keep to his bed for a few days. Clearly, he had caught a cold during a walk in the rain, and his throat was very sore, the membranes inflamed and almost closed. The next day, the doctor came again, found his patient shivering from chills, his throat much worse, and his breathing difficult. Leeches were applied, and his servants, alarmed, sent word to Highbury that Weston should return at once. His condition worsened rapidly. By the time Weston returned, his father was failing and almost unable to speak. All he could say was, "I am not afraid; I am going to join your dear mother," leaving his son and all his vast wealth and properties in Enscombe.

The news was sent to Highbury, greeted by all with shocked surprise. Mr. Frank Churchill, after all, was not an old man, somewhere in his mid-forties. Yet those who recalled his demeanor at the Donwell celebration for the vicar spoke of how he had looked aged and not quite himself. Emma thought her own husband, at least ten years older than Frank, looked younger and far more fit. Well, she had thought, that's what years of happiness will do for you. Frank had been grieving after Jane's death. But what of Weston now? Surely so young a man would find it lonely to stay at Enscombe. She hardly dared suggest inviting him to Donwell. But she was sure Mr. Weston would do something. He would not leave his grandson alone during his time of grief.

When Mr. Weston received the news, he was once again stricken with grief and regret. He went back again, in his mind, about the decision to permit his wife's sister to rear his son. "And I lost all those years with him," he said to Anna. "And just now, when he finally had spoken the truth to me, and we became completely reconciled, he is gone. It is almost too hard." He turned to her. "It means everything to me now, that you will stay with me, even though we must put off our own wedding for a bit," he said. "I must leave for Enscombe immediately to be with Weston for the funeral and burial services. Thank goodness you will be here with the girls. But after that, I must bring him back here. It's too much for him to be alone at this time. When I return, dear Anna, we will go ahead with our wedding plans. If you move from the rooms you shared with Edith into my chamber, we could have a room prepared for Weston. That is, if you are in agreement with me."

"I will do as you wish," she said. "Of course, you must go to Enscombe. Meanwhile, I and the girls will arrange things to accommodate Weston, if he wishes to come here." She felt more hesitation than did Mr. Weston. The old secret was rearing its head once again. Weston and Edith were half-brother and sister. Fortunately, he had shown no particular interest in her. Anna was sure the girl had already given her heart to George Knightley. Although Mr. Weston believed it was possible to put all the past behind them, she continued to bear it in her deepest heart and thoughts. It would be best if Weston were to come to Highbury, that he set up for himself nearby, she was sure. Since he could afford almost anything, she immediately set about inquiring about small properties in the neighborhood. She knew of two within a mile of Randalls which, she thought, might be suitable.

The next morning, as Mr. Weston was ready to leave, she stopped him. "My dear Mr. Weston. I have been thinking that it would, perhaps be best for Weston to have a place of his own. While you are away, the girls and I will look around and see what is available. I do think it would be better, do you not, all things considered, that he set up on his own, near you, of course, but not at Randalls. I hope you will not think me too interfering. If you disagree, remember, you can still change your mind about our relationship, and then, my suite would be available to him." This was all still so recent and raw, she hardly knew how to face it all.

"My dear, of course, you are right. Do find something for him, and I will discuss it with him, as soon as he is ready. You do always know what is best to do," he said, holding her hands tightly. "And I am not changing my mind about our plans. They might just have to be somewhat delayed. Dear Anna, the horses are ready and I must be off. I will be back as soon as possible and right." He donned his greatcoat and hat and left her to meditate on all that had happened. As soon as Mr. Weston left, she rode out to review the properties, taking the girls with her, as they would help her decide.

At Donwell, the news was received like a bolt out of the blue, so unprepared had they all been for such tidings. Of course, the young hardly knew him, but for Emma and Knightley, Frank's sudden death was totally improbable, dropped on them from out of nowhere, without any warning, except for how old he had looked at their party.

"Don't you think it's almost as if he had had a prevision? I mean, don't you think," said Emma, "that he must have been behind those bequests to Edith and Miss Sharpe? He had a presentiment, a premonition of some kind."

"Emma, please do not invent some fantasy about the bequests. If he did it, what prompted him was guilt, of course, old guilt. That he chose this moment, just before his own death, does not make him clairvoyant."

She was silent. Whatever he said, she had her thoughts and could not rid herself of them.

"Is it so unlike his purchasing that expensive piano for Jane, and keeping everyone guessing as to who had sent it?" said Mr. Knightley. "He always was a man for secrets. If he did give the money, I suppose it was his way of making amends for his past actions. Though true amends can never be made merely with money."

"Well, let us change the subject for a moment," said Emma. "Has George approached you regarding Edith?"

"No. I suspect he wants to marry her. I don't think he would marry her without my approval, however. And so, dear Emma, we are at a bit of a standstill. A standoff, might be more appropriate. The matter will require further consideration and talk. I still hope he will choose a different kind of alliance." he concluded. "Yet I can't help feeling that he is managing me, in some way. Ambushing me, almost. But he will not come upon me again from an unexpected quarter. I

265

will be ready for our future encounters."

"You make it sound like some kind of duel," she said, her always enchanting eyes upon him. Why could he never get used to them, he wondered.

"Don't look at me like that. It's not a duel. We must talk it over before a final decision is taken."

"He has all your charm, you know, my dear," she warned. "Remember how you overwhelmed my dear father. He was all against our marriage too, if you recall. Even after you disarmed him by moving in with us at Hartfield. Yet before long, I thought he was preferring your company to mine. Your brother remarked on it at that first difficult dinner, after we had returned from our honeymoon. 'Such a charmer,' he called you, watching you lead my father upstairs to his bed. Well, George takes after you. Better watch out, especially if he starts taking your arm to assist you onto your horse or coach." She smiled teasingly.

"I can still mount old Bessie on my own," he said, smiling back at her. "And should I need help climbing into my coach, James will be at hand. Now that you've warned me, I'll be on my guard," he said, giving her hand a kiss.

CHAPTER 26

John Knightley had never been much of a horseman, even in his youth, leaving that kind of outdoor activity to his older brother. He spent the fourteen years of his young manhood in law studies at Oxford, and after that worked in law offices in the city, becoming very much a London man. So it was, that entering upon his residence at Hartfield, after Emma's marriage to his brother and eventual move to Donwell, he had not kept stables at the Hartfield residence. Horses required much maintenance. Apart from food, water, grooming, stabling, harness, and veterinary care, they needed to be properly shod. He was not sufficiently interested to embark upon these tasks. When his oldest son Henry wanted to ride, it was his custom to go up to the Donwell stables, where he cared for his own mount.

Henry was still living with his family at Hartfield, much to his father's distress. It was high time, his father told him on many recent occasions, for him to move to London and get his career started in one of the many law offices there. But Henry continued to linger, going up to the city several days a week, where he had procured a part-time position in the chambers of Dodson and Grimsbury. It had been enough to content his father for a while, but Henry was cognizant of the fact that such an arrangement could be only temporary. He was, truth to be told, not quite comfortable in the legal profession, trained in it, though he had been. He was not naturally argumentative by nature and had been thinking, recently, of investigating some other career, perhaps in the Post Office, which was recently expanding and developing its focus to include the requirement for many of its employees to travel abroad. Travel was something Henry thought he might enjoy but hesitated to bring this idea out in the open as yet, though he had arranged a few interviews for himself, about which no one knew. After all, his legal training had come at considerable expense to his father, and he was sure a change in career would not meet with joyful approval. And he was as yet himself unsure.

It was with such thoughts that he decided to walk over to Donwell to take a ride on his horse. It was a fine day, and he longed for exercise, for a way to clear his thoughts. When he arrived, he found his cousin George also mounting up for a morning ride. Though there was a difference of some six or seven years in age between them, they had always gotten along well, two oldest sons in families headed by strong fathers who were brothers and mothers who were sisters. Invited to join him, Henry willingly agreed, and the two headed out across the fields, and into the surrounding forest lands and paths for a pleasant morning's canter. The roads around Highbury were often uneven and sometimes treacherous, but in the vicinity of Donwell, Mr. Knightley kept them in good condition.

After a good long ride, the two young men pulled up in an open field, dismounted, tied their mounts to a nearby tree, and sat down to take some breath. Before too long, the subject of last night's dance and party arose.

"The Crown looked quite capital, didn't you think," began George. "And imagine, Mr. Weston and Miss Sharpe making a marriage of it after her years of governessing."

"Yes, indeed. Adelaide always seems to have liked her, though she wasn't always the most serious pupil," said Henry. "She has told me she has merited quite a few scoldings, but, you know, Adelaide never minds that. I know that from my own experience."

"Have you often scolded her?" asked George, somewhat taken aback by Henry's words.

"Often, I admit. She is a most annoying girl, sometimes. Often quite puts me out of temper, I admit."

"About what?" inquired George, still curious. "You are certainly not her tutor. And from what I have noticed, she's not much of a reader. Is it her conduct about which you have scolded her?"

"Perhaps I should have chosen a better word. I have had to

correct her, from time to time, about her behavior. She is quite irrepressible, you know, and says all kinds of things one never expects to hear from the mouth of a young lady."

"Do you mean—excuse me—vulgarities?"

"Oh no. Quite the opposite. But she does have a temper and a ready tongue. I sometimes tell her, resorting to slang, that she should keep her tongue between her teeth. She says just exactly what she thinks, though it is often what one would never have expected in polite conversation." He paused. "But to tell the truth, I have come to rather like it. She's never dull, you know. Never boring. She quite picks one up, you know."

"Do you like her? I mean, you know, like her in more than only a friendly way?"

Henry gave pause. "I hardly know how I feel about her. One day I am angry with her, the next something she says or does is the pleasantest thing in my day."

"Well," said George. "I don't mean to presume to give you advice, as you are my senior in years. But there is one way to find out, you know."

Henry eyed him. Here he was, getting tutelage about his deepest and most unresolved feelings from his young cousin. "Are you about to instruct me, cousin," he asked, with a grin.

"Well, I think even one kiss would tell you how you both feel. Of course, you'd have to find the right moment, and that's never easy in the Highbury world, is it? We are either out for walks with a crowd of people, or at a party having a picnic or picking strawberries up at Donwell in a crowd when it's the season. Even when you're dancing with a girl and holding her tight, there's a bunch of nosy bodies around you, watching from the sidelines. I admit, it will be hard. But if you put your mind to it, you can arrange it. Trust me, I know."

Henry looked at his cousin with some amazement. "You seem to have given the matter some serious thought. Or have you perhaps done it?"

George made no answer. "I tell you, it's the only way to know for sure. For one thing, you'll know at once if she likes you or not. Whenever we meet ladies, there's so much bloody etiquette one has to observe, for both us and for the ladies. They must always be so polite, so condescending, one never knows if they really like one, or if their behavior is the product of years of training by some governess or teacher at Mrs. Goddard's. I think that for girls, knowing how they feel is even harder. They need to marry for money and social advantage. You can be a lawyer, and I can run the Donwell estate. But girls don't have even that much freedom of choice. That's why I recommend trying a kiss, to see whether she likes you or not," he concluded.

"Well, I can see that my younger cousin has given this matter much thought. I will not ask you if you have also given it an actual try."

"Of course, cousin, and I thank you for your discretion. But I would not try unless I were myself first sure of my own feelings. Otherwise, that would be disgraceful. I am no rake!" he said with some indignation.

"Of course, you are not. I did not mean to suggest such a thing. With the fathers we both have, we would never be disrespectful to a woman. Still, what if the lady in question did not like your experiment?"

"Then it must be apologized for and forever forgotten. I surely would never speak of it again. After all, a woman's reputation is among her most important assets."

"I see. Well, I thank you for this most interesting lesson. I will most carefully consider what you have said. I think I'm ready for a return ride. Shall we gallop back all the way?"

George nodded. He was sure Henry fancied Adelaide. She was such a lively girl; he thought she would not take such an attempt amiss. He felt he had given good advice. His cousin was an older man, but he had listened very attentively. More he could not do for him. For now, his own problem was securing his father's permission for him to offer marriage to Edith. For that, he himself needed strategy, and except for his own father, there was no one he could ask. He would have to brave the daunting task on his own.

CHAPTER 27

All the funeral obsequies were finally completed at Enscombe. Young Weston and his grandfather had been together at the old estate for two weeks and Mr. Weston was ready to return to Randalls. It was a good time for them to be alone together, for they had seen one another only on brief, if regular, visits over the years of his youth and young manhood. Having so reluctantly given up his son to the care of his aunt Churchill in the old days, Mr. Weston was resolved not to do the same with his now orphaned grandson. Anna had written to say she located two properties in the neighborhood of Randalls that she thought would suit Weston, and his grandfather began to talk to him about returning to Highbury

"Weston. My Anna—who will soon become your step-grandmother—has been looking in Highbury for a property you might purchase or lease so that you could be near me and your other new friends. Enscombe is quite large and a lonely place, I think, for you to stay by yourself. Of course, you should keep it and, perhaps someday, when you marry, say, you might want to return here. But for now, I hope you will come back with me to Randalls and choose a suitable place in Highbury for yourself."

Weston was for a moment silent. He had grown closer to his grandfather over the past two weeks. They had talked together about his father and his mother for, of course, his grandfather knew much about them before they married and removed to Enscombe. Truth to tell, he did not relish the thought of staying here alone. He had warmed to the Highbury society in the brief time he stayed there. He felt adrift now, his own father having been so much in control of his life during the recent past, he was hardly accustomed to think for himself, let alone manage this large estate. His grandfather suggested hiring a Bailiff to reside there and manage the place. Yes, it seemed the best thing to do. He knew he was now a rich man, and could do as he liked.

"Yes, grandfather. I do think it might be the best. I am ready to go back with you. Though at my age, setting up household will be a formidable task."

"My Anna will help you. And we will find servants to help and a good housekeeper. Mr. George Knightley's wife will help as well, I am sure. You will be surrounded by more assistance than you could even desire."

Weston nodded in agreement. He was not accustomed to having authority over anything in his life to this point. After Uncle Churchill passed away, his father managed the estate. And his mother, always frail, was so hovered over by his father, that he knew her only as a gentle, giving person who, he knew, loved him very much, as did his father, but who was often unwell. He was well-educated, of course, but had not yet chosen any career for himself, since his father wished him to come back home after his education was complete. He would be the lord of Enscombe someday, he was told, and that was quite enough for any young man. After his mother died, his father kept him even closer to home. His longest trip had been that recent visit to Highbury, and the reluctantly granted week-long visit with his grandfather, at the Crown. He was ready to go elsewhere, at least for a while. He was a good-looking young man, with dark hair and eyes, though he did not resemble his father much. Tall and slim, with good shoulders, he had not his father's flair for dress or his dashing horsemanship. He had pleasing manners, yet was not bookish, nor a sportsman. It was hard to say in what direction he would take his life. But he was ready to leave Enscombe behind, at least for a time.

On their return, Weston went out almost immediately to inspect the two properties Anna had found. One was in open country, the house rebuilt somewhat pretentiously, in the so-called Georgian style, and in need of minor repairs. The other was larger and newer, with a nice brick terrace, beautifully situated on sloping fields, with attractive gardens, and the inside white-washed and nicely wall-papered, with high ceilings and many windows.

"There will be plenty of tax on all those windows," cautioned Anna.

Feeling himself for the first time in charge, he replied that it did not matter to him. And the house had a name—Dove's Nest—he found appealing and which finally decided him.

"Dove's Nest it will be for me," he said. "I will make my nest in Highbury right here."

And so it was that Mr. Weston Churchill became a resident of Highbury, in a house near Randalls and the vicarage, just on the edge of the town. He would stay at the Crown until the house was made ready for his arrival and residence.

This news quickly spread all over town. Hetta Knightley found it exciting. "Have you heard, mother, that Weston Churchill is coming to Highbury to live! What fun it will be to have him here. Everybody liked him very much at the vicar's party."

Emma spoke quietly. "You must remember, Hetta, that he has just recently lost his father. Don't be thinking of social occasions and parties, and that sort of thing. He will be wearing a black band and gloves in his mourning for a time now." Her husband was out and about, and she imagined would be hearing the news himself. He must learn to regard this young man objectively, and not as some kind of reincarnation of Frank Churchill.

"I know that Mama, but he can still be asked to dinner here sometimes, can't he?" pursued Hetta.

"We will see, Hetta. He will have much to do getting settled in his new residence. We must leave him alone for a while. His grandfather will need to be with him and will help with his arrangements." She wondered where George and Charles were just now. When she thought about George and the problems he was presenting to his father, she wanted no new issues at present. She sent Hetta over to Mrs. Goddard's for her piano lessons and set about deciding on the day's menu. She needed a walk but would await her husband's return. He would need a walk too when he learned the news, she thought. It looked to her like some uncomfortable situations might be in the offing.

CHAPTER 28

Soon after his return from Enscombe, Mr. Weston contacted Reverend Brewer and arranged for a wedding ceremony at the parish church for himself and Anna Sharpe. He had spent so much time during his life mourning the dead, he was not about to wait any longer for his marriage to Anna. He knew that both Frank and Jane would have wanted him to go forward with his life, already so jolted and rudely interrupted by past griefs. It was to be a modest ceremony, with refreshments following in the gardens at Randalls. The list of those invited was small. The Knightleys, of course, all of them, his two girls, Mrs. Goddard, the Reverend Brewer's children. Amazing, he thought, how small the circle of friends around him now was. Yet they had all, in one way or another, sustained him. A man of sixty now, he was grateful for the gifts that life had given him, not the least, these last weeks with his grandson at Enscombe. New life, it seemed was coming to him again. He hoped he would share many years at Randalls with Anna.

Reverend Brewer led the way through a modest ceremony. His talk was short, taking as his theme, the blessings of finding happiness in unexpected places. "We must always be ready to seek happiness," he said, "for ourselves and for others. We must be alert, on the lookout, for often we might pass it by, sometimes because we are too focused on ourselves and our foolish preoccupations, sometimes because we have not held out our hands to those in need, or have continued to nurse old grievances. We must never stand in the way of anyone's genuine happiness. Still, happiness is always there and available, to be sure. Always there, because God in his wisdom is always good."

That was all. And yet, it struck Emma, it seemed aimed at her and, truth be told, at her dear husband. It had taken her so long—almost a year full of blundering mistakes—to realize her love for Mr. Knightley. And he too, an objective and right-thinking man, had almost missed his chance for happiness with her. One must be careful, she thought, not to place obstacles in the way of others seeking their own happiness. She must remember to talk to her husband about the sermon tonight.

Sitting beside her in the small church, holding her hand, as he often did during services, he looked uncommonly serious and thoughtful. Though he was not an especially spiritual man, he always endured these Sunday observances, more difficult in the Elton times, to be sure, when the talk was ringed round with flourishes, embellishments, and often inexplicable Biblical quotations. But there was no missing the directness of Reverend Brewer's talk.

Sitting beside his father, George also looked very serious. Of all her children, he was the most like his father, she thought. And though one never talked of or confessed to having favorites, he was surely hers. Not only was he like his father in temperament, but he resembled him in face and feature. How painful it was, often, to love one's children. She hoped he could resolve his difficulties with his father.

Edith, sitting in the front pew with Adelaide, looked very pretty in her poke bonnet, its brim framing her face, but also solemn and serious. They were a good pair for each other, Emma thought, endlessly talking about their books together, always seeming to find one another at gatherings. She and her husband had some literary talks together too, she remembered, though she had not been very fond of Milton. Dickens had been a better companion, for he was often very funny. Next to Edith sat Adelaide, her bonnet trimmed with ribbons and lace, head upright and a wide smile on her face throughout, always sprightly, full of verve and fun. Emma knew from her sister that Henry liked her very much. How different they were, though. Of course, Henry was older. Not too old, though, a bit younger than her Mr. Knightley when they were married. Adelaide was close to her own age at the time. She always thought they were a youthful version of themselves. Maybe they would marry someday.

There she went again, matchmaking. She wondered if the young Mr. Weston Churchill might be a problem for Henry. She must watch and see.

Then, the service was over, and everyone was walking back to Randalls for refreshments. Everything was prettily arranged. A cluster of people had already gathered and were welcoming young Weston. He was very much—after the bride and groom, of course—the focus of attention.

"So you will have your own house," said Adelaide. "How exciting for you! Have you furnished it as yet?"

"Well no, not yet. I need to go to London, I think, to choose furniture for a start. Aunt Anna—I'm to call her that now, I was told—will go with me to help." said Weston.

"We were very sorry to hear of your father's death," said Edith. "How hard for you it must be. I know how it is to have no parents, though you will have a loving aunt now, as I have had all these years."

"Yes, he said. I look forward to knowing her better now that I'm here in Highbury. And to being with grandfather."

Henry walked over to the group. "Accept my condolences too, Mr. Churchill," he said. "I was very sorry to hear of your loss."

"Thank you, Mr. Knightley. But I am glad to be here with you all in Highbury. So much better than being all alone at Enscombe."

Henry nodded, though with a look that seemed to say that being alone at such a time might have been a more appropriate choice.

Adelaide was annoyed at Henry's demeanor. He looked vaguely disapproving, as he so often did when she had done something amiss. She knew him so well and threw him one of her looks, whose meaning he readily interpreted. Sometimes they hardly needed to speak to know what the other was thinking. But she could not have known all of what he was, at that very moment thinking. It was George's advice to him. How ridiculous that was, recalling it at this inappropriate moment. He tried to banish it from his thoughts, but for the moment could not. He bowed, turned, and moved away, joining another small cluster of guests. He had not yet met the Reverend Brewer's son and daughter. It was time he introduced himself there and put away from him all such inappropriate thoughts as those his cousin George had introduced. It was all so ridiculous, he told himself. He could never do something like that. Still, as he began conversation with the two young Brewers, the thought lingered, still not eradicated, at the back of his mind.

"Henry?" said Hetta. "Saul Brewer just said something to you. Did you not hear?"

"So sorry," he answered. "I was a bit lost in thought. By the by," he said, recovering himself. "I thought your father's talk was very good. So nice to have something helpful said briefly and to the point."

"Yes," answered Saul. "That's father all right. Brief and to the point." But he did not look as if he meant his statement to be a compliment.

"Does he sermonize at home?" asked Henry.

"Don't all fathers?"

"I suppose so," said Henry. "But I'm a bit past that now. You will be too, someday."

The young man made no answer, and Henry moved away, again lost in his thoughts, as he looked over to see Adelaide, still regaling Weston Churchill with something or other, gesturing with her violet-colored gloves in the air. Perhaps he would try George's suggestion. Though how or when he had not an idea. Pity that he couldn't shake the thought just now.

Hetta joined him. "Of what on earth were you thinking," she asked. "You looked so strange just now."

"Of nothing at all," he said. "Let's talk of something else. Are you liking the looks of young Mr. Churchill too?" he asked.

"So that's it," she said, remembering the day George had employed her to ask Edith out for a walk. "Would you like me to go over to Randalls tomorrow and ask Adelaide out for a walk? I did this once for my brother George and Edith, after which he took over. I'll be glad to comply. I love being a go-between."

"Hetta, I have not asked you to do that."

"No, but I think you want to. Anyway, I'm ready when you are," she said with a smile, moving away from him.

Could it be possible his mind was so transparent as to be visible to a girl of seventeen? But it was not such a bad idea, he thought.

CHAPTER 29

Mr. Knightley had indeed heard the news of Weston Churchill's removal to Highbury and of his impending residence in the vicinity of Randalls. As he rode from Abbey Mill Farm to Donwell, his thoughts were, for almost the first time in his life, totally confused. He would have to face his oldest son's desire to offer marriage to Edith Sharpe, natural daughter of Anna Sharpe and Frank Churchill. And now, Frank's other progeny was returning to Highbury, in the person of his son. He thought he knew himself to be a fair-minded man. Was it right to continue fostering his dislike of Frank Churchill even beyond the grave? Ridiculous, of course. He must rid himself of this, once and for all. And yet, here he was, spoiling what promised to be a delightful ride with Bessie with these dark thoughts. He supposed Emma knew of Weston's plans also since she was never far behind the town gossip. He would talk with her. He was still meditating on Reverend Brewer's talk at the Weston wedding—an odd circumstance for him, a rational man, who had always instantly dismissed the cant he found in most of the sermons he heard across the years. But the Reverend Brewer's talk still rang in his ears. Was he about to prevent his children from finding happiness? He had found so much in his time, in his courtship of Emma, even with the various scoldings and lectures with which he had sometimes peppered their time together. Then, the unbelievable happiness he had found with her in marriage, first at Broadstairs, at their seaside retreat in the Albion, and then, over all the years together, of the children she had born to him, in the many hours of shared talk and companionship.

No. He had resolved, almost before he returned to the stables, and was brushing down old Bessie, to tell his wife that he was getting himself ready to permit George to court young Edith, when George himself appeared, walking toward him.

"Hello sir," he said, smiling. "Have you enjoyed your ride? I do think, however, that you should be looking out for a replacement for Bessie. Don't you think she's served you long enough and would enjoy being put out to pasture?"

"You see George, it's always hard for me to relinquish the companionship of those I love—and that, I fear, includes Bessie," he answered, smiling back. "Have you come out to continue our conversation about your future plans?"

"No, sir, not exactly. I was on my way to ride over to Randalls and offer Weston the use of one of our horses," he explained. "Mother suggested it, and I thought it was a decent idea."

"Very well. Be on your way. I actually was on my way to have a few words with your mother. Perhaps you will favor me with your company after lunch for a talk."

"Capital. I'll be back for lunch, and will see you after that."

No doubt it was not only the offer of the horse to Weston but the hope of seeing Edith that drew him to Randalls at this hour. It was just as well that he have some time with Emma first, to consider what he would say to his son.

He watched him cantering away. A fine horseman was George. He would make a splendid lord of the manor one day. And, he supposed, he needed to take a closer look at Edith. But Emma would know about that, he thought. And so, he walked down to the house, looking for his wife.

He found her with the housekeeper, preparing menus and shopping lists. "Emma dear," he began, "Would you come into the drawing-room for a few minutes? I have something I'd like to talk with you about."

"You've heard that Weston Churchill is coming to live in Highbury," she said, making a guess at the subject of their conversation.

But he stopped her. "No, not that. I was wanting to discuss George and his wish to offer for Edith. I will be meeting with him this afternoon, and need to come to some kind of conclusion." He paused. "I admit to having been rather moved by Reverend Brewer's sermon last Sunday."

"Well," she said. "That is a novelty. You usually barely make it out the church door before you start outlining the various faults in logic, ignorance of current scientific truths, or factually unsupported claims. We are all used to it by now, of course. I add, to give you justice, you are usually right. But it does so put one out of the spirituality of Sunday services." She twinkled a smile at him.

"I am an awful fellow, I admit. How do you manage to put up with me?" he asked, drawing her down beside him on their favorite sofa.

"I work hard at it," she said, putting her hands to his shoulders, and giving him a kiss. "But let's talk of George instead. What are you going to say to him?"

"As I was starting to say, before being so rudely interrupted with your catalogue of my spiritual sins, I have been giving the matter much thought. What do you think if I told him they must wait six months before any formal betrothal. Then, if they feel the same way at that time, I would give my approval to the match. He will soon be twenty-one, so I thought it a good time for me to set."

"And nothing to be said in the interim?" asked Emma. "They are still living in a small and close neighborhood, and people have already noticed the attraction, I think. Won't they feel hampered by the waiting period? Could they not announce their intention to be betrothed now?"

"No, Emma. What if he—or she—were to change their minds? It would be very awkward. No, I do not like that idea. I will make my pledge to George not to withhold my approval upon his 21st birthday. Then, they can announce their betrothal and set a wedding date."

"Did you ask me to join you to learn about your decision? Or did you want to hear what I think?" Emma was readying herself for battle, he could tell.

"What are your objections to my plan?"

"It puts them in a false position. People will talk—and they always do—and George will be able to say nothing about their future plans. I think it would be better if they were asked to wait three months, and then, if they still feel the same way, we can announce an engagement, to last for three more months. That way, you will have your period of waiting, but not so much secrecy about it. I thought you didn't like secrets."

"How you always do find my weak spots, dear Emma. I do see your argument. But there must still be the three-month wait, with no announcement."

"Do you fear George will change his mind? Speaking for myself, I do not. Don't you recognize your own son's likeness to yourself? Once you saw your way clear, you left London and immediately proposed marriage to me. I can't imagine anyone having required you to wait three or six months before making your relationship with me known."

"I was much older than George, and my parents were gone. I needed no approval from anyone. He is younger and somewhat dependent upon me for his allowance. Were he to marry, I would make a financial settlement on him."

"You are forgetting Edith's recent good fortune. He will not be in need of such a settlement. And he will one day be heir of Donwell. That he already has."

"You have an answer for everything, my dear, do you not. I would like more time to look at Edith in this new light."

"You are not marrying her, my dear. He is. And apparently, he needs no more time. He will not care what you learn about her during the next three or six months. He has already made up his mind. I think we must respect that. My suggestion is that you agree to the betrothal, and then ask them to wait the six months, until he comes into his maturity."

Mr. Knightley knew he had been defeated. "Very well, my dear. I concede. Of course, the question of where they are to live, after they marry, must also be decided."

"But not just now. Donwell is such a huge place. Surely there would be plenty of room for them here, don't you agree?"

"I will ask him what he plans to do. For now, I would like a bite of lunch to ready myself for my meeting, the outcome of which, it seems, you have already decided." He took her in his arms.

"You were ready to move to Hartfield, to live with me and my father," she said. "There were those who predicted disaster about that living arrangement. But it worked nicely, I think. And we are far easier parents than my dear father. We won't insist that they dine on gruel. It didn't take you long to charm Father, did it? I'm sure you will do the same with this young couple." She rose. "I'll see to lunch.

Something sturdy to ready you for your upcoming task."

"No," he said, with a smile in his eyes. "Just some of Serle's boiled eggs will do for me."

CHAPTER 30

The impending residence of Weston Churchill was greeted with even more enthusiasm and speculation than had the coming of his father over twenty years ago. Of course, his grandfather Weston and all the Knightleys knew of his planned residence in the neighborhood for weeks. But as the news spread through the town, almost everyone had something to say or think about what this new outsider might bring to the community.

Since Highbury was still such a relatively small country village, adding a new eligible male to the population—and a rich one, even more—was of great interest to the young ladies, of whom there were more than a few. At Randalls, there were Adelaide and Edith, and at the John Knightleys even the usually uninterested Bella was excited. Hetta Knightley, Emma's daughter, felt a flurry of interest, having already liked young Weston at the vicar's celebration party at Donwell. Even Reverend Brewer's daughter Susan wanted to hear more of the young man. Mrs. Goddard's older girls and a few of the teachers also found the coming of Weston Churchill a subject for much conversation and conjecture. The Coles and Perrys had a few unattached daughters to add to the congregation of ladies waiting to be introduced to the new Highbury resident.

During the first weeks of his arrival, Weston continued to stay at the Crown, visiting at Randalls frequently, and occupying himself with regular trips to London with his step-grandmother to buy furniture for his new home, Dove's Nest. And although there was not such a thing as a coming-out party for young men, Mr. Weston had already determined to host a dinner dance at the Crown for friends and family, to formally introduce his grandson to the Highbury community.

"Mr. Weston is an amazingly social man," commented Mr. Knightley. "A gigantic celebration for the new vicar, a dinner at Donwell, a supper, and a dance at the Crown are clearly not enough to satisfy him and his grandson."

"Now, now," said his wife. "It's always good to have the opportunity to get out and meet friends. We've always known how dear Mr. Weston loves company. I must say, it's what I like about him. He has suffered so much loneliness in his life. One must excuse his desire to assemble people around him."

"Yes," agreed Mr. Knightley. "Except that I must be part of the assembly, I see. And no doubt, our most dear and difficult children."

"Of course. We're all difficult in our own ways, are we not, my dear? Except for you, my husband, who never is."

"I've told you many times, dear Emma, that flattery will not work with me. And now, if you have ordered my boiled eggs, I will ready myself for my encounter with young George this afternoon."

The hours passed with household accounts and ledgers, and much business from the Donwell properties which needed his oversight. And then, as he was seated in the library, working, George opened the door and entered.

"Hello, Father. Here I am," he said. "Ready for our conversation." He looked resolute and stood very tall in front of his father.

"Be seated, son. Don't stand on ceremony with me." Mr. Knightley always had trouble softly making his way into a difficult subject. And so, once again, he entered it with no attendant small talk or nice phrases.

"So, you want my permission to address Edith, to ask for her hand in marriage."

"That is correct, Father. I realize I am a bit short of attaining my majority, but in any case, this is a step I am resolved upon, needing only your blessing—and mother's, of course," he added, his blue eyes steady upon the gray ones of his father.

"Well, I have given it much thought, and have spoken with your mother on the subject. Though it is not the match I might have sought for you, you may proceed with your intentions and approach the young lady in question. Marriage must be postponed, of course, until you at least reach your maturity." There. He had said it and was done.

"Thank you, Father. I must admit it takes a bit of the pleasure out of it for me that you add that you yourself do not like the match. Nevertheless, you may think better of it in time, I hope. I do want you to love her as I do," he concluded, both happy about the permission and a bit rueful at his father's reservations. He could not help wanting his father's full approbation. But he could wait. He had gotten the permission he wanted, if not the blessing which would have been even more desirable.

"I hope so too, George."

"I've heard mother say that her father was not happy at her marrying you, father."

"Mr. Woodhouse never objected to me personally, George. Indeed, I was almost an inhabitant of his house during the years of your mother's young girlhood. It was marriage itself he objected to, as an agent of change and the possible removal of your mother from Hartfield. Hence we lived the first two years of our married life with him at Hartfield."

"And how did you get along with him during those years?" asked George. "Maybe there are some lessons for me in your behavior." His eyes now contained the hint of a smile.

"Well, it happened gradually that he came to depend on me, and then, finally, I think, to love me as he loved your dear mother. I can't say that I did anything particularly notable. Of course, he liked it when I led him up the stairs each evening. He needed to lean on something, and my arm was always there. Soon it became a habit to both of us. We each of us came to miss that moment, whenever it was taken from us."

"That's not much help, father. Edith can hardly help you up the stairs. You must have done something else. I'm serious, in wanting to know," said George.

"I think above all, he saw how necessary my presence was to dear Emma. And then, all the rest just fell into place."

"I hope you will see too, then, how necessary Edith's presence is to me, father."

"I have already had some intimations of that, my son. I will keep an eye out. Meanwhile, let us go and tell your mother the news. She will be very happy for you. And I suspect, will have no reservations whatsoever."

As they exited the library, George turned to take his father's hand. "Thank you, Father." Then, emotion welling up in him, he turned back and led the way into the house, seeking his mother. He well knew how this approval had been wrung from his father and was grateful. He did wonder at his reluctance now, though, especially since Edith had received her large inheritance. But he knew that would have made no difference to his father, either way. Perhaps it would be something else he would never know. But he did not care. Edith was going to be his.

CHAPTER 31

After leaving his parents, George went to the stables, saddled up, and headed for Randalls. He supposed he must talk to Mr. Weston first, though he had no doubt of his approval. About Edith, however, he was not totally sure. It was like a riding course full of hurdles. He knew how to guide his mounts over that kind of obstacle. He had often enjoyed the thrill of a cross-country gallop with hedges, stone walls, ditches, gates, and watercourses to jump. This was a different sort of challenge. He had, he thought, mastered the first and most difficult, his father. Of course, it still rankled him a bit that he had attained permission but not a blessing. He hoped that would still be forthcoming. But his mother had been so kind and enthusiastic. Now, the next jump would be Mr. Weston, an easy one, he thought. It was how to approach Edith that would be the last. She might still hold back from him, and it behooved him to be careful and tread warily there.

Pulling up in front of Randalls, George dismounted, knocked, and when the door was opened, gave his horse to the servant and went in. Mr. Weston greeted him heartily, as usual, and led him into the drawing-room. "Anna is busy just now," said Mr. Weston. "How good to see you, George. No doubt you've been told of the party I'm giving Weston. Hope you can come, along with your family."

"Oh yes, sir. But that's not what I've come about," he said, seating himself across from his host. "Actually, it's about Edith." He was no better than his father at making preliminary small talk.

"Indeed?" said Mr. Weston. "About Edith. Are you wanting to

take her out for a ride? I know the two of you enjoy riding together, and today is an especially good day for it. Cool and lovely. So good of you and your family to make your mounts available to us." Mr. Weston looked at him expectantly.

"No sir. I've come on another errand. I want to ask your permission to address Edith with a proposal of marriage. I suppose Mrs. Weston should be here as well, but I thought I might as well tell you directly why I've come."

Mr. Weston was at first filled with delight for the girl—and then, when he recalled all he knew about her parentage, he wondered. He must ask.

"Have you spoken to your father?" he inquired.

"Yes sir, and he has given me permission to present myself to Edith. And, of course, first to you and Mrs. Weston." He wondered why the hesitation from Mr. Weston. He was normally the most agreeable of men, falling in with whatever suggestions were made to him. Of course, this was important, but he was a bit surprised at Mr. Weston's hesitancy.

"Can you excuse me for just a moment?" he said. "I do think Anna should be here as well. After all, she has been Edith's guardian all these years. It would be best that she also be involved." He rose and disappeared.

George felt himself at a loss. Was it the new bequest that held Mr. Weston back? Was he hoping for an even more important alliance for Edith? But surely, he did not seem that sort of man. Before he could further assemble his thoughts, the new Mrs. Weston was with them. She smiled and sat down beside her husband.

"Mr. Weston has told me of your purpose in coming," she said.

Why this formality, he wondered. "Yes, I have come to make a proposal of marriage to Edith." He decided to say no more.

"Have you talked with your parents?" she asked. "More specifically, with your father?"

"Indeed, I have and have secured his permission to make my addresses. I thought it best to see you next." He watched her face carefully. This meeting was so much more reserved than he had anticipated.

"Of course, you are both so young," she said. "I knew you liked Edith—so many exchanges of books, so many rides out," she said as if listing their encounters for consideration. "Are you sure you know your own mind? There need be no rush, I think," she added, repeating, "You are both very young."

"I am most sure," he said, a bit testily. "I would not have come here were I not sure. Is there some obstacle in your mind? I do think Edith enjoys my company and perhaps even more," he added firmly. "I will have much to offer her, as I am the heir of Donwell, as you may know. She need not touch her own new inheritance if you wish. I am quite ready to agree to that in a marriage settlement. I am not interested in her bequest." He was heating up and had to try controlling himself. He had not anticipated this reluctance on the part of the Westons.

"It has nothing to do with any financial consideration," she said. "More with your youth, and your future position here in Highbury."

He was silent. He waited for them to speak further. He had had his say.

"Can you give us a little time to discuss your offer together first? I promise you, we will not be long in giving you our decision," she said. "You may return tomorrow, and we will be ready. Meanwhile, please do not present Edith with your offer as yet." She looked steadily at him.

He could see there was nothing for it, but to leave. He rose, bowed somewhat stiffly, and left. The interview had not gone as he had anticipated. He would say nothing of it to his father until the morrow. If he were not granted permission, he would be ready to do battle. This was an obstacle he had not anticipated.

Later that same day, the Westons called at Donwell. Emma guessed at once why they had come. "So, George has been over to see you about Edith?" she asked, smiling.

"Indeed, he has," said Mr. Weston. "But we wanted to speak with you regarding his visit. Is your husband about? We would like to see him as well."

"I'll send someone up to the stables to fetch him," she said. "I suppose George has told you he means to ask for Edith—in betrothal for now, and ultimately in marriage. He spoke to us, and we gave our approval." She looked at Anna, who looked quite somber. "Are you not pleased?" she said.

Before she could answer, Mr. Knightley entered, bowing to Anna and extending a hand to Mr. Weston.

"Mr. Knightley, we have come about George's proposal to Edith.

We can talk frankly about this, as we all know the facts of her parentage. Becoming the wife of the heir to Donwell will be serious business. George says you have given permission, but we wanted to hear more from you."

Before he could answer, Anna spoke. "Edith is a very good girl, Mr. Knightley. I would not want her to be part of a family that did not welcome her. I'm sure you understand me. I do not wish to be impertinent, but I, of course, can never entirely put all that past behind me. Edith is so young and so innocent. I do not want her to bear my burdens, which she would, were she not freely accepted by you."

"Of course, we accept her," said Emma, breaking into the conversation. "She has nothing to do with the past. And George is very determined, you know. A bit like his father. He is settled and sure of his feelings for her, else he would not have so presented himself."

Finally, Mr. Knightley spoke. "I confess, I had not wished for their attachment. And I must be honest with you. Once George told me of his wish to marry Edith, I did some research with my brother John, who knows the law better than anyone I know. Some years ago, one needed special permission if a person with a biological, but no legal father, should seek to marry by license, especially if one of the personages should be a minor of natural parentage. Even legacies in that situation were considered invalid. But all that has been changed. Since 1822, there are no longer any such obstacles in the law. There is no need for special licenses or any problems of inheritance for any children they might have." He paused. "Given George's eventual inheritance of Donwell, I had to be sure that all was in order. So, I have no reservations regarding their eventual marriage. Of course, George does not know the issues concerning Edith's parentage, nor does she. And they need not. Together, you remember, we decided to put all that past to rest forever."

Mr. Weston looked at Anna, who still was silent. "Well, my dear? What do you say? I think we should let the young people make their choices themselves. Obviously, Mr. Knightley has looked into the legalities, which is as it should be. Speaking for myself, I think we should let the young man make his addresses. It is really up to Edith now."

Anna was still silent. Then, she spoke directly to Mr. Knightley.

"Are you quite sure, sir, that you will welcome my daughter into your family without always wishing that your son had made a better choice?"

"As my dear wife told me when we first discussed this matter, I would not have permitted my father, had he been alive when I approached Emma with my own proposal, to stop me. Of course, I was older, and both my parents were gone. But my prospective father-in-law was not keen on Emma marrying. As you know, Weston, I had to move to Hartfield to secure his reluctant approval of the match. I can hardly interfere with George, in good conscience. When they marry, my wife and I will welcome Edith to our family. When a man decides to marry, there is only one correct choice for him—and that is his own."

Emma went over to the Westons and embraced them both. "Let's be happy with them. I will tell George you have come over to give your blessing—as we have, as well." Mr. Knightley rose, took Anna's hand, and kissed it. "Have no fear. She will be safe with us." After shaking Mr. Knightley's hand, the Westons departed.

"Well done, my dear. You are, as always, a man who gets the facts of the matter first. I'm glad you did, though it might have been better if you had told me what you were doing over at Hartfield with John yesterday. You brothers—always so confidential with one another. But I understand. And you spoke very graciously to Anna. As I said to you once before, for a man who can't make speeches, you do very well at it." She went to her husband and gave him a long kiss.

He held her tightly. "How could I take his happiness from him?" he said. "But I had to make sure there would be no trouble when he was ready to marry—licenses, inheritances, and all that. I tell you the truth, Emma, it was the legalities that held me back, not any lingering memories of Frank Churchill."

"Let's go find him. Was he at the stables when you were there?"

"Out for a ride. When he returns, we'll tell him the way is clear for him. I hope, after all this, that Edith will accept his offer."

"Trust me, she will," said Emma. "As usual, I think I knew about this first. But I swear to you, I haven't done any matchmaking—though I haven't given it up entirely."

"Ridiculous girl," he said, returning her kiss. "But let's talk for a moment of something else that has been bothering me. I hope you will agree with me that Weston Churchill should be kept away from Hetta, as nearly as possible."

"You are changing the subject," said Emma.

"I am. But it's a subject that needs to be discussed," he said, with a serious look on his face. "And the common ingredient is, I am sorry to say, Frank Churchill. I have agreed to welcome Edith into our family, knowing all we do about her parentage. Now comes Weston, also Frank Churchill's child. I can't tell you how little I am prepared to bring another of his children into our family."

"Weston only enjoys flirting," said Emma. "I'm sure it's nothing serious."

"That may be true, but he clearly likes our Hetta. I see that he often comes over here to ride with her, and I don't like it."

"I'm sure it's harmless," said Emma. "But I'll talk to Hetta tonight, and give her some warning about her behavior. She's a good girl, and will listen to me."

Mr. Knightley had to be content. What he did not know, was that at the very moment he raised the matter with Emma, Hetta and Weston were enjoying a longer ride together than usual. She had told him about Box Hill, and when he said he wanted to see it, she agreed they could ride there and be back well before dinner. It was, she thought, a delightful escapade, and no one would ever find it out.

When they arrived, both in need of a rest, they stopped near Burford Bridge, at the foot of Box Hill, to watch the little river going on in the midday golden sunlight. They had just reclined on the grass when all at once Weston, unlike the more gentlemanly Henry Knightley, took Hetta in his arms and kissed her.

She hardly knew what to say or do, this being a new experience for her. She pulled away from him.

"Are you angry with me?" he asked, smiling. "It was hard to resist, you know."

"I don't think I'm angry," she said. "But I don't want you to do it again if you please."

"I'll ask first, next time," he said with a smile, and she smiled back, uncertain about any other reply. As they sat there, she began to be uneasy. She knew her father would not have liked it, and his image came up powerfully in her mind, even more than the face of the young man who so carelessly smiled at her.

"We'd better go back," she said. "I hope no one has been looking for me. That might be trouble."

He agreed, feeling annoyed. It seemed like everything he wanted to do meant trouble. But he acquiesced, and they trotted back to Highbury, with nothing more said about what had happened.

When they brought the horses back to the stables, one of the grooms saw that they had been ridden far and hard. And when Mr. Knightley came by later to check on Bessie, he mentioned the condition of the horses Hetta and Weston had taken out.

Back at Donwell, Mr. Knightley asked Emma for Hetta.

"She's gone up to her room to rest," his wife said. "She came in quite tired and hot from her ride with Weston. Did you want to see her for something?"

Indeed, he did but decided to wait until after dinner. And when he inquired about her afternoon ride, Hetta told her father where she and Weston had gone.

"I do not want you doing that again," he said somewhat sternly. "Riding about the grounds here is fine, but Box Hill is too far for you to go alone with a young man."

Hetta looked contrite and said she would not do it again. Fortunately, her father did not ask for further details. Not that she could have told him what happened. The more she thought about it, she was sure she could not. She thought of talking to her brother George, but that was sure to stir up trouble. It would be best to be quiet and hope the subject would not come up again.

For his part, Mr. Knightley told Emma that she should keep a watchful eye on Hetta. He did not want her welcoming young Weston for rides here unless others were present.

Emma merely nodded. Before retiring, she went into her daughter's room. "I've just only come to say goodnight. I thought you were looking somewhat strange when you returned from your ride. Was anything wrong?"

Hetta was immediately disarmed. "Oh Mama, please don't tell Father. When Weston and I were resting near the bridge, he suddenly kissed me. I was surprised, and to tell the truth, I didn't like it much. I don't think it will happen again. I really don't want to talk about it." She was near tears.

"You know, my dear, you must not permit any young man such liberties with you," said Emma. The fact that Hetta said she hadn't liked it, was encouraging. "You are far from being ready for something so serious as matrimony. That's where kisses lead, you know. But even if he made you an offer, your father would not accept, since you are too young."

"I don't want to be married," said Hetta, still teary-eyed. "I don't want anyone to kiss me again! I just wanted to have a ride to Box Hill. I never dreamed what would happen."

"Of course, you didn't," said Emma soothingly. "Now, let's just forget all about it." She looked thoughtful. "I think young Weston is really interested in Adelaide, who will be very able to manage him, I fancy. But that's beside the point. I want only to tell you—to ask that you do not permit him to have your unchaperoned company again. Do not worry, my dear. One kiss, however inappropriate, is not definitive. Some day you will perhaps find yourself liking being kissed. But for now, look for some other interests. And there is no need to burden your father with any of this. Wipe your eyes, my dear. Just think, we will soon have another evening of dancing at the Crown. You may dance with Weston, should he ask you. But do not give him a second, please. There. That's all for now," said Emma, embracing her daughter. She would reassure her husband that Hetta was fine, and there was no need to worry about any further expeditions with Weston Churchill.

For his part, though he had enjoyed a number of flirtations with some local girls, and liked Hetta Knightley best, Weston Churchill was not ready for settling down. Their Box Hill escapade had been delightful, but he was sure he had offended. Actually, the small country town, delightful as it had been for a while, despite its assortment of young friends and proximity to his grandfather, was beginning to feel more confining than the grand Yorkshire estate of Enscombe. While there were diversions in Highbury, there were more social restrictions, he realized.

He was sure the Knightleys learned of his and Hetta's excursion, for he felt himself newly unwelcome at Donwell. There was no remedy, as he had little taste for the confinements of matrimony, and was not about to make Hetta an offer, even had the Knightleys been persuaded to accept it. When his grandfather learned of it, he said his behavior had compromised the young lady. Even worse, the Reverend Brewer made some pointed references to his conduct. He felt himself hedged in. It would seem that further enjoyments would be forbidden. Making an offer was the only way he would further succeed with young Hetta, guarded by her own proprieties and the watchful eyes of her father, the redoubtable Mr. Knightley whose favor, he knew very early, never rested very firmly upon him. He did not think it possible either to procure Hetta's unchaperoned company again or if he were to propose for her, to be accepted.

The next best prospects, Edith and Adelaide, seemed destined for the two older Knightley cousins. He liked Adelaide and thought she might be fun, but in her direct way, she let him know that though she might enjoy a dance with him, she was not interested in further attentions. Returning north began to look good. He might try his fortunes there. He had some of the restless nature of his father and was ready to experiment with being master of the grand estate. He fancied that at Enscombe he would be more in charge of his own life and developing tastes. Its location promised broader possibilities, he thought, with the seaside resort of Weymouth not far away. His mother and father had met and fallen in love there. Perhaps that would eventually be his fate as well, though certainly not for some time. Thus, the news was soon out that Dove's Nest would again be vacant.

CHAPTER 32

Once again, they were destined to spend an evening at the Crown Inn. As Mr. Knightley reminded Emma, it was the second time in only a few weeks. "We are becoming dancing mad in Highbury, I think," he said, only half-joking.

"I love it," said Emma. "Dancing is always a source of happy memories to me and a time for meeting friends and watching the young people have such good times. Mr. Weston told me there would be waltzes, a few country dances, and the quadrille. It was fun watching Hetta dress herself up in her best gown, a white Chinese crepe with embroidered flounces. I gave her my sash of silk tulle to wear, and one of my gold bracelets."

"It isn't a coming-out party, Emma. Just a country dance at the local inn."

"Yes, but she's had this dress for a while and no place to wear it. She is so excited."

"At least we didn't need to take two carriages, as George offered to ride over. He is always aware of finances, I'm glad to say. If we had left it to you Charles, you'd have had us arrive in a parade of coaches," said Mr. Knightley.

As they waited for James to settle the horses, Emma told her husband quietly, "George told me he hopes to ask Edith tonight. How romantic a memory that would be for her. And for George," she continued, her own thoughts racing back to the moments when her husband had first proposed to her. 'Have I no chance of ever succeeding?' he had said, so hesitantly at first, it had taken her a moment to realize he was proposing to her. Of course, he had gone on to say more, but it was that first magical moment that gave her the first inkling of his love for her. So wonderful it had been. She would never forget it. She hoped George would find the right words to bring his suit to Edith. How he would manage it, she did not know, amid the press of the dance. But she was sure he would try. Like his father, he would not await a better moment. He would speak just as his father had spoken, even if the moment seemed unlikely of success.

"Are you ready to step up, Emma? What are you thinking of, my dear," asked her husband. "You have such a far-away look in your eyes. You are somewhere else, are you not? I know that look."

She could not tell him just now, with Charles and Hetta so near. "Nothing much," she said. "Just some old memories."

When they arrived at the Crown, people were gathered in groups, talking and laughing. The musicians positioned themselves in the loft, and the inn looked again a bright and welcoming place. Emma entered first, showing to best effect, her evening dress of pale green crepe, embroidered with silver, trimmed with festoons of silk and tied at the waist with a tasseled cord. Mr. Knightley and George had taken extra time arranging their snowy white cravats and wore the usual coats and knee-breeches. Emma thought they both looked very handsome.

Mr. Weston came over to welcome them, along with Anna and young Weston, by now affectionately dubbed "Wes" by his young friends. He had bespoken the first dance with Hetta, and George was on his way over to ask Edith to join him for the first. Henry Knightley stood at the entranceway, watching everyone assemble, but not moving forward to seek a partner. Mr. Knightley went over to greet Robert Martin and family, and Emma was chatting with Anna Weston. Then, the first dance was announced, the music began, and the partners assembled on the dance floor.

The couples moved in lines, first one way, then the other, parting and coming together. When they joined hands, George spoke quickly, "During the supper break, I would like to speak with you privately," he said, managing the sentence before the dance steps once again took them apart from one another and down the line. There would be one more coming together, and he hoped she would speak then.

As they took hands, stepping down the center of the dancers, she said, "Yes, I will look for you then," and smiled at him.

They finished the dance and bowed to one another, though her eyes were averted from his, and then they both looked up and applauded the musicians. That was all. He would find her later.

Meanwhile, young Wes danced the next with Adelaide, a lively country dance with much circling and clapping of hands. When it was finished, she walked over to Henry Knightley. "Aren't you going to ask me to dance, Henry?" she said with a smile.

"I thought your card was full already," he answered.

"How would you know that," she replied. "As it happens, I do have one more space. It's after the next. The waltz. Shall I put your name down for that?" she said, giving him one of her sauciest looks. "Unless you are not in favor of waltzing. Are you or are you not?"

"Adelaide. If you will give me a chance, I will ask you to dance the waltz myself. Be quiet for a moment," he said, in a tone of reprimand. "It's the man who is supposed to invite the woman—and most especially to the waltz."

"Oh bother. Go ahead. I'm waiting. You can pretend I said nothing. That way it will be proper," she answered.

Ask her he did, bringing color to his face. "It's supposed to be the woman who blushes," she said. "I'll be waiting for you."

And after the next set, he approached her, taking her around the waist, waiting for the music to start. "You can hold me a bit closer," she said. "Don't be afraid."

"You are the most nonsensical girl I ever met," he said but smiling. "I'll hold you just as close as I want."

"Good. That sounds better," she laughed. And so, they started whirling about the floor, his eyes full on hers. For a moment, she too blushed but returned his look full on.

Once again, George's words about trying to kiss Adelaide came back, sounding in his ears in time with the music. Of course, he could not do that now. It was all he could do to keep dancing with his eyes on her.

And then, suddenly, the music stopped. They were looking at one another when she turned, clapping her hands in tribute to the players. He followed suit. "Adelaide," he said.

"Yes?" she replied. But he said nothing. "You wanted to say something to me?" she asked. "Did you enjoy the waltz?" She had recovered herself, he saw, though he had not.

"No. I only wanted to thank you for the dance." Of course, that was not what he wanted to say. Not at all.

"Do you want another?" she said, looking up at him with some laughter in her eyes. "You'd better ask now, before the supper break. Who knows how many other invitations I may have by then."

How could she be so bold? He had the advantage of years and experience. And yet, he found himself always at a loss with her. "Yes, if you'd be so kind, if there's room on your crowded card, add my name to those many other admirers of yours." He felt himself getting heated up, and knew it was ridiculous.

"As you wish, Mr. Knightley. Unless you want to first scold me for being too forward."

"I have given up scolding you," he answered. "You never listen to me, these days. It was better when you were a chit of a girl."

"Those days are over, I fear. Still, I give you permission to go on with your lecturing. I always learn something, though it may not be what you intend. Though you may no longer give me a shake, or box my ears," she said.

"I'm sure of that," he replied, with a smile, and somewhat recovering himself. "I'll look forward to our next dance. Is it to be another waltz?"

"I don't know yet. I have to consult my card. But just be ready when I come over to you and remember to ask me first. We must be proper, is that not correct?"

"Indeed. I'll be waiting for you."

"You should practice, dance with some other ladies first."

"I don't need practice. Besides, there's no practicing that will ever make me prepared for you."

"I like that. Well said," she said, dropping him a curtsey. "I will see you again soon."

He bowed to her. His cousin George walked over to join him. "I see you are making progress with Adelaide," he said, with a grin. "Are you remembering what I told you?"

"Indeed. I find it is an annoying memory which I cannot get rid of."

"One way to get rid of it. Just do it. Then you'll have another, to replace it. I'm going to meet Edith at the supper break. It's your best chance then, old boy."

"Enough from you, youngster. I see you have danced twice with

Edith. Will I be congratulating you soon?"

"Tonight may tell the tale," said George. "Wish me luck."

"I don't think you need luck. I wish you happy, instead," said Henry. "I think I'm going to ask Hetta for a dance now, if you'll excuse me."

"Then I'll wish you luck instead," said George with a knowing look. "But do remember, fair heart never won—You know the rest, I'm sure."

CHAPTER 33

The supper break at the Crown Inn dance usually lasted an hour at most. George would need to make swift work of his proposal. And yet, he must also be cautious. He had been taken aback by the reaction of the Westons. Was it because they knew Edith might refuse him? He did not want to wait any longer. He took her hand and led her outside, hoping that no one noticed. Behind the Crown was a patio with chairs, sometimes used in warmer weather. He motioned her to sit down and pulled a chair close by.

"Edith. You must know what I am going to ask you. When I spoke of this last, you talked of the vast difference in our position. You said you had nothing to offer. Of course, now you have an inheritance, not that I am in the least interested in that. You said I needed to talk to my parents. I have done that and secured their permission for our betrothal. Marrying you will make no change in my future position as master of Donwell. I have done all you asked. Now it is time for you to answer me directly. Will you be my wife?"

Edith was somewhat overwhelmed by his recital of the considerations he had overcome. Yes, she now had a dowry to offer. Yes, his father had given permission. Yes, he would continue to be heir of Donwell. But he had not spoken of his parents' feelings about this most unequal match.

"George. I know you can be quite firm and demanding, even with your father, I suppose. But I do not want to feel as if you have compelled your parents to accept me. Will your father accept me as a daughter, or as an upstart? I am as familiar as you are with the social hierarchy in Highbury. Though Mr. Weston is among the leading citizens, and now my aunt has married him, they still cannot approach the standing of the Knightleys."

"This isn't a social transaction for me, Edith. My father will come around. He has already given his permission. The rest will come. I love you and don't care about hierarchies just now. All I care about is if you love me. If you do, please accept my offer, and everything else will follow that."

"You tell me your father will come around. That makes me feel that you have compelled him to accept me." She stopped. She saw he was growing impatient. Perhaps he should have chosen a better time and place for this conversation. But he needed no more time. And, he thought, neither did she, if she were truthful with herself.

"I don't know what else you want, Edith," he said compellingly.

"If your father will tell me that I shall become his daughter, should we marry, then I will become your wife," she said.

"We will soon have to go back inside, Edith. I can't very well ask him to do that right now. Please give me an answer." She looked at him, loving him, and not wanting to harm him in any way. She saw that not answering him honestly, would do the greatest harm.

"Yes, dear George. I do love you with all my heart. Do you promise me that he will do that before we marry?"

"I promise," he said, hardly knowing what he was saying. He stopped her from speaking further, pulled her to him, and kissed her.

"So," he said. "We are in agreement. Let's go inside and tell everyone we are to be married."

"What?" she gasped. "Now?"

"Yes, now. I want everyone to know. Come on, Edith. You'll have to get used to me. I don't like putting things off. No need for the grapevine tomorrow. We are going to make our announcement tonight." He kissed her again, took her hand, and led her back inside.

After the stir of good wishes had ceased, Mr. Knightley and Emma came over to congratulate them. Emma kissed them both, and Mr. Knightley offered his hand to his son and bowed, then putting both arms around Edith in an embrace.

"There," said George to Edith, when they went back to the side benches and were seated. "There's your answer. Once or twice Father might have kissed a lady's hand, but I have never seen him embrace any women except his wife and daughters. I want to hear no more reservations from you. Actions speak louder than words. You are now officially part of the family," he smiled at her.

He noticed his cousin Henry talking with Adelaide. George hoped he too would meet with some success in forwarding what was obviously his feeling for the girl. Perhaps he might take his advice about a kiss, but no, the two stood politely at a distance while they spoke. It seemed as odd to him, as no doubt it seemed to his cousin, that he was so much more at ease in making progress with a girl—but so it was. That was the older generation for you, though Henry was not so very old, he mused. Well, he had tried to help; the rest a man must do himself.

Had George been able to overhear their conversation, he would have been only a little pleased. Henry had asked Adelaide to take a ride with him on the morrow, and she agreed. He would bring the horses over to Randalls, after picking them up at the Donwell stables. Having secured her agreement, Henry had bowed politely and left her side. But George saw that they danced another waltz after supper, so there was hope, he thought. Meanwhile, for the remainder of the evening, he was consumed by his own happiness and delighted to accept the congratulations of all present.

The next day, Henry arrived at Randalls with the horses, a groom bringing Adelaide's mount, and he on his own horse. Having made his greetings to the Westons and his congratulations to Edith, they mounted and rode off into the hills and fields which spread behind the Randalls and Hartfield properties.

At first, they trotted along pleasantly together, no real talk being possible. After a brief canter, they stopped at a tree-covered spot, and Henry dismounted and helped Adelaide off.

"Time for a bit of a rest," he said, spreading his coat for her to sit on.

"Yes. What a beautiful day it is! I do love riding when the sun shines brightly, don't you?" she said, taking off her cap and smoothing her riding habit, its jacket cut masculine style, he noticed, looking at her closely, even buttoning it left over right. She arranged her cut-away skirt nicely and looked up at him with that smile which always so disarmed him. She waved her riding crop, inviting him to sit down beside her.

"Isn't it wonderful about Edith and George?" she said, giving him another of her lovely smiles. "I'm so happy for them. Aren't you?"

"Yes, of course, I am. I think they make a perfect couple. Lots of the same interests—books and such," he said, unsure how to make a start for himself.

"Oh, do you think that's what it's all about—common interests?" she asked. "I mean, whatever it is that brings people together and makes them fall in love. Do you think that is the whole thing? Isn't there something else? Some kind of feeling? An attraction that is somehow larger than an interest in books?" She had that mischievous look about her. He was becoming uncomfortable again.

"Yes, I suppose you're right. Maybe one can't really put words to it, you know. Foolish to try, I suppose," he offered.

"My father and Miss Sharpe that was," she said. "They don't talk about books. At least, I've never heard them."

"What do they talk about?" he asked, having been given some sort of lead, he thought.

"I don't think it's about talking at all, Henry," she said, still looking up at him with her perplexingly steady eyes. "Do your parents talk about books? Or farming, say?"

"I've never really given it much thought," he said. Where was this conversation going? Nothing to do but follow her lead, he supposed.

"My Aunt Emma says that when she was younger, Uncle George used to lecture her a good bit. I've heard it said she liked it," he offered.

"You lecture me a good bit, truth be told," she mused. "Why do you do it? Is it that you think I like it?"

He was silent. "I don't lecture you very much anymore," he said. "That was when we were younger. After all, I am at least ten years your senior in age. It was appropriate then."

"But you're older than your sisters and I've never heard you lecture them," she said, smiling. "Are they all so much better behaved than I?"

He felt this conversation was getting out of hand, and did not know how to extricate himself from it. "Let's talk about something else," he said. "Tell me how you enjoyed the dance last night. It looked to me as if your dance card was full all evening long."

"Yes, it was. Though I must say that I had a few favorites. Especially the waltz. Did you enjoy waltzing with me, Henry? I was surprised at how well you did. You're quite an expert," she joked.

"One needs a good partner," he said. "After all, one gets so close. It's easy to tread on a girl's toes if you're not careful."

"You didn't tread on mine," she said.

"No. I'm always careful with you," he answered.

"Why is that? Should you always be so careful with me?" she asked, looking up at him, some kind of invitation in her eyes.

For a moment he was silent. It seemed to him that if he was going to do it, this was the moment. And so, he reached out, pulled her close to him, and resoundingly kissed her.

"At last," she said, holding tightly onto his arm. "You've taken long enough! I thought you'd never get around to it!"

CHAPTER 34

Henry Knightley wasted no time in proposing to Adelaide after taking that first kiss which, as she often reminded him, had taken him so long to deliver. After that, he had been quite taken aback by Adelaide's suggestion that they marry immediately. He was almost as much surprised as she was by that first kiss he had taken—though, truth to be told, it was she who, in the end, brought him to it. He had been shocked by his own behavior but once begun, it seemed quite natural and, as his cousin, George, told him, he would know at once if she liked him enough to return his own feelings for her. And it was clear she certainly did

He had always been shy with her, a product of being so much older, he thought and knowing her first only as a girl. In those early days, they had been thrown together much, as there always was abundant visiting among the Hartfield, Randalls, and Donwell families. At first, he found her a little annoying, always hanging around him, asking provoking questions, and making comments he found precocious and even impertinent. In time, he became accustomed to her lively presence. When she asked him, almost pleadingly, he taught her how to ride. She was a natural and was as good as he was by the time she was fourteen.

Then, he had gone away to London, to train himself as a lawyer, acceding to his father's wishes that he follow in his footsteps. But Henry had not enjoyed the law. His whole nature rebelled against the argumentative nature of the profession, and the need to spend hours buried in ancient laws and practices. But he persevered and even did respectable work. But he never became a London man, hating the clubs at night, the dirt and congestion of the streets, and his confinement in dreary chambers all day long. The press of study left him little time for socializing, and he made few friends in London, always coming back to Highbury on his vacation breaks, enjoying far more visits with his Highbury friends and family, his rides, often with young Adelaide, in the rolling countryside around Donwell. She rode easily, side-saddle, the long veils wreathed around her small top hat, flowing on the breeze behind her as she trotted along. What a picture she made!

When he came back home, Adelaide was always there, waiting for him, asking him to take her riding. He fell into the habit—which he regretted—of becoming a kind of mentor to her, lecturing her on her manners, and her increasingly unladylike boldness. Then, as the years passed, and she became more a young woman than a green girl, he became uncertain how to handle himself around her. To be sure, her manners did not change as she grew older. She remained outspoken and completely devoid of the careful conduct usually cultivated by girls of her age. He reasoned it was because she thought of him as of a brother. And, he told himself, so he was.

In recent years, he began to have other feelings for her and found himself unable to repress them. Thankfully, his cousin George challenged him to act on them. And, with Adelaide's help, he had. Now, quite suddenly and rather miraculously, he thought, they were married. He planned, at the time of his proposal, that she would continue to live at Randalls until he should have established himself in his new career. He had informed his father that he was not about to pursue the legal career his family hoped he would assume. Instead, he interviewed for a position at the General Post Office at St. Martins-le-Grande, where a reorganization of the postal services had just been accomplished, including specific reforms recasting the whole system. There had been a creation of a new body of officers called surveyors' clerks, seven in England, two in Scotland, and three in Ireland. To each surveyor, a clerk was attached, whose duty it was to review postal conditions. The clerks were to "travel about the country under surveyors' orders." reviewing the practice of postal offices and improving and regularizing the delivery of mail. He hoped he had not made a terrible mistake, giving up the law, but he was willing to try out the position in Ireland to see if he warmed to it. He always loved riding and travel, and no doubt with his father's reluctant assistance, was appointed to a post in Ireland. The only drawback was telling her that he was to go away, for how long, he did not know. Never had he contemplated taking Adelaide there. Pronouncing herself equally fond of riding and travel, she suggested that now that he had proposed to her, they should marry and she would accompany him. And so it was, a second Highbury wedding occurred, and the bridal couple spent their honeymoon in Ireland's west country. "We can learn to hunt," she said, "something I have always wanted to do." And they made it their practice to ride to hounds as often as time and finances permitted. Henry's law degree proved to be of great assistance in reviewing the postal master's accounts and investigating public complaints. He was glad to be free of the multitudinous forms to which he had been subjected at the law offices in London. He would have to find a place for them to live, transport both of them into unknown territory, and begin work which was totally new to him. An adventure, to be sure, both personally and professionally.

They landed in Dublin and took lodgings in Banagher on the Shannon. From there, Henry was to set out on his inspection tours of the outlying districts. Since neither he nor Adelaide knew anyone in the neighborhood, she suggested coming with him, an idea which he at first declined.

"I don't want to sit in this old hotel all day with nothing to do," she said. "I will enjoy the rides with you, and you can always find a place for me to wait for you while you do your business."

"Adelaide. I know you are the best of riders. But I cannot permit you to travel by horse on these rough roads as I go about my interviews."

"Well, if you won't let me ride, get me a small carriage so that I can go on beside you in the most ladylike of ways. I always did like driving a curricle."

She would not be discouraged from this plan, and Henry thought the best way to disabuse her of it was to try it and show her how little it would answer. Ireland seemed a rather wild country to him, and to tell the truth, he did not fancy leaving Adelaide alone, either at an inn or in a rented lodging, while he did his work.

"I am quite good at writing and figures," she said. "If possible, you can take me with you into the offices you visit and introduce me as your clerk. Freed of all the paperwork, you can better concentrate on solving the problems of the people you have been sent to visit. Or, failing that, I can just wait for you in my curricle."

"Adelaide, I don't think it will do. A young man I could bring with me, but a lady?"

"That's all right," she said. "You must of course introduce me first as your wife and then as your clerk and amanuensis. I will see to it that your reports will be neatly written, your figures correctly calculated, and with you by my side, no one can question the appropriateness of my bearing you company in your tasks," she said.

He was not so sure. Nevertheless, as always, she won her way. He told her it would be only a trial, and that he must first consult with his superiors in the office in Banagher. He must also apply to his father for help in securing a proper vehicle for Adelaide. Or perhaps Mr. Weston would assist. He ran his hands through his hair as if to smooth it out along with his disordered thoughts. The Irish used jaunting cars, which were not covered and were very uncomfortable. He sat down at a small table in their rooms and began to compose a letter home which, he knew, would be received with many remonstrances from his father. But that did not signify any longer. He was a married man now, and Adelaide's happiness must be his first concern.

Soon they were able to move out of their hotel room to a rambling old house on the High Street, that was more comfortable and capacious. And the curricle arrived. One of the other surveyor's clerks was another Englishman, one Anthony Trollope, himself only recently married and who was an acquaintance of Henry's in London.

They had met under rather odd circumstances—though the circumstances had served to bond them together. It was in the first days after Henry had arrived at the London Post Office. He was waiting to be shown in to meet one Colonel Maberly when he heard quite a bit of shouting coming from in the office. It seemed the Colonel was missing a letter and a check. A young man stood at his desk. "The letter has been taken," roared the Colonel. "And by God! there has been nobody in the room but you and I." He thundered his fist upon the table. "Then," said the young man, "by God! you have taken it." He too thundered his fist down, unfortunately hitting a large bottle of ink, which flew up and stained the Colonel's face and shirt. In the midst of the fracas, the Colonel's private Secretary entered with the letter and the money. Henry thought the Colonel should apologize, but he merely sent the young man out of the office. It seemed as if the incident would be held against him. Outraged by the Colonel's behavior, he spoke to the fellow, introducing himself and offering his consolation. Afterward, the two of them went out into the streets and had a drink of ale together, along with a good laugh.

After that, they saw each other a few times in London, and when both were posted to Ireland, they naturally fell in together, having many common interests, and missing the English countryside and people. Mr. Anthony Trollope also soon married Rose Heseltine, daughter of a bank manager in Rotherham. She was a different sort of girl than Adelaide, more of a homebody, and not taking at all to the business of riding, either on a horse or in a curricle, which Adelaide now drove. Undaunted, Adelaide often invited Anthony's wife for a ride, and though Rose was a bit nervous at first, for being driven by a woman was unusual, she went along and soon accustomed herself to what was obviously Adelaide's skill and pleasure in driving. They too became friends.

"Rose, do you not feel bored staying at home all day while your husband rides all around the country?" asked Adelaide.

"It took some getting used to," Rose admitted. "But now, I have work to do, while he is gone. My husband has started writing a novel, and he leaves me his completed chapters each day, to read, edit, and when they are finished, write a fair copy. I like the work, and think he will be good at this," she said, somewhat shyly.

"What does he write about?" asked Adelaide, curious. "Could I ever take a look?"

"Oh no," said Rose, quickly. "He says I am the only one to see what he has written. He's a bit shy about his writing. That's because he comes from a very accomplished writing family. You have perhaps read the novels of Mrs. Frances Trollope, his mother? He worries he may not be good enough, though I think he is even better than his mother and brother. He thinks they will laugh at him when he tells them he has completed a novel. After all, his mother has already published several, even some best-sellers. I'm surprised you have not heard of her."

"I fear I am not much of a reader," confessed Adelaide. "But I would like to read the work of your husband. Maybe when he has his work published, I shall. As for me, I prefer riding out with my husband and most particularly love to join him when he hunts. I have noticed that Mr. Trollope often hunts with Henry. Do you think he will include some hunting scenes in his novel? Then, for sure I shall read it," said Adelaide with a smile.

"Yes, Tony loves to hunt. It's his passion, I think. I'm always a bit sorry that I can't join him, for I don't like it at all. Someone must be very good on horses, to even imagine hunting. And then, I don't enjoy thinking about the fate of the poor fox."

Adelaide and Rose continued their meetings and grew to be close friends as the months wore on, as did their husbands. For Henry and Mr. Trollope, there was much common ground in discussions of their postal duties and their mutual love of hunting. Not long after, both ladies discovered they were in a child-birth way, and Adelaide had to give up her horses and curricle. No more riding, no more hunting. It was a dismal prospect. Embroidery or sewing she had no use for, nor did she play the piano, even if they had one. Rose said that her husband awoke at four each day to write before he went to work. That wasn't appealing to Adelaide.

But keeping to a schedule was a good idea. She was always well-practiced at writing. She started copying her husband's notes, assembling and organizing the records of his many meetings with local officials. Her governess had tutored her in mathematics, an unusual subject for young ladies at the time, unlike the regular curriculum at Mrs. Goddard's, which did not feature such unfeminine subjects. She heard stories that the fierce reformer Florence Nightingale was using the new science of statistics to prove to the bureaucracy back in London that nearly seven times as many British soldiers died of disease in the Crimean War than in combat, and had seen to it that hospitals at the front were cleaned up. Miss Nightingale also rode on horseback while making her rounds, a practice that endeared her to Adelaide's heart. While Miss Nightingale's role in the campaign was not yet generally known, Adelaide had seen copies of dispatches that came through Post Office channels on their way to London and believed she too could make a difference in the world of communications. Using statistics could make Henry's well-written reports stronger, more compelling. And so it was that backed by graphs and numbers, his investigations proved to be the impetus to reforms in mail delivery, and one of the secrets to his rise in the Post Office.

Meanwhile, her husband and Mr. Trollope further developed their friendship.

"So, when did you start this business of writing novels," asked Henry of his friend.

"Right after we took that walk to Drumsna," Trollope said, sitting across from Henry at one of the tables in the inn where they stopped for a rest and some refreshment. "You may not remember it as clearly as I did. We went out for a walk, looking for some good scenery, where Drumsna stands on a bend in the Shannon. We asked the maid to show us where we could find something beautiful to look at, but she was not very helpful. So, we went off on our own and walked over the bridge, following some pretty bad roads. We took a chance going across the stepping stones of a bog stream and found a broken down entrance into a kind of woods. It looked like it might have been a gentleman's seat."

"I do remember now," said Henry. "There was some kind of fallen-down wall, with a footpath around it. A ruined house stood there, a large one, two stories high. The whole roof was off, as I recall."

"Indeed. I think you wanted to go back, but when I saw the knocker was still on the door, I pulled it and went in. Much of the floor of the hall had been stolen for firewood. Everything was so damp and rotten, I didn't try to go upstairs, for the timbers of the roof that were left were threatening."

"Yes," said Henry. "It reminded me—not exactly, but somewhat—of Donwell Abbey, had its owner deserted it and left it to ruin."

"Do I know that place?" asked Trollope.

"Oh no," answered Henry. "Donwell's my uncle's place in Surrey. Quite beautiful. So many windows, my aunt told me, that when a little girl, my uncle—now her husband, you see—challenged her to count the number of windows on the front."

Trollope went back to recalling the Irish scene.

"There were no windows left here," he said, a far-away look in his eyes.

They looked out back into what had once been large gardens. Everything was covered by rubbish heaps and potato patches. Out front, they discerned the remains of a drive and places where some poor Irish family had propped a cabin against a deserted wall.

They continued reminiscing. "We sat," said Henry, "lighted our cigars, and though I was ready to go back, you wanted to sit and meditate on these ruins, specimens of Irish life, you said."

They both remembered, then, that a man came up and told them the place was called Ballycloran, and that a family called the Macdermots had lived there some time ago.

"I was eager to leave," said Henry, "as the evening was drawing on, and so we walked back to the inn, boarded our mounts, and headed home. I could tell you were still thinking about the place, all the way back."

Within the year, Mr. Anthony Trollope's first novel, *The Macdermots of Ballycloran*, was in print.

"You never told me about the novel. I only found out about it by chance," said Henry to his friend, somewhat reprovingly. "You see, Edith, wife of my cousin George, reads everything. When she heard an Irish novel had just been published, she ordered it from London, as she wanted to know more about the land Adelaide and I had come to. When she finished, she sent it to us."

"I'm surprised she was able to get a copy," said Anthony. "It got hardly any notice or reviews. You are the first person, I think, I have ever spoken with who has taken any notice of it. I wonder if your cousin's wife actually read it. Indeed, I only got it printed through the good grace and help of my mother, though I think she thought it absurd that I should wish to enter the sacred precincts of the writing Trollopes. You see, my father was a great scholar who wrote an Ecclesiastical Dictionary—which he never completed, by the way—and my mother is still quite a best-seller, and my brother writes very respectable academic and travel books. Even my married sister has completed a novel. No one in my family even read my effort. They thought my attempt was simply an unfortunate aggravation of the writing disease which had been much more successful in others. If it hadn't been for my dear Rose, who supports me so stalwartly, I don't know that I would have had the courage to go on. But go on, I have."

"One's family is not always the best judge of one's talents," said Henry. "My own father was quite crestfallen when I abandoned a career in the law. Of course, he had paid for fourteen years of training—and is himself so successful in the law, that he is now a judge. I know I was a disappointment to him. But my case is a bit like yours. My wife was supportive of my wish to change my career and eager to come to Ireland with me. She has also been a tremendous help to me in my efforts here."

"Then we are both lucky dogs," said Trollope. "Rose is the only person in the world to whom I entrusted my first effort. And I mean to make some more. Indeed, I have already published a second, also accepted, no doubt as an act of charity, by my mother's publisher. This one was actually reviewed but called coarse. The publisher wrote me that readers don't like novels on Irish subjects, and added in a devastating postscript, "Thus you will perceive it is impossible to give any encouragement to you to proceed in novel-writing." So, there we are. And, unfortunately, I've been posted to Clonmel now, and I will have to lose your good company. But perhaps you and your good wife will be able to pay us a visit there. It's a prettier town than Banagher, a center for horse sales. No doubt your wife will enjoy such a trip. We will have a larger house there, so we can put you up. Do come. Rose will like it very much."

And so, when Henry had a brief break, they went traveling to the picturesque valley of the Suir, sheltered by three small mountain ranges, one famous in legend. Adelaide was delighted, and they took a whole week away visiting the Trollopes.

Then, fate intervened to bring the Trollopes and Knightleys together again. Both men were posted to Mallow, a busy market town on the River Blackwater in County Cork. Each had advanced in the service and now resided in their own homes. Mallow was in the center of hunting country, and both families found it a pleasant place to rear their children. The Trollopes by now had two sons, as did Adelaide and Henry. It was here that Anthony's mother made her first Irish visit and found Anthony and his excellent wife as happy as possible. The Trollopes were caring for a child of Anthony's sister Cecilia, who had just succumbed to tuberculosis. But when her widowed husband soon remarried, the child was brought back home to England. Anthony always thought his mother had made the visit mainly to see Cecilia's little girl. The shy Rose always had a somewhat difficult time with her mother-in-law, but the old lady had quickly taken a great liking to Adelaide, so the Henry Trollopes were constant visitors, especially during Mrs. Trollope's stay with her son.

"I never talked to my mother about novel-writing," confided his friend. "After those first two Irish ones, my next two were both failures. Sometimes I wonder that I kept on with it," he said. "But Rose said if I stopped, she'd have nothing to do. So, I kept trying to think of something else for a subject."

Then, fate intervened again, and Henry Knightley again had a role, this time in the first great success of Anthony Trollope. Both men were still doing the work of the General Post Office, but on a business trip, they contrived a brief visit to London, and en route, visited Salisbury Cathedral. One evening, wandering round the purlieus of the cathedral, Henry was prompted to speak of the Reverend Rufus Brewer.

"This place puts me in mind of a man I knew in Highbury. He came to us as our new vicar, whose first task was to marry a friend of our family to a woman who had been governess to Adelaide since she was a small child. Reverend Brewer was that rare thing, a totally good man, you see. That day, his sermon had a great effect on my uncle, not himself a particularly spiritual man. Strange the power that simple goodness has, no?"

Anthony absorbed this conversation while standing that hour on the bridge at Salisbury while Henry continued to tell him stories about the Reverend Rufus Brewer's work in Highbury which, along with that view of the Cathedral from the bridge, became the source of the story of *The Warden*, with its bishops, deans, and archdeacons, which finally cemented Trollope's fame as a novelist. Though he later claimed that all these clergymen came whole from his brain, he did admit that he picked up as he went on whatever he could learn about them. And Henry was always sure Trollope had absorbed the stories about the Reverend Rufus Brewer on the bridge at Salisbury, inspiring him to paint his picture of the Reverend Septimus Harding, a man also good, sweet, and mild. That novel was Trollope's first success, and when Henry and Adelaide read *The Warden* and its successor, *Barchester Towers,* they always said that Septimus Harding bore much resemblance to Reverend Rufus Brewer of Highbury.

CHAPTER 35

Inspired by how swiftly Henry had made Adelaide his wife, George Knightley moved quickly to arrange his own marriage. On the day he gained his maturity, George and Edith were married at the local church. George had often heard the story of how his mother had always wanted to visit the seaside, and so his father had taken her to Broadstairs as a surprise on their honeymoon. It was his suggestion that George do something similar for his bride. And so, following in his father's footsteps, he planned a mystery honeymoon for Edith. His Edith had always longed to hear 'the Inimitable', so, he took rooms in London where, starting in April 1858, the great Charles Dickens had begun giving public readings, and was performing at St. Martin's Hall once or twice a week. As a special treat for Edith, George booked two performances of the *Christmas Carol*, one with the story of Little Dombey, and another, with Mrs. Gamp, from *Martin Chuzzlewit*. They stayed a week in the city, making visits to the British Museum and other favorite places. It had, indeed, said Edith, been magical! Going up to London to hear the great Dickens read became an annual event for the George Knightleys.

One evening at dinner, when John Knightley mentioned casually that one of his clients was Mrs. Letitia Austen, a younger sister of Dickens, and that she was coming to Hartfield to consult with him, Edith begged for an introduction. Mrs. Austen's late husband Henry had been an architect and civil engineer much interested in sanitary conditions in London and other cities. He became General Secretary of the Board of Health. Certain legal cases had brought Mr. Austen into the orbit of John Knightley, now a judge presiding over several issues related to sanitary conditions in overcrowded London. Dickens was devoting himself to procuring a government pension for Letitia, the legal aspects of which had been turned over to John Knightley. The case took over two years to settle. Edith wondered if this complicated case had been the inspiration for *Bleak House,* one of the greatest novels written by 'the Inimitable.'

Letitia had remained close to her brother, even after his scandalous and public separation from his wife, which was just then being talked about all over England. She idolized her brother and refused to hear anything detrimental about his behavior. On her visits to Hartfield, she found a sympathetic listener in Edith, who also continued to revere her favorite author.

"People can say whatever they want," said Letitia to Edith, one evening when she had come on business. "My brother is a good man. Consider all the good he has done for our family, supporting my indigent brothers and demanding parents, and, indeed, the good he has done for the nation itself. His social commentary has begun to change the world for the better."

Edith completely agreed. She told Letitia that reading the great Dickens together had been a large part of George's courtship—though, at the time, she hardly knew what was happening—most especially their reading together of *David Copperfield.*

"Later," said Edith, "we read *Hard Times* as it came out in the *Household Words* magazine. It was certainly a masterpiece, though not with his usual happiness and good humor throughout."

"True," said Letitia. "And you know, writing it in just seven months exhausted my poor brother. He told me it had left him feeling three parts mad, and the fourth delirious. All things considered, he did get a bit darker in his later works."

Edith invited Letitia to Donwell, to meet Emma and Mr. Knightley. At present, she and George lived in one of the large wings of the Donwell Estate, and she was happy to show the house off to her new acquaintance.

"You know," confided Edith. "Evenings I often read aloud to the family from one of Mr. Dickens' ever-forthcoming masterpieces. And every Christmas, it's always selections from the *Carol.* When his day's responsibilities are over, my husband always joins in, often commenting on the plot or character. My father-in-law says his comments are worthy of the great Croker himself." She brought Letitia into her father-in-law's Donwell library with its complete collection of Dickens publications.

"He's becoming almost more famous for his readings, than for his novels," said Letitia. "But I fear he is overdoing it a bit. He is often exhausted by his tours. They have to lay him down for at least a quarter of an hour after the more demanding ones. His daughters are trying to persuade him to give them up, but you know how these headstrong great men can be difficult. I often fear my own dear husband worked himself to death over trying to reform these dreadful sanitary conditions. Be sure, my dear, take care of your own husband. It's not easy to be left alone." And so, things at Donwell went along well, with Edith rapidly becoming one of Mr. Knightley's favorites.

George finally persuaded his father to put his old Bessie out to pasture, but Mr. Knightley continued to ride on a new mount—not, he often remarked—the equal of Bessie, and continued his energetic walks around his properties. As his father grew older, George was assuming more of the responsibilities of the estate management, riding out to Abbey Mill Farm and the other properties, and overseeing many of his father's managerial responsibilities in the town. Mr. Knightley still worked with William Larkins, but George was often present at those meetings, learning the intricacies of the complicated finances of his father's large ownership of land and properties in Highbury.

Emma mothered the rest of her brood of children, paying particular attention to Hetta who, she knew, had been more than a little unsettled by her adventure with young Weston Churchill. But she was still young, and Emma would soon take charge of finding a suitable match for her daughter. Though Emma made some matchmaking mistakes before, she was now a matron with two daughters to marry off, and finding proper partners for her children would surely be an appropriate activity. Their circle was small, but the world was expanding. She had not as yet told her husband but had an eye to a London trip with Hetta in tow. She also asked George to invite some of his old Oxford friends to Donwell for a visit. Edith suggested an invitation to Weston Churchill, but whether it had been made or not, the young man did not come.

When *Great Expectations* made its appearance in weekly

installments, Edith began reading it evenings to the family at Donwell. They all liked it very much, but its events started Edith thinking again about her own mysterious bequest. She often wondered about it, but her aunt seemed determined not to discuss it or engage in speculation. Thus, as far as she knew, there had been no Miss Havisham in her past. She hoped her fortune had not come from a convict, and though she rather liked Magwitch, she never met or ministered to one. Her life provided no likely candidates, as her aunt had told her so little about her mother or father. There was nothing for it, she thought. The past must remain shrouded in mystery.

"You know," she said one evening, when her reading was finished, "I have often wondered if someone, somewhere, knew something, some clue that could unravel some details of my own parentage or even the secret of my mysterious bequest."

"Much as we love these novels of the great Mr. Dickens, my dear Edith, we must not expect to find such happenings in our own lives," said George. "You always were one to identify with his characters, more than anyone I have ever known," he continued, lovingly. "But alas, here at Hartfield there is only Uncle John to keep our legal secrets. Here there is no strange Mr. Jaggers to help. You already know all that is to be known, and all I need to know about you, my dearest."

Emma regarded them with great satisfaction but saw that a cloud passed across her husband's brow. She knew that look and would ask him about it when she could.

Upstairs, Mr. Knightley began before she could make her inquiry. "Emma, my dear, I was very troubled by Edith's last remark about her own past."

"I knew that was what you were thinking about. But put it away from yourself, my dear. It was only an idle comment, prompted by reading a novel."

"I know that. But sometimes words, whether in sermons or novels, can enter our minds, and stimulate what has been hidden there. I know we have agreed to free the children of this generation from the secrets of the past. But Edith wants a mother and father, just as George has his. I have felt it for a time now. I am going over to see the Westons tomorrow. Though I still agree that the old secret must be kept, I think I see a way of giving Edith what she so desires."

He would say no more that night, despite Emma's questions. He must first bring his idea to Randalls, where he rode, early the next morning, finding Mr. Weston and Anna just leaving the breakfast table.

Never one to waste time getting to the point, he began. "I am sorry to disturb you so early, but I have something on my mind which I must discuss with you."

They repaired to the drawing-room. Mr. Knightley looked very serious.

"What is the problem, my friend?" asked Mr. Weston. "Is something wrong? How can we help?"

Mr. Knightley recounted the scene of the previous evening and Edith's revealing remark. "I know we have agreed not to burden these young people with old secrets," he began, looking anxiously at Anna, who sat with downcast eyes. "Nevertheless, it is clear to me that Edith wants her past explained, her bequest revealed. She is a sensitive girl, I think you know better than I. It has occurred to me we can do something for her if you will agree."

Anna looked up. "I told Mr. Weston at the time of our marriage, how I wished I could tell her I was her mother, but we have all concluded it should not be done. I live with that, and have made my peace with it."

"Yes," said Mr. Knightley, "but I fear she has not."

"What possible solution could there be?" asked Anna.

"I propose that you and Mr. Weston formally adopt her. John can easily do the legal work, and then you must tell her that she now has a mother and father of her own. Tell her to call you by those names, and the words will soon become reality for her."

Mr. Weston smiled broadly. "You know, Knightley, I had often thought of that myself. It is a capital idea. Especially now, since she has told Anna she thinks to be expecting her first child. She will be telling you soon, I know, as soon as she is sure. What do you think, my dear?" he said, taking Anna's hand.

She was too moved to speak at once, but rose and took Mr. Knightley's hand in both of hers.

And so it was, that Edith Sharpe Knightley took another name, and became Edith Weston Knightley, and was told, with some truth, that her bequest had come from a distant dear friend of Anna's who stipulated that she remain anonymous. A few days later, after John

Knightley completed the paperwork, Edith and George went over to the Westons for their first formal visit to her new parents. When Anna opened the door, Edith greeted her with a warm embrace. "At last, I have a true Mama, as you have always been to me," she said. "And Mr. Weston—I mean Papa, as you too have always been to me." She turned to her husband. "I know you will think me silly," she said. "But this is as good as the ending of a Dickens novel."

"We've come full circle now," George said, with a smile. "Let's go in and have a toast on it. Then we can go to Donwell and have another, for my own mother and father are waiting for us!"

EPILOGUE

Much in the fashion of Septimus Harding, the Reverend Brewer became a much respected and beloved member of the Highbury community. His good works continued to have their effect, the first of which had been that important sermon on the subject of happiness, so often found in unexpected places, and the moral duty of those who encountered it never to obstruct its workings. It is often said that deeds are more important than words, but in this case, the Reverend Brewer's words had a powerful effect on Mr. Knightley. Soon after, he gave his blessing for the marriage of his son George to Edith Sharpe. It was noticed by the residents of Highbury, that thereafter, Mr. Knightley and his wife Emma never missed one of his Sunday services.

Reverend Brewer's fame as a preacher spread even as far as the Enscombe area where Mr. Elton and his wife had settled. Elton had been appointed Vicar of Ravenswood, a small, but historic town near Rotherham in Yorkshire. Mr. Elton owed his preferment to Frank Churchill's uncle, because of the service he had performed in marrying Jane and Frank at Enscombe. His parish was undistinguished, its one claim to fame being six alabaster tombs of undetermined date which nevertheless were regularly described in guidebooks as the main attraction of the area. Mrs. Elton thought her own husband by far the better preacher since his sermons abounded with richly embellished and arcane biblical references. "The Reverend Brewer," she said to her cara sposo, "has no idea of the eloquence appropriate—indeed, demanded—in weekly preaching. On the few occasions we heard him, I thought I was listening to a shopping list."

Of Reverend Brewer's influence at home, like many a father, he was sometimes less loved by those who saw him more frequently than at Sunday services. Of course, he was always respected by his children, though his son Saul found his father's moralizing something of a burden. His daughter Susan became a friend of Hetta Knightley, and they sometimes rode together, visiting with the Goddard girls and the Robert Martin family.

Weston Churchill remained at Highbury only a little longer. There were some more dances at the Crown, courtesy of Mr. Weston, and a picnic at Donwell, but at none of them did Weston Churchill make any noticeable advances to Miss Hetta Knightley. After another month, news came that young Weston was returning to Enscombe where he felt himself more in charge of his own life and developing tastes. He was given a dinner at Randalls so that he could make his fond farewells to his Highbury friends, after which he once again journeyed north to his great estate and a future beyond the bounds of Highbury. His departure seemed to signal the end of the Churchills' complicated relationship with Highbury and its principal residents.

Mr. Weston and Anna welcomed visits from Adelaide and Henry Knightley whenever they were in England, and even more frequent visits from their newly adopted daughter Edith and her husband George. They also regularly saw Hetta and her sister Caroline, giving Mr. Weston the excuse to illustrate the practical application of Reverend Brewer's Sunday talks by scheduling more dances at the Crown and thus further increasing the supply of happiness at Highbury.

As for Emma and Mr. Knightley, with the marriage of George and Edith, followed by that of cousin Henry and Adelaide, they were free to concentrate on the younger members of the family. Whether Hetta, Caroline, or her brother Charles ever caused as much concern to their parents as had their older brother—that is a matter outside the province of this account. But it can be said of Emma and Mr. Knightley that nothing further ever disturbed the condition in which their marriage had begun, now so many years distant. It continued to be a union of 'perfect happiness.'

ABOUT THE AUTHOR

Helen Heineman graduated as valedictorian, Phi Beta Kappa, *summa cum laude* from Queens College, New York, and earned her Master's Degree from Columbia University and Ph.D. from Cornell University. She was awarded two Woodrow Wilson Fellowships, an Andrew Dickson White Fellowship from Cornell, an American Association of University Women Fellowship, a Fellowship from the Radcliffe (now Bunting) Institute. She has received several awards as a distinguished teacher, one from Radcliffe College and one from Framingham State University, which awarded her an Honorary Degree and named its Cultural and Ecumenical Center after her. During her presidency, she was named Woman of the Year by the Metrowest Daily News. She was married for 55 years to Dr. John L. Heineman, Professor of History at Boston College, and has four sons: John, now retired as a vice president at Fidelity, Michael, a lawyer in Framingham, George, Professor of Computer Science at WPI, and Joseph, a Urology Surgeon in Rhode Island. She has ten grandsons.

Made in the USA
Middletown, DE
07 September 2023

38159682R00198